ZONE DEFENCE

Petros Markaris was born in Istanbul in 1937.
Having studied Economics, he made his literary
debut in Greece in 1965 with a theatrical work,
The Tale of Ali Retzo. This was followed by
several other plays and film scripts. Markaris
recently published a Greek translation of
Goethe's Faust to critical acclaim.

PETROS MARKARIS

Zone Defence

TRANSLATED FROM THE GREEK BY
David Connolly

VINTAGE BOOKS
London

Published by Vintage 2007

2 4 6 8 10 9 7 5 3 1

First published with the title *Amyna Zonis* by Samuel Gavrielides
Editions, Athens, 1998

First published in Great Britain in 2006 by
Harvill Secker
Random House, 20 Vauxhall Bridge Road,
London SW1V 2SA

www.vintage-books.co.uk

Addresses for companies within The Random House Group Limited
can be found at: www.randomhouse.co.uk/offices.htm

The Random House Group Limited Reg. No. 954009

A CIP catalogue record for this book
is available from the British Library

This publication was made possible by the support of the Greek
Ministry for Culture

ISBN 9780099466741

The Random House Group Limited makes every effort to ensure that
the papers used in its books are made from trees that have been
legally sourced from well-managed and credibly certified forests. Our
paper procurement policy can be found at:
www.randomhouse.co.uk/paper.htm

Mixed Sources
Product group from well-managed
forests and other controlled sources
www.fsc.org Cert no. TT-COC-2139
© 1996 Forest Stewardship Council
FSC

Printed in the UK by CPI Bookmarque, Croydon, CR0 4TD

... Les vices à la mode passent pour vertus

Don Juan

DRAMATIS PERSONÆ

Costas Haritos	– Inspector, Homicide Division
Adriani	– his wife
Katerina	– his daughter
Eleni	– Adriani's sister
Christos	– brother of Adriani's brother-in-law
Stavria	– Christos' wife
Aspa	– Eleni's daughter
Yangos Kalokyris	– mayor of holiday island
Karabetsos	– police officer on island
Thymios	– truck-driver on island
Hugo Hoffer	– German tourist
Jerry Parker	– British tourist
Anna (Anita) Stamouli	– Jerry's girlfriend
Ghikas	– Chief-Inspector, Athens Security HQ
Koula	– Ghikas' secretary
Sotiris Vlassopoulos	– Police Lieutenant, Homicide Division
Yorgos Dermitzakis	– Police Lieutenant, Homicide Division
Markidis	– coroner
Kyrilopoulos	– coroner
Korkas	– coroner
Konstantinos Koustas	– nightclub owner
Elena Koustas (Fragakis)	– his second wife
Makis Koustas	– his son
Niki Koustas	– his daughter
Stellas	– Inspector in Anti-Terrorist Squad
Papadopoulos	– owner of stolen Yamaha
Lambros Madas	– doorman at the Bouzouki Strings
Haris	– one of Koustas' heavies
Vlassis	– one of Koustas' heavies

Renos Hortiatis	– manager of the Bouzouki Strings
Kalia (Kalliopi) Kourtoglou	– singer at the Bouzouki Strings
Marina	– singer at the Bouzouki Strings
Karteris	– singer at the Bouzouki Strings
Kardassis	– sergeant at Haïdari Police Station
Karabikos	– young police officer at Haïdari Police Station
Aristos Moraïtis	– owner of car-repair business
Fofo	– his wife
Argyris Koutsaftis	– best man at Aristos and Fofo's wedding
Prodromos Terzis	– owner of children's clothes factory
Lambridou	– female reporter
Yannis Stylianidis	– Koustas' accountant
Sakis	– Koula's fiancé
Menis Sotiropoulos	– TV reporter
Hartmann	– Ghikas' contact in the German Police Force
Fanis Ouzounidis	– Haritos' doctor. Katerina's new boyfriend
Panos	– Katerina's former boyfriend
Kyriakos Sarafoglou	– player for Falirikos FC
Christos Petroulias	– referee
Marianthi Kritikos	– Petroulias' neighbour
Dimitris	– forensics officer
Klairi Stratopoulou	– manager of San Marin Yacht Chartering Company
Hatzidimitriou	– official at Athens' Association of Referees
Nassioulis	– sports correspondent
Frixos Kaloyirou	– owner of Homelectronics and of Falirikos FC
Obikoue	– Nigerian centreforward for Falirikos FC
Manos Kartalis	– Haritos' second cousin. Director at Ministry of Finance

Stavros Kelesidis	– tax inspector
Stratos Selemoglou	– manager at offices at Triton FC
Arvanitakis (Mrs)	– director of R.I. Hellas
Loukia Karamitris	– Koustas' first wife
Kosmas Karamitris	– Loukia's husband. Cabaret singer and record company owner
Antonopoulos	– new officer in the Homicide Division
Stefanos	– Elena Koustas' illegitimate and disabled son
Kaiti	– woman who looked after Stefanos
Serafina	– Elena Koustas' Filipino maid
Methenitis	– Reality TV show host
Kondokostas	– officer at Nikaia Police Station
Balodimas	– officer at Nikaia Police Station
Koutsaftis (Mrs)	– former Minister's private secretary
Maria Stathakis	– girl on motorbike
Stratos	– her boyfriend

A NOTE ON THE CURRENCY USED IN THIS BOOK

At the time it was written the exchange rate was approximately 1GBP = 500 drachma.

CHAPTER 1

It began with a slight rumbling, like someone running on the floor above.

'Earthquake!' screamed Adriani, immediately in a panic. Droughts, earthquakes and floods are her forte.

'In your head!' I said to her, looking up from the Dimitrakos dictionary, in which I was perusing the entry under *diatherizo . . . = spend the summer, break off, interrupt, in contrast to* paratherizo, *the verb we use today, and which originally meant 'cut off the end of something'*.

We were taking a holiday on the island and were staying at the house belonging to Adriani's sister. I had rather half-heartedly agreed to go. I do not like being a guest in someone else's house, having always to be on your toes. But Adriani wanted to see her sister and also we had to economise because with Katerina, my daughter, studying in Thessaloniki, there was no money left over for a hotel of the demi-pension type or for a room with a bathroom across the yard of the rooms-to-let type such as are advertised on the signs hanging outside every old barn on the island. In the old days the barns had donkeys in them. Now they have tourists.

It was a two-storey house, not beside the sea, but high up, not two minutes' walking distance from the main village. Adriani's brother-in-law had built it in partnership with his brother in the golden age of the EEC agricultural subsidies. My wife's brother-in-law was an ironsmith and *his* brother owned a café. Neither had any connection whatsoever with the noble farming life, but they had inherited a field from their father, put sundry Albanians to work on it, took the crops, buried them in the local tip and collected the subsidy. And that is how they had built the house. A brick shell, that is, and plastered over. On our first afternoon there, I was taking a nap when

I was suddenly awoken by a deafening noise coming from above. The house was creaking at its very foundations and a woman was screeching: 'Aagh . . . aagh . . . aagh!' Because being a policeman is in my blood, I thought at first that my brother-in-law's brother was beating his wife. It took me a while to realise that he wasn't beating her, but bonking her and that it was her groaning that had awoken me.

'Shh, don't listen, it's not right,' Adriani whispered to me. She has a sinful mind, which is why she fasts all through Lent.

'Four in the afternoon – where do they find the energy?'

'It's not hard to understand. The kids are out of the house.'

The kids in question were two boys – a shrimp of about ten and a runt of about eight, who both wanted to be basketball players. And their father, who had heard on the television about the millions earned by sundry beanpoles, nationals and foreigners alike, had rigged up a frayed basket for them in the middle of the living room so that they could learn to sink three-pointers like Michael Jordan from the edge of the china cabinet. Training was rigorous twice a day, morning and evening, with jumping, shouting, fighting, and a ball. I took myself off to the café owned by their father, who charged me five hundred drachmas for a coffee, when he should have been compensating me for the mental stress.

That is why I had said to Adriani that the earthquake was in her head, because of the training, but developments proved me pitifully mistaken. The house leapt up from its foundations, hovered indecisively and then dropped back down again with a deafening bang. The picture of the lambs at the spring fell from the wall, and the two goat bells hanging above the picture began ringing demonically.

The force of the earthquake abated for a moment, only to return yet more violently and in a different form. The house rocked, with the furniture sliding to and fro. The wall I was facing cracked apart somewhat, as though the Peloponnese were separating from continental Greece, and its fragments tumbled on to the three-piece suite – the colour of raw liver, with lamé braid – bought by my brother-in-law from Furniture Factories United. As it crumbled, the wall took with it the Corinthian vase with the gold artichokes, and the cathedral chandelier that they had hung from the ceiling as a light fitting began swinging like a censor in the hands of a brawny priest.

I watched Adriani jump up from the armchair and brace herself beneath the door frame.

'What are you doing there?' I shouted

'During an earthquake, they say you should stand in the doorway. It's the only place that's safe,' she said, shaking like a leaf.

I cast Dimitrakos aside, grabbed her by the hand and began tugging her towards the street while the walls around us bent and straightened in turn.

As we were crossing the threshold of the front door, a piece of the ceiling became dislodged and crashed to the floor. I felt its fragments showering me and thousands of tiny needles piercing my hide.

Once outside, I heard a woman crying: 'Help, help!'

'Get as far from the house as you can!' I shouted to Adriani as I ran in the direction of the voice.

Stavria, the wife of my brother-in-law's brother was standing at the top of the stairs. She was clutching hold of her two boys and screaming hysterically for help.

'The kids, Costas, take the kids!'

As I ran up, I could feel the stairs shaking, ready to collapse beneath my feet. I snatched the two creatures, but the younger one, the little runt, started kicking me.

'My ball, I want my ball!'

'You go and I'll throw the ball down to you!' Stavria shouted from above.

'Don't go inside!' I told her, but she had already vanished inside the house.

As we reached the last step, the ball came whizzing down from above. The boy let go of me and ran to take it, even as from inside the house came the deafening crash of shattering glass along with Stavria's despondent cries.

'My light fitting!'

3

The shaking all of a sudden stopped and the ground calmed itself as though needing to take a rest.

Stavria emerged on the top step, her hair ruffled. 'That's my chandelier gone!'

It was identical to the one my brother-in-law had. I don't know why they had twin ones. Perhaps so that they could celebrate the Resurrection at home. You light them, light your Easter candle from them, say 'Christ is Risen' and you save yourself the trouble of climbing the 350 steps to the Church of Our Lady of the Golden Grotto.

'Never mind the chandelier. Come down here before there's another tremor,' I told her.

'Is the basket OK?' said the shrimp anxiously.

'I couldn't care less about your basket,' she said like a spiteful child.

'Anyway, that last basket of yours doesn't count. You'd committed a foul,' said the runt to the shrimp.

CHAPTER 2

The main square in the village was built on a stone wall and looked to me like a setting for concerts played by a town band. It was dissected by three narrow streets. One led out of the village, one led to the stop for the bus that did the run between the village and the harbour, and the third was a dead end that stopped in front of the church. Squashed in the streets to the right and left of the square was the entire life of the village, which amounted to a grocer's, a combined butcher's and greengrocer's, and a shop that sold everything from popular art to farm boots. The rest consisted of the café belonging to my brother-in-law's brother, a taverna, an old-style restaurant and two kebab joints, the one international, the other Greek. The international one was distinguished from the Greek because its sign said neither 'grill' nor 'kebab takeaway', but

4

rather 'kebaberie'. The owner believed that in this way he would attract the French, who were in the majority as regards tourism on the island, though he was probably wrong, because the Greeks who read the sign preferred the grill to the kebaberie, while the French, who might have preferred the kebaberie, could not read the sign because it was in Greek. The shops in the square were the only ones not to have suffered damage from the earthquake because they were huddled close up to each other. They were saved by their solidarity.

Three hours had passed since Adriani and I had rushed out into the street. I was sitting on the square's stone wall, across from the kebaberie, but I was unable to read its sign as it was pitch black. The electricity and telephones had been cut off. From the transistor, we learned that the earthquake's epicentre had been off the coast of Crete and its strength had measured 5.8 on the Richter scale. During those three hours the island's inhabitants had counted thirty-seven aftershocks, but a dispute had broken out concerning the last one. Half the people claimed that it should count, the other half said not, that it was simply an extension of the previous one, a sort of special offer: two for the price of one. So they went on discussing it, to give full vent to their masochism.

'After the earthquake in Kalamata, they counted fifty-two tremors in the first three hours,' said the man sitting next to me on the wall, seemingly upset that the island had failed in its bid for first place.

The whole village had gathered in the square. Some were sitting on the chairs belonging to the tavern and the restaurant, both of which were shut, and others were in the café belonging to my brother-in-law's brother, which was open and serving orange juice, Coca-Cola and iced coffee. Those who hadn't managed to book a seat in these establishments were roaming the square among all the children, who were chasing each other, playing football and fighting. The noise was deafening because it was not only the young, it was also the grown-ups who were shouting from the café to the square, from the square to the tavern and from the tavern to the restaurant. The two kebab joints were doing a roaring trade. The children were hungry and there was no way they could eat at home. They had lit a charcoal fire and were grilling kebabs on wooden skewers, which they handed over with a lump of bread as fast as they could. In the end, they ran out of bread and passed out the kebabs on their own. The charcoal fire was the only source of light in the square.

The few tourists who were still there in September had been pushed out of the square and had found shelter in the bus stop. They would have gladly left, but the bus, which was drawn up alongside, did not dare set off and they did not dare go back indoors to collect their luggage. Some were queuing outside the kebab joints, waiting their turn, which never came, because the locals kept shoving in front of them.

As the night progressed and the tremors continued, fear stifled the cries and the din died down. As if all this was not enough, a light rain began to fall, which gave rise to a new wave of protest. The Electricity Board van passed by for the fourth time, honking its horn furiously in order to make its way through.

'What's going to happen, Lambros? When will we get the electricity back on?' the man beside me called to the van driver's colleague.

'Don't get your hopes up. There's a fault in the underwater cable and it's going to take some time,' he replied, pleased that for once there was an explanation as to why the electricity had been cut off. Usually it goes off twice a day without any explanation.

'You should be ashamed, you good-for-nothings!' the man beside me shouted after the van.

There was more he was going to say, but a tremor caused him to lose his balance and slide off the wall. A clamour of various tones rose up from the square. From the 'Uh-oh, here it comes again' of the braver ones, to the high-pitched screaming of a number of women.

'So here you are. We've been looking for you all around the square.' I heard the sound of Adriani's voice beside me.

She was with Eleni, her sister, and Aspa, Eleni's daughter, who is in the third year of high school and is a quiet, bright girl, the most likeable member of my sister-in-law's family.

'Everything all right?' I asked Eleni, mostly out of courtesy as I could see that everything was all right.

'I'm still shaking. I was at the community centre at a meeting to decide what we're going to do about that old rascal Theologou. He wants to build a hotel at the tip of the island and close off the beach, when suddenly I felt the ground going from under my feet. By the time I'd run to the school to make sure Aspa was all right, I'd been to hell and back.'

'You're the cause of it with all your nagging. Why go away, we're all right at home, why do we need to go on holiday? With all that moaning, it's little wonder that we had an earthquake come down on us,' said Adriani, and all at once I had become the fault line that gave rise to the earthquake.

I was about to come out with a few well-chosen ripostes, because I had been right and she should have listened to me about staying at home, whereas now we would be hunting for our socks among the rubble, but again I felt that stabbing pain in my back and I leapt up in agony.

'What's wrong? Are you hurting again?' said Adriani, who for the past twenty-five years had been monitoring my every movement. 'Serves you right, since you won't see a doctor. You're paying all that money into the health scheme for nothing.'

'She's right, why don't you go and see a doctor if you're in pain?' said Eleni, tipping more fat on to the fire.

'Because he's afraid, like all men! A full-blown, top-notch police officer, head of the homicide division, who all day long is dealing with murderers and muggers, and he's scared stiff of the doctor!'

'It's just a crick. I'm not going to the doctor's over a crick.'

'Well, well, he's even come up with the diagnosis,' said Adriani disdainfully.

The whole conversation took place amid a slight swaying, as though we were in a fishing boat, and with the rain starting to get heavier. It had been about a month since I'd last felt that sharp, sudden pain, starting at my left shoulder blade and running down my arm. It lasted about ten minutes and then went away of its own accord. I don't go to the doctor's, because once you start looking, they always find something worse.

I stopped thinking about it, not because of any iron will, but because of the mayhem in the square. I turned and saw the mayor standing on the wall, trying to make himself heard over the crowd.

'Quiet. Let me speak!' he shouted and the din abated somewhat. 'I've spoken with the prefect. They're going to send us tents and blankets,' he continued, obviously pleased with himself, but his satisfaction went for nothing, because instead of reassuring the people, the news only infuriated them.

'When will that be? In three months' time?'

'Do you know that in Kalamata they're still living in caravans ten years on?'

'So much for State help! All they know is how to increase taxes!'

The mayor made another attempt to reassure them. 'Come on, have a little patience. We're not the only ones to have suffered damage.'

'We might not be the only ones, but we'll be the last, no question, to get the tents and blankets. Because of you.'

'I told you not to vote for him, but you wouldn't listen to me,' someone beside me said in a voice that everyone would hear.

'They'll be here, it's been decided, and you have my word on it,' the mayor told them, plainly worried that votes were at risk. He looked around for support and spotted me.

'You see what we have to go through, Inspector? Everything here is an Odyssey. Unfortunately, your people in Athens don't realise that.'

'The people are right,' Adriani intervened. She likes protecting cats, dogs and the downtrodden so long as she doesn't have to have them in her house. 'Why don't you send a helicopter to fetch them? Seeing as there's a heliport on the island.'

'A heliport is all we have, dear lady,' replied the mayor, shaking his head sadly. 'Without any helicopter. They built the heliport for us and we've been waiting six years for the helicopter. When we have an emergency case, a helicopter comes from Athens to take the patient to the hospital.'

It seemed as though everyone and everything was out to prove him wrong. Even as he spoke, the sound of a helicopter could be heard overhead.

8

'There it is, it's on its way! Didn't I tell you so?!' he yelled.

We could make out the black shape of the helicopter in the distance, with its lights flashing as it got closer. The island's entire police force, one lieutenant and two officers that is, was there, trying to maintain order. They linked arms, but there were only three of them, and with the first onrush they were swept aside. Without saying a word, I went and stood in front of them.

'There's no need for any trouble,' I said peaceably to the crowd. 'Those bringing the supplies will distribute them and there will be enough for everyone.'

I don't know whether it was my personality that imposed itself on them or the whirlwind created by the helicopter as it landed, but they began to draw back.

The helicopter came to rest on the concrete strip, the door opened and a young woman, no more than twenty-five, climbed out. All dolled up, she was the kind that in my village we would call a minx.

'We're here!' she shouted, thoroughly pleased with herself.

The people began to clap and she swayed coquettishly. But behind her, instead of tents and blankets, they saw a bearded man stepping out with a camera on his shoulder, and two other men who began unloading boxes, tripods and spotlights.

'They're from the TV,' said a disappointed voice and the clapping fizzled out like the froth on lemonade.

'Are you from the TV?' The mayor went over to the girl, ready to blow his top.

'Later, later,' she replied, in a rush herself. 'First I want to see the houses that were destroyed. Do you have any houses destroyed here?'

'No, fortunately, we don't, but –'

'I told you we wouldn't find any,' said the cameraman to the girl reporter. 'We've wasted our time, let's go.'

'No way,' she replied, snatching the microphone. 'We're behind schedule and I'll miss the live link-up.'

'So all that matters are the houses that were destroyed?' shouted the mayor angrily. 'We've been five hours in the street, in the rain, without electricity, without telephones, we don't dare go back inside our homes and no one cares about us. What are we supposed to do? Pull our houses down so that somebody will show some interest?'

'The criminal indifference shown by the State!' cried the minx excitedly. 'Who's the mayor? Do you have a mayor here?'

'I am the mayor.'

'Oh, it's you.' He was not what she had hoped for, but any port in a storm. 'What is your name?'

'Yangos Kalokyris.'

'OK, Mr Kalokyris. Stay close. In a while I'll call you to say what you told me into the camera.'

She took hold of the microphone and waited on her toes for the live link-up and for her spot on the screen. And because nowadays everyone works in television, including God, two claps of thunder were heard and it began to rain cats and dogs.

'Good evening, Yorgos . . . Good evening, ladies and gentlemen . . .' said the minx into the microphone, from which I understood that she was now live.

'The situation is tragic in this outlying island. Its inhabitants fled from their houses at the first strong tremor of 5.8 on the Richter scale. Five hours have passed since then and the emergency services are conspicuous only by their absence. As you can see, it's raining torrentially and the inhabitants have been waiting in vain for a blanket or a tent in order to get through the first night of the disaster . . .'

'Is there any damage?' asked the newscaster.

'No doubt there is, Yorgos, but at this point in time it's impossible to assess the extent of the damage as the electricity network has collapsed and the island has been plunged into darkness. However, I have standing beside me the mayor of the island, Mr . . .' She had forgotten his name.

'Kalokyris . . .' the mayor supplied.

'. . . Mr Kalokyris, who will give us an exact picture of the situation prevailing here. What is the situation at this moment, Mr Mayor?'

'As you said yourself, the situation is tragic. Once more we find ourselves having to put up with the criminal indifference of the State. Five hours have passed since I phoned the prefect to report the situation to him. He promised to send help, but no help has yet arrived. The aftershocks are continuing, our children are outside in the rain because we do not dare return to our homes . . . We run the risk of illnesses, of epidemics . . .'

I saw the inhabitants nodding their heads in approval and I admired his shrewdness at the way he had retrieved the initiative. At that moment he would have been voted in unanimously.

'I appeal through your channel to those in charge –'

'No need to go on, we're off the air,' the reporter said. 'Let's go, everybody,' she said to her crew, who began gathering up their paraphernalia and making for the helicopter.

'Thank you,' said the reporter, and she made off too. Halfway there, her heels got caught, she stumbled and only just escaped landing face down in the mud. Before climbing into the helicopter, she half turned as though remembering something.

'Hope you're soon back on your feet,' she called out.

'Back on our feet?' exclaimed one young lad. 'What have we got, a virus?'

It was the only sensible comment that I had heard all night.

CHAPTER 3

Eventually, around midnight, the tents and blankets arrived. By that time most of the inhabitants were soaked and towels would have been more useful. The mayor suggested that they set up the tents immediately, but the people were at the end of their tether and told him to set them up himself, that was why they had elected him mayor. Some who offered to help banged their knuckles with the hammers as they could not see the pegs in the dark and so gave up. In the end, everyone curled up somewhere – some squashed into their cars, others wrapped themselves in the blankets and some, the more daring ones, decided that after all they were better off returning to their homes.

We put up in my brother-in-law's ironmonger's shop, together with his wife, his daughter, his brother's family and a gaggle of other villagers he had rounded up at random from the square and offered refuge. The company, the conversation and the recollections of the quake exorcised the fear of the night and I began to miss the halva that my mother used to make when she invited the neighbours round for a soirée. The only sourpuss was Christos, my brother-in-law's brother, who gave him a mouthful under his breath, saying that the next day half his stock would be gone, because the villagers would steal it from him to repair their houses and that that was why he always got a raw deal and was taken for a sucker and why half the island owed him, whereas, despite all the fuss, he himself had not been taken for as much as an orange juice.

Now it was ten in the morning and everything hidden by the night was revealed in the light of day. On the surface, nothing had changed; the village was as it always had been. Except that from inside the houses could be heard the sounds of grieving, lamentation and bewailing, not in chorus, but separately in crescendos, because a team of assessors had arrived from Athens to inspect the houses and the grieving went up from those that were declared uninhabitable.

My sister-in-law's house looked like a house in Bosnia after the civil war. The plaster had fallen from the walls and the bare bricks were exposed. The chandelier from the cathedral had lost half its baubles and was maimed and hanging askew. A section of the ceiling had fallen and smashed the glass front of the cabinet and bits of plaster had found their way between the treasures: a vase in the shape of a flowering rose, three silver dishes and two murrhine candlesticks dotted with gold. Only the TV was intact and it stared at us blankly. Eleni, my sister-in-law, was silently brushing the liver-coloured suite with a will, as though she were spring-cleaning.

'Leave it, Mum,' her daughter told her. 'Cleaning's the least of our worries.'

Eleni turned and gave her a look as though she were about to tear her to pieces. 'Do you know how many years I had to wait to get that suite? And look at the state of it now. Just look!' she screamed at her daughter, as though she were to blame for the earthquake.

'Eleni, why not wait till those people come from Athens?' her husband said to her gently, for fear of riling her even more. 'We don't want them to see a tidy house and stop the 200,000 they're handing out for compensation.'

'Not to mention that they might declare it uninhabitable,' said the daughter.

Eleni looked at her with an expression that brooked no objections. 'I'm not leaving my house again. Not even if it collapses around me.'

Adriani made the smartest move of all. She said nothing, but simply went over to her and held her tight. Eleni put her arms round her sister's waist, rested her head on her breast, and all her rancour dissolved and she broke into sobs.

And at that very moment, while the sisters were wrapped in each other's arms and swaying, the chief from the police station arrived and defused the emotionally charged atmosphere. He stood in the entrance to the living room, cap in hand, and stared at me with a perplexed expression.

'What is it?' I asked him.

'I'm sorry. It's not a good time, I know, but could you come with me for a moment?'

'Now?'

'Yes, I need to show you something.'

I glanced at Adriani, who still had her arms round Eleni. She nodded and appeared to share my thoughts: that it was better for me to leave as I was only the odd man out there.

'Let's go,' I said.

Waiting for us outside was the island's only patrol car. The lieutenant sat in the front seat beside the driver and let me sit in the place afforded to VIPs – the back seat.

We took the uphill road towards Palatini, which is a mountain village and the only agricultural area on the island. The road was narrow and winding, hardly wide enough for two cars to pass.

The rain washed over the landscape. Below, the placid sea

stretched out and burrowed into both sides of the island in tiny coves, in crevices and niches in the rocks. Not that I have any particular love of nature; when I was small I was always bored stiff of it, and its solitude, and I would count the days before going back to Athens, but the view was breath-taking and carried me away.

I was brought back to reality by the voice of the chief. 'As if the rest weren't enough, we also had landslides,' he was saying.

'Is that why you've brought me out here, because of the landslides?'

'No, not because of the landslides. There's something else I have to show you. We're almost there.'

I was ready to start cursing him, because his evasiveness had begun to get on my nerves, but the patrol car turned left into a gorge that led down to the sea. On the way down, I noticed that the upper part to the right of us had come away, slid down and was at the bottom, only a hundred metres from the bay.

Beside the mound made up of the rocks and earth that had fallen, one of the station's two officers was standing guard. The driver of the patrol car, the second officer, pulled up nearby.

'Come with me,' said the chief, striding ahead towards the mound.

After a few paces, I halted. Something bulky was buried there. But for the head sticking out, I would not have recognised it as a body.

'This is the reason I brought you here,' I heard the lieutenant say. 'It was found by some English hippies, those unsavoury types that rent rooms out here in the wilds so they can get stoned in peace.'

The body was lying on its front with the face buried in the earth. The only thing visible was the short, black hair, from which I gathered that it must have been a man. I looked up at the hill. The whole slope had come away, as if sliced with a knife.

'We haven't touched him at all,' the chief said, proud that he could still remember the basics from the academy.

'Even if you had, it wouldn't have changed anything. He's been moved regardless. He was buried up there and his body has been brought to the surface by the landslide.'

I picked up a broken root and began scraping the stones and earth

14

from around the body. Worms wriggled in alarm and a lizard, perhaps another victim of the landslide, scuttled to find refuge elsewhere.

The chief stood beside me, watching. 'It may have been an accident and I have wasted your time bringing you here.'

Gradually, the body of a man was revealed. He was wearing only underpants – no socks, no shoes, no shirt.

'Accident?' I said to the chief. 'What about his clothes? Did he take them off so they wouldn't get creased?'

He looked at me, as he might have looked at that moustached Hercule Poirot, the one who concealed the fact that he was really a Cretan. 'That's why I called you, because you're with the Homicide Division and you know about these things. We've never had to deal with a corpse on the island before.'

'Lend me a hand so we can turn him over,' I said to the officer who was keeping guard. His face turned yellow like an autumn leaf and he began shaking from head to toe. 'Come on. He won't hurt you, he's dead.'

'Karabetsos!' said the chief in a commanding voice, though he did not offer to help me himself.

I bent down and took the dead man by the ankles to set an example and appeal to the officer's sense of shame. It was like lifting two pillars of ice; the rigor mortis made it impossible to lift him. I managed to shift him only a little and stood there holding him, waiting for the officer to swallow his vomit. After much ado, he came over and took hold of him by the tips of his shoulders, at the same time turning his gaze towards the sea.

As we turned him, a second swarm of ants and insects scattered in panic. The corpse fell on its back with a thud. The officer let go of it at once, ran to the nearest tree and began rubbing his palms on its bark. I stood over the dead man and stared at him. He was young, about five ten in height. His eyes were open and his glassy gaze was fixed on the sun above as though he were surprised to see it again. His cheeks were half eaten away. Undeterred, one worm continued to burrow inside a nostril, like a worker doing overtime in the metro. At first sight, I was unable to make out any signs of violence, but this was not necessary. The fact that he was all but naked was enough to persuade me that it was murder.

The chief turned and ran to the patrol car. He opened the boot and took out a white sheet. He unfolded it as he came back, covered the body and breathed a sigh of relief.

'How are we going to move him?' I asked.

'That's easy. I'll send Thymios. He has a truck and shifts stuff from the harbour. The difficult thing is finding somewhere to store him. We've nowhere here. I even brought the sheet from home with me. Now it's not fit for anything and I don't know who to charge it to.'

His accounting procedures were of no concern to me. 'Where are the ones who found the body?'

'There.' He pointed to a two-storey summer hostel some ten metres back from the pebbled beach. The ground floor was a taverna. The upper floor had five or six rooms in a line, their doors and shutters painted blue. Tables and chairs were spread out in front of the taverna. A fair-haired, bearded youth was lolling with his backside on one chair and his feet on another. He was your typical beach bum: half naked, barefoot, denim shorts. He had a guitar resting on his belly and he was causing it distress. I could just about make out his strumming.

'Luckily they hang out here and don't come down to the village,' the chief said.

'Let's go and see what they have to say.'

As we approached, I saw a young, dark-skinned girl with crinkly hair coming out of the taverna. From a distance, she looked no more than eighteen. She was wearing a bikini top, shorts and sandals. She stood over the bearded youth and began rubbing his back. I don't know if she was massaging him or rubbing him to get rid of the filth. At any rate, the youth appeared to be enjoying it. He put the guitar down and stretched his head back. The young girl leaned down and kissed him on the lips. He finished with the kiss and went back to strumming his guitar, which he seemed to consider more important.

I reflected that I would have to resort to my broken English to communicate with them and I felt my spirits sink. We went up to them, and it was as if they had not seen us. Indifferent, the bearded

16

youth went on strumming and the girl continued to massage his back. From close up, she looked older, maybe twenty-five.

'You found the dead?' I asked straight out, because I had practised the question on the way.

He half looked up and glared at me in annoyance, as though I had interrupted him in his conversation with Beethoven. The girl kept up her work.

'No, Hugo did and then he called us. Anita, would you fetch Hugo, darling?'

The girl went to summon Hugo, while the bearded youth went back to his guitar.

I turned and looked at the chief. He shook his head resignedly. 'You don't have to say anything. I get this every day.'

'What's your name?' I asked the youth. So long as I keep my sentences short, I'm all right. Five words and upwards, and I start to stammer.

'Parker . . . Jerry Parker.'

Anita came down the steps from the upper floor followed by Hugo. He was a tower, nigh on seven feet tall, with shaved head, a moustache that hung down to his chin, a ring in his left ear. He was wearing a sprigged kaftan, so he was a junkie. If he had been wearing a fleece, he would have been a lion-tamer.

The same question, to get into my stride. 'What's your name?'

'Hugo Hoffer.'

'You found the dead?'

'Yes,' he said.

'Explain, please.' And that is where the good and the bad began. Good, because he was German and his English was no better than mine, so my confidence rose. Bad, because I could not understand a word he was saying to me in that pronunciation of his.

I turned to the chief. 'Did you catch that?'

He shrugged in bewilderment. 'Not a word.'

'Listen . . . I'll tell you, so you'll understand,' Anita said in fluent Greek.

I could have belted her round the ear. 'Are you Greek?'

'Yes. Anna Stamouli.'

One Brit, one German and a Greek girl. Fine, I thought to myself, relieved. At least when it came to riff-raff, we had achieved the goals of the Maastricht Treaty. That was something.

'So tell us then what happened,' I said, getting cross.

'We stayed out all last night because of the earthquake. It was impossible to get near the shore because of the huge waves breaking on it. And then, it must have been around ten, we saw the hill shaking and splitting in two following one of the aftershocks. I can't describe it; I've never seen anything like that before. We watched it falling and were sure it was going to crush us all. Fortunately, we got away with it at the last minute. This morning, at around nine, Hugo told us he was going for a ride on his bike to the village to see what was happening. Within two minutes, he was back here. Come and let me show you something, he said. We went and there was the body. Hugo rode to the police station and informed you. That's all.'

Concise and to the point. 'You'll have to come down to the station to make a statement,' I told her.

'I see, I'm to be the interpreter. Though I don't know how it will help. That man's been dead around three months.' She looked me in the eye with an ironic smile. 'If you examine his neck, you'll see signs of a struggle,' she said.

'How would you know that?' I asked out of curiosity.

'I'm studying medicine in London. Jerry's reading maths. We're together. We met Hugo here. He's doing a doctorate in philosophy and he's here to get away for a bit.'

'Why didn't you say you were Greek instead of pissing around?'

'I saw the look on your face, that's why. I knew you'd taken us for junkies.'

She still had the same ironic smile. She knew she had got one over on me.

'Come and show me those signs,' I said to her. 'And then you and the German are coming to the station with me to make a statement.'

We set off to go back to the scene of the landslide. The officer was leaning against his tree, smoking, his back half turned to the corpse. I went up to the body and pulled back the sheet.

'Show me.'

She knelt beside the body. 'Here, look,' she said.

I bent down to look. On the left side of his neck, the side facing the hill, there were a few, barely perceptible, scratches. I swallowed with difficulty, annoyed with myself. Because we had found him naked, I had been certain that it was murder and I had searched no further. I had to admit that the girl was right, but her manner had got on my nerves and I said nothing.

I heard the roar of a motorbike approaching and stopping behind us. I turned and saw Hugo on an antiquated motorcycle, the kind used by the Germans in the war. No doubt his grandfather had been a Nazi and he had inherited it.

'We'll take you in the patrol car. You'll be more comfortable,' I said to the girl.

Again, the ironic smile. 'I prefer the bike. If I come with you in the patrol car, the whole village will say that you nabbed me because I'm a junkie.'

She climbed on behind the German and the bike sped off with a deafening roar.

CHAPTER 4

Three blasts of the ship's horn were heard and its smoke appeared from round the cape. Presently, its prow came into view; the white bulk grew larger, blocking the entrance to the small bay. The ship swung to the left and began coming astern to the quay as its ramp slowly descended.

About thirty people and five or six cars, the final remnants of the summer, were waiting to embark for Piraeus. Only four days had passed since the earthquake, but there in the harbour, with its few houses and two seafront tavernas, there was nothing to recall its passing.

The sea was like a millpond; the sun's rays glistened upon it and two speedboats were darting in and out of the bay.

If it hadn't been for the unidentified body, we would have left the day after the earthquake so as not to be a burden to my sister-in-law's family. The house had not been declared unsafe, but they were going to rebuild it from scratch. So, the opportunity was presented to us on a plate; on the one hand we were able to appear discreet and on the other we were able to return home.

But it was the corpse that spoiled it for us. I telephoned police headquarters in Ermoupoli, but they had their hands full on account of the earthquake and had no time. They did not want to know.

'At least look to see if there's anyone missing who fits the description.'

The police chief agreed to give me five minutes of his time. 'I have a Frenchman, two Brits and a Dutchwoman. I also have an eighty-year-old gone soft in the head. Any good to you?'

'No.'

'One more reason for me not to get saddled with him. He's most likely one of yours who came on holiday and got bumped off.'

I saw that I was getting nowhere and phoned my superior in Athens, Chief Superintendent Ghikas.

'Reminds me of the Jew who decided to go to market and it turned out to be the Sabbath,' he said to me, laughing. 'For once in your life, you go on holiday and you find yourself up to your neck in earthquakes and corpses.'

'I always go to market on the Sabbath, you simply never noticed. What do you want me to do about the body?'

'Bring it back here and get on the case, seeing that you've got yourself involved already.'

I wavered between two possible reactions. The one was that of the public employee who comes out with a stream of abuse under his breath. The other was that of the masochist police officer who is intrigued by the case. The latter prevailed and I decided to call Markidis, the coroner in Athens.

'You must take me for a lunatic if you think I'll make a ten-hour trip to an earthquake-stricken island to look at a corpse disgorged by a landslide,' he said. 'Send it in by freight and I'll see what I can do.'

So, there I was, standing on the quayside, with Adriani and three suitcases, waiting to board the ship. The crowd jostled forward in anticipation of the harbour official opening the gate. They were in a hurry to charge into the saloon to grab a table for playing cards or an armchair for watching TV.

Thymios' truck, with a coffin containing the unidentified corpse in the back, arrived at the last minute, as we were about to board.

'Oh no, we're not travelling with a corpse, are we? As if the earthquake wasn't enough!' exclaimed a fat, middle-aged woman in green tights, crossing herself energetically.

'It'll be the man they found up in the hills after the earthquake,' said her friend, who had the same figure, and was wearing skintight jeans.

'And do they have to send him on the passenger ferry? Couldn't they find any other way?'

'Greece, what do you expect?'

'Why does it bother you to have to travel with the corpse?' said Adriani, intervening, as I tugged at her blouse from behind to get her to keep quiet, though I knew it was pointless.

'What do you mean, dear?' said the one in the green tights. 'Merciful Lord, it's bad luck! We're about to cross the sea!'

'Of course, the sea, what was I thinking of. Bad luck doesn't strike you on the land.' Her sarcasm dripped sweetly, as though she had laced it with honey.

'As you don't seem to mind, you keep it company, we won't stand in your way,' said the one in jeans as she walked up the companionway.

Adriani chose two plastic seats in the stern so that we might get a bit of sun, and we parked ourselves down. On the benches various foreigners, wrapped inside their sleeping bags, had sprawled themselves out and were dozing blissfully. Opposite us, sitting on the deck, Anita and the Brit were shamelessly cuddling. At one moment, the Brit turned and our eyes met, but it was as though my face meant nothing to him.

Adriani took out her paraphernalia and began embroidering. I watched her and wondered where she would find room for the new handiwork. She had always had a craze for embroidering, but after

Katerina had left to study law in Thessaloniki and she was left on her own, things had got worse. After a while her gaze wandered over the foam churned up by the propellers; she sighed deeply and abandoned her embroidery.

'What's the matter?' I asked.

'I'm thinking of Eleni. What's she going to do now?'

'She'll clean the suite or help Sotiris to hang the chandelier.'

She looked askance at me because she knew what I was leading to. 'It's called a light fitting.'

'All right. Like the light fittings hanging in the cathedral.'

'Anyhow, you're just plain mean. I wonder what you say about our house.'

Better that she did not know. Anita and the Brit had tired of canoodling and were locked in embrace, like the fossils of burnt trees in Evia. I leaned over and took Dimitrakos out of Adriani's bag. I thumbed through it and came upon the entry *doneo = 1. quake or tremble with or as with fear. 2. to convulse or quiver as with instability.* While looking further down to see if it had anything to say about earthquakes, as I had had enough of fear and quivering, I heard a voice above me.

'What did you do with the body?'

I looked up and saw Anita. My gaze searched for the Brit and I located him sleeping on his back with his mouth open, inhaling the sea breeze.

'It's below. Do you want to see it?'

'No, I've seen it twice. That's enough.'

Adriani glanced up from her embroidering, looked at us, concluded that a girl with a figure like that couldn't possibly fancy a policeman and went back to her needlework.

Yet Anita did not seem to want to go away. She glanced at the sleeping Brit, then she turned back to me and stared as if trying to make up her mind.

'If there's something you want to say, why don't you come straight out with it?' I said.

'Hugo told me something on the day he left.'

'What did you tell you?'

22

'That he'd seen the guy, before he was killed.'

'Where?'

'In Santorini. With a girl.'

'A girl? What girl?'

'I don't know. At any rate, she must have been local because she spoke Greek.'

From bad to worse. A pity it wasn't some tourist that he had picked up in Santorini. 'And why didn't he mention this at the time?'

'Because he had to wait an hour to make his statement and he was fed up. If he'd told you about the girl, you'd have kept him there even longer and he wanted to get it over with.'

'Why? Was he in a hurry to feed the lions?'

It took her half a minute to bring to mind the philosopher-cum-lion-tamer with the earring and she burst out laughing.

'Don't judge on appearances. He's far from stupid.'

'If he had any brains, he would have told me about the girl. Do you have his address in Germany?'

'No. These are summer friendships. Come autumn, you forget them.'

Perhaps she did not want to give it to me so as not to get him involved. The Brit had opened his eyes and was stretching. She saw him, left me and went to him – in case he missed the caress of her breath, I suppose.

'Do you think it might be a crime of passion?' Adriani said to me.

So many murders take place every day in Athens – junkies who knife you for a fix, Albanians who butcher you for a dishcloth, Russian mafiosi who kill for an old Datsun – and she still thinks that murders can be crimes of passion. Enough to make you quake, as Dimitrakos would say.

'Yes, indeed. She strangled him, undressed him because she wanted his clothes as a souvenir, then she got hold of a pick and shovel, dug a pit and buried him.'

'Is it really so improbable?'

'I don't know. That policeman you watch on TV who's always yelling his head off most likely wouldn't find it improbable.' He's the policeman in a series that she watches religiously every evening.

'I don't watch him any more,' she said. 'Nor any other soaps. So don't waste your ammunition.'

I was taken aback, but I did not let it show. 'That's something. Of course, it took you three years to realise he was a complete fake.'

She glared at me. Then she gathered together her embroidery, got up – clutching the plastic chair to her backside – and went to sit five yards away in the sun.

At such times, her temper does not bother me at all, because I get some peace. I was beginning to like the business with the unidentified corpse less and less. If the man really had been with a girl and if the girl had been a local, so what? And why hadn't she gone to the police to notify them of her friend's disappearance? One explanation would be that the murderer had buried her as well, somewhere nearby, but she had not been unearthed by the landslide. If the German giant had told me about *her* on the island, I would have had the area dug up so we could have been sure. Now, I would have to send a message to the police station and how would I know whether they would search properly? If they did not find her, it would mean either that they had separated or that she was in on it and that she was afraid and in hiding. And as if this wasn't enough, I would have to send a message to the German police with particulars of the philosopher-cum-lion-tamer, so that they could track him down and get a further statement from him. And all this because he could not be bothered to sit ten minutes longer at the police station.

I sank into my thoughts with the rhythmic sounds of the boat lulling me to sleep. I did not know how long I was asleep, but when I awoke, it was already getting dark and I needed a second or so to realise that the boat had stopped in the middle of the sea. I looked at Adriani's chair. It was empty. Nor were Anita and her Brit anywhere to be seen.

I got up to go and look for Adriani. I found her in the saloon sitting in an armchair in front of the TV and watching a man in a green jacket, brown shirt and grenadine trousers talking to a woman who was distraught and sobbing buckets, while on the right side of the screen there was someone giving a commentary from inside a tiny frame rather like a skylight. It was pandemonium all around in the saloon, what with the smoke, card playing and shouting and I could not catch what they were saying. Adriani was lost to the world. She was hanging on every word. I touched her on the shoulder and she jumped like a frightened bird. She saw that it was me and turned at once back to the screen.

'So you've woken up?'

'Why have we stopped?'

'Mechanical problems, they said.'

'Broken down'

'What else?' It was a white-haired man nearby. 'No wonder, when they're still operating these wrecks. It's happened to me twice before on this same old barge.'

'I told you it was bad luck to travel with a corpse on board, but you wouldn't listen to me!' The fat lady in tights was standing in front of me and gloating because her prophesy had come true.

The bad luck lasted another hour and a half. Eventually we reached Piraeus three hours behind schedule. The ambulance was there, with the driver and stretcher-bearer by now weary of waiting. I made sure they got the corpse inside the van and then, together with Adriani, I joined the queue for taxis. One came about every five minutes. There was no police officer around at that time to keep order and it was a free-for-all. I had thought about taking the Mirafiori with me but, like the boat, it too was an old crock and it would not have stood up to ferryboats and dirt roads. We got to the front of the queue, but that meant nothing because people kept jumping out from behind, getting into the taxi and going off. One taxi driver had already found one couple and was looking for a second fare.

'Where are you going?' he asked me.

'Pangrati.'

'Not on my route,' he said and got back into his taxi and drove off.

'Why didn't you show him your badge so he'd have to take us?' said Adriani angrily.

'Are you off your head? So he'd turn round and call me a fascist?'

'So what? Would it bother you if he'd called you a commie? The good old days are long gone,' she added with a sigh.

Fascists, communists and liberals, they had all gone. There were just the two of us left with our three bags waiting in the hope that some taxi might go out of its way and take us.

CHAPTER 5

The Mirafiori was waiting for me just as I had left it ten days earlier. It must have been annoyed that I had not taken it with me on holiday because it played up on me for a good five minutes before starting up. As I turned from Aristokleous Street into Aroni Street, I came face to face with a low hill, rather like a miniature of Lycabettus Hill. I braked sharply and an old man leapt aside in a panic to save what was left of his life.

'Are you blind! As if the piles of rubbish aren't enough, you want to cripple me too!' he shouted, banging on my windscreen with his fist.

It was only then that I saw that it was not a hill but rather a mountain of plastic bags, empty banana boxes, pizza boxes, meat bones for dogs, fish bones for cats and silver food containers. On top of the mountain, where normally there should have stood the tiny church as on Lycabettus, there was a clapped-out mattress, presumably for climbers who needed a rest.

'What's going on? Are the refuse collectors on strike?' I asked him.

'Where've you just come from? From the EEC?'

'No, from a holiday.'

'Welcome back to Athens,' he retorted and turned his back.

In Hymettou Avenue, the piles of rubbish reached as high as the first-floor balconies. In the morning, when you opened the shutters, instead of fainting from the smell of the thyme, as the song goes, you would faint from the stench of the rotting meat and fruit. Some people had heaped it against the saplings planted by the City Council

26

to fool us with supposedly tree-lined avenues. It reminded me of the pine needles and cones that we heaped around the pines in my village.

I arrived at the police headquarters in Alexandras Avenue and went up to the third floor to the Homicide Division. The corridor was empty. Before going into my office, I glanced across to where Vlassopoulos and Dermitzakis, the division's two lieutenants, were sitting.

Dermitzakis had replaced Thanassis, the police sergeant who had committed suicide virtually before my eyes. Sometimes, while I'm driving, the windscreen suddenly turns into a television screen and I see his head on the pillow with his left arm dangling from the bed and his right hand still holding his service revolver.

Dermitzakis has the same rank as Vlassopoulos; both are lieutenants. When you see them side by side, you would think that I had chosen them deliberately, because the one is a variation on the other. They are the same height, though Vlassopoulos is broader in the beam, while Dermitzakis is narrow and thin. They are both dark-haired, though Vlassopoulos' hair spreads out like a halo around his bald patch, while Dermitzakis' is thick and ends on the fringes of his brow.

'Back already, Inspector?' said Vlassopoulos. 'Was it the earthquake or did you miss us?'

'The earthquake, plus a corpse. I didn't miss you two at all. Now, come with me, we've got work to do.'

They followed me into my office and sat in the two chairs while I phoned Markidis, the corner.

'Why are you calling me at nine in the morning?' he said to me, annoyed. 'Did you think I'd be up at dawn to carry out an autopsy on your corpse?'

'When will you have something for me?'

'I may have something now, but you won't like it.'

'I guessed as much.'

'If you were intending to establish his identity from the fingerprints, you'll be disappointed.'

'Why?'

'Because his fingertips have all been burned off.'

His words made my stomach sink. We had the corpse of an unidentified man whose fingertips had been burned, and who had been seen on the island in the company of some unknown girl. Things were certainly going from bad to worse.

'I've done you a favour in order to sugar the pill for you,' said Markidis at the other end of the line. 'I've notified Forensics and they're coming to photograph him before I cut him open.'

'Thanks. As soon as you have anything, call me.' I hung up and put my two assistants in the picture.

'Other people come back from their holidays with a stick of rock, you've come back with a stiff,' Vlassopoulos said.

I let it pass, as I always do, when my subordinates are right. 'Call Forensics and tell them to get a move on with the photographs. And send a message to the island police to start digging on the hillside where the landslide happened in case they come up with the body of the girl who was with him.'

'They can dig, but they won't find anything,' said Dermitzakis with absolute certainty.

'How would you know that?'

'It's obviously a case of summer sex. Screw and scram.'

I hoped he was right. We went out together. They went back to their office and I took the lift up to the fifth floor, where Ghikas' office was.

Koula, the uniformed model, who acted as his secretary, jumped up from her seat as soon as she saw me.

'What happened to you? Such bad luck! You go on holiday after two years and you run into an earthquake!'

'What can I say?' I said, assuming the mandatory sorrowful look when you are obliged to cut short your leave, even though you are actually pleased to be back.

'It's the eye. Someone's put the evil eye on you, mark my words.'

'Who would have put the evil eye on me, Koula? Not the Chief. He takes his leave like clockwork.'

She smiled conspiratorially, as always whenever I said anything remotely disobliging about Ghikas.

'Never mind, I've got something nice for you.' She opened the top drawer of her desk and took out an island-style box. Painted in the middle of the box was a heart pierced by an arrow. It was stuffed with wedding confetti.

'Is somebody getting married?' I said innocently.

'No, engaged. I've got engaged.' And, beaming from ear to ear, she showed me the ring on her left hand.

'Well done, Koula, congratulations. And who's the lucky groom? A colleague?'

'You must be mad,' she retorted indignantly. 'I became a police-woman to secure myself a permanent job somewhere, but not to get married to a policeman. He's a building contractor with an office in Dionysos.'

Look what we've come to, I thought: lower than constructors of illegal residences in Dionysos.

'All the best.'

I gave her a friendly pat on the back and darted into Ghikas' office before it occurred to her to ask me to be the best man. I shut the door behind me as my feet sank into the lush carpet. Ghikas was sitting with his back to the window and talking on the phone. He turned and looked at me. His desk was oval-shaped, nine feet across. It reminded you of a hotel reception because the west end of it was marked by the Greek flag, the east end by the American flag and the south-east end by the flag of the EEC. The central plains were a desert, given that there were never any papers on his desk.

'What's happening with the body you landed us with?' He was his usual welcoming self.

Not a word about how I got through the earthquake, how my wife was; not even a word of appreciation for my cutting short my leave and returning to work. Nothing.

'I sent it to Markidis for the autopsy.'

'Do we have anything to go on?'

'The only new item of evidence is that we won't be able to identify the man from his fingerprints because his fingertips have been burned.'

He did not like that at all and as always, when he did not like something, he took it out on the nearest target.

'And why didn't you notice that? You had the body for three days on the island.'

'He was covered in earth and I didn't want to touch him. I wanted to hand him over to Markidis exactly as I'd found him.'

Then I told him about the philosopher-cum-lion-tamer and the girl that he had seen with the man. 'I intend to send a message to the German police to take an additional statement from him,' I added.

'Do it. And I'll call Hartmann to speed things up.' He lifted the receiver. 'Call Hartmann for me in Munich,' he said to Koula.

I assumed that the Hartmann in question was his counterpart in the Bavarian police; one of those acquaintances of his that he trots out every so often. Because he had six months' training in the FBI, he reckons himself a specialist in international relations. Which accounts for the flags on his desk, so that the uninformed might get the picture. As soon as he gets a hint of a trip abroad, he swings into action. And it is from these trips abroad that he comes up with various names, without anyone being able to establish whether they are in fact acquaintances of his or whether he has simply heard of them. Most probably he did meet them but did not make any impression on them, so these so-called colleagues rack their brains trying to remember who he is every time he calls.

'Start with the missing persons,' he said, as if, left to myself, I would begin with the army recruitment base at Corinth. 'Find out whether there's anyone who fits the description of the victim.'

'Of course. As soon as I get hold of the photographs.'

'Because this case is going to take some time, I've got something else for you, to keep you busy in the meantime.'

He took a file from his desk and handed it across to me as though he were handing me a birthday present. 'It was sent by the Anti-Terrorist Squad this morning.'

'Why is the Anti-Terrorist Squad involved?'

'The victim is someone by the name of Koustas. Someone shot him four times at point-blank range with a .38 in Athinon Avenue as he was leaving his office. At first, they took it for a terrorist job. But now they have decided that it was more likely a settling of accounts and so isn't their concern.'

I put the file under my arm and turned to leave. 'Keep me informed,' he shouted after me.

'As soon as there's any statement to be made.'

It was the only thing that interested him. Summoning reporters and making statements. I felt a sudden pang of hunger and remembered that I had forgotten to have my morning coffee and croissant. I reflected that it wasn't right for me to strain my nerves on an empty stomach and so I pressed the button for the first floor, where the canteen was.

In the past, it was Thanassis who always brought me my coffee and croissant every morning, but I can't ask the same of Dermitzakis. I miss Thanassis, and not only on account of the coffee and croissant. Perhaps this is what's behind the slight antipathy I feel towards Dermitzakis, because he was the one who took Thanassis' position. I have no other reason for either liking or disliking him. A good professional relationship is based in part on mutual respect, though above all on mutual indifference.

'Welcome back, Inspector,' said Aliki, who served behind the counter.

She handed me a croissant wrapped in cellophane. Then, taking hold of the coffee pot, she threw in a couple of spoonfuls of Greek coffee, a spoonful of sugar, added hot water from the espresso machine, put the coffee pot under the mechanical whisk and stirred the mixture. The coffee soon began to froth, possibly from indignation at being made in that way. She took it from under the whisk, added tinned milk and handed it to me. The traditional Greek coffee is a thing of the past. Now we drink it like the Greeks we have become: neither one thing nor the other.

'Ah, you got it, did you?' I heard a voice behind me.

I turned to see Stellas, one of the officers from Anti-Terrorist, pointing to the file under my arm.

'What's the case all about?'

He laughed. 'If you want my opinion, file it and forget it.'

The second case in a row that people have told me to file. 'I'll have a look into it first.'

'You won't get anywhere with it. A settling of accounts, rival gangland bosses . . . someone did him in and made good their escape. You'll never find them.'

'If I need anything, I'll call you.'

'No need to call. I've told you everything I know. What little there is is in the file.'

I sat at my desk, took a bite of the croissant and opened the file. The first thing I saw was a photograph: paving stones with the chalk outline of a body. They shot him from in front and he fell on his back with his right arm stretched out to one side, just like when you sleep in the July heat and you let your arm hang from the bed because you don't want it touching your body. His right leg was straight, his left bent at the knee. Next to the outline of the body could be seen the wheels and lower part of a car with the driver's door open.

There were two similar photographs taken from different angles. In one, there was a better view of the car. A big car, an Audi or a BMW, something of that sort. The fourth photograph was different. It showed a man of about fifty-five, with a thin moustache, lying on a stretcher. His eyes were closed, Koustas dead at the hospital.

Before turning to the results of the coroner's examination, I read the police report. Konstantinos Koustas was a figure well known in night-time Athens. He had two clubs: the Night Flower, a chic place in Poseidonos Avenue, just up from Kalamaki, and a more moderate one, the Bouzouki Strings, in Athinon Avenue where it entered Haïdari, as well as an expensive restaurant in Kifissia, the Canadré – whatever that might mean.

Koustas had left the Bouzouki Strings the previous Wednesday at two thirty in the morning. The club's doorman had found it strange that he should leave alone without his bodyguards, but when the doorman had bade him goodnight, Koustas had said that he wasn't leaving, but that he simply wanted to get something from his car and that he would be back. As he was opening the driver's door, the doorman saw someone going up to him from behind. He was unable to make out his features in the dark. All he could remember was that he was wearing a T-shirt and jeans. He must have said something to Koustas because he turned round. At that point, the doorman heard the sound of gunshots and saw Koustas collapse to the ground. The assailant ran towards an accomplice waiting on a motorbike with the engine running. He jumped on to the pillion and the bike sped off. The whole business had barely taken a minute. It was then that the doorman had gone over to Koustas, found him lying in a pool of blood and had rushed to call the police and the Emergency Ambulance Service. By the time they had got him to Tzanneio Hospital, Koustas was already dead.

I picked up the coroner's report. The autopsy had been carried out by Kyrilopoulos. He was not as experienced as Markidis, but how much experience does it take to locate four mortal wounds from a .38 automatic? Two of the bullets had pierced his heart, another his right thorax. Those three bullets had passed right through him. The fourth had lodged in his liver.

I lifted the receiver and called Markidis again. 'It's about the autopsy on Koustas. It was carried out by Kyrilopoulos.'

'Yes, and we sent you the report.'

'I've seen it. But I want to see the body.'

'You can't. We've given it for burial.'

I read the coroner's report again. Something was not right. Professionals have a steady hand, they know where to aim a bullet, two at most just to be sure, and they have you. This murderer seemed to have been shooting blind, wherever: two in the heart, one in the right thorax, one in the belly. At first sight, it did not seem to me to be the work of a professional. And if it was, he must have been either a greenhorn or a bungler.

At the bottom of the file there was a second report. The bike had been found abandoned in Leonidou Avenue in Haïdari, near to the Haïdari tax office. It was a 200cc Yamaha, registration number AZO-526, and had been stolen two days earlier in Maroussi. Someone by the name of Papadopoulos had bought it two months previously for his darling son because he had passed his university entrance exams.

I gazed out of the window and reflected. The theft of the bike suggested that it was a professional job, the shots not. Did Koustas know the murderer and so turned to speak to him? Or did the murderer simply know his name and call out to him? I put the brake on my thoughts because it was still too early to come to any conclusions.

If the Anti-Terrorist Squad were right, our only hope of getting anywhere was in the underworld. I lifted the receiver and told Vlassopoulos to come to my office.

'We've got ourselves a second case. Koustas.'

'Why aren't Anti-Terrorist dealing with him?'

'Because it isn't a terrorist job. They only deal with the pick of the pile.'

'One unknown and one well known. Good combination,' he said, laughing.

'Find out if there's any dirt going round that we should know about.'

'If there is something, I'll find it.'

On the balcony opposite, a young girl was hanging out the washing. She was wearing a miniskirt and as she bent over to pick up the clothes from the bowl, I could see her shiny blue knickers. Until a year ago, an old woman had lived there with her cat. One morning, while I was sitting in my office, I had seen a coffin through the balcony door. Two other old women were leaning over it. Before long, the hearse came and two men took away the coffin. The old women accompanied it to the front door of the apartment block. Within two months, a couple had appeared in place of the old woman. The young girl and a big hulk with hair down to his shoulders and a 1,000cc bike. I do not know what became of the cat. It might at this very moment be scrimmaging through the rubbish piled against the saplings.

CHAPTER 6

There was a sea breeze blowing; the sea was glistening, but the exhaust fumes rushed in through the open window and prickled my nostrils to remind me that I was not on board a boat but in a patrol car being driven by Dermitzakis along Poseidonos Avenue. The city stank of rubbish, the coast road of exhaust fumes. All along the coast, people were splashing in the shallows or sunning themselves and filling their lungs with pollution. A tall, gangling woman had grabbed hold of her son and was dragging him towards the shore, and he was wriggling like the fish in the Saronic Gulf before they migrate. In front of us, a rubber-dinghy seadog had loaded his craft on to the roof rack and was off to launch it in somewhere like Varkiza or Porto-Rafti.

We were on our way to the home of Konstantinos Koustas in Glyfada. Besides, I had nothing better to do. The business with the unidentified corpse would indeed be a long, drawn-out one. It would take at least a week before we came up with anyone who knew him – if we found anyone at all, that is. There was no point in our going to the Bouzouki Strings, where Koustas was shot. It would be closed at this time. So our only hope was Koustas' house.

Dermitzakis turned off Poseidonos Avenue and parked in front of the Night Flower, Koustas' other club. I had suggested that we take Vouliagmenis Avenue, which is the shorter route, but he had wanted to go along the coast road in order to take a look at the Night Flower. Like all the nightclubs where you go to be fleeced, it was a flimsy construction of prefabricated concrete covered in white plaster. The entrance was strewn with gravel and above it was a metal construction taller than the building on which were written the names of singers. Dermitzakis rang the bell a couple of times, but no one opened the door. The Night Flower was closed, like all night flowers at that time of the day.

'We've drawn a blank,' he said, disappointed.

'What I expected, but I saw you were determined and I didn't want to dampen your enthusiasm.'

Taking Vassileos Yeoryiou Street, we arrived at Psarrou Street where Koustas' house was. It looked like a fortress behind a high concrete wall, on which were set iron railings topped with barbed wire. The double gate was also of iron and cased with thick sheet metal. Beside the house was the garage door, also closed. I rang the bell and a tiny screen immediately lit up. Obviously so that they could see your face and, if they liked the look of it, let you in.

'Who is that?' came the sound of a woman's voice.

'Inspector Haritos.'

Apparently she was not impressed, as I got no answer. She let us stand there a couple of minutes and then the gate half opened. At the same moment, a bulldog in a security guard's uniform appeared and blocked the opening before we had time to enter.

'May I see some identity, gentlemen? We would normally frisk you, but if you are police officers, that won't be necessary.'

'If you so much as dare to lay a finger on me, I'll have you locked in a cell till your boss gets you out on bail,' I snapped.

He backed down and did not even check our badges.

In contrast to the outside, the inside resembled in size a neighbourhood allotment, except that instead of tomatoes and cucumbers, they had planted statues: a discus thrower, a caryatid, a Cycladic idol, a satyr, and three more that I didn't recognise – all of clay. You passed through the graveyard of statues, climbed three steps and were at the entrance to the house. An Asian girl, one of those that got us to swap bean soup for soya, was waiting for us at the door and ushered us into a pitch-dark sitting room. She opened the blinds a fraction, just enough to enable us to make out our shadows and not bump into each other. The light penetrated through the slit and formed a dividing line on the floor between Dermitzakis and me.

The floor was marble and covered with rugs – not everywhere, only in places: beneath the suite of blue sofa and armchairs, beneath the round table with its four chairs, and beneath the two high-backed wooden chairs, where King Arthur was sitting with Lancelot, a telephone stand between them. I went to the blinds and peered through the slit opened by the Asian girl. Now I understood why the garden in front was only a few feet wide. At the back, an enormous green expanse reached as far as the next street, with flower beds and a few scattered palm trees. The high wall stretched all the way back, though instead of a moat and drawbridge, the castle had a swimming pool with deckchairs and umbrellas.

The purring of a cat distracted me. It was coming towards me, its rump swaying aristocratically, and if I had not seen its eyes, I would not have been able to make it out against the floor because it was pure white. It looked more like a lamb than a cat – perhaps it had just come out of hormone therapy. It stood there in front of us and continued to purr, not pleased by our presence. Now that I was able to see it close up, I noticed two grey marks on its forehead.

'Calm down, Mitsi,' came the sound of a woman's voice, and I turned.

In the doorway was a woman of around fifty, but with the body of a thirty-year-old and a tired beauty. She was wearing a black blouse and white linen slacks. Her face was familiar to me and I racked my brains trying to remember where I knew her from.

She smiled at me without offering her hand. 'I'm Elena Koustas, Inspector.'

'Haritos. This is Lieutenant Dermitzakis.'

'I apologise for keeping you waiting, but I wasn't expecting you.'

It wasn't a reproach, simply a statement. The cat positioned itself in front of her, sitting motionless and looking into her eyes, just like lovers look at each other for the first month, before the hard looks begin. Koustas stretched out a hand and stroked it. I was still racking my brains, trying to remember where I had met her. She understood and burst out laughing.

'Are you trying to remember where you know me from? You're not the only one. Everyone remembers me from somewhere, but they don't know from where. Do you like musical reviews, Inspector?'

I was about to say no, that I preferred the cinema, when it came to me. When I had first entered the Force, I had been assigned to guard a minister of the junta, who had a thing about musical reviews. That was where I knew her from. Her name was not Koustas in those days, but Fragakis. She wore a black lamé evening dress, with a low cleavage, and a slit that served as a curtain for her legs. She liberally revealed both and the audience went wild. 'What a woman, what a woman,' murmured the minister in admiration, though with a note of sadness, as though he regretted that she wasn't a communist so that he could have had her locked in a room in Security Headquarters and have given vent to his admiration.

'You are Elena Fragakis,' I said.

She was pleased and smiled coquettishly. 'You know, it's been fifteen years since I gave up singing. It was when I got married. That's why I'm pleased when people still remember me. It's a sort of consolation,' she added with a slight bitterness in her voice.

My recollection of her caused me a mental block and I didn't know how to begin. Her experienced eye caught sight of my perplexity and she decided to help me. 'If you've come to ask me questions, I can tell you that I said everything to your colleagues in the Anti-Terrorist Squad. You can read my statement.'

'Do you mind saying it all again to me? I'd like to hear it from you.'

'By all means, Inspector. Besides, there's so very little I know that it won't take a minute.' She crossed her legs, but she was wearing slacks so the curtain did not open to allow me to see what her legs were like now. 'Konstantinos left at around eleven. He told me he was going to drop by the restaurant first and then go to the Bouzouki Strings. And because whenever he went to both establishments he usually didn't get back before three in the morning, I watched a little TV and then went to bed. I was awoken at four by the telephone and someone told me that my husband was dead. That's all I know.'

'Is that what your husband did every night?'

'Yes, unless we were going out. But usually he only went to one or the other.'

'Did he have any special reason for going to both that night?'

'I wouldn't know, Inspector. Konstantinos never talked about his work.' The bitterness returned to her voice, though I could not tell whether the bitterness belonged to Elena Koustas, whose

38

husband had left her in the dark, or to Elena Fragakis, who from being in the spotlight and the public view had found herself shut up in Alcatraz.

'When you say the restaurant, are you referring to the Canadré in Kifissia?' Dermitzakis joined in the conversation. He had noted the name of the restaurant on a slip of paper so as not to get it wrong and he read it out with some difficulty.

'How did you say it?' Koustas burst out laughing.

'Canadré. That's what I have written down.'

'Le Canard Doré, Lieutenant. The Golden Duck. My husband gave it a French name because it has French cuisine. He'd spin in his grave if he heard you call it the Canadré.'

The thought seemed to alarm her. Dermitzakis had turned bright red and I was furious.

'Our officers don't have any problem with English,' I said, thinking of my own failings in that quarter. 'But they don't know French. The State doesn't pay them to learn French just so they can read restaurant signs correctly.'

'I don't know French either. But I've heard it so many times that I've learned it. If you did know French, you'd realise that my pronunciation is that of a bumpkin.' Her sincerity was disarming and you could not but like her.

'Did your husband have any enemies?' I asked, to get back to the subject.

'Don't you?'

'What?'

'Have enemies. Colleagues who envy you your position and do all they can to undermine you, criminals who would like to kill you. Don't you? I left the theatre fifteen years ago and they're still saying behind my back that I slept with the impresario to up my salary and that I dressed provocatively to flirt from the stage with the rich and famous. I've been married for fifteen years to the same man and they still call me a whore at every opportunity.'

She had succeeded once again in flummoxing me, because I had thought the same thing myself when I had seen her onstage. 'I didn't mean that,' I said as though apologising for my long-ago thoughts.

'I know what you meant. If he had enemies who wanted to kill him . . . Underworld bosses . . . Protection racketeers . . .'

'Yes. Your house that's built like a fortress would seem to suggest something of the sort.'

'No, Inspector. It simply shows that Konstantinos took precautions, that he knew how to protect himself.'

'I'm off. I'll take the car.' It was a voice behind me.

I turned and saw a young man of no more than thirty, tall and unshaven. He was wearing jeans, black boots with spurs and a motley shirt. But the most striking thing about him was his gaze. It was bleary and lifeless, and had difficulty in focusing. It tried to fix on something and slipped away.

'Your dad didn't want you to take the car.' Koustas' voice was soft and friendly.

'My dad's dead. Come on, give me the keys.'

'You know I can't give them to you.'

Her soft tone was still there even in her refusal. For a moment, the young man's gaze livened and fixed itself angrily on her. I thought he was going to lunge at her and I readied myself to prevent him. Then his gaze became bleary again and slipped off Koustas. He spun round and made for the door.

'My husband wasn't killed by gangsters, Inspector.' Koustas turned back to me. 'I know that's what your colleagues think, but they're wrong.'

'Bullshit.' Koustas' son had changed his mind and come back. 'Bullshit, it *was* gangsters who did him in. You're barricaded up in here with your swimming pools and your Filipino maids and you don't know what goes on outside. He knew, but he acted the tough guy behind security guards who were a joke.'

I did not like this boy, but what he said was not without logic. Most people pay and they put their minds at rest. On the other hand, I remembered Koustas' wounds and I was still bugged by the idea they were not the work of a professional.

'Do you know whether your father had received any threats from gangsters?' Dermitzakis asked him.

'I know nothing. I was simply stating my opinion because it seems logical to me. But don't ask me because I'm in the dark.' The tone of the expert had gone and he was trying to cover himself.

'In any case, you'll be required to make a statement. If you know something, let's have it now and be done with it.'

'I saw nothing, I heard nothing, I know nothing. Write it down and bring it to me to sign.' He hurried off before we had time to ask him anything else.

'That was Makis, Konstantinos' son from his first marriage,' Koustas explained. 'Please don't be offended by his manners, he's been through a lot. He's just come out of a rehabilitation clinic for drug abuse.' She paused as if waiting for a reaction from me, saw that there was going to be none and went on: 'I hope he won't slip back again. He's been clean for six months now.'

'Did your husband have any other children?' I asked.

'A daughter, Niki, younger. The two are like night and day. Niki went to university, did a master's in England and works for an opinion-poll agency, R.I. Hellas.'

Dermitzakis took out his notebook and wrote down the name. He would hardly get that one wrong.

'What makes you so sure that your husband wasn't murdered by underworld interests?'

'No reason in particular. I just think it unlikely. Are we through?' she asked impatiently. 'Please excuse me, but I'm not in such a good way.'

She did not wait for me to tell her that we were through. She simply left us and the cat got up and followed her, its tail taut like an antenna.

The Asian girl saw us to the door and from there the security man escorted us to the garden gate. He played the austere and silent guard, but something told me that he was doing it in order to avoid my gaze.

When we got outside, we found Makis leaning against the patrol car waiting for us.

'Do you want to know whether my father had enemies?' He looked at me, but his gaze slipped away again and dropped to my belt.

'Did he?'

'Yes. Her in there,' he said, pointing towards Alcatraz. 'From the day she arrived, everything changed. She knew that he was madly in love with her and she twisted him around her little finger. But all she cared about was his money.'

An empty taxi came down the street. Makis hailed it and got in. The taxi drove off before I could ask him anything else. He had thrown us a bone – the wife who kills her husband for his money – before running off. I would have to think about it, but, on the other hand, I liked Mrs Koustas.

CHAPTER 7

'Have you called the doctor?'

Adriani was sitting at the kitchen table. She had a pile of newspapers in front of her and was cutting out the coupons to get a new set of pans. So far, she had acquired a rug that was in the living room and stood out like a sore thumb, an electronic notebook that she did not know how to use because the instructions were in English, a cookery book that she threw away because it had nothing in it about how to make moussaka, and a set of nice glasses, the only things to have proved to be of any use.

The previous evening, I had promised that I would make an appointment with the doctor at Security Headquarters about the pain in my back. But that morning, I had got straight down to work on the case of the unidentified corpse, and then I had been given the Koustas case and I had forgotten all about it.

'I phoned him, but his line was engaged,' I said, hoping to make my escape from the kitchen before she started grumbling.

'And why didn't you call again later? Or are you going to tell me there was a fault and the lines weren't working?' she said in a caustic tone.

'I got caught up in work and forgot about it. Anyway, I'm fine, my back's not been giving me any trouble.' One reason I had forgotten was precisely that: it hadn't bothered me for days. And when something doesn't bother you, don't bother it – it's a hard and fast rule.

'If it's spondylitis and you're doubled up for the rest of your life, you'll have only yourself to blame. And what if it's not spondylitis, but a slipped disc? Did you hear what happened to Manthos, my friend Anna's son? A strapping young man of thirty-five and now he has to go round in a wheelchair.'

'Stop nagging me!' I shouted at her. 'There's nothing wrong with me, it's just a twinge. You'll put a jinx on me and I'll end up with bone cancer!'

'Whatever you end up with, it'll be because of your own pigheadedness!' And instead of me escaping from the kitchen, she was the one who stormed out, leaving me to begin cutting the coupons from the newspapers, just to unwind.

From the time we got married, Adriani has been living with the fear of my falling ill. During the first years of our marriage, she would put her ear to my heart while I was sleeping, or glue her face up against my open mouth so as to be able to feel my breath. At first I was flattered by her fears, as when she would stroke my hairy chest or make me stuffed tomatoes, my favourite dish.* After about five years, her hand on my hairy chest started to tickle me, after ten her ear against my heart woke me up with a feeling of discomfort, and after fifteen the stuffed tomatoes began to give me indigestion. But because happy marriages thrive on contrariety, Adriani is terrified of illnesses and I of doctors. At the first twinge, she rushes for tests whereas I, even when in a lot of pain, prefer to leave things as they are and wait for it to go. Until now, I am the one who has been proven right.

Cutting out coupons started to get on my nerves and I gave up. As I went through the living room, I saw Adriani sitting in her usual spot in front of the TV, with the remote control an extension of her arm so that she could switch channels as soon as the adverts came

* A recipe for stuffed vegetables is included on page 334.

on. She was watching the same man I had seen on the boat, except that now he was dressed in a grenadine jacket, green shirt and brown trousers. He was sitting in an armchair, had his hands to his mouth and was listening very attentively to a woman's voice over the telephone. Sitting opposite him was a couple, both of them dressed in department-store bargains and both of them staring at him anxiously.

'What's that you're watching?' I asked Adriani.

'A reality show,' she replied without taking her eyes off the screen.

I suddenly recalled Koustas' Canadré that turned out to be Canard Doré and it occurred to me that she, too, was pronouncing it wrongly.

'What's that?' I asked again to be sure.

'Reality show,' she repeated testily. 'Where have you been hiding? It's the latest thing in TV shows. They get the dirt on people and bring it out into the open. More or less the same as you do.'

'You can be sure that if they had any evidence, they'd come to us first and then they'd go on the air to criticise us for not doing our job.'

'Well, it's not far from the truth, is it? We've got security firms and security systems everywhere because you people don't do your job properly. Who goes to the police today for security? No one.'

What she said put me in mind of Koustas' security guard and I felt the anger rising in me, but I decided not to give way to it. I went into the bedroom and from the top shelf of the bookcase where I kept my dictionaries took down Liddell & Scott. It was my moment of relaxation. I lie on the bed, open a dictionary and know peace. Adriani's nagging, problems at work, even murders, all disappear from my mind. I sink into the bliss of my solitude. I am particularly fond of my Liddell & Scott. It's the four-volume edition, published in 1907, and it was given to me by my godmother, who had inherited it from her father. She was the daughter of a renowned lawyer and lived in Athens, though they had a place in the village and would come every Easter.

When I was born, my father tried to get round a politician to persuade him to be my godfather. But my father was a mere police sergeant: he had no pull with politicians and so he settled for a lawyer's daughter, who was a spinster and at least wanted a godchild. Every Christmas she sent me a pair of trousers and every Easter a pair of shoes and an Easter candle. If the trousers got holes in them, I would wear them patched till the following Christmas; if the shoes got holes in them, I would go barefoot till the following Easter. And in both cases, I would get my ears boxed twice in succession, first by my mother and then by my father. She gave me the Liddell & Scott when I entered the Police Academy. I had never actually needed it, but I became hooked on words.

I looked up the word arthritis. I found that *arthritis = inflammation of a joint or joints characterised by pain and stiffness of the affected parts, caused by gout, rheumatic fever, etc. [from Greek* arthron, *a joint].*

Well, my joints were not inflamed or stiff, I thought to myself. It was just a twinge that came and went. After all, Hippocrates was a doctor, too. He made everything out to be worse than it was to drum up custom.

'It's Katerina on the phone. Do you want to talk to her?' I heard Adriani's voice from the doorway.

She knew very well that whenever my daughter calls, I invariably take the phone, but she deliberately asked because she did not approve of my passion for dictionaries and wanted to make the point that my addiction might even take precedence over my daughter's phone call.

I brushed past her without giving her so much as a look, went into the living room and picked up the receiver.

'Hello, dear, how are things going?'

She laughed. 'Fine, if you ignore the fact that I'm up to my neck in laws. I'm collecting material for my doctorate.'

'Don't worry, if a thing's worth doing, it's worth doing well,' I said, supposedly to give her some encouragement, while I restrained myself from audibly bursting with pride that she had managed to get accepted for a doctorate and that her lecturers were delighted with her.

'What about you? Did you go to the doctor?'

There followed a pause as I tried to stop myself from shouting.

'Why would I go to the doctor?' I said calmly, no change in my voice.

'Because your back's hurting you.'

I looked around. Adriani was nowhere to be seen. She had primed her daughter and then vanished so as not to get a flea in her ear.

'It's nothing for you to worry about.'

'I do worry when there's something wrong with you and you don't go to the doctor. So, will you go or shall I go on worrying?'

'All right, I'll go.'

'I'll call tomorrow to see whether you've made an appointment. Don't force me to come to Athens and stop my studies.'

'How's Panos?' I asked, because my temper was starting to get the better of me.

'He's fine. He sends his regards,' she answered briskly and then rang off.

That was one way I had of showing her I was annoyed. Panos was Katerina's boyfriend. They had been together for two years, but I did not like him at all and Katerina knew it. He was not a bad lad; he was studying to be an academic greengrocer, in other words an agriculturalist. But he was a muscle-bound hulk who wore T-shirts and trainers. We had types like that in the Force and usually their brains were smaller than the olives they cultivated in the School of Agriculture. So my daughter and I gradually developed a code. I did not ask her about Panos and she did not mention him, but on the rare occasions that I did ask her, it meant that I was annoyed with her.

As I had given Katerina my word, it was pointless to get into a row with Adriani, so I sat down to watch the news in case there was anything about Koustas. Adriani did not so much as poke her head round the door. She was waiting until I was absorbed in the news. Presently, I sensed her entering without a sound, like Mrs Koustas' cat, and sitting on the edge of the armchair. Her eyes were fixed on the screen and she avoided looking at me.

The bulletin had nothing new about the murder and, as usual, when there's nothing new, they play the video with the old report again. The opposite of the cinema. At the cinema, they show what is coming next, on the news bulletins they show what went before. It was only at the end of the report that they mentioned that the investigations were being carried out by the Homicide Division. This was followed by the day's medical discovery. A team of doctors in Iceland or Greenland had discovered that, apart from lowering blood pressure, garlic also prevented heart attacks. A researcher appeared, dressed all in white, with a medical mask, chopping garlic as if she were making tzatziki. It seemed that everyone was out to get on my nerves.

'What, every night they have a new medical discovery? Such progress, it's beyond belief,' said Adriani. She was pretending to be indignant in order to play up to my dislike of doctors and win me round.

'They've got so much money for research that they've ended up spending it at the greengrocer's,' I replied. We laughed and the ice was broken.

But I had had enough of medical matters and I needed to go out for a walk, amid the rubbish, to get a breath of fresh air. Instead, I decided to go to the Bouzouki Strings to put my questions to the doorman and Koustas' henchmen. I'd be sure to find them there at that time.

CHAPTER 8

The traffic in Athinon Avenue was light. Apart from the car showrooms with their brightly lit glass fronts, everything was pitch black. In the darkness the rubbish looked like fortifications left over from the battle of Athens. A few lorries and a couple of intercity buses were in the lane going towards Athens. Half the passengers had their heads resting on the windows and were dozing, the others were looking out and admiring the view.

I saw the Bouzouki Strings to my left as I turned into Haïdari. I drove past and made a U-turn at the first traffic light in order to park outside. This place, too, was plastered white. White seemed to be the dominant colour in Koustas' life: white clubs, white garden statues, white marble in the house, white cat, white umbrellas round the pool, as though, before becoming a businessman, he had been a paramedic. This place, too, had a metal construction at the front, though not nearly as big as the one outside the Night Flower.

The doorman was a thirty-year-old giant. He was wearing the classic overcoat with gold buttons and a cap with braid. He took up the entire entrance with his bulk.

'Are you Lambros Madas?' I said.

'Yes. Who's asking?'

'I want to ask you a few questions concerning Koustas' murder.'

He looked me up and down. 'A million,' he said.

I stood there staring at him, but he did not give me time to recover from my shock. 'Listen, I'll do more than just answer your questions, I'll re-enact it all for you step by step. I'll tell you how these gangsters go about their killing. I can even sketch the outline of the body on the asphalt for you. And if you're willing to throw in another two hundred thousand, I can get you a BMW just like the boss's so that it looks real.'

'And since when has the Greek State handed out a million drachmas to interrogate eyewitnesses?'

He was taken aback and stared at me. 'Aren't you from Hellas channel?' he said.

'Never mind the channel, you be careful you don't find your-self in the gutter. Inspector Haritos, Homicide Division. What did you think? That I'm here from a reality show?' I was secretly grateful to Adriani for just having explained to me what this was.

'I don't know why you're here, but I've nothing to say. I said it all in my statement.'

'And what about what you just said about the gangsters?'

'Hot air. I took you for a TV reporter and I thought of spinning you a yarn to make a bit extra.'

'We'll do something else,' I told him. 'I'll take you in for questioning. When you come out, all the reporters in Athens will be waiting outside and they'll get it out of you for free.'

It did not take him more than a second or two to say: 'Ask your questions.'

'What time was it when Koustas came out of the club on the night of the murder?'

'Around two thirty. I thought it strange that he came out alone and I said to him –'

'I know what you said to him. What did he do?'

'He walked to his car and opened the door.'

'Where was the car parked?'

'Over there, on the pavement.' And he pointed to where a red Ford Escort was now parked. 'He always parked it there. I made sure that the space was empty.'

'And what did he do?'

'He opened the door and stooped to get something. Then I saw someone going up to him.'

'Did he come on a bike?'

'No, on foot. The bike was there already, but I only made the connection afterwards.'

'Forget the bike for the time being. Let's turn to the murderer. From which direction did he come?'

'From over there.'

He pointed in the direction of Skaramangas. The area around the Bouzouki Strings was open on all sides. To the left there was a dark alleyway, wide enough for a small van. Beyond that, there was a warehouse built of concrete slabs, and then a garage. The man must have waited in the alley and approached when he saw Koustas going to his car. The question was how did the murderer know that Koustas would come out of the club alone? Normally he left with his two bodyguards. It would have been too much of a risk to take on all three of them.

Unless the thing he went to get from the car had some connection with the murderer, who knew that he would come out to get it. But nothing had been found, either in Koustas' hands or in the car, that would support this theory. At least that's what the official report said.

'What did the gunman do?' I said to the doorman.

'He went up to him from behind. He must have said something to him. Not that I actually heard him speak, but Koustas turned round, and so that was my conclusion.'

'Never mind your conclusion. When Koustas turned round, was he holding anything in his hand?'

'Not that I saw.'

'Then what happened?'

'The man shot him three or four times . . . four, I think . . . then ran to the bike.'

'So he didn't bend down to take anything from the car before leaving?'

'No, what would he take?'

'His coat – how should I know?' I said irritably, as though he were to blame that my theory didn't stand up. 'The man who killed him, can you describe him?'

'Average build, pretty tall. He was wearing a white T-shirt, jeans and dark glasses.'

'Did you see his face?'

'No, it was dark. Only his hair, which was white.'

'That wasn't in the statement that you told me to go away and read if I wanted information.'

'I forgot about that.'

Perhaps. Perhaps he had also kept it back in order to remember it later in exchange for a million. 'Do you mean that he was old?'

'I told you. It was dark and I couldn't see his face. Only his white hair.'

That did not make him old necessarily. Some quite young people have white hair. 'Let's turn to his accomplice. What time was it when he arrived on the bike?'

He thought a moment. 'I can't tell you exactly. Motorbikes and scooters go past here all the time. I noticed him because I saw him waiting with the motor running. But that happens often, too.

Because the club is well known, people make appointments outside, so I assumed he was simply waiting for someone.'

'How long was he waiting?'

'If I count backwards from the time the boss came out, it must have been three or four minutes.'

So he was on time, too. They must have known when Koustas was going to come out. Otherwise the accomplice would have been there earlier, or would have driven round the block so as not to attract attention to himself.

'How was he? In appearance, I mean.'

He shrugged. 'He was wearing a helmet and a leather jacket. I can't recall what trousers he was wearing.'

He let out a deep sigh, either because he was getting tired, or because he thought the worst was over. If for the latter reason, he was on the wrong track.

'What was it you were going to tell the vultures from the TV channels about gangsters?' I asked him, adopting my stern manner once more.

'That they were the ones who killed him. What else?'

'How do you know?'

'Come on. It was a professional hit,' he said.

His conclusion matched that of the Anti-Terrorist Squad. 'How did they know that he would come outside alone?'

He laughed out loud. 'If he'd come out with Haris and Vlassis, they'd have plugged them too. They were lucky.'

Perhaps he was right. Professionals always bank on the element of surprise. By the time the bodyguards have pulled out their guns, the hit man has shot them. I left him and went inside the club.

For a moment I had the impression that I was inside the house of my sister-in-law on the island, except that here, in place of the liver-coloured three-piece suite, there was a liver-coloured wallpaper covering the plywood walls. Liver-coloured with gold baklava slices. The tables began at the foot of the stage, in the shape of a half-moon, and were arranged all the way back to the entrance. There were very few customers; no more than three or four tables were occupied. To the right was a bar with high stools. The booming sound of the band was coming out of four enormous speakers and reminded me of cannon fire on Independence Day. Onstage, a forty-year-old woman in a black dress and bulging bust had the microphone glued to her mouth, as though it were an ice-cream cornet, and was singing:

> 'Happiness cannot be
> Divided into three,
> But in our case, OK,
> There's no other way.'

Her case did not interest me one bit and my eyes fixed on Koustas' bodyguards, who were standing at the bar, sipping their drinks.

'Inspector Haritos,' I said to them, before they too demanded a million from me. 'What did Koustas say to you before going outside on the night of the murder?'

They looked at the woman onstage, who continued to lick the microphone. 'That he was going to get something from his car and would be right back,' one of them said.

'We wanted to go with him, but he said not to bother,' said the other.

I didn't know who was Haris and who was Vlassis, but it hardly mattered. What mattered was that a man who was so cautious, with a house like Alcatraz and with bodyguards in his club, had decided to go out unprotected.

'What time did Koustas usually leave the club?'

'Normally around three, never before two.'

He had been killed midway – at two thirty. The girl behind the bar was wiping the glasses, not interested in our conversation. At that moment, a man, thin as a toothpick, wearing a light brown suit, blue shirt and bow tie, came rushing over to us. He held out his hand to me from ten yards away in case I missed it and did not shake it.

'Renos Hortiatis, Inspector,' he said as I shook his hand. 'I'm the club's manager. I was only just informed that you were here. Can we offer you something?'

'No, thank you,' I said.

'How can I be of help to you?'

'I want to know whether Mr Koustas took anything with him when he left here on the night of the murder.'

'Such as?'

'I don't know, that's why I'm asking. The day's takings for example.'

His expression told me that he took me for an idiot. 'No, Inspector. No one would carry that amount of money around with him. I lock the takings in the office and the next morning a van from City Protection comes and takes them to the bank.'

'Who did Mr Koustas talk to before going out on the night of the murder?'

'To Kalia,' one of the bodyguards chipped in.

'She had just left the stage and was going to her dressing room. Koustas took her aside and they talked for a while.'

'Where can I find this Kalia?'

'She's inside now, putting on her make-up,' said Hortiatis. 'Follow me, please.'

He hustled me down a narrow corridor. On the left were four partitioned spaces, each closed off by curtains. Hortiatis drew back the second of these and instead of finding myself confronting a family of Kurdish refugees, I found myself looking at the back of a girl in front of a mirror, putting on her make-up. As soon as she saw us, she left off what she was doing and stood up. She was wearing a dress of silver scales. I looked at the hemline and wondered how many inches higher it could go before her underwear became visible. She could not have been more than twenty-five, but the heavy make-up made her look older and cheaper.

'The Inspector would like to ask you a few questions,' Hortiatis said to her. Then, turning to me, he gave me an ingratiating smile and remained fixed in his place.

'Leave us alone,' I said to him.

His smile vanished, but he left. The girl was still standing and looking at me with a blank expression.

'Are you Kalia?' I said.

'Depends. For the customers I'm Kalia. For the police I'm Kalliopi Kourtoglou.'

'And you're a singer?'

'Is that what they told you?' A cynical smile spread over her face. 'No, I'm not the singer, I'm the stage-dressing.' She saw that I didn't understand and went on. 'Marina and I go out on stage with Karteris, who's the star turn. One of us stands on the right and the other on the left. In theory we're there to accompany him, but we don't sing anything. The customers, you see, don't only want to hear Karteris' latest hit, they also want something to look at and we provide our thighs and our bums. Every so often, we come out with a rehearsed "yeah-yeah-yeah" . . . if that's what you call singing . . .'

That much I understood. What I did not understand was what Koustas might have to talk about with this nightclub Lolita.

'What did Mr Koustas say to you on the night of the murder, when you came off the stage?'

She stared at me as if trying to fathom my gaze. 'I don't remember him saying anything to me,' she replied, though I'm certain she must have thought of several answers before she chose that one, which was the most harmless one.

'He stopped you and took you aside to talk to you. His body-guards saw you together.'

'Now that you mention it, I do remember something. He wanted to tell me that I don't swing my hips enough onstage. And I told him he ought to have us up there in our birthday suits and be done with it.'

'Is that all he said to you?'

'No. He said that if I ever talked back to him again, he'd take me off the stage and have me scrubbing the floor. And he would, you know,' she added bitterly. 'I need the money.'

'He told you he'd have you scrubbing the floor and you don't remember?'

She shrugged. 'You hear all sorts of threats in this place, almost every night. From Koustas to Karteris, and from Karteris to Hortiatis, they're always threatening to show us the door. Who can remember all they say?'

'Are you finished, Inspector? Kalia is due onstage.' Hortiatis was

54

in the doorway. His eyes were on Kalia and he had an enquiring expression. As soon as I left, he would press her to find out what I had asked and what she had told me. The girl flew out. I followed. Behind me I could hear Hortiatis' footsteps.

In the meantime, the club had filled up. The two bodyguards were no longer in their place, and the girl behind the bar was desperately serving drinks. A photographer was wandering among the tables and taking shots of the people. Up onstage was a gypsy with sideburns all the way to his lips. Kalia and another girl, with a similar figure to hers but in an auburn version, were on either side of him. I stood at the back of the club and watched the show for a while. It was just as Kalia had described it. The girls swayed non-stop, forwards, backwards and around. Their mouths opened and closed, but not a sound could be heard. Between them, the gypsy sang with his eyes closed, sealed shut by his pain.

'Next time you come around asking questions, let us know in advance.' I heard a voice at my back.

I turned and saw Makis, Koustas' son. His gaze – no longer all over the place as it had been that morning, but, glaring and wild – was trained on me. He was wearing a leather jacket and jeans which he had tucked into pointy, patterned cowboy boots. We used to have machos who danced the zeibekiko, now we have cowboys who dance the tsiftetelli.

'What are you doing here?'

'What do you mean what am I doing? Now that Dad's dead, I'm in charge of the place. And I don't want policemen here in business hours, they ruin the atmosphere.'

I was thinking that what he wanted was a belt round the ears to wake his ideas up, but at that same moment Hortiatis came tripping over.

'Take it easy, Makis,' he said almost imploringly. 'We've got enough on our plate, we don't want any more trouble. Please excuse the misunderstanding, Inspector.'

He succeeded in soothing me, but made Makis furious. He grabbed Hortiatis by his brown-suit lapels and began shaking him.

'Shut up!' he screamed. 'I'll get rid of you, do you hear? You've had your way long enough. If the old man had listened to me and left the management to me, you'd have been long gone!'

Hortiatis stared at him in surprise for a moment. Then he broke into a mad, almost paranoid laugh. His slender body shook like fruit jelly, his steel-rimmed glasses were about to fall off his nose, but he was unable to put a stop to his laughter. Makis looked at him dumbfounded. The photographer had stopped and was watching the scene. Hortiatis turned, still in stitches, and walked away. I was curious to know what he had found funny, but it was not the moment. The spectacle had lost its interest and I went outside.

'Where's the Haïdari police station?' I asked the doorman.

'Take Karaïskaki Street towards the city. Turn into Iera Odos Street. You'll see it in front of you, on the corner of Iera Odos Street and Neas Fokaias Street.

'If he takes over, we'll be closed in two months and I'll be looking for a job,' he called after me.

I left him with the prospect of approaching unemployment and went over to my Mirafiori.

CHAPTER 9

The lorries and trailers went up and down Iera Odos Street with the speed of a VIP escort. With headlights blaring, they jumped on the patches in the asphalt and at every jolt honked their horns.

It was extremely humid and my clothes were sticking to me. At the beginning of the third block, I saw on my right the only building with any lights on. In the past the choice was simple: if you saw lights in a building at that time of night it was either a bordello or a police station. Now, with bars and all-night clubs having sprung up everywhere, it was more complicated. I got closer and saw that I was in luck. It was the Haïdari police station.

'What do you want?' asked the guard at the entrance.

'Inspector Haritos. I want to see the duty officer about a stolen motorbike.'

He looked me up and down suspiciously. It was too much for him to take in that from the whole of Athens a senior police officer had come down to Haïdari in the middle of the night to get information about a stolen motorbike instead of waiting for God to bring a new day or, better still, obtaining the information through official channels without moving from his chair.

'First floor, first door on the left, Inspector,' he said hurriedly, to make up for the time he had lost gaping at me.

The lift was busy. I thought of taking the stairs, but my tiredness was taking its toll on my legs so I decided to wait. It was more user-friendly than our lift at HQ and in less than a minute I was up on the first floor.

The duty officer was a sergeant; one of those who believe that everyone and everything is there to harass them for no reason and without any solution. He was chatting to a younger officer standing beside his desk. 'Wait outside, I'll call you,' he said on seeing me entering.

'Inspector Haritos, Homicide Division.'

He sprang to his feet, while the officer slipped out.

'Sergeant Kardassis. I'm sorry, Inspector, but it's a madhouse here.'

'So I see,' I replied, glancing round the empty office. 'I need some information about the bike used in the murder of Konstantinos Koustas.'

'Of course,' he said, only too willing to oblige and went over to a filing cabinet. 'Here we are. A 200cc Yamaha, registration number AZO-526. Stolen two days previously –'

'I know all that,' I said, interrupting him. 'I read it in the report. I've not come down here in the middle of the night for you to read me what I know already. I want to know how you found it.'

'A patrol car found it the next day abandoned in Leonidou Street, next to the Haïdari tax office. At first, they paid no attention to it, but when they passed again in the evening, it was still there. They became curious and checked it out. That's how it came to our attention.'

'And how did you ascertain that it was the bike used in Koustas' murder?'

'The doorman at the club recognised it.'

It was to be hoped he had recognised the right one and not confused it with another. Of course, the bike had been hovering for a full three or four minutes while waiting for the murderer. During which time, the doorman had had it in full view. He would have been unlikely to get it wrong. Anyway, the fact that they had abandoned it meant that someone else had been waiting there with a car. How else would they have got away at that time of night? A murder with three men involved was a professional murder, whether I liked it or not. I tried to put the timing into some kind of order. The killing had been carried out at two thirty. At most, it would have taken them ten minutes to reach Leonidou Street. They could have been at home in bed by three after their night's work.

'Did anyone see a car speeding along Leonidou Street at any time before three o'clock?'

The duty officer shook his head. 'No, Inspector. We made the usual, routine inquiries, but no one saw anything. It's mainly working people who live round here. They sleep early and get up early. Don't be fooled by Koustas' club being always full. His customers aren't from this area; they come from elsewhere.'

'Do you know whether Koustas had ever received any threats from the underworld protection racketeers?'

Before he had had time to hear my question the door to his office burst open and a couple staggered in. The man, a fifty-year-old, was beside himself. He was holding a bright red handkerchief to his nose and the two middle buttons were missing from his white shirt. His companion was a plump, curvaceous woman, no doubt the pick of the local talent. She was wearing a white dress that was tight across her plentiful bust. Her mascara had run because of her crying and was trickling down the bags under her eyes.

'You again?' the duty officer groaned.

'I want to lodge a complaint,' the man shouted.

'Who's it against this time and why?'

'Argyris Koutsaftis.' The man went on bellowing. 'He made a pass at my wife and then punched me.'

'Where did this take place?'

'At the Bouzouki Strings.'

I recognised them. They had been sitting at a table at the back, together with a man who was younger than them.

'Aristos, *please*,' the woman said imploringly. 'Drop it. We'll end up in court and we'll be made a laughing stock.'

'Shut up! Shut up, you whore! It's all your fault! If you didn't swing your hips so much, that punk wouldn't have got so cocky!'

And he gave her a backhander. As a result of this manoeuvre, the handkerchief fell from his nose and drops of blood dripped onto the balcony created by the woman's bust so that she began to screech. I could not work out whether she was screeching because of the slap or because her dress was stained. Probably the latter, because she seemed more accustomed to backhanders than to expensive outfits.

The officer pushed the man away from his wife. 'Simmer down,' he said severely. 'In here, you'll keep calm and say what you have to say in a proper manner.'

'Don't listen to him, Officer.' The woman was doing the rounds, imploring. First her husband, then the officer. It would be my turn next. 'Don't pay him any attention. He's our best man, he was at our wedding.'

'At our wedding and in your bed!' the man squealed.

'Let me give you a bit of friendly advice,' said the officer. 'Go home and when you've cooled off think about it and if, tomorrow, you still want to lodge a complaint, I'll be here.'

'No! I want to do it right now!'

'Very well,' said the officer and called out: 'Karabikos!' When the young officer came in, he pointed to the visitor. 'Hold him in custody. And give him some cotton wool and spirit to stop his nosebleed.'

'Me?' said the man, astonished. 'You're going to hold *me*?'

'Yes, you! For assaulting your wife, before my very eyes. Now you're going to spend a night in the cooler and tomorrow morning we'll both lodge our complaints: the police's against you and yours against your best man.'

Given the way he handled the matter, I reconsidered my first impressions. It was easy to handle criminals, you lock them up and you're done. The real knack was dealing with law-abiding citizens, and he had it.

The man deflated like a balloon. 'I prefer to cool off at home,' he said in a timid voice.

'Get him out of here,' the officer said to the woman. 'And the next time I see you in here, I'll lock you up come what may, because I'm sick and tired of you!'

'Come on, Aristos, let's go,' the wife said. Now that he was back in his shell, she started with her swaying again. 'Look what you've done to my dress.' And she pointed to the bloodstains.

'I'll buy you another one,' he replied. 'I'll buy you ten, but you're still a whore and you don't deserve them.'

'You wouldn't believe what I have to go through because of his jealousy,' the woman whispered to me. It was my turn now.

She did not appear to be suffering from it. On the contrary, from the way she wiggled her behind as she went out, it was rather as if she enjoyed it.

'Every so often, he comes to lodge a complaint,' the officer said to me crossly. 'He was here just the other day. Someone had blocked his drive with their car and he had a go at him. But he was the one who came off worse and they both ended up here to lodge complaints. It was as I was taking their statements that we got the news of Koustas' murder.'

The matter was of no interest to me at all. I wanted to finish with the motorbike and get home to bed. Fortunately, the sergeant did not need me to remind him of it. 'But what was it you were asking me about? I've forgotten.'

'Yes . . . About whether Koustas had ever received threats.'

He burst out laughing. 'Are you serious, Inspector? Who would ever dare threaten Koustas?'

'I don't know. That's why I'm asking you.'

He leaned over and lowered his voice, although the corridor was empty. 'No one would dare go anywhere near Koustas. He always went around with two bodyguards. They took him home and then went back and slept in the club, along with the doorman. To tell you the truth, if he were paying for protection, it would have cost him less, but his pride wouldn't allow him. He spent a fortune on bodyguards and security systems and, even so, he got done in.'

'Those heavies of his, what sorts are they?'

He shrugged. 'What can I tell you. Hired bodyguards. You know the type.'

'Do they have a record?'

He laughed again. 'They've never done time if that's what you mean. They're former police officers who were discharged. They weren't out of work for as much as a day. Koustas hired them right off.'

Even police officers are taken on as security men, albeit only the cast-offs. Whatever the case, I was beginning to accept that Anti-Terrorist had been right. Koustas had got their backs up with his security systems and they had bumped him off. They may have not had any gripe with him, but killed him like that anyway as a warning to the others, to show them that no one was beyond their reach, not even Koustas.

There was nothing more for me to do. I said goodnight to the duty officer and left. My eyes were heavy with sleep.

At the next traffic lights on Iera Odos Street, I made a U-turn and got back into the lane heading into Athens.

When I reached home, it was three thirty. Adriani was sleeping. I undressed and got into bed without turning on the light so as not to wake her. She sensed my presence and stirred.

'What time is it?' she said.

'Go back to sleep.'

CHAPTER 10

The photographs of the unidentified corpse were on my desk; a whole pack of them. I sipped my Greek and not-Greek coffee out of a plastic cup and examined them one by one. In three of them he was in the ground, as we had found him. In the others, in which he was washed and cleaned, he looked to be not more than thirty-five, with a well-knit, athletic body and a fine face, even though his skin looked like parchment, with a colour ranging from grey-green to pale grey and brown – a veritable reality show.

I took a bite of my croissant and picked up the phone to call Markidis. His 'Hello' sounded, as always, as though he had just woken up, or hadn't had his morning coffee yet.

'When am I going to get my report?' I asked him.

'By midday, though I can tell you now what's in it. And there's not much.'

'Go on.'

'First of all, it's impossible to ascertain the exact date of his death. But you're a lucky bastard.' The way he said it, you would have thought I had won the lottery.

'Why?'

'Because they buried him on an island. They burned his fingertips, but they didn't know that the air and damp preserve the body. That makes recognition easier. My estimation is that he must have been in the ground two and a half to three months.'

That meant that he was killed between the middle and the end of June. 'How was he killed?'

'That's the problem. There are no traces of any murder weapon or object. No knife, no razor, not even any sign of his skull being cracked with a rock, nothing. All I came up with was some rupturing to the fibrous ligaments between the second vertebra and the base of the skull together with a displacement of the discs between the vertebrae. That leads me to conclude that they killed him by breaking his neck.'

'Is that why he has marks on his neck?'

'No, those are indications of a struggle.'

I could have kicked myself for taking Anita for a junkie when she had come up with the correct autopsy diagnosis.

'As you can see from the photographs, he was an athletic type. He didn't go down without a fight,' Markidis said. 'He has the same marks on his forearms. They were preserved because his skin is like parchment, as you will have seen. That's the good thing about summer. Because everyone goes about half naked, you only have to touch someone and your marks remain.'

He said it as if he included it among the delights of holidays, like swimming, sunbathing and ouzo on the beach.

'How many of them were there?' I asked.

He stifled a laugh and immediately became serious again. 'I knew you'd ask me that. In my opinion, there must have been two of them. One of them held his arms behind his back, while the other twisted his neck. It would have been very hard for one man to achieve on his own.'

'That's cold comfort.'

'I know. I explain it all in more detail in my report,' he added with the familiar sadism of the coroner.

'Right now, I'm not interested in the details. What you told me is enough.'

I hung up and took another sip of my coffee. Wonderful, we had an unknown victim and two unknown assailants. As if Koustas' murder weren't enough. I had been landed with another professional murder. Robbery was out of the question. No robber would have gone to the trouble of burning his victim's fingertips and burying him without his clothes. They would have thrown him into a ravine or off a cliff. At any rate, he must have been staying somewhere on the island, either in a demi-pension or in rooms-to-let, with the girl or without her. Accordingly, somebody must remember him, apart from the philosopher-cum-lion-tamer. And the same was true for his two murderers. They too must have stayed somewhere. It would have taken them some time to track him down, lure him away and kill him. You can't do that in a day.

I was about to call Vlassopoulos when I remembered that I had to call the Security out-patients surgery to make an appointment. Unless I wanted Katerina and Adriani nagging at me all evening. I didn't know the number and so I called the switchboard to have them connect me.

'Which department do you want?' the girl asked me.

'I don't know. I'm having problems with my back and I want to see a doctor.'

'Let's start with a pathologist-rheumatologist and see how we go. The earliest appointment is in ten days. Tuesday 26 September, at 11 a.m.'

Now that the moment had come for me to say 'OK', I found myself tongue-tied. The girl took my silence to be displeasure and said hesitatingly: 'If it's urgent, Inspector, I could put you in place of someone else.'

'No, no, no need for that. It's not so urgent.'

If she could have delayed it another ten days, I would have thanked her. My mind was still on the appointment with the doctor when Vlassopoulos came in.

'The mob is outside waiting for you,' he said. He meant the reporters.

'OK. On your way out tell them to come in. In the meantime, take this photograph with you.' And I gave him one of the shots of the man looking clean and photogenic. 'Send it to the police station on the island. Have them ask around the hotels and the rented rooms to see if anyone recognises him. If he stayed in a hotel, they must have his particulars. And also have them ask if two men, probably ex-police, were staying anywhere on the island during the same period. They would have rented a room so as not to have to give their particulars. Take another print with you and have it run through the computer in case it comes up with a match.'

'It'll come up with at least a thousand,' he said resignedly.

'Better search through a thousand than look for a needle in a haystack. And tell the ruminants to come in.' I call them ruminants, because they come here, swallow their fodder and then go back to their stations and channels and regurgitate it. 'Have you turned up anything on Koustas?'

'No. Nothing yet.'

As soon as Vlassopoulos was gone, they cantered into my office all together, Sotiropoulos at their head, and lined up before me. Sotiropoulos was the oldest of them all and had been rightfully assigned the role of leader. He was, as always, wearing an Armani shirt, a pair of Harley-Davidson jeans and Timberland moccasins. His hair was cut short, almost shaved, and he was wearing round, metal-rimmed glasses. He reminded me of those old two-sided gabardines that we once wore: gabardine on the outside, overcoat on the inside. That was Sotiropoulos. In his dress he was like an American, in his features like an SS officer.

'We gather that you've been assigned to the Koustas case, Chief,' he said.

That was his other trademark. His complete lack of respect. He believed that in this way he was genuinely expressing the conscience of the people and it never crossed his mind that this was how the commissioners spoke at the courts martial convened by the junta.

'Yes,' I replied abruptly. I knew what the next question would be.

'What news do you have for us?'

'None. I was assigned to the case yesterday and I'm still gathering information. In two or three days, I'll be able to tell you more. In the meantime, I have something else for you.'

I took the photographs of the corpse and handed them out. Ghikas' tactics in reverse. He had landed me with Koustas; I was passing on to them the unidentified island victim. They stared at the naked body on the mortuary table, couldn't take their eyes off it. I knew that my trick had worked and that in the evening I would see the man's face run all over the TV screen. That way, there was a real hope that someone would recognise him.

'Who is it?' said Lambridou, a short, knock-kneed female in a mauve miniskirt.

'We still don't know.' And I gave them the full story. The only thing I held back was the information about the girl who had been seen with him, because if she were to find out that we knew about her, she would take to her heels. We were better off letting her sleep soundly.

I saw all the men's hands reaching towards their belts. In the old days I would have thought they were going to draw their guns, but now I knew that they were simply taking out their mobile phones. Before they had reached the door, I could hear the murmured beep-beep-beeps of the numbers they were calling.

Sotiropoulos let the others go and then shut the door. 'There's more, but you're keeping it for yourself, Chief,' he said.

'Cut the "Chief", Sotiropoulos, it gets on my nerves. Call me Haritos, Costas, whatever you like, but don't keep calling me Chief.'

'Would you rather I call you "Mr Implement of the Law"?' he replied ironically. 'That's what I called you when I was a student.'

'And what did we call you?'

'Commie,' he said, raising himself to his full height.

I looked at the Armani and Harley-Davidsons he was wearing and thought how blind we had been back then. Except that we realised it eventually. Whereas he was still a long way off.

'I know nothing about the corpse. When I do, I'll inform you.'

'And what about Koustas?'

'Anti-Terrorist believe it was a settling of accounts.' I didn't like him, but he had a nose for it and I wanted to see his reaction.

'It's possible. But I'll tell you one thing: when it comes to Koustas, don't go digging with a shovel. Use a trowel and dig discreetly.'

'Why so?'

'Because you've got a lot of surprises in store for you and you might find yourself in hot water.'

Before I could ask him what he meant by that, he opened the door and was gone.

I picked up the phone and called the head of Forensics. 'Did you find anything in Koustas' car?' I said, after introducing myself.

'Nothing, inside or outside. The glove compartment was open, that was all.'

'What was in it?'

'The usual: car registration, insurance and a pair of gloves.'

It was unlikely that he had opened it to get his gloves, or the registration. Could he have taken something else? And what was that something else?

'Did you find anything on him?'

There was a pause as he searched through the file. 'A handker-chief, a wallet containing thirty thousand and three credit cards, and a Motorola mobile phone. The car keys were in the door.'

Unless the glove compartment had opened while he was driving and he hadn't noticed it. Another idea flashed through my mind.

'Did you find any clues on the bike?'

'No, it was as clean as a whistle.'

At such moments, when everything seems to be leading nowhere, the office is too small for me and I need to get out on to the street. The offices of R.I. Hellas, where Koustas' daughter worked, were in Apollonos Street, just after Voulis Street. I told Vlassopoulos to order up a patrol car. The phone rang as I was about to leave. It was the chief from the police station on the island.

'I received the photograph by fax, Inspector, and I'll set the inquiries in train,' he said.

'It's urgent. Begin with the hotels. We might get lucky and find they have kept his particulars. If you don't get anywhere with the hotels, ask everyone who rents rooms.'

'All right. As for the other two, can you give me a description?' he asked, sheepishly.

'If I had a description and their names, I'd go and arrest them. I've nothing, I'm searching in the dark. They might be tall or short, fat or thin, anything. Whatever the case, it won't be hard for you to track them down. There can't have been many male couples staying on the island.'

'You're mistaken, Inspector. In summer there are lots. They walk around the village arm in arm or hand in hand, or sun themselves on the beach in pairs. You understand what I mean.'

'What are you trying to say? That he was killed by two romantic faggots?'

'What can I say, everything's possible. The way the world is today.'

Without warning, the heatwave came back. Each year the heat plays the same trick on Athenians. To get a little relief from it, they rush to the islands and the coasts in July and August when the meltemi is usually blowing, and as soon as they get back to Athens at the end of August, they find the heat lying in wait for them and, not being able to get away again, they end up sweltering till November.

The traffic flowed fairly smoothly as far as the Hilton, but started to back up at the park in front of the Evangelismos Hospital. In the past, Athenians spent their day in the café playing cards and backgammon. Now they spend it in their cars toying with the driving wheel and the gear lever. In the café they used to discuss everything and anything. In their cars they can go anywhere. That's why they all go to the city centre, because there they can find everything, from public services to sweet-smelling rubbish.

Suddenly, without my realising it, Vassilissis Sophias Avenue in the direction of Syntagma Square had filled with dustcarts. At first, there were just one or two, then more appeared, and eventually they were occupying all three lanes. The cars were squashed in between them and were going at a snail's pace. Probably at best two got through each time the lights changed to green.

'Where are all the dustcarts going?' I asked Vlassopoulos in amazement.

'I've no idea. Most likely the strike is over and they're out to collect the rubbish.'

At Koumbari Street, the traffic ground to a complete halt and the carts were all honking their horns, sharply and rhythmically. A traffic policeman asked us where we were making for.

'Philellinon Street,' Vlassopoulos told him.

'Well, you've chosen the right time.' And he threw his hands up in despair. 'The rubbish collectors are driving their dustcarts to the Ministry of Finance to demonstrate.'

In front of us, the whole of Syntagma Square, as far as the eye could see, was an ocean of dustcarts and we were stuck in the middle of them like a buoy. Beside me, a driver of one cart had taken out his mobile phone and was giving a report in a voice so loud that it must have reached the back benches of the Parliament building alongside.

'Where am I? Jammed in next to the Parliament. No one has seen the like of this before, we've blocked the whole of Athens. There's not a thing moving from Omonia to Ambelokipi. We've sent a message to the minister that if he doesn't meet our demands, we'll bury Athens in rubbish. And when we do start carting it off, we'll cart him off too.'

He said he would call back and rang off. Then, seeing that I was watching him, he turned to me and held his mobile out of the window.

'Call home and tell them you'll be late,' he said. 'I can't see you getting away from here before the evening.' And he slapped his driving wheel, delighted at how comical he was.

I held my tongue and watched the scene through the windscreen. If I had said what I thought, he might have thrown me in the rubbish and then I would have had to wait till they carted me off together with the minister.

A dozen or so traffic policemen were pacing to and fro between the dustcarts. They were looking around, speaking into their walkie-talkies and doing nothing, because there was nothing they *could* do.

'What's happening?' I asked one officer standing beside me, the same one who had spoken to us before.

'What always happens,' he said fatalistically. 'They're creating havoc, a public prosecutor is negotiating with them to open up the square and we're on duty and getting all the abuse.'

I could not see the riot squad anywhere, but if they had been called out, they would be lined up around the square. At Papandreou's funeral, they had us ready and waiting at the corner of Mitropoleos and Philellinon Streets. I was still a rookie then. I watched the sea of people pass by with the coffin at the front and prayed that they would not order us to break up the procession, because with that impassioned crowd, God alone knows who would have come out alive. It would have been a toss-up whether we charged or ran. Now, in place of a sea of people, there were the municipal rubbish trucks;

they swear at us, we whistle at them and the only thing we're afraid of are the germs from the rubbish.

The sound of the truck driver's mobile phone brought me back to reality and I marvelled at the craft of the manufacturers to come up with such a piercing sound that you can't fail to hear it even if the world's going to hell in a handcart all around you. The driver put the phone to his ear, put his finger to his other ear and began screaming. 'Just because the minister agreed to see us, we have to clear the square? First let him agree to our demands and then we'll disperse, that was what we said!' He flung down the phone, opened the door of his dustcart and began shouting to everyone and to no one: 'You've sold out! You yobs! How much did it take for you to back down, eh? How much did it take?' He grabbed the phone again. 'I'm going to their office right now and I'm going to rip it apart! Do you hear?' he yelled.

And as if wanting to show that he meant what he'd said, he put his truck into reverse and backed into the one behind. 'Steady on, brother!' shouted the driver of the one behind. 'You'll put a dent in it and I'll be the one to have to foot the bill.'

The car was like an oven, my head felt as though it were about to burst and I sensed my sweat stinking like the rubbish. Beside me Vlassopoulos took out a paper handkerchief and wiped his face. On the other side, the truck driver had his elbows resting on the steering wheel and his head in his hands and was gazing at the Hotel Grand Bretagne. Probably he was thinking of those he ought to shoot as traitors.

Another quarter of an hour went by and the rubbish trucks slowly began to move, as though a light breeze had started to blow. Another quarter of an hour and we too got going and edged our way towards the square. As we turned into Philellinon Street, I looked at my watch. Three hours had gone by from our leaving Security Headquarters in Alexandras Avenue and it was now two o'clock.

The offices of R.I. Hellas were in an old three-storey block. The walnut door opened into a quiet and warm space. No liver-coloured carpets here, or modern metal constructions, or security guards. The walls had wood panelling and scenes from Greek islands and seas.

The girl in reception fitted in with the rest of the decoration. She, too, was dressed simply and was without make-up, and the only piece of modern equipment in view was the computer on her desk.

'How can I help you?' she said politely.

I introduced myself and Vlassopoulos and told her that we had come to see Niki Koustas.

She picked up her phone, informed Koustas and told us to go up to the second floor. The lift had been an afterthought and it barely managed the two of us.

When we got out of the lift, we found ourselves in a large room, like an old dance hall. To the left was a wide, wooden staircase leading up and down. The dance hall had been divided into six by means of plywood partitions with three cubicles on each side, just big enough for a desk and a chair and a second chair for visitors on the thin side. Working at their computers in the cubicles were two men and four women. In the past, these cages were for messengers or doormen. Now they use them for refugees and company employees.

The corridor with the cubicles on either side led to another one where the offices were two on each side and one at the end. Koustas' office was the first on the right. The door was open and inside I saw a girl with short, black hair, and with her eyes glued to the computer screen. She was dressed in black and had no make-up whatsoever. I knocked on the open door and she looked up.

'Inspector Haritos. This is –' I said.

'Yes, I know. Come in, Inspector.'

Her office was not exactly large, but nor was it a cubicle. Several noticeboards covered with notes and graphic designs hung from the walls.

'You're late,' she said, as she offered us the two chairs in front of her desk. 'I was expecting you sooner.' She had an innocent, almost childlike smile, which made her look even younger.

'It's just a routine visit, Miss Koustas. It was something that could wait.'

'You're right. What could you possibly learn from me? I know absolutely nothing. I learned about my father's death on the radio

71

in the morning.' She said it with the same childlike smile, but hastened to add: 'I'm not saying it out of spite or anything. In her distress, Elena simply didn't think to call me. Or perhaps she didn't want to upset me in the middle of the night and was waiting for morning.'

'Were you at home all night? Perhaps she called you and didn't find you in?'

'No, I was at home with my brother.'

This surprised me. 'With your brother? Do you live together?'

'No, but Makis has one or two problems and –'

'I know about his problems. I was informed about them by –' In my mind I saw Mrs Koustas as Fragakis, with the plunging neckline and the curtain for her leg, and somehow it didn't seem right for me to say 'your stepmother'. 'I was informed about them by Mrs Koustas.'

Her childlike smile returned. 'You've saved me my embarrassment, Inspector. Makis is fine now, of course, but sometimes it becomes too much for him and he's ready to slip again. It's then that he needs support. The night of the murder was one such occasion. He was with me all night and I took care of him.'

He may have got through it on the night of the murder, I thought to myself, but not last night. He had had his fix and he was high.

'Is that how it always is? Does he always come to you when he needs support?'

'My father was a man of old-fashioned principles. He believed that a firm stance and severity could cure all weaknesses. Makis slipped back three times, but my father persisted with the same tactics.' She paused and then added reluctantly: 'And Makis doesn't get on at all well with Elena either.'

I played the fool, as if being unaware of it. 'Why? Is there some specific reason why they don't get on?'

'Makis has never got over the trauma caused by our mother.'

'What trauma?'

'Don't you know?' She seemed surprised. 'Our mother abandoned us.'

No, I did not know. Without anyone actually having told me, I was under the impression that their mother was dead.

It seemed that Vlassopoulos was under the same impression because I heard him ask how, in what circumstances had their mother left them.

'She ran off with a singer. As far as I know, she's still living with him. He doesn't sing any more but he has a record company I believe. From the time she left our father, she never wanted to see us again.' She said all this without any hate or bitterness, as though she were giving an account of someone else's life. 'Makis has never got over it. He was fourteen at the time and I was twelve. And when Elena moved in, he directed all his hate on to her, as if she were to blame.' She stopped, as if wanting to rethink what she had just said and then continued, with that same childlike smile. 'Perhaps I'm doing him an injustice, because it was easier for me. You see, I cut all ties, I rarely go to my father's house: in fact, only at Christmas and on the feast days of St Constantine and St Elena when my father and Elena celebrate their name days. And if it weren't for Elena, I wouldn't even go on those few occasions.'

'Why? Were there problems between you and your father?' Given that she had said that she only went to her family home on account of Mrs Koustas, I assumed that must be the case.

'No. Quite simply, I'm an independent person and I prefer to get by on my own. When I finished my studies abroad and returned to Greece, I asked my father to let me have a flat he owned in Fokylidou Street in Kolonaki. It was the first one he'd bought. Since then, I've been living there. Afterwards, I got this job and I've made my own life.'

'What work do you do exactly, Miss Koustas?'

'In England, I studied market research, but here I also work on TV ratings and opinion polls. For example, at the moment we're conducting a poll on the popularity of politicians. Would you like to know who's the most popular politician?'

I was not particularly interested, but she was extremely polite and I did not want to seem discourteous. I leaned over the computer. I could not make any sense at all of the figures, but I did not have to, because I read the name of a former minister and Member of Parliament for the Opposition. In a column next to his name was the figure of 62 per cent.

'Does he have a popularity rating of 62 per cent?' I asked as though in disbelief.

'Yes. Higher than his party leader. Of those asked, 62 per cent want him for prime minister.'

He was one of those politicians who are always on the TV screen or with a microphone in their hands talking about everything and nothing. More often than not, he was critical of his leader; he 'differentiated his position' as they put it now. Each time I hear him, I want to tear my hair out with his inanities. In the past, all roads led to Rome, now all roads lead to the screen and, if you prattle on enough, you can even get to be prime minister. He knows that only too well.

'Thank you, Miss Koustas. If I need anything else, I'll contact you,' I said and made for the door before I came out with anything I might regret. After all I am a civil servant and if tomorrow, God forbid, he were to become Minister of Public Order, I could find myself transferred to some village constabulary.

I was at the door and she was saying goodbye when I remembered something and turned. 'I saw your brother last night,' I told her. 'He was at the Bouzouki Strings and was telling Hortiatis that he intends to take over now that his father is dead.'

She ran her fingers through her short, black hair and let out a deep sigh. 'That was always Makis' dream,' she said. 'Something he's wanted for years. If my father had agreed, perhaps Makis would have taken a different path. He was on about it all the time, but my father wouldn't hear of it. Now that he's dead, Makis has his hopes up again, but nothing will come of it.'

'Why?'

'Because our father wanted us to have everything *ab indiviso* and neither Elena nor I would agree to Makis taking over the management of a nightclub in his present state. It would be the end of him and the end of the club.

'Perhaps your father left a will with other provisions.'

She burst out laughing. 'My father? No way!' She saw the astonishment in my eyes and hastened to explain. 'My father loathed anything in writing, Inspector. He loathed written agreements, contracts and all forms of documents in general. Even the singers in his clubs had only verbal agreements. They knew that he kept his word and that made them trust him.'

'Yes, but he had so many businesses. Accounts . . . receipts . . . invoices . . . tax returns . . .'

'He never had anything to do with all that. That was the job of his accountant. Do you want to meet him?'

'If it's not too much trouble.' To my surprise she picked up the phone and started talking to someone by the name of Yannis. 'Does your father's accountant work here?'

'Yes, I was the one who recommended him. He's a good, honest lad. My father got a trustworthy accountant and Yannis got an extra salary. And they were both happy with the arrangement.'

Perhaps her use of the word 'lad' was somewhat exaggerated, though he could not have been more than about her age. He was a young man, unassuming and withdrawn. He stood in the doorway and didn't turn to look at us. His gaze was fixed on Koustas. He looked at her and melted.

'Yannis,' she said to him tenderly, 'these gentlemen are from the police and want to ask you a few questions about my father's accounts.'

I wanted to ask him more than a few, but I preferred not to ask them in front of her and so I confined myself to the most pressing. 'All I want from you for the time being are Konstantinos Koustas' bank account numbers,' I said.

He turned and looked at us for the first time, then his gaze went back to Koustas. He remained silent.

'Listen,' I said to him, 'I can find out the banks where Mr Koustas had accounts and have them opened. I'm asking you to make our job easier, so that we don't waste time.'

He still said nothing and continued to look at the girl. 'Give them to him, Yannis,' she said with her innocent smile. 'If my father had any secrets, he certainly didn't keep them in his bank accounts.'

'You know, these things are confidential.' It was the first time he had opened his mouth.

'But you have my permission to give them to him.'

Yannis hesitated for a moment, then said, 'Give me a moment,' and left the office.

'I told you he was trustworthy and honest.' Koustas smiled smugly because her diagnosis had been confirmed. 'The best thing Makis can do is to invest his money somewhere and live off the interest,' she continued, as though Yannis had not appeared at all.

I refrained from saying that whether he took his share of the inheritance or lived off the interest, his future was bleak, because he would squander it all on drugs.

The phone rang and Koustas picked it up. 'Do you want to note it down?' she said.

I nodded to Vlassopoulos to take out his notebook. She gave me two bank account numbers, one at the National Bank of Greece and the other at the Commercial Bank. I thanked her and we left.

Once we were outside in Ermou Street, we saw that Syntagma Square was back to normal. It was four o'clock and my lack of sleep the previous night suddenly caught up with me.

'Drop me off at home,' I told Vlassopoulos. 'There's nothing more we can do today.'

CHAPTER 12

I woke up in terror and saw Adriani leaning over me.

'What's wrong?' she asked me anxiously.

I thought it was morning and I leapt out of bed, but when I looked around me I realised that I had fallen asleep in my clothes and with Dimitrakos in my hands.

'What time is it?'

'Half past seven. You've been asleep for three hours. Are you feeling ill?'

'Of course not, what on earth gave you that idea?'

'Because you never sleep in the afternoon, that's why?'

'I was late to bed last night and I've been rushing round all day today. I must have fallen asleep while I was reading.'

'It's not enough that you refuse to see a doctor, now you're staying up all night as well.'

'That's where you're wrong,' I said, getting up from the bed. 'I've made an appointment for the 26th.'

She stared at me dumbfounded. She could not believe it at first. Then she hugged me tight and planted a kiss on my cheek. 'Well done, Costas. At last, I can relax. It's nothing, you'll see, but why suffer for no good reason? They'll give you something to cure you. In fact, while you're there, why don't you have a general check-up? Blood test, urine, X-rays, so we know where we are.'

'Do you want me to cancel the appointment?' I snapped.

'No, no,' she said reassuringly. 'Let the doctor see you. That'll do for a start. Though if you do cancel it, you'll have to deal with your daughter, because she was the one who got you to make the appointment,' she said, sounding as if she wanted to take her kiss back.

'I made it on account of both of you, because you were both nagging at me like twins.'

'Never mind,' she said laughing. 'What matters is that you decided to go.'

I watched her going out of the bedroom with a broad smile and then I had an idea. 'What would you say to our going out tonight to celebrate it?' I said to her.

She spun round and stared at me in surprise. 'Celebrate what? Going to the doctor's?'

'That I made the decision.'

'And where would we go?'

'To a French restaurant.'

'French? What's got into you? The few times we ever do go out, you never want to go anywhere other than the taverna.'

Somehow she was not cut out for playing patience, but I had no intention of telling her the real reason. 'I thought we'd have a change, try something new.'

'The doctor is doing you good already,' she replied enthusiastically. 'What time shall we leave?'

'I want to watch the news first.'

It would take her at least an hour to decide what to wear, so I went into the living room. The news bulletin had not yet started. I saw a new hairspray being advertised and I wondered whether the market research had been carried out by Niki Koustas. Just as the news was about to start, the phone rang. It was Katerina.

'Well, Dad?'

'Yes, OK,' I said. 'I've made an appointment with a rheumatologist.'

There was a pause and then she whispered: 'Thank you.'

'What is there to thank me for?'

'Because now I can stop worrying and I won't have to abandon my work and come down to Athens when I'm up to the eyes in it. Isn't Mum there?'

'She's getting ready. We're going to eat out tonight.'

There was another pause. 'I envy you,' she said.

'Why? Because we're going out to eat?'

'No. Because I'm not coming with you. I miss you both.'

When she comes out with things like that, I become all emotional and the words stick in my throat. 'We miss you too, dear,' I said, with not a little difficulty.

'I know, but I can't see myself coming before Christmas.'

My warmth turned to irritation, though it was like this every year. We only see her at Christmas, Easter and for two weeks of the holidays. It's Panos who steals the other two weeks from us. It's not enough, it seems, that he's with her all winter, he wants her to go with him to the countryside for holidays, so that he can gaze at vegetable patches.

Katerina hung up just as the photograph of the unidentified man appeared on the screen. Magnified like that his features looked much plainer. The sight of his parchment skin was repulsive, which is why they kept it on screen for quite a time so that people would shudder, but that suited me. The reporter described how he was found, where, which gorge, the shore, as if he were trying to

78

contribute to the island's tourist trade by turning the corpse into one of the local sights.

I was about to turn it off when the poll carried out by Niki Koustas was displayed. That morning I had only seen a slice of it, now I had the whole cake in front of me: which party was ahead in the preference of the voters, what percentage thought the government successful, what percentage wanted to sling it out with the rubbish (which was ready and waiting), what percentage of popularity was enjoyed by the prime minister and what percentage by the leader of the Opposition, and so on and so forth. A pile of figures, colours, charts with tables that seemed all the same to me, whether they were measuring the Chernobyl disaster or the popularity of politicians. Whereas the prime minister was the most popular politician in his party, the leader of the Opposition party was only the second most popular in his, trailing behind the 62 per cent of the former minister. The same figures pointed out to me by Koustas that morning. The newscaster, together with the opinion-poll analyst, was trying to explain the phenomenon.

'I'm ready.' I heard Adriani's voice behind me.

She was wearing the dress that we had bought together for her birthday in the sales, a string of pearls, false ones but exquisitely fashioned, and she had a brown handbag and brown shoes. I was amazed at how she managed to maintain her modest taste with all those frumps that she saw every day in the soaps, dressed like Christmas tree fairies.

'Let's go,' I said, getting up.

'What? Is that how you're going?'

'What's wrong with me?'

'Put something else on, please,' she wheedled. 'You can't go out in the suit that you wear every day to work.'

I had a second lightweight suit that I wore only on special occasions, but it was a light colour and I always got stains on it, whereas the one I had on was dark and didn't show the marks. I opened the wardrobe and saw it hanging on a metal hanger in its plastic cover, exactly as we had got it back from the dry-cleaner's. I put it on and found a matching tie, the same one each time, as I only had one that went with it.

'That's better,' she said when she saw me. She straightened it on my shoulders and then strode jauntily to the door.

CHAPTER 13

The Canadré, or more properly, the Canard Doré, bore no resemblance whatsoever to any other of Koustas' establishments. It was a neoclassical building from the beginning of the twentieth century, the kind built by politicians, merchants and doctors so that they could spend the summer months in Kifissia. In front was a large, well-tended garden with lights in the shape of mushrooms. The building was floodlit from below by lights hidden in the flower beds. The iron garden gate was open and on the old wrought-iron frame above it was a sign in the shape of a duck, not illuminated but painted: 'Le Canard Doré'. It was a humid night and the people were sitting at tables in the garden, among the illuminated mushrooms.

I felt uncomfortable leaving the Mirafiori among the Mercedes, BMWs and Audis. I parked it a little further off, among the pine trees.

Before we went in, Adriani stood admiring it. 'Very glamorous,' she said, beside herself with enthusiasm. The first time she had used that word, I hadn't known what it meant and I had to look it up in the *Oxford English–Greek Learner's Dictionary*, the only English–Greek Dictionary I have. Now I know what it means: alluring and fascinating, beautiful and smart.

Adriani took my arm and we went through the open gate. The head waiter, wearing a cream-coloured jacket, black trousers and a bow tie, spotted us and hurried over.

'Good evening,' he said very politely. 'Do you have a reservation?'
'No.'

'I'm afraid you're going to be disappointed.' He looked so

80

distressed that you would have thought he was going to commit hara-kiri.

I was about to tell him who I was, which really would have led him to commit hara-kiri, the very idea of a policeman at the restaurant at that time of night, but I didn't have to.

'It's OK, Michel, he's a friend.'

I turned and saw Elena Koustas coming over to us. She had fixed her hair and was wearing a simple white dress, but that was more than enough to make you prefer older women to twenty-year-old girls.

'Good evening, Inspector Haritos.' She held out her hand.

'I didn't expect to find you here,' I said to her, at the same time introducing her to Adriani, who was open-mouthed in admiration.

'You know, Konstantinos was particularly fond of the Canard Doré. It was his pride and joy. I thought that if I were to come and take care of it, it would be the best thing I could do in his memory.'

She accompanied us as the head waiter led us to a table a little aside from the rest. Adriani continued to feast her eyes on Mrs Koustas. In the end, she could no longer restrain herself.

'Aren't you Elena Fragakis, or am I mistaken?' she said.

A smile spread over Koustas' face. 'Thank you for remembering me after so many years,' she said, with undisguised emotion in her voice.

'You're not easily forgotten.'

Koustas spontaneously reached out her hand and touched Adriani on the arm. I realised that Adriani had displayed her admiration, Koustas her coquetry and within the space of a minute they were getting on like a house on fire.

The head waiter opened the menus before us. On the right-hand side it was in French and on the left-hand side it was in French transliterated into Greek, with the result that I couldn't understand a word. Koustas immediately sensed my predicament and said to the head waiter: 'What would you recommend, Michel?'

'I'd recommend the seafood platter,' he said without hesitation. 'But, if you prefer something more classical, I would suggest the *pâté de foie gras*, unless you prefer the mushrooms *provençale*, and for the main course I would recommend *boeuf bourgignon*, garnished with new potatoes, or *coq au vin*, which is our *spécialité*, or an *escalope*. If you want fish, then the John Dory *à la crème* is the very best we have to offer.'

'You decide for me. I have complete faith in you,' Adriani said, and I watched the head waiter puff out like a cockerel, ready to bathe in her wine. At times like that, I have to admire her. Though she had understood nothing of what he had said, she had a way of getting away with it.

'What of all the things you said is grilled?' I said.

'The *escalope*.'

'That for me.'

The head waiter had barely left when another waiter appeared with a basket of various breads. Slices of hot brown bread, slices of cold white bread, breadsticks and rusks. The basket itself was more than enough to feed a family of Albanians.

'What would you like to drink?' he asked.

'Wine?' asked Adriani, looking at me.

'A Chablis '92,' said Koustas breaking in. Then she turned to me: 'So, Inspector, are you here for the food or on business?'

She had a way of making me feel continually ill at ease. 'For the food, though I hope to mix it with a bit of business,' I said. 'Besides, it's not really important. Just a question I have for the restaurant manager.'

She did not appear to think it strange, because she smiled. 'He's inside,' she said. 'You can ask him anything you want. Please forgive me. I'll be back when I've done the rounds.' I watched her at the next table, chatting with that same disarming smile.

'Have you brought me here on business?' Adriani said.

'No, I brought you because I wanted to take you out. We could have gone somewhere else, of course, but I thought of coming here because I want to ask the manager something.'

She was having such a good time that she was easily persuaded, and she smiled at me. At last, I had an opportunity to look around me. The customers were all roughly the same age, between forty-five and sixty, not younger. They were all smartly dressed and I had to admit that Adriani had been right to insist I changed my suit. Every table was taken and we would not have been able to hear ourselves think if we had been in a taverna, but here everyone was speaking in low voices, as if they were eating in the National Library.

The waiter returned with an ice bucket and a bottle of wine. He turned the wine round in his hands like a conjuror and uncorked it. Then, he wrapped it in a cloth, let two drops fall into my glass and, as if suddenly changing his mind, stood still, with the bottle hovering over my glass and with him looking at me.

'What are you looking at? Fill it up,' I said.

He gave me a rather strange look and filled the glass. The wine had a sweet smell and a soft, bitter-sweet taste. And then, in the middle of the garden, I caught sight of the former minister with the high popularity ratings. He was sitting at the head of the table and eating with five other people, three men and two women. Every so often, he looked around him, as though waiting for someone to greet him or shake his hand. But the clientele at the Canard Doré could not have cared less about ministers, particularly former ones; it had dealings only with prime ministers. His popularity rating was wasted on his fellow diners despite it being higher than that of his party leader.

The escalope was dripping blood. I looked at Adriani's plate and from the new potatoes realised that he had brought her that bourguignon or whatever it was called.

'Is it good?' Adriani said.

'Yours?'

'Delicious.'

My escalope stuck in my throat because I felt as if I were eating a murder victim, like those I saw every day, and got up to go and find the manager. As I was going towards the neoclassical building, I passed close to the former minister. He looked up and saw me. He waited for me to greet him, but I could not have cared less about him either. It was not a former minister I had to answer to, but Ghikas.

On entering the neoclassical building, I saw to the right and left two rooms, which must have been where people ate in winter. A wooden staircase led to the first floor, where there must have been yet more rooms. The walls were wood-panelled and with one or two paintings. Apart from the head waiter, there was another man in the hallway; a tall, thin man who was expensively dressed. I immediately assumed that this was the manager, but I wanted to be sure.

'I'd like to speak to the restaurant manager.'

'That's me.'

'Inspector Haritos.'

'Ah, yes,' he replied. Mrs Koustas had spoken to him. 'And what can I do for the Inspector?' he asked, stressing the word 'inspector' on the final syllable and rolling the 'r'.

'I'd like to ask you a few questions. I won't take up much of your time.' It seems that I had been infected by the ambience of the restaurant and I was more polite than usual.

'I am at your disposal.'

'On the night of Mr Koustas' death, he first stopped here, before going to the Bouzouki Strings, isn't that so?'

'Yes.'

'What time did he come, do you recall?'

'I didn't check my watch, but he generally came at the same hour. Around eleven.'

'And what time did he leave?'

He reflected. 'Mmm . . . Midnight . . . half past midnight?'

'When he left, did he take anything with him?'

'Like what? A doggy bag?' He laughed at his little joke, whereas I was starting to get irritated by the way he answered every question of mine with one of his own.

'I don't know, that's why I'm asking. Well, did he?' Becoming more direct usually works with Greeks, but it was lost on him.

'A doggy bag, no.'

'Did he take anything else? Money perhaps?'

'This is not a bank, Inspector. No.'

'I didn't say it was a bank. But perhaps he took the day's takings with him.'

'O, mais non.' His French escaped him. 'He never did that. The security company comes to collect them every morning in a van.'

'City Protection?'

'That's the one.'

The security van followed a regular route every morning: Kifissia–Kalamaki, Kalamaki–Athinon Avenue, Athinon Avenue– bank. A regular bus route.

'That's all. Thank you.'

'My pleasure. I hope you enjoyed your meal.'

I confined myself to a smile, which could be taken for a yes. I didn't want him to think I was ready to turn somersaults because he'd served me a raw fillet as if I were a cannibal. At any rate, Koustas had not taken any money with him from either the Canard Doré or the Bouzouki Strings. My one hope was that he had withdrawn money from the bank. And if he had, where was it? And if it wasn't money but something else that he had gone to fetch from his car, why had it not been found, why should it have disappeared? Unless all this was coincidence and the murderer had simply been waiting for him. He had known his routine and his itinerary and had known that he would come out of the club at around that time. If we discovered that he had not withdrawn any money, then this was the most probable explanation, though it still left open the question of what he had been going to get from his car, and whether it was a gangland killing.

When I returned to the table, I found Adriani talking to Mrs Koustas as though they were old childhood friends.

'Have you finished?' Koustas asked.

'Yes. In any case, it was nothing important. A detail. Is your manager French?'

'Yes, and the chef too. It is as I told you: Konstantinos wanted a real French restaurant.'

'With you here it acquires a different kind of glamour,' said Adriani with a honeyed tongue.

Koustas laughed out of embarrassment, but it was clear that she liked what she had heard. 'Don't put temptation before me, Mrs Haritos. I decided to try it for a few days, but I'm not sure I want to take it on in the long term. You know, Makis is right about one thing,' she said to me. 'I've spent too many years shut up in that fortress with my Filipino maids and now the outside world really alarms me.'

'If you do take it on, then there'll only be the Night Flower left to be taken care of.' She didn't understand where I was leading and looked at me in surprise. 'Makis was at the Bouzouki Strings last night and making it clear that he was the one in charge.'

She reacted just as her stepdaughter had. She sighed and sat back in her chair. 'Then he'll want to take charge of the Night Flower too. Those two clubs were always his dream. He got into epic arguments with his father, but Konstantinos was unyielding.' She fell silent and sighed again. 'Someone ought to talk to him, to explain – but who? The one person he listens to is Niki. He hates me, as you saw.'

'I saw it and heard it from Makis himself.'

'When?'

'When we left your house he was waiting outside, to tell us that you had trapped his father into marrying you and that you had him wrapped round your little finger.'

I came out with it bluntly to see what her reaction would be, but all I got was a wry smile. 'He's not too far wrong,' she said, thoughtfully. 'Not that I had him wrapped round my little finger. Konstantinos would never have allowed that. But that I trapped him, perhaps . . .'

She fell silent again and her gaze wandered, resting on the trees beyond. As if she were examining the past, to determine whether she had actually hoodwinked Konstantinos Koustas. 'Do you know how I met my husband?' she said. 'I was singing at the Acropol. At the time, he only had the Bouzouki Strings and the Night Flower was just opening.'

'Wasn't it the Night Flower that opened first?'

'No. First was the Bouzouki Strings, then the Night Flower. Last of all was this place. My husband was a self-made man, Inspector, and he climbed the ladder rung by rung. Anyhow. At that time, the microphones for the musical review had long wires, so that we could pull them behind us and go down into the stalls. Konstantinos would often come to the theatre. He always sat in the second or third row next to the aisle. Whenever I saw him, I'd go down from the stage, give him a smile and brush against him as I walked past . . .'

And you opened the curtain to show a bit of leg, I thought to myself, but I said nothing so as not to embarrass Adriani.

'I didn't want to be his mistress,' she said, as though reading my mind. 'That's what everyone said, but it wasn't true. I wanted him to notice me, to hire me for the Night Flower. On the third or fourth occasion, he sent flowers to my dressing room and then took me out to dinner. His wife had just left him and the two children. We went out together a few times. He was good company and I liked him, but there was no mention of the Night Flower. In the end, instead of proposing that I go and work for him at the Night Flower, he proposed marriage to me. So, from one point of view, I suppose I did trap him.'

'Why?' Adriani asked her. 'Because you gave up your career?'

'Because I was in my thirties, Mrs Haritos. In my line of work, either you've made it to the top by then, or you risk ending up doing tours in the provinces. And I hadn't made it to the top, no matter what anyone says.' She paused and smiled at me. 'I've told you all this, Inspector, so that you can hear it from me before others tell it to you in the way that suits them.'

When I took out my wallet to pay, she flatly refused. 'Next time,' she said. 'Tonight, you are my guests. Who knows, you may bring me luck so that I find my feet here.' Though I had known they would not let me pay, even if Mrs Koustas had not been there, I had brought money with me.

'I had a wonderful time,' Adriani said as I was starting the Mirafiori and she planted a kiss on my cheek. The second one that evening. She was spoiling me of late.

'How did you find Elena Koustas?'

'Wonderful woman. Not at all stuck-up despite her talent.'

'And what she said about her husband?'

'What? That she had trapped him? If nothing else, I admired her sincerity. All women do the same. If I told you what I'd done to trap you . . .'

I put my foot on the brake and stared at her. She smiled triumphantly. I was minded to ask her what it was she had done, but I let it go. Better I didn't know.

In the three hours we had been out, rubbish had appeared and covered the whole of the pavement in Aristokleous Street and had spread right up to our door. Adriani let go of me, jumped over two plastic bags, and reached the door.

'Ignorant people,' she said angrily. 'Don't they listen to the experts telling them all day long on the radio and TV not to put their rubbish out on the street?'

'They hear so many things that they forget all of them,' I said, negotiating the hurdle, and following in her steps.

CHAPTER 14

Koustas' accounts at the National Bank and the Commercial Bank had both been opened at their Glyfada branches. I decided to drive down there before going to the office. I wanted to see if I could persuade the managers to show me the accounts without having to get a warrant. It would take me a couple of days to get a warrant issued. If Koustas had withdrawn money from his accounts, then it could have been to give it to the man who killed him. The question remained: what had happened to it? If he had not withdrawn any money, then there was still the probability that Koustas had an appointment with the man and wanted to talk with him alone in the car. That was why he had opened it and why he had not let his bodyguards come with him. When the murderer had called out to him, he had turned to talk to him. Whether he was going to give him money at two thirty in the morning, or whether he had a rendezvous for some other reason, the whole business stank, because how was anyone going to find out what shady dealings Koustas had had and with whom, in order to discover who might have murdered him?

From Hymettou Avenue, I turned into Vouliagmenis Avenue. The heatwave of the previous day had given way to a dull sky with thick clouds and a humidity that was stifling. Every so often I took out my handkerchief to wipe my palms because they were sweaty and the wheel was slipping in my hands. Fortunately, the traffic eased up after Brahami and so did I, because I could drive quicker and there was a slight breeze coming in through the window cooling me down.

It took me around forty-five minutes to reach the Commercial Bank and to park. It was one of those modern buildings, decorated in blue and white like the Greek flag. The desks were all identical, with two chairs for the customers, all of which were empty. Apart from three people waiting in line at the counter, I was the only customer. I counted at least ten department heads, assistant managers and managers and only two clerks, and the teller. I went up to one clerk, who was poring over a document, and asked her where I could find the manager. Without looking up, she stretched out her arm and pointed to the stairs.

I don't know if he took me for some slick businessman who had come to open an account in his branch, but the manager welcomed me with an airy and sunny smile. When I told him who I was and what I wanted, his smile faded and he looked at me grimly.

'What you ask of me is subject to banking confidentiality,' he said.

'I know. But you know, too, that Koustas was murdered. I'm neither a relative nor an heir. I'm a police officer and I'm asking for assistance in our investigations.'

He was in a tricky position, but he did not try to be difficult. He simply weighed the consequences. 'I can't let you have a detailed statement, but you can look at it here.'

'That's all I want.'

'You realise that if this gets out, I risk losing my job.'

'It won't get out. You have my word.'

He picked up the phone and instructed that a printout of Koustas' account be brought to his office. The girl whose arm had pointed me in his direction eventually appeared with it.

I took the statement and examined it. There were daily deposits of around five million, but there was no large withdrawal either on the day of the murder or on the day before. I handed the statement to the manager and took my leave. If Koustas had withdrawn money to pay someone off on the night of the murder, he had not withdrawn it from the Commercial Bank.

The National Bank branch was only a couple of minutes' walk further down, but it was in complete contrast to the Commercial Bank. Here the managers were few, the clerks many and the queues at the counters reminded me of the tax office on the last day for the submission of declarations. The two chairs in front of the manager's desk were taken and I waited outside.

When I finally saw him half an hour later, and told him what I wanted, he raised his arms in a gesture of despair. 'Unfortunately, there's nothing I can do. I'm bound by banking rules.'

'I know that, but your client was murdered and we are doing our best to track down those responsible.'

'Our client is dead, yes, but he left heirs, and at this moment in time I have no idea who they are – officially, at least.'

'I'm not asking for a copy of his account. I don't even need to look at it. All I want you to tell me is whether Koustas made any substantial withdrawals on the day he died or the day before.'

'I'm sorry.'

'I can get a warrant and have the account opened.'

He smiled. 'Since you know the proper procedure, why don't you do it so that we're both covered?'

'Fine,' I said, getting up. 'I'll be back tomorrow with the warrant. Kindly arrange to have two of your clerks put at my disposal.'

'Why?' he said, surprised.

'Because I'll go through the account from the day it was opened and I'll require the receipts for every deposit, withdrawal and transaction. It will take us at least two days.'

'You just told me that you only wanted to be told of significant withdrawals for the last two days of his life.'

'You want to observe the strict formalities, so do I.'

Obviously he was taking into account the queues of people at his counters. Outside, thunder rolled and lightning lit up the darkening sky. The manager picked up his phone and asked for Konstantinos Koustas' account details. He put the phone down and stared at me. He would have gladly thrown me out. When they brought him the file, he took off the last sheet and handed it to me. Koustas had made one withdrawal of fifty thousand on the day before the murder. He had gone through twenty and we had found the other thirty in his wallet.

'Thank you for your help,' I said, giving him the sheet back.

He did not say anything as I went out, and neither did I. Not out of impoliteness, but because my mind was on Koustas. His having withdrawn money to give to the man he would meet could now be ruled out. The alternative was that he had had a rendezvous with the man and had gone to his car for that reason. When we found the murderer – if we found him – perhaps we would find out what it was they had planned to talk about. I made a mental note to tell Dermitzakis to check what phone calls Koustas had made from his landline and from his mobile phone during the days before he died.

It was raining cats and dogs. By the time I got to the Mirafiori, I was soaked and I cursed the weather and Koustas for having his bank accounts in Glyfada and the manager of the National Bank for having kept me waiting.

Vouliagmenis Avenue was blocked from the airport turn-off and cars were moving at a snail's pace. The traffic lights were not working; drivers were losing their tempers and taking it out on their car horns. My wet clothes were sticking to me and I was quivering like a fish out of water. It could not have been raining for much more than half an hour, but at the junction with Ilioupoleos Street, a torrent of water was rushing down from the mountain. A Yugo, a Renault Clio and a Fiat Uno had become waterlogged. Their drivers were sitting at their steering wheels and gazing at the rivers of water like tourists on a trip to the Niagara Falls. If the Mirafiori were to stop now, I would never be able to start it again, I thought, and I would have to spend all day travelling around by trolley. I wound the window down and signalled to the other drivers that I wanted to pass from the middle to the left-hand lane. The driver behind me on my left put his head out of the window and hurled a string of abuse at me for cutting in, but the rain was coming down in sheets and hitting him in the face. He soon would up his window. At the first opportunity, I turned left and parked on the pavement. I switched off the engine, shivered and waited for the downpour to end. The night before I had been playing the wealthy Greek ship owner in a French restaurant, that morning I was a shipwrecked Pakistani from a Greek tanker in Vouliagmenis Avenue.

CHAPTER 15

The centre of Athens was strewn with the rubbish that had been swept off by the rain. You arrived at your destination by crossing the National Rubbish Park: cartons of chocolate milk, plastic Coca-Cola bottles, beer cans and empty tubs of yogurt. Never mind what the radio said about the refuse collectors' strike being over, the piles of rubbish remained consistent. Evidently they were waiting for the sun to dry it all first before going out to collect it.

The journey to Security Headquarters in Alexandras Avenue took as long as it would to get to Volos: three hours. My clothes had dried on me. Vlassopoulos saw me heading for my office and ran to catch up with me.

'The Chief wants to see you.'

'All right. Come inside.' I left Ghikas for later, to allow myself time to calm down. 'Have you got anything on Koustas?'

'In the way that you ask, no.'

'What's that supposed to mean, Vlassopoulos? How *should* I ask you? Why not at least say "Nothing to report", which is what all the slackers say?' I was grateful he had given me an opportunity to let off steam before going to see Ghikas.

'What I mean is that no one knows anything concerning Koustas.'

'They know, but they're not saying, is that it?'

'No, Inspector.' This time he looked puzzled and paused before saying: 'There was something strange about the man. Not about his murder, but about him.'

'What sort of thing?'

'I can't put my finger on it. When you talk to people about the murder, they seem OK, whereas when you ask them what kind of man Koustas was, they clam up.'

'Less psychoanalysis, Vlassopoulos. Our job is all drudgery and there's no room for psychoanalysis. Keep looking, turn the screws a bit.'

'I will keep looking.' I saw that I had not convinced him, because he added: 'Of course I'll keep looking.'

'Good boy. Now send in Dermitzakis.'

I had ticked him off, but what he said set me thinking. If he was right, then word had got round, not because they were afraid of Koustas, who was dead, but of his associates. The second alternative was beginning to take shape. Koustas had left the Bouzouki Strings alone on the night of the murder because he was expecting 'an associate'. As much as it rankled, I was beginning to think that the Anti-Terrorist boys had been right. The killer might not have been a professional hit man, but he was a hired man all the same.

'I want you to check all Koustas' telephone bills,' I said to Dermitzakis when he came in.

'How far back?'

'Two weeks minimum, just to be on the safe side. Start with his mobile phone.'

I left him and went to see Ghikas. Koula was all smiles when she saw me.

'When's the wedding set for?' I asked her.

'Well, Sakis wants us to get married right away, but I'm not in any hurry.'

'Why so?'

'Let him sweat a bit. Show too much willingness and men get above themselves.' She looked at me as if to say that I was lucky Adriani had got to me first and I had escaped falling into her hands.

'Is he in?' I asked, wanting to make a quick getaway.

'Yes, and he's been hunting for you since early this morning.'

She wasn't exaggerating because the moment I went in he jumped down my throat.

'Where have you *been*? No one informs me of anything.'

I told him a bit about the investigations since I had taken over the

93

case and where I had been that morning. He studied me sceptically for a few moments.

'I'd rather you turned your attention to the matter of the unidentified corpse,' he said afterwards. 'Hand Koustas' murder over to Vlassopoulos.'

I was dumbfounded. I struggled to fathom what his motive was, but his face remained expressionless.

'Why?' was the only word that came out of my mouth.

'We'll keep him on the case for a month; he'll come up with nothing, and then we'll file it with the unsolved crimes.'

I recalled what Sotiropoulos had said: that if I were to dig too deeply into the Koustas case, I would land myself in hot water. I knew Ghikas well. He had us going through much less important cases with a fine-tooth comb. For him to be in such a hurry to get rid of it into 'unsolved crimes' meant that he had had his orders from above. I thought that I had let off all my steam by snapping at Vlassopoulos, but I felt my temper rising again.

'Did Stellas give you the idea?'

'What's Stellas got to do with it?'

'Because it was he who told me from day one to file it.'

'And you think that I wait for Stellas to tell me what to do?' He barked, partly because he thought I underestimated him and he was full of complexes and partly because he wanted to put a lid on the matter. 'We have our hands full here with the forty tribes of Israel. We're overrun with Albanians, Serbs, Romanians and Bulgarians, all of whom kill for a crust of bread and can't be found. We'll file it now and if we're lucky, we'll catch the culprit in a year or so for some other murder and get his confession to this one too.'

He waited to see whether I would object. I kept my mouth shut and he calmed down. 'Besides, we have some developments in the matter of the unidentified corpse.'

He picked up two pages stapled together and handed them across the desk to me. The first page was in German. I could see from the stamp that it was an official document.

'The German's statement. It came by fax this morning. In less than a day, they had traced him to the University of Berlin.'

I turned to the second page and saw that it had been translated into Greek. 'So soon?' I said it only to prime him because I knew what would follow.

'When you know the right people . . .' he said smugly. My prediction was confirmed.

'Your contact in Germany?'

'Yes. Hartmann.'

Who knew whether it was Hartmann or my own message that had resulted in the supplementary statement. In any case, all the documents would first go through Ghikas.

'You know, since we began our inquiries into Koustas, we find that everyone is afraid and no one wants to talk. The business might go much deeper than we thought at first. I think we should go on digging a bit, to see what we come up with.'

He immediately adopted that friendly expression that he always produces when he wants me to understand something without his actually saying it. 'Costas, I know where you're heading. Hand the case to Vlassopoulos. Don't give me a hard time.'

We looked at each other for a moment without another word being exchanged. Then I opened the door and walked out.

'Tell me,' I asked Koula, 'what really happened with Hartmann?'

'Who's he?'

'That German you were supposed to phone in Munich.'

'Oh, him! We couldn't find him and gave up.'

If I could solve crimes as easily as that, I would have been Chief of Police by now.

In the lift I tried to think who would have given the order to Ghikas to bury the case and for what reason. What grubby business was Koustas involved in? It couldn't have been drugs. Nothing that had to do with drugs would be swept under the carpet. Drug cases are first uncovered and then those who are convicted find a way to buy their freedom. The only possibility I could think of was that he might have been a loan shark. If some well-known businessmen had been involved, they might have pulled strings to get the case closed before their names were bandied about on TV or in the press. However, from the swift look I had had at Koustas' Commercial

Bank account, I did not have that impression. And if I were to obtain a warrant now to open his accounts, I would no doubt find myself in hot water after what Ghikas had said.

I sat at my desk and read the German's statement. It was just a few lines.

'*I saw the unidentified man walking with the girl in the square of the main village in Santorini. They were walking hand in hand. The girl was medium height and had long, blonde hair tied in a ponytail. I can't be sure about her age. She looked about twenty, but she was probably older. I saw them again later. I was eating at a taverna and they sat at the table opposite. I did not see them again.*'

The only new piece of information was that the girl had long, blonde hair. In other words, neither here nor there. The world was full of blondes. The statement did not even say whether her hair was naturally blonde or dyed.

On the balcony across from the office, the hairy hulk had his arms round the young girl and was caressing her. She was glued to him, while he held her round the waist and kissed her on her hair, her neck and her lips. The telephone interrupted me from my absorption in the spectacle. It was the chief from the station on the island.

'He wasn't staying on the island, Inspector,' he said. 'We've done a search of all the hotels and houses, one by one.'

'Did anyone recognise him?'

'Only the café owner in the square. He had sat there for a coffee with two others.'

Something stirred in me. Those two must have been his murderers. So, he knew them. 'Do we have a description of the other two?'

'Only vague. One was brown-haired, the other darkish. But the café owner thought they were foreigners.'

'And the girl?'

'He didn't see any girl. Only the two men. You understand, I'm sure,' he added, as though trying to make excuses. 'With all the people on the island in summer, how is anyone going to remember faces?'

96

'Thank you, Lieutenant,' I said and hung up.

If he was not staying on the island, then how had he come to be there? Had he gone there on a boat together with his murderers? It was not out of the question, given that he knew them. Perhaps he had gone by ferry to meet them there, but they murdered him before he had had time to rent a room. And the girl? The German had seen them together in Santorini. Perhaps Dermitzakis was right. Maybe it had been just a one-night affair. Unless the killers had set him up with her so that they could follow his movements.

An image started taking shape. The unidentified man had gone to the island. Or he had gone there with the girl, but had not had time to find somewhere to stay because he had bumped into the killers. Or they had all gone there together – he, the girl and the killers. This last version seemed to me to be the more likely. The girl was in on it and had left them to talk. They had sat at the café, talked, but had not managed to work it out, whatever it was. They had taken him into the hills, killed him and buried him. Then the murderers and the girl had vanished.

CHAPTER 16

The pain in my back came back and this time was even more acute. It pierced me through to my chest. I did not need to think long to find the cause. It was the hours I had spent soaked to the skin in the Mirafiori. I sat in front of the TV and bit my lip, because if I said anything, I would have to put up with Adriani's scolding.

The news began with its favourite topic: the torrential downpour. The roads turning into lakes, the hundreds of calls received by the fire brigade, the chairs and tables floating in living rooms and people emptying out the water in buckets and cursing the government for doing nothing.

'They're right,' said Adriani crossly. 'They can't be bothered to build a proper drainage system. All they're interested in is votes.'

I was in no mood for conversation. The political news, which usually comes fifth or sixth in line, like athletes who never manage to make the podium, held nothing of any great interest. Only the former minister with the high popularity ratings appeared before the cameras to state that he disagreed with the party line over Greek–Turkish relations. You would think he was about to begin bombarding the Turks from the expensive French restaurant where he ate every night.

We had already got to the day's medical report and they had not yet said anything about either Koustas or the unidentified corpse. I got up quietly and went into the bedroom. I took down Volume II of Dimitrakos and lay on the bed. I was searching for an interesting entry to take my mind off things when I realised that my left arm had gone numb and I could not hold the dictionary. I let it drop and remained still while I felt the pain shooting through me.

'What's wrong? Why are you lying down?' Adriani was at the door and looking at me with a worried expression.

'My back's hurting again. It must be from the rain this morning. And my arm's gone numb –'

'What!?' she cried. 'You're arm's gone numb?'

She turned and ran out. 'Where are you off to?' I called after her.

'Stay where you are. Don't move.'

I heard her making a phone call and rapidly giving her name and the address. She came back and looked me over. She was trying to guess from my appearance how I was.

'Who did you call?'

'Emergency. They'll be here in fifteen minutes.'

'Are you in your right mind? Do you think I'm going to go to hospital just because I've got a pain in my back? I told you I've arranged to see a rheumatologist.'

She tried to hide her fear. 'Costas, dear,' she said. 'It might not be your back. It might be your heart.'

'My heart . . . don't be stupid! My heart's fine. It's my back that's hurting. If the Emergency Services ever come, I'm not going with them, I can tell you that right now.'

'Please. Do it for my sake. Can't I ask that of you as a favour?'

She begged me, and even though I was trying to put on a brave face, I had started to feel alarmed too. 'All right, but I'm not having an ambulance. We'll take the car.'

As soon as I tried to get up, my heart started pounding like an outboard motor and I surrendered to my fate. Adriani looked even more worried.

After exactly fifteen minutes, we heard the sound of the siren and she ran to open the door. Two paramedics came in with a stretcher. They tossed me on to it as though I were a bundle of washing, covered me with a blanket and rushed me through the front door.

'Where are you taking him?' Adriani asked.

'To the State General Hospital. The emergency ward. Are you coming with us?'

'Of course.'

Two or three passers-by stopped to watch the spectacle. I wanted the ground to open up and swallow me because I felt as though they were looking at an old man who reckons his days in the journeys he makes to the hospital. Adriani sat beside me, holding my hand. The doors closed, the ambulance siren started and we set off.

It took us about ten minutes to reach the emergency ward at the State General. The paramedics left me in a corridor.

'Wait here, the doctor will be with you soon,' they said to Adriani and disappeared.

I looked around and could see only stretchers lined up against the walls of the corridor and red doors. Lying on the stretcher across from me was an old woman, all skin and bone, with eyes closed and mouth open. A phantom. At her side was a thin woman, looking around her with the same bored expression that the regulars in the corridors of Security Headquarters have. The old woman let out a groan and the thin woman leaned over.

'What is it you want, Mum?' she said irritably. I could not tell how the old woman communicated without moving her lips, but evidently she managed it, because her daughter said: 'All right, be patient. We're not the only ones here.' And she fixed her eyes on the ceiling. Nothing else appeared to hold any interest for her.

I turned and looked at Adriani, who had taken out her

handkerchief and was mopping the non-existent sweat from my brow. I wondered how many more times she would be able to bear coming here with me before she started cursing me like the woman who was with her mother. I felt frightened, a carcass helplessly shoved this way and that. If Vlassopoulos or Dermitzakis were to interrogate me now, I would have confessed to everything, even to things I had not done.

A red door opened and a couple came out. Adriani left me and went inside, leaving the door open behind her. I could not hear what she was saying, but I understood from the man's reply.

'Don't be impatient, madam. We'll see him as soon as it's his turn.'

'Imbeciles!' Adriani shouted, slamming the door behind her.

She walked back to my side, but she avoided looking at me, as though ashamed that she could do nothing. The pain had spread down both my arms and I was unable to get comfortable on the stretcher. Sitting on a plastic chair beyond the thin woman was an old man. He was bent forward and blood was trickling from his nose to the floor, drop by drop, like a tap that needed a new washer. The man had his eyes fixed on the puddle being formed by his blood, not such a big one that the Mirafiori would get stuck in it, but a puddle nonetheless. The chairs to the right and left of him were empty, but the people around him avoided them and preferred to stand.

Two hours must have gone by when I heard voices, shouts, crying and the sound of wheels speeding down the corridor. When the stretcher drew up in front of me, I saw a gypsy lying on it, moustache and stubble. He was wearing a worn, shiny jacket and old jeans, his shirt was ripped and above his liver was a huge wound gushing blood. He was gasping for breath. One for Markidis, I thought to myself. Over him, five women, wearing pleated skirts and scarves, were wailing and lamenting fit to wake the whole hospital.

The door of the surgery opposite opened and a doctor came out. He was tall, dark and had wavy hair. A real good-looker.

'A little less noise,' he berated the gypsies. 'This is a hospital. We have other patients too.'

As soon as Adriani saw him, she rushed over to him. 'Please,

Doctor,' she said. 'Take a look at my husband. At least make sure it's not serious.' She stood on tiptoe and whispered something in his ear.

The doctor was undecided for a moment and then turned to look at me. I do not know what he saw in my appearance that concerned him, but he did come over.

'What do you feel?' he said.

'A pain in my back.'

'In your back or in your chest?'

'I'm not sure if it's in my back and hurting me in the chest or vice versa.'

'Is there any pain anywhere else?'

'My arms. At first it was my left arm that went numb, now both arms are hurting.'

'Upset in the stomach?'

'Yes. Like a swelling.'

The concern was now plain in his eyes. He saw a nurse who was hurrying by and stopped her.

'Nurse, help me to push this bed into the surgery.'

A look was all they needed in order to communicate. 'Hold this a moment,' she said, handing a plastic container of urine to a woman who happened to be standing there.

'Well, I never,' the woman shouted. 'It's not enough that we have to wait three hours to see a doctor, we end up having to look after somebody else's urine as well.'

The nurse paid no attention. With the doctor, she took hold of the bed I was on and they rolled me into the surgery.

A chubby woman in black was holding the shirt of an old man sitting on the bed there and helping him to put it on.

'Get dressed outside please,' the doctor said.

'We're not done yet,' the woman protested. 'You still haven't told us whether we need more tests or medicines or what.'

'I'll call you in five minutes. I have an emergency here.'

'Come on, Dad.' She helped the man to his feet, picking up his clothes from the chair at the same time. As she walked out, she gave me a look. 'So what connections does he have?' she asked the doctor. Her look and her words were full of venom. If I sat you down for interrogation, I thought to myself, you would need more than connections to save yourself.

No one else appeared to pay her any attention.

'What medical insurance do you have?' the nurse in the surgery said.

'Police Insurance,' Adriani chipped in. 'He's a senior police officer.'

The woman overheard as she escorted her father out of the door. 'That explains it,' she cried out. 'They have all they need because they're on the take from the drug dealers.'

I didn't know what hurt more: my back or the humiliation. I waited for someone to stand up for me, but once again no one paid any attention, not even Adriani, who was helping me to undress. From which I concluded that she must by now be terrified.

Out of the corner of my eye I watched the nurse wire me up as though I were a generator. I wondered whether the needles scratching patterns on the paper were also monitoring my anxiety along with my heart rate.

'It's an acute ischaemic attack and I'm going to keep you in for observation,' the doctor said.

It was what I'd been afraid of from the beginning and I felt myself breaking out in a cold sweat. If he had said he was keeping me in for interrogation, I would have accepted it more cheerfully. The interrogation rooms were a hell I was familiar with.

They took me to a room with two beds and to my great relief I saw that the other one was empty. It was only then that I noticed the large plastic bag that Adriani was carrying. She took out my pyjamas and a pair of slippers.

'I packed them while we were waiting for the ambulance,' she said as though apologising. 'I thought they might want to keep you in.'

She helped me into the pyjamas, then sat on the bed facing me and stared at me. I thought that I should say something, a thank you, or that I was feeling better and she should not worry, but the words would not come. Adriani smiled at me sheepishly, just as on our first date. Who would have believed it, I thought, the illness had brought us back those little tender moments. She reached out her hand and laid it gently on mine. Now that everything was under control, she seemed likely to burst into tears to relieve her pent-up feelings, but she restrained herself. Her hand gave me reassurance, the pain gradually went away and I fell asleep.

CHAPTER 17

When I opened my eyes, I could not at first work out where I was. The place was completely unfamiliar to me. It was not until I saw the white walls round about me and the tube coming down from the serum and ending in my arm that I remembered I was in hospital. Katerina was sitting on the empty bed and smiling at me.

'Are you awake?' she said.

'What are you doing here?'

'Mum phoned me last night. I caught the morning flight and came.'

'What, you mean she called you in the middle of the night?'

'What do you expect? That they'd take you to hospital without her telling me?' She got up, leaned over and kissed me on the forehead. 'So, in the end, you succeeded in getting me to Athens.' She smiled. 'How do you feel?'

I explored to see where the pain was, but there was no pain, anywhere. 'Fine. I'm not in any pain.'

Her eyes wandered over me, as though she wanted to make sure that I was telling the truth. She was dressed casually, in a blouse and jeans. Her brown, wavy hair wrapped itself round her head like a garland and her eyes, when they did not have that investigative, worried look that they had then, gazed at you foxily, cheekily. She was a good-looking girl, though perhaps she wasn't – perhaps I simply saw her like that because I was her father. Everyone thinks their fart is frankincense, as my dear old mother used to say.

'Where's your mother?'

'I told her to go home to get some rest. She'll be here after lunch.'

I had no time to ask her about herself before the doctor came in.

Smiling, he came out with a good morning, then his eyes turned to Katerina and remained fixed on her. Katerina acknowledged him with a nod and then turned back to me. She was a modest girl and felt uneasy when men looked at her in that lecherous way.

'Would you please wait outside while we examine the patient?' said the nurse accompanying the doctor, as she wheeled in the cardiograph machine.

'It's all right, she's not bothering us,' the doctor said.

Katerina retreated into a corner so as not to be in the way and the nurse pushed the machine up to my bed.

'So then? How are we doing?' the doctor asked.

'Better. I'm not in any pain.'

'Let's see.'

Once again, the needles scratched their shapes. I don't know whether my anxiety showed on my face, but I could certainly see the anxiety in Katerina's eyes. The doctor, on the other hand, seemed calm and the nurse looked merely bored.

'Splendid,' the doctor said in a satisfied tone. 'The cardiograph is much better today. You should be very grateful to your wife.'

'Why is that?'

'Because she had the good sense to get you to the hospital straight away and we were in time to prevent anything worse happening.'

'Did you tell her that?'

'Naturally.'

I felt like punching him on the nose, because now there would be no stopping her.

'When did you first feel the pain in your back?'

I did my calculations. 'It must have been about a month ago.'

'You should have gone to see a doctor immediately.'

'You don't know my father,' Katerina muttered from her corner.

'Are you afraid of doctors?'

'Afraid! Ask him which he prefers, a doctor or a murderer, and he'll say the murderer.'

They looked at each other and laughed together at my expense. The nurse remained unsmiling and she went up in my estimation.

'They'll be coming to take you for a chest X-ray and a scan soon,' the doctor said. 'I'll see you again tomorrow morning.'

He gave me a friendly tap on the shoulder, smiled at Katerina and went out with the nurse at his heels. Katerina ran after them. Presently, she returned holding a huge plant looking like a plane tree in a pot.

'What's that?'

'Ghikas sent it. Best wishes for a speedy recovery.'

I took the card and read it. His writing was a scribble. He would not be coming to see me, of course, but nevertheless I was moved that he had thought of me because by and large we got on each other's nerves.

'Did you ask the doctor when I'll be out of here?'

'Dad, you must be out of your mind. He'll think I'm mad. You've not been here twenty-four hours yet.'

I knew, but the burning question for me was just how many twenty-four hours I would have to be in there before I tasted freedom again. The door opened and in walked a male nurse with a wheelchair to take me for the tests. He helped me up, and Katerina hastened to take my other arm, then the two of them sat me in the chair as if I were an invalid being taken for a walk in the park.

'Are you going to keep me company?' I asked Katerina.

'Of course.'

I said I wanted her for company, but it wasn't true. I wanted her beside me because I was afraid. I was afraid of the hospital, the doctors, the machines, and I needed support.

The X-ray room resembled the Glyfada branch of the National Bank. It was packed with people, all pushing and shoving, some in their everyday clothes, others in pyjamas and others wandering around with their wives or daughters holding their serum up high to let it drip. Would they find anything wrong with my lungs? I wondered, as I entered the X-ray room, and I trembled to my slippers.

When we got back to my room half an hour later, I found Vlassopoulos and Dermitzakis waiting for me. Vlassopoulos greeted Katerina like an old friend since he had known her for years.

Dermitzakis, who was new to the department, was meeting her for the first time and after a formal handshake avoided looking at her out of fear that I might misconstrue his intentions, which I certainly would have.

'So what do you think you're up to, Inspector?' Dermitzakis said.

'There's nothing wrong with me, I'm fine. If you think you're going to be rid of me, you're wrong.'

'We don't want to be rid of you. You might grumble at us every now and again, but all the others are much worse.'

'Is there any news?'

'Never mind the news for now,' Vlassopoulos said. 'Tell us how you are.'

'I want to know. I'm going crazy in here. At least let me hear something of interest. What have you found out about Koustas?'

I saw Katerina discreetly leaving the room.

'Only one person we questioned said anything of interest.'

'What did he say?'

'"Drop it, don't ask."'

'What the hell is that supposed to mean, Vlassopoulos?' I said, and sat bolt upright in bed. I felt my heart begin to pound violently, and sat back, terrified.

'No, you don't understand,' said Vlassopoulos. 'I'm telling you what he said. We were alone, but he looked about him, frightened, as if he was being watched, and he whispered, "Drop it, don't ask".'

What was Koustas involved in? Who was he dealing with so that everyone was too scared to talk? I no longer doubted that his death was a settling of accounts, but not an underworld thing as Anti-Terrorist supposed. This business was deeper than that and we would have to drill to get to the bottom of it.

'What about his phone calls?' I asked Dermitzakis.

He looked at me for a moment before answering. 'Did Koustas have any connection with politics?'

'Why?'

'Because if I exclude the calls to his home and his clubs, the others were all to politicians.'

'Politicians?' My curiosity was aroused again and I sat up, more carefully this time. 'Which politicians?'

Dermitzakis took a sheet of paper out of his pocket and referred to it. 'Three government MPs, two Opposition MPs and a former minister. He called the last one five times in three days.'

The former minister with the high popularity ratings who ate every night at the Canard Doré. I thought of Ghikas. Now I understood where the pressure on him was coming from, and why he wanted to have the case filed 'unsolved'. He could not close the case, but if he filed it 'unsolved' and we eventually happened to discover the murderer, he would confess to the killing without revealing the true story behind it and we would have him committed without having to dig too deep, and that way the case would be swept under the carpet. As for Koustas, it was dirty business on the one hand and dealings with politicians on the other. Apparently, Sotiropoulos knew something about all this, or at least he suspected something, but even he was too afraid to vouchsafe what he knew.

'What other calls had he made?'

'He made two calls to mobile phones, but I haven't been able to identify the owners of the numbers. They're foreign numbers.'

The calls abroad may not have been of any significance. He could have been talking with agents to book dancers or singers for his clubs. But they may have had to do with other kinds of dealings. Impossible to know.

'File it with the unsolved crimes and cease all investigations,' I said.

A silence followed. 'Don't you want us to look into his dealings with the politicians?' said Dermitzakis timidly.

'What would you do? Go and interrogate them? They'll say that they were on friendly terms with him and that he took them out for dinner. And the minister will come down on us because we're badgering politicians without a shred of evidence. File it. Maybe in a couple of years we'll get the killer for some other crime.'

Rarely do I have recourse to Ghikas' arguments, but this time he was right. If it was not the best solution, it was certainly the most innocuous. Any other would have landed us in hot water. And I had no intention of coming into conflict with Ghikas without a leg to stand on. Not to mention that the man had sent me a potted plant.

They went and left me deep in thought, and this went on until Adriani and Katerina came into the room.

'So even in here you can't stop discussing your beloved murders?' she said with a stern expression.

'What do you want me to talk about with Vlassopoulos and Dermitzakis? What Vlassopoulos' Hyundai does to the gallon or if Dermitzakis is down in the dumps because Panathinaikos lost last night? It's all they're interested in.'

'You'd do well to forget the department and the murders for a while.'

'Are you trying to wind me up?'

She fell silent. I was beginning to discover the benefits of being ill. They flatter you, nothing is too much for you, and when you say 'shut up', they do just that.

'If I can hear your voice from outside in the corridor, it must mean you're feeling better.'

I saw the doctor in the doorway. 'I came to tell you, before I go off, that the X-ray is clean. In general you're doing fine.'

The news cheered me up no end and I thought I was through with it all. 'When can I leave, Doctor?'

'Ah, starting to get impatient,' he said, but without committing himself. 'I've seen to it that they won't put anyone else in the room, so you'll be left in peace.'

Together, with one voice, we said 'Thank you'. He acknowledged us with a smile, first Adriani and me, then Katerina, and left.

'I think I'd like a little sleep.'

'Of course, it'll do you a world of good,' Adriani said, as though she were talking to a child who for the first time had decided to do the correct thing. 'Katerina and I will go for a coffee.'

I was not sleepy. I simply wanted to be alone because it had pained me to have the case filed with the unsolved crimes and I needed time to come to terms with that.

CHAPTER 18

Klysma = a purgative drug or agent, the action or result of purging. See
catharsis, *purging particularly of the intestines or womb with water or*
various other liquids (milk, water and oil, etc.) containing certain
substances with a laxative effect, depending on the ailment and the
organ to be purged.

The entry was neither from Dimitrakos nor from Liddell &
Scott, but from the *Hermeneutical Lexicon of Hippocratic Terms*
edited by Panos D. Apostolidis. Katerina had given it to me as a
gift. It was all of nine hundred pages and it must have cost her an
arm and a leg. I told her off for spending so much money, but she
said that now she was staying with us in Athens, she was not
spending as much as in Thessaloniki and so she had money to
spare to buy me a present.

It was my fifth day in the room with two beds – one empty, one
occupied. The doctor and I had become chums. I had learned his
name, Fanis Ouzounidis, but all this was neither here nor there,
because each morning I asked him when I would be let out and he
answered only with an enigmatic smile, like a tricky politician who
was not about to make a statement. The previous day, I had
badgered him and he had finally given a response.

'Look on it as a holiday, my dear fellow. I gather you were obliged
to cut yours short. Think of your stay here as the holiday you didn't
have.'

I had a mind to tell Ghikas to put Adriani on the pay roll.
Squealers like that are in great demand in Security. Anyhow, I had
completely recovered and you could see as much from the way
Katerina and Adriani had changed. During the first two days, I
would open my eyes and see them there, next to me. Now they were
coming at around twelve, after they had finished the household
chores. Unfortunately, when it came to my being discharged, they all
pretended to be deaf, and I passed my time by means of a
preordained series of trips: room–toilet, toilet–room. And since I
was fed up to the back teeth with these, that day, at around ten in the

morning, I was sitting on my bed and reading the entry under 'purgative'.

'If you bring home those marks next term, I'll give you a purgative.' That's what my father used to say whenever I brought my school report home. I could never understand why a purgative was a worse punishment than a clip round the ear or being confined to my room. It was only when I entered the Police Academy that I discovered it was the favourite form of torture during the time of the Metaxas dictatorship. Of course, my father was only a simple gendarme and I very much doubt that he had ever used an emetic on a prisoner. After all, whenever we were ill, the doctor would bring the purgative with him. But my father used it as a threat, seeing as it was approved of by his superiors.

'May I come in?'

I looked up and saw Vlassopoulos. He was waiting in the doorway, smiling. 'What are you doing here so bright and early?' I asked him in a sour tone to underline my displeasure at the fact that he had not visited his ailing superior for several days.

'I have a surprise for you.'

'What surprise?'

He came in and sat on the other bed. 'We've found someone who recognises the body.'

I immediately forgot my sourness and the grievance of the patient who takes pleasure in feeling continually ignored, and I was ready to spring out of bed.

'When?'

'This morning. I had asked Sotiropoulos to run the photograph again on TV. Yesterday, this man went to his police station and from there they sent him to us.'

'Come on, who is he?'

Vlassopoulos looked at me, still smiling. 'I took a statement from him, but I thought that you'd want to hear it for yourself. I don't know whether I've done the right thing, but he's waiting outside.'

'Stop playing games with me. Bring him in.'

He got up and went out. He soon reappeared with a stocky young fellow, average height and with stubble. There was nothing to distinguish him other than his bandy legs, rather like two slices of melon. He was carrying a plastic bag.

'Good morning,' he said, sheepishly. 'The lieutenant told me you were in hospital so I brought you a few oranges.' A few only in a manner of speaking – there must have been three kilos of them.

'Thank you, but there was no need.'

'Vitamins are good for you. Trust me, I know,' he said, as though feeling the need to apologise for his gesture.

'Tell me, what's your name?'

'Sarafoglou . . . Kyriakos Sarafoglou . . .'

'And you know the man whose face you saw on TV?'

'Yes.' He collected his thoughts. 'Look, I'm a footballer. I play for Falirikos in the Third Division. That's where I know him from. He was a referee for matches in the Third Division. His name was Christos Petroulias.'

'And why didn't you come forward earlier? Did you see him yesterday for the first time?'

'No, I'd seen his photograph a few days ago, but I couldn't have sworn that it was him. You know, the way he was . . .' He tried to describe him, but could not find the words. He was a footballer, after all. 'It looked like him, but I couldn't be sure. The other lads said the same thing: that it looked like him, but that it was a coincidence, that it couldn't be Petroulias. You know, it's not easy to go and say that someone is dead. You keep your thoughts to yourself. Because what if the next day it turns out he's alive and well? He might sue you or something. But when I saw his photo again yesterday, I was sure about it being him.'

'When did you last see him?'

He did not answer straight away. He thought about it. 'It was at our game against Triton in mid-May. I remember it because Triton were heading for the championship and in the last minute Petroulias gave a penalty against them, which wasn't a penalty by any stretch of the imagination, and it lost them the game and the championship.'

'And you haven't seen him since then?'

'No, but he refereed other matches because I kept hearing his name up to the end of the season.'

'Do you know if he had another job, apart from refereeing?'

'He must have. The refereeing lark is supposed to be for amateurs and all the refs have some other job.'

'Do you have any idea where he lived?'

'No, but he belonged to the Athens Association of Referees. You should be able to get it from them.'

Vlassopoulos reached into his pocket and took out his classic notepad, where he wrote everything, from his notes on the course of his investigations to his shopping list, and jotted it down.

'Tell me, Kyriakos,' I said to Sarafoglou, 'do you know whether Petroulias had any enemies?'

He burst out laughing. 'There's no such thing as a referee who doesn't have enemies, Inspector. In Greece, you lose a match and you think it's the end of the world. Everybody is to blame: officials, players, coach. And above all the referees who sold out the side that lost.'

'Why do you say that? Was Petroulias on the take?' Vlassopoulos said.

He had been talkative until then; now he became uneasy. He was about to say something, then changed his mind and shrugged. 'Everyone has their own side of the story. After almost every game, there's always someone who will say that the referee sold us out. Most of it is lies, but some of it is true. It's impossible to get to the bottom of it.'

Even if he knew something specific, he wasn't going to tell. He makes his living by kicking a ball and if he were to say to a police officer that a referee had fixed a result, he might very well find himself kicking pine cones like the kids in my village.

'OK, Kyriakos,' I said gently. 'That's all. We have put you to some trouble, but you have helped us a great deal.'

He got up at once. In his eyes I could see his relief that he had got through it without our putting pressure on him to tell us more.

'I hope you get better soon,' he said. Vlassopoulos thought it unnecessary to accompany him. Now that he had told us what he knew, we no longer had any need of him, so he was economising on the niceties.

'Call the Referees' Association and find out where Petroulias lived,' I told him. 'Take a look at the place and ask round the neighbours in case they know anything. Call me and tell me what you find.'

'All right.'

He got up to leave. 'Sotiris,' I called to him when he had got to the door. 'Well done, you did a good job.'

He beamed. 'I'll phone,' he said, and was gone.

I laid the lexicon aside and tried to put what Sarafoglou had told us into some sort of order. Fine, Christos Petroulias was a referee in the Third Division and he was bumped off. Let's say that he was on the take and had fixed a result or two. Was that why he had been killed? Was there so much interest vested in what happened in the Third Division? If someone does you out of fifty million, you might see red and do him in, but not even the Albanians would kill for a lousy five grand. And even if someone had killed him because he had fixed a game, they would have done it at night, as he was going home, or on some lonely street corner. They would not have taken him to an island to bump him off, undress him and bury him, having first burned off his fingertips. There was something else going on here, something not connected with refereeing, but with his real work. We needed to find out what that was. I reflected that the two cases which had fallen to me of late had a common characteristic: at first sight they presented one picture on the surface, but there was in each case a lot hidden underneath.

The development with the hitherto unidentified corpse made me feel like a fakir on a bed of nails, so that when the doctor came in I almost jumped down his throat. 'So what's going on, Doctor? When am I going to get out of here?'

He smiled reassuringly, with the confidence of someone with an ace up his sleeve. 'Today is Wednesday. On Saturday you can leave.'

I decided to use whatever pull I had. 'Listen, Doctor,' I said. 'Either there's something that you're holding back from me or there isn't and I can't see why you're keeping me here, taking up two beds too, for no good reason. From what I know, the health service doesn't have leeway for such luxuries.'

'No, no. You don't have anything else. But –'

Why did he have to add that 'but'? If I didn't 'have anything else', it meant that my heart wasn't as good as I felt it to be and I broke into a cold sweat. 'What's the "but" supposed to mean?' I said, while I felt my heart starting to pound again, this time like an outboard motor gathering speed.

He held back for a moment, but eventually he came out with it. 'Your wife has told us that you're not someone to take sick leave and stay at home. She's afraid that as soon as you get out of here you'll go straight back to work. So she asked us to keep you in a few days more.'

I did not know how to react. Whether to fly off the handle because Adriani was organising my life behind my back or to be amazed at her ability to get round everyone, even the hospital doctors, and always have her own way.

'Please don't compromise me because of something I told you in confidence,' Ouzounidis implored me. 'Put it this way: I think that by staying here a few days more you'll have to spend less time at home.'

To be honest, the prospect of staying at home with Adriani driving me up the wall did not fill me with enthusiasm. 'All right, but if you don't let me out on Saturday, I'll leave of my own accord.'

'No, no. You'll definitely be let out,' he said, giving me a friendly pat on the back.

That friendly pat on the back was starting to get on my nerves. Usually, I was the one to give a friendly pat on the back – to the suspects when they confessed.

He left and I got down to some serious reckoning. Let's say that Vlassopoulos would spend all that day finding out where Petroulias lived. The next day, he would go to the house, take a look around, talk to the neighbours or his flatmates. Which meant that by Friday he would have finished the legwork and that I could take it from there.

The phone call came as Katerina and I were thumbing through the *Lexicon of Hippocratic Terms*. I was sitting on the edge of the bed in my pyjamas and slippers with Katerina beside me and I was pointing out to her various unusual words such as *metakata-psychomai, nychtalopikos, spermologeo.*

The phone rang and I lifted the receiver. 'Hello,' I said sharply, thinking it was Adriani and I wanted to show her my underlying vexation, even though I had promised the doctor I would say nothing. But it was not Adriani, it was Vlassopoulos.

'I've got Petroulias' address, Inspector. He lived at 19 Panga Street in Neo Filothei.'

'Well done. Now get over there and take a look round.'

'I'm calling you from there. I mean, not from his house, but from one of his neighbour's. His phone has been cut off. Inspector –' Whatever it was he was about to say, he stopped himself.

'What is it? Out with it.'

'We're talking about a luxury penthouse with a huge balcony. And he must have spent a fortune furnishing it. Except that someone's taken it apart.'

'What do you mean?'

'Someone's been in and turned the place upside down. Looking for something, obviously, but I don't know what, or whether they found it.'

I remained silent, taking in what he had said. A Third Division referee with a luxury penthouse, expensively furnished. Perhaps I should have asked at the Canard Doré whether they knew him. Probably he ate those raw steaks that they serve there. Katerina had put down the *Lexicon* and was looking at me inquisitively and with some concern.

'Right. Say nothing to Forensics yet. Lock it up and leave it so I can see it as it is. And find out which tax office Petroulias was registered at. I want a copy of his last tax declaration.'

I put the phone down and turned to Katerina, who was now looking at me with undisguised suspicion. 'Katerina, dear,' I said to her sweetly, 'I have to leave hospital today. Something extremely urgent has cropped up.'

'You must be out of your mind.' It was all she could think of to say. 'You know what will happen when Mum finds out.'

'No, but I do know what your mother cooked up with the doctors.

I squeezed it out of Ouzounidis. I told him I wouldn't say anything to your mother about it, but I can tell you.'

I saw her look away and I realised that she had been in on it too, or at any rate she knew about it.

'So you knew, eh?' I said. 'You knew and you said nothing.'

'What do you want me to say? She arranged it herself. You would have got into a row and I can't stand your fights. Anyway, it won't do you any harm to stay in a couple of days longer.'

'I'm getting out of here today. Whether you like it or not.'

'All right. Wait a moment,' she said, rushing out of the room. If it had been her mother, they would have heard us across the street. The good thing about Katerina was that she knew when to stop.

Presently, she returned with Ouzounidis. 'What's all this I've been hearing? I thought we had an agreement,' he said to me, not pleased.

'Because I like you, I'll give it to you straight, so you'll understand. There are two ways I can leave here. One is for you to discharge me, so that I can leave normally. The other is for me to get dressed and leave of my own accord and for me to arrest you for obstructing a police officer in the course of his duty if you try to stop me.'

I explained to him in a few words about Petroulias and what we had found. He calmed down and smiled. 'You can leave, but first you have to give me your word that you won't smoke.'

'OK. Not more than three cigarettes. One after each meal.'

'Not even one. You smoked your last cigarette before you were wheeled into this hospital. From now on, smoking is forbidden. And secondly, you'll take the medicine I prescribe for you and you'll come back in ten days so I can have a look at you.'

'OK, agreed.'

'And thirdly, you won't tire yourself out. Three or four hours of work each day at most and then you go home to rest.'

'Agreed.'

'And fourthly, you won't drive for a while. You will use only taxis or public transport.'

'I'll drive him around,' Katerina offered.

'Where did you learn to drive?' I asked her when Ouzounidis had gone to write my prescription.

'I took my driving test because Panos has a car and he lets me use it from time to time,' she said, defensively.

I wanted to ask her whether it was a car he had or a lorry for carrying farming produce, but she had behaved very decently towards me and I did not want to upset her.

When Adriani arrived, she found me dressed and ready to leave.

'Why are you dressed?' she asked, poised to start yelling at me.

'Because I'm being discharged and I'm leaving.'

'You were due to leave on Saturday.' She bit her lip for letting the cat out of the bag, but it no longer mattered now.

'I got round the doctors and they're letting me out today.'

She was flummoxed and I basked in my triumph.

CHAPTER 19

Petroulias' balcony, the size of a two-room flat, overlooked half of Athens. It was a view that was immense but qualitatively mediocre. Your gaze spread unhindered over rooftops and the terraces of apartment blocks, over dots of green scattered here and there, over clothes hung out to dry and – a block away – over a girl sunning herself on her terrace.

In its heyday, his balcony must have been a whole garden. Geraniums, daisies and chrysanthemums in boxes and narrow cement flower beds; saplings in huge pots; lemon and tiny cypress trees. It was a veritable nursery. In place of awnings, the balcony had two huge white umbrellas, with tables and garden chairs beneath. It reminded me of those roof-garden cafés you find nowadays in hotels. Only the waiter was missing. But the way it was now, the white umbrellas had turned yellow, half the saplings had withered and the flower beds were singing: 'Where have all the flowers gone?'

Vlassopoulos had been right. The flat had been richly furnished with couches and armchairs of leather and metal, a glass dining table, spotlights and standard lamps with silver plates that shone the light on to the ceiling.

If Petroulias' balcony looked like a drought-stricken arboretum, his flat looked like my sister-in-law's after the earthquake, except that he was no longer alive to straighten the place up. The armchairs were overturned; the couches had been slashed open; the books had been dislodged from the shelves on the wall, as had the TV, which was lying on the floor, its screen smashed. The hi-fi was in pieces and with its cables pulled out. Only the glass dining table had been spared the devastation.

I left the living room and went into the bedroom. The same scene. The wooden floor had swollen from the water. Perhaps they had not noticed that the mattress was filled with water before they slashed it open. I imagined how they must have cursed when it had drenched them and I almost laughed out loud. The wardrobe drawers were all on the floor and spread around them were underwear and socks, shirts and T-shirts, all designer-wear and expensive. His suits, which were lying in a heap at the bottom of the wardrobe, on top of his shoes, were all striking colours, like the suits worn by TV presenters. What I was seeing here was another form of reality show, with Petroulias dead and buried on top of the island and his flat a rubbish dump of modern furnishings. No knowing what they had been searching for, but they had searched with a vengeance. You could see that at a glance. Hanging behind the other door of the wardrobe, I found two shiny shirts and two pairs of black shorts – the regulation kit of a referee.

I remembered that I must not tire myself. I took hold of the only chair still standing, put it in the hallway and sat down. It was the quietest place in the house and I avoided getting in the way of the forensics people who were eager to get to work on the chaos.

Katerina had taken me round there at ten that morning. I had chuckled to myself after a week of depression when I saw her having a hard time starting up the Mirafiori and then struggling to turn the wheel, which was tighter than a water hydrant. 'Dad, I don't know why you don't sell it and get a steamroller,' she said indignantly at one stage. She left me at 19 Panga Street and said that she would pick me up from Security Headquarters in Alexandras Avenue at one o'clock. I realised what was going on. On the one hand, she wanted to drive me around so that I wouldn't have the hassle of using public transport, but on the other hand it was her way of monitoring my routine so that I didn't go AWOL.

'Have you found anything?' I asked Dimitris from Forensics.

'A lot of fingerprints, but I don't expect that they'll be from the villains. They're sure to have worn gloves. And footprints in the living room and in the hallway. They trod in the water and left tracks everywhere.'

'How many of them were there?'

'Two and they were wearing different kinds of shoes. One had trainers, the other was wearing shoes with smoother soles.'

'Any of Petroulias' personal papers?'

'An electricity and a telephone bill pushed under the door. Nothing else.'

The bills must have come after the break-in. The would-be thieves had taken all the other personal effects with them, either so as not to leave any evidence or to go through them in their own good time. After so many days of lying in bed, I was fed up sitting down and I decided to make a round of the neighbours in case I might come up with something, although Vlassopoulos, who had tried the previous day, had failed to do so.

I rang the doorbell opposite, under the name 'Kritikos'. No one had answered when Vlassopoulos had tried, but I was in luck. After ringing a second time, I heard footsteps and a youthful voice asking: 'Who is it?'

'Police. Inspector Haritos.'

The door opened immediately. The woman standing before me in the doorway sounded young, but she wasn't. She must have been seventy and had white hair and blue eyes still full of life.

'It must be about Mr Petroulias,' she said straight out.

'Yes. I'd like to ask you a few questions.'

'Of course. Come in.' And she stepped aside to let me in.

Petroulias had started his interior decoration from scratch, but she had collected remnants from all the houses she had ever lived in.

Her flat was filled with old family furniture. There wasn't an empty space anywhere, but it was all prettily arranged and the flat was cosy. She showed me into the living room and I noticed that her balcony was not an imitation forest with saplings; it had only flowers, like all the old Athenian balconies, and it had an awning rather than umbrellas.

'May I offer you something?' she said.

'No, thank you. Tell me: when did you hear about Mr Petroulias?'

'Last night, on the late-night news. I've been in London for a month, staying with my daughter, who lives there with her husband, and I only got back yesterday. I decided to watch the news before going to bed and that's how I heard about him. How tragic, good Lord!'

'How well did you know him?'

'As well as anyone knows their neighbours in an apartment building. Good morning, good evening, chit-chat about the weather . . . You know . . . He was a polite person. Whenever he saw me coming back from the supermarket loaded with bags, he always carried them in for me.' She smiled and her eyes had an ironic glint in them. 'Of course, that's not always a good thing, because it reminds you that you've grown old, nevertheless it's still polite.'

She was one of those people who win you over immediately. And she was not garrulous. She said exactly what was necessary and no more. The ideal witness.

'Did you ever happen to see anyone else going into or leaving his flat?'

'No. He once told me that he was an only child and that his parents had been killed in a car crash. No, I never saw anyone. Apart from –'

'Apart from?'

'A girl who was always with him in the last few months.'

'What was she like? Do you recall?'

She thought, in silence, bringing the image of the girl to her mind. 'Blonde, younger than him . . . long hair . . . Very courteous and always a smile on her face.'

The blonde again, I thought. Would I ever find out who she was?

'Did you catch her name?'

'No, he never introduced us. To tell you the truth, I thought it uncivil, but young people today attach little importance to social formalities.'

'When was the last time you saw him?'

She reflected again. 'It must have been at the beginning of June. We were in the lift and he asked me where I was going for my holidays. I told him that I never went on holiday in the summer, because I loathe the crowds. He told me that he himself was leaving the next day on a cruise round the islands.'

I felt like getting up and banging my head on the wall. I had been searching the hotels and the rooms-to-let and they had arrived on the island by yacht. If the yacht had been his, then things were easy because we could trace it through the shipping register. But if it was chartered, then I prayed he had chartered it in his own name and not in that of the blonde.

'Do you know what work he did?'

'Something with football, I rather think.'

'Apart from refereeing. That much we know.'

'I can't be sure, but I don't think he had any other work.'

'Why do you say that?'

She looked at me and she clearly felt perplexed. As with all ladies of the old school, she had no wish to be indiscreet, but eventually she made up her mind. 'Because a man who leaves his home at twelve or one in the afternoon doesn't work, Inspector. Unless he works an evening shift in a factory or is a waiter, and Mr Petroulias didn't look like either one of those.'

I was tormented by the question of where he had found the money for a flat like that and for cruises on yachts. I was impatient to see his tax return, in the hope that it would provide me with the answer. I had done with my questions. I wrote down her particulars – her name was Marianthi Kritikos – and I left her in peace.

Normally, I would have taken the stairs down to the ground floor, but because I had promised Ouzounidis not to tire myself, I waited for the lift. I rang the bell of the flat that was exactly below Petroulias'. The door was opened by a dark-skinned girl with an

Afro, all dolled up. Gone are the days of the old dressing gowns and housewife's aprons. Now they all wake up decked out in all their finery. But I may have been doing her a disservice. She may have got dolled up in the hope that the TV cameras would come to get an interview from her about Petroulias.

'Yes,' she said sharply, in case I was selling Tupperware door to door.

'Inspector Haritos –'

'If it's about the man upstairs, I said everything to you people yesterday. Don't make me go over it all again.'

'Just a couple of questions. It won't take long.'

'There's no need for you to ask me any questions. I'll show you so you'll understand.'

She ushered me into the flat. 'Look,' she said, pointing to the ceiling in the corner of the living room. It had swollen and was ready to come down. 'There was a leak in his flat and the idiot's ruined our ceiling. We told the caretaker, another dozy bastard, but he told us that he couldn't force the door of the flat or he'd be in trouble. We waited for Petroulias to come back to tell him to sort it out and now we've found out that he's gone and got himself killed. So how are we going to get compensation from his heirs?'

Here we had a man who was murdered, buried, then unburied by the earthquake, and all she cared about was her ceiling. 'Did you know him?' I said.

'We saw him, but we never said so much as a "Good morning" to him. Because when he was here, he used to deafen us with his music and when he wasn't here, he flooded our house. Not the kind of neighbour you want.'

'Why was it only now you learned that he'd been killed? Didn't you recognise him on TV?'

'Why would I have recognised him? Every night they show you ten different bodies on the box till in the end it's all a blur. Why would I pick out the man upstairs? It's not as if he were anyone special.'

I saw that I was not going to get anything more out of her and I turned to leave. She stopped me in the doorway. 'Tell me, you're a policeman and you should know. If I sue for the damage, will his heirs have to pay up?'

'I'm a police officer not a lawyer,' I said. Obviously she didn't like my answer, as she slammed the door behind me.

CHAPTER 20

I do not know who tipped them off that I was better and coming back to work, but the whole herd of ruminants was in the corridor waiting for me, Sotiropoulos at their head, their permanent reserve officer. 'Hope you're recovered,' they all called out, in chorus. Then I began to distinguish the solo parts: 'Take care of yourself', 'We missed you', 'Don't overdo it', 'Cut down on the smoking'. I replied with a general 'Thank you, all of you', as though I were greeting the crowds. I refrained from the usual 'I'm very touched', because I wasn't.

'Come in, but only for a moment. I mustn't tire myself, you said it yourselves.' In fact, only one of them had said it, but what did it matter, who would argue?

I walked into my office and stood for a moment looking around, taking in the familiar environment. The mob pushed past me and began setting up their microphones and their cameras. Like street vendors playing hide-and-seek with the municipal police. I was already regretting having invited them to come in. I should have remained alone for a while, rejoicing in my kingdom, but it was too late now and all I could do was to give them their dose and send them on their way.

'As to the hitherto unidentified corpse, you know everything already. Don't make me say it all again. The murdered man lived in a penthouse at 19 Panga Street. Someone broke in and turned the place over. We don't know yet whether the break-in occurred prior to the murder or after.'

'Do you exclude the possibility of robbery?' It was the first time I

123

had set eyes on the one who asked. His plastered-down hair shone as though he had polished it.

'No, we don't exclude it, but we regard it as unlikely. Nothing appears to have been stolen. Those who broke in were looking for something else, but, no, we don't know what that was.'

'Have you found out how he got to the island?' Sotiropoulos said.

'By yacht, we think. We're investigating.'

'Do you think his murder has to do with his being a referee?' asked the knock-kneed woman in the mauve mini. 'Perhaps he was involved in fixing football matches?'

'That, too, is under investigation. That's all, ladies and gentlemen. I have nothing else to tell you.'

To their credit, they went off quietly. Sotiropoulos waited till they had all gone, in keeping with his usual practice. He liked to show that he had a personal relationship with me, one not shared by the others. He believed that he reinforced his role of leader in that way.

'From what the sports correspondents have told me, your Petroulias was an out-and-out rogue,' he said. 'He was forever on the take.'

'Maybe. If it's true, we'll get to the bottom of it, you can be sure.'

'What's happening about Koustas?'

'No progress.'

'Don't expect any.'

'Why do you keep hitting me with that, Sotiropoulos? Just what is it that you know about Koustas?' I came out with it abruptly in case I caught him off guard.

'Rumours, hearsay, nothing concrete. Perhaps what I could tell you is claptrap, and I may also land myself in it.'

He made for the door. 'I'm glad you didn't have anything seriously wrong with you. What would I do without you?' he said as he left. You would give my successor an equally hard time, I thought.

I closed the door and breathed a sigh of relief. I had never felt so much joy, not even when I set foot in that office for the first time when I had just been promoted. I was dying to light up a fag, but I had given my word to Ouzounidis and I gritted my teeth. Adriani had also wanted me to cut out coffee, because, she said, it increased my heart rate, but I told her that the only thing that affected my heart rate was her constant nagging. The problem with marriage is that you start off fine and finish up badly in exactly the same way: from the rapid heart rate of the first date with the woman of your dreams, you progress to the rapid heart rate of living permanently with the woman of your nightmares.

I reached into my jacket pockets and began lining up medicines on my desk: digoxin 0.25mg, Monosordil 20mg, Salospir-A 500mg, Inderal 40mg. Adriani had insisted that I have two sets, one at home and one at the office. I agreed, because now they were part of my life, like my suits, ties and shoes. And you always have at least two of those. Last of all, I took out the paper on which he had written what I had to take of each and when. I tried to learn by heart what it said so that I would not have to take it out and read it each time like an incompetent pupil cheating in his exams.

I phoned Koula to find out whether Ghikas was in. She told me that he was in a meeting and would be free in fifteen minutes. With Katerina watching me like a hawk, I had to make use of every second. I called in Vlassopoulos and Dermitzakis.

'What happened with Petroulias' tax declaration?' I asked Vlassopoulos.

'I found out the tax office where he was registered. We'll have a copy today.'

I turned to Dermitzakis. 'Search every shipping register in the region of Attica and all the agencies that charter yachts. I want you to find out what vessel it was that took Petroulias to the island. Whether it was his or chartered.'

'If we're lucky and it was his, we're bound to turn up something to help us,' he said.

Perhaps, but I was not so sure. If it had been his, it would have been left moored in the island's harbour and somebody would have notified the authorities. Unless it was brought back by the blonde, which wasn't impossible. I called the police chief on the island and told him to ask at the harbour whether any craft had been left there since the summer, but I was not optimistic.

The lift was playing games with me, but I was determined not to give in. I waited patiently until it came.

'Glad to see you've recovered,' Koula said, happy to see me again. 'When did you get back?'

'This morning.'

'And when did you get out of the hospital?'

'Yesterday.'

She looked at me as though she had seen an Albanian in morning dress. 'What? You got out yesterday and you came back to work today? Why don't you spend a few days at home? You're a state employee, remember?'

'What does that have to do with it, Koula?'

'It has a lot to do with it. Who's ever heard of a state employee not taking all of his sick leave?' she replied indignantly.

I muttered something about having urgent matters to deal with and hurried into Ghikas' office. He was on his feet collecting some papers from the conference table. Not even he expected me back so soon and he seemed astonished to see me.

'Back so soon?' he said.

'Yes. And thank you for the plant.'

'I'm sorry I couldn't come to visit you, but, as you know, I'm up to my ears here.'

'I do know. I came because there have been some developments concerning the identification of the body.' I hastened to justify myself before he referred me to the disciplinary board for violation of the code relating to state employees.

I briefed him on Petroulias' flat, our investigations concerning the yacht that took him to the island and concerning our attempts to pin down the source of his income.

'Do you rule out the possibility that he was killed because he was fixing matches?'

'No, but I don't think it likely. They would have got rid of him in Athens before he went on his cruise, or they would have waited for him to come back. They wouldn't have gone to the expense and risk of killing him on the island and they would have had no reason for breaking into his flat or burning his fingertips.'

'The unsophisticated answers are often the correct ones,' he said smiling. 'You don't know what those hooligans are capable of when they get excited. They might have had it in for Petroulias, run into him on the island and decided to deal with him there. Without it being planned. They simply did away with him.'

'What about the two foreigners who were seen talking with him on the island?'

'A coincidence. They talked at a café and then went their separate ways, and the murder was committed afterwards, by others.'

'And the blonde?'

'How do you know that it was the same one who was regularly at his flat? He was young, the physical type. He may have met her by chance on the island, spent a couple of nights with her and then gone on his way. Why should the girl care what happened to Petroulias?'

His theory was unsophisticated, neat and might even be correct. But it was too neat for me. Maybe because I had spent too long with Adriani. Damn it, how come all the coincidences had come together in this case? But because there was always the possibility of his being proved right and of me losing face, I left myself a way out.

'Very likely you're right,' I said. 'We'll keep on it and see what we come up with.'

He stopped me before I got to the door. 'What did you do about Koustas?'

'I filed his case "unsolved".'

'A score draw, in football terms,' he said, smiling.

'What does that mean?'

'That in the case of Koustas you did what I told you. And in the case of Petroulias you'll do as you please.'

If I had had a little more evidence concerning Koustas, I would have answered him in kind. Vlassopoulos saw me going into my office and galloped after me with a photocopy.

'Petroulias' tax return.' He stopped me before I had even looked at it. 'Let me save you the trouble. All he declared were his fees for refereeing and the rent from a two-bedroomed flat he owned in Maroussi. The flat in Panga Street was his. He did not own a yacht or any other vessel or he would have declared it. He owned an Audi

80. He declared so little that he was taxed according to his presumed income.'

A glance at the declaration confirmed what Vlassopoulos had told me. Petroulias' annual income was no more than four million drachmas, including the rent from the Maroussi flat. 'And on that income how did he manage to buy a massive penthouse in Panga Street, a flat in Maroussi and go cruising on a yacht?'

Vlassopoulos flung up his arms. 'What can I tell you? I've no idea.'

Ghikas had got it wrong. The case was not so neat and clear-cut as he chose to believe. He was right about one thing, though. When you do not have anything else to hold on to, it is best to start with the obvious.

'Call the Association of Referees and tell them to expect us tomorrow morning to have a look at Petroulias' file.'

'All right.'

On the opposite balcony the girl and the hulk were arguing. From their gestures I was afraid that they were about to come to blows. The hulk tried to grab her by the arm, but the girl managed to push him away. The man must have said something nasty to her because I saw her raising her arm and slapping him across the face with such force that, if my window had not been closed, the sound would undoubtedly have carried into my office. Then she turned and ran off.

The phone rang and interrupted the spectacle. It was from downstairs. They told me that my daughter was there waiting for me. I looked at my watch, it was one o'clock. Exactly on time. She was not going to give me one minute over my limit.

As I got up from my desk, I saw the girl coming out of the apartment block. She had thrown a coat over her shoulders, was carrying a bag and was walking off at a rapid clip. The hulk was leaning over the balcony railings and shouting to her, but she did not look back. She turned the corner and disappeared. I saw the hulk leaning against the wall of the building, covering his face with his hands. His body shook from the sobbing. It used to be that men had short hair and women long hair, and it was the women who got slapped and burst into tears. Now women have short hair, men long hair and it's the men who get slapped and burst into tears. All very symmetrical, but you cannot feel sorry for a man who grows his hair like Samson and still finds himself on the receiving end.

CHAPTER 21

I would never have imagined that six days in hospital would have so changed my daily routine. When I got home that afternoon, I felt as though I had been carrying bricks round a building site all day. I ate my lunch and went straight to lie down. I woke up at eight, watched a little TV, ate my supper and then slept straight through until seven the next morning.

I was with Katerina in the Mirafiori and we were turning from Ambelokipi into Alexandras Avenue. 'There's no need for you to stay in Athens,' I said to her, half-heartedly. 'I'm fine now. You can go back to Thessaloniki.'

'Are you in a hurry to get rid of me?' she said, smiling.

'No, but I don't want you to get behind with the work for your doctorate because of me.'

'I'm not behind with it at all. Besides, I needed to come to Athens to chase down some of the bibliography. I thought I'd do it at Christmas, but as I'm down here for you, I've already started. As soon as I leave you in the morning, I go to the library in the Law School or to the National Library, then work until I come to pick you up.'

Her excuse filled me with a sense of relief. 'And how much longer do you intend to be here?' I said. That's how it is when someone offers you a finger, you want to eat their whole hand.

'It depends on how long it takes me to get the bibliography together,' she replied vaguely. 'I'll be here to collect you at one.'

'How about two?' She wagged her finger negatively and drove off so as not to allow me any room for bargaining.

I went to the canteen first to get my frothy Greek and not-Greek coffee. I had cut out the croissant because Adriani insisted that I eat a wholesome breakfast 'and not that plastic stuff from the canteen', as she called it. She got up before me and fed me two slices of toast and butter with marmalade that she herself had made while I was in the hospital. She had not made any stuffed tomatoes for me yet, because they were heavy, she said. But how long would she get away with it? I'd start huffing and puffing, playing the poor unfortunate, and in the end she would make them for me to raise my morale, and for fear I would take a turn for the worse.

Dermitzakis was waiting outside my office. He ran to meet me, as if I were getting out of a train.

'We've got a lead on Petroulias' yacht,' he said, beaming. 'He chartered it from a firm in Piraeus. I asked the manager to stop here on her way to her office. Her name's Stratopoulou. She's waiting for you.'

'Show her in,' I told him.

Before I had had time to take a sip of my coffee, he came back with a short, fat woman. She was wearing a light blue two-piece, a blue shirt and six-inch high-heeled shoes that brought her height up to four feet nine.

'Klairi Stratopoulou, Inspector,' she said, holding out her hand. 'Manager of San Marin, yacht chartering.'

'Was it from you that Christos Petroulias chartered a yacht?'

'Yacht, no. It was a sailboat with an auxiliary engine, Inspector,' she said condescendingly.

'Whatever, a sailboat, then. Did he charter it from you?'

'Yes. When the lieutenant phoned me yesterday, I looked at the contract. We chartered it to him from 10 June to 10 July.'

'When did you learn that the vessel had been abandoned?'

'A woman called us. She said that Petroulias had been taken to hospital and that there was no one to bring the boat back to Piraeus.'

'When exactly did she call you?'

She took a Filofax from her bag and consulted it. 'On 21 June.'

At least we now knew by when Petroulias had been killed. The blonde had phoned the charter company on the 21st. She was in on

130

it, as I had guessed. They had carried out their contract on Petroulias and then she had called the company.

'What did you do when she told you that they couldn't bring the boat back?'

'We sent one of our skippers to bring it back for us.'

'Is that all? Didn't you ask for any compensation?'

I asked her in the hope that I might learn something more, but Stratopoulou burst out laughing.

'Why would we ask for compensation, Inspector? We had chartered the boat till 10 July, we got it back on 22 June and chartered it again. We had the extra revenue for eighteen days that had already been paid for. The vessel was in extremely good conditions, my records said. Even if it hadn't been, we wouldn't have chased anyone.'

'Why?'

'Because the fee includes an amount to cover reasonable damage to the boat. We rarely have cases where the damage is any greater.'

'How did Petroulias pay you?' Dermitzakis asked her.

'In cash. The whole sum in advance.'

'Do you know how many people were on the boat?' I asked her.

'No. It's not our concern. All we have to be sure of is that the person chartering the sailboat has a master's licence. Otherwise, we require that they take a skipper along.'

'And did Petroulias have a licence?'

'Most certainly. We checked it before signing the charter contract. I have it with me, if you would like to see it.'

I saw nothing unusual. It gave Petroulias' name, his address, the fee, one and a half million, the duration of the charter.

'Did you find any personal items on the boat when you took possession of it? Clothes, identity cards, documents?'

'Nothing at all.'

'I'd like to take a look at the boat.'

'It's on charter now and it's practically impossible to locate it. I'll be happy to notify you when it's returned.'

It wasn't important. From the moment it had been chartered to others, it was of no use to me. Stratopoulou made a show of looking at her watch.

'Thank you for taking the trouble to come, Mrs Stratopoulou,' I said.

She got up immediately. 'If you need anything else, the lieutenant has my phone number.' She said goodbye and was gone.

'Find out at which banks Petroulias had accounts and get a warrant issued so that we can get into them,' I told Dermitzakis. I couldn't use the same ploy here as I had with Koustas' accounts. I wanted to examine them as far back as they had them, and right to the end.

'God knows what we'll come up with.'

'What do you want me to do? File him along with the unsolved crimes?' I snapped at him, as though he were to blame for Koustas being filed with the unsolved crimes.

He immediately back-pedalled. 'No, no.'

The door opened and Vlassopoulos came in. He too had a big smile on his face. Everyone, it seemed, was hurrying to bring me good news.

'We've located his car,' he said. 'I've notified Forensics to have it picked up. It seems he went to Piraeus by taxi to get the boat. We can probably find the driver who took him.'

'Leave it, it's a waste of time. We have a description of the blonde. We won't find out any more. Any news from Forensics on the flat?'

'A lot of fingerprints. Most of them from the same person, most likely his. All the others are unidentified.'

The blonde's, the cleaner's, friends', there was no way of knowing. 'And the footprints?'

'Most likely men's. One was size nine, the other size ten.'

'Did you speak with the Referees Association?'

'Yes. A Mr Hatzidimitriou is expecting us.'

'Fine. You two go and see what you can get out of him. And bring me the file on Petroulias.' OK, I may not have taken sick leave, but I was not going to do all the legwork.

They had both reached the door when I had an idea. 'Tell me, is Sotiropoulos outside?'

'I caught sight of him somewhere,' Vlassopoulos said.

'Tell him I want to see him. But discreetly, without the others getting wind of it.'

While he was looking for Sotiropoulos, I drank the rest of my Greek and not-Greek coffee and reflected on what we had so far on Petroulias. He had a penthouse worth around sixty million, a two-bedroomed flat worth around thirty at a conservative estimate, he drove an Audi 80, declared an annual income of four million and spent a big chunk of it on a cruise round the islands. Whoever leads a life like that has signed his own death warrant, because sooner or later he is going to get his comeuppance, and we get the mess to unravel, the mugs working for our measly salaries. The only advantage we have over Petroulias is our sick leave and, dimwit that I am, I had not made use of it. Koula was right.

The blonde was my other problem. If I could find her, at least. But something told me that first I would find the murderer, or murderers, and then I would get to the blonde.

'How come you asked to see me alone?' Sotiropoulos said. 'Can't you manage by yourself? Perhaps you want to take me on as a consultant?'

'No, but I do want your help. Could you introduce me to one of your sports correspondents to clear up a few things?'

'Yes, but –'

'But?'

'What's in it for me?'

'If anything sensational comes of it, you'll be the first to know, given that you'll be present.'

'Right, why didn't I think of that?' he said. 'Monday at ten, we'll be in your office.'

I had an idea that I would learn more from the channel's sports correspondent than I would from the Association of Referees.

CHAPTER 22

I spent one and a half days, the whole of Saturday and half of Sunday, poring over Petroulias' file. I had everything before me, referee's licence, curriculum vitae, match reports, evaluations by the official observers, but I could not find any lead. Perhaps because actually there was nothing reprehensible, perhaps because I haven't a clue when it comes to football, I don't know. I do not have an office at home, so whenever, very occasionally, I have to study documents from the department, I spread myself out on the kitchen table – in my pyjamas to be more comfortable. Adriani kept coming and going, claiming she had jobs in the kitchen, and nagging all day long: that the doctor's good work was going to waste and that I was doing as I pleased again, that I was tiring myself even more now that I was taking work home and that the only arrest it would lead to would be of the cardiac variety. In the end, I threatened to take my papers and go to the office to get some peace, whereupon she piped down.

Hatzidimitriou from the Athens Association of Referees had told Vlassopoulos and Dermitzakis that Petroulias had been an unreliable referee. He would turn in excellent performances in some matches and be on track for promotion, then he would make a cock-up. This was why he had been stuck in the Third Division for ten years. He had immediately and vigorously denied the possibility of Petroulias having been on the take; there had never been any accusation against him apart from the usual accusations systematically levelled at all referees.

On the Monday morning, I came out with my second bombshell: I put my foot down and insisted on driving the Mirafiori again. Besides, Ouzounidis had only said not to for a few days and I had kept my word. Adriani started nagging but I shut her up by saying that Katerina was staying even though she had work at the university and it was not right that she should abandon it to act as my chauffeur. To tell the truth, I felt a flutter or two when I sat at the steering wheel. I took half an Inderal to put my mind at rest.

Fortunately, everything went like clockwork and I found myself sitting opposite the sports correspondent Nassioulis. He was young, casually dressed, and seemed to be quite serious. He had the file in front of him and was leafing through it. Sotiropoulos was sitting in the other chair, watching.

'You're not going to find what you're looking for here, Inspector,' he said. 'You're right to have your suspicions. We have them too – after almost every game – but we can't prove anything. Without a well-founded accusation, there is nothing you can do.'

'If you had to single out the games where Petroulias could have been bought off, which ones would you choose?'

'There's rarely a case for any buying off unless the points are vital.'

'Which games this last season refereed by Petroulias were vital ones?'

He took a newspaper cutting out of his coat pocket and began comparing the reports from Petroulias' file with the cutting. 'At first glance, the game between Falirikos and Triton.' I was surprised that this was the one he should pick out first. 'That defeat cost Triton the championship. The game between Argostolikos and Anamorphosis Tripolis. From what I recall, Petroulias sent off two Anamorphosis players so that Argostolikos won and avoided relegation. The official observer reported that one of the sendings-off was unjustified. And the game between Atromitos Sfakion and Halkidaïkos. Atromitos Sfakion were second in the league behind Triton; Halkidaïkos were in the relegation zone and managed to defeat them on their home ground. Of course, everything is possible in football, but personally I found it surprising. Petroulias awarded a penalty against Atromitos in the last minute, just as happened with Triton. The official observer evaluated his refereeing here as poor, but that doesn't mean a lot.' He looked at me apologetically, as though afraid that his information would not satisfy me and I would stop him. 'I could go on, if you gave me time to examine the records,' he added.

'Are you out of your mind, Inspector?' interrupted Sotiropoulos, who, against all expectations, had until then succeeded in keeping his mouth shut. 'What are you after, exactly, Inspector? Club officials who grease palms and club officials who murder referees – and where? In the lousy Third Division? The money involved is a mere pittance. Do you understand what we're talking about? About the dregs of the football league.'

I knew he was right, but it annoyed me to hear it from Sotiropoulos. 'I'm certainly not saying that it was club officials who had him killed. He may have been killed by fanatical supporters. Possibly they ran into him on the island and did him in.' I said this not only because I had no other theory, but also because I wanted to check out Ghikas' hypothesis.

'Football maniacs are usually fans of one of the major teams,' Sotiropoulos said. 'That's where they give vent to their fanaticism – on Panathinaïkos, or AEK, or Olympiakos. In the lower divisions they support their local team out of a sense of pride, but they couldn't really care less.'

I turned to look at Nassioulis. 'That's the truth of it,' he said.

'And where did Petroulias get the money from to live the high life? The only income he declared was some rent and his refereeing fees.'

Sotiropoulos laughed at me. 'Wake up. From moneylending, of course. Do you know what the rates of interest are on the street? More than a hundred per cent. Let's say a hundred. If he had five million, he'd turned it into ten in a year, twenty in two years. All untaxed. There, that's where the money came from for the high life.'

I had had the same idea at the beginning, but about Koustas. What if it was not Koustas who had been involved in a money-lending racket, but Petroulias? 'Even so, he must have got the interest on his money from his own circle. And his circle was the teams in Division Three. So that's where we have to start looking.'

'Do you know what zone defence is, Inspector?' Nassioulis said.

'No.'

'It's lining up the defence in a zone formation, making it difficult for the forwards of the opposing team to get close to the goal. The club officials in the Third Division stick together. You'll find yourself facing a zone defence and it's going to be very hard for you to break through.'

Up against it again, it seemed. 'Things aren't going well for you, Inspector,' said Sotiropoulos, preparing to leave.

'Why's that?'

'Because you got nowhere with the Koustas case. And I'm afraid you're barking up the wrong tree with Petroulias. It's your illness. It has turned your world upside down.'

I felt my tongue starting to twitch, about to give him a lashing, to tell him that I came from a hospital bed straight back to work, without taking any sick leave, so that he could appear on the evening news and reap the rewards of someone else's sweat. But I restrained myself because he had helped me by enlisting Nassioulis' wisdom.

'Thanks for your help,' I said to Nassioulis. 'If I need anything else, I'll call you if I may.'

I watched them going out and reflected that I was wrong to be offended. There was something about Petroulias' murder that didn't seem right to me either, just as with Koustas' murder. My logic and such evidence as I had told me that he had been killed for fixing matches. Yet Sotiropoulos was right, the theory was full of holes. But I had no other tree to bark up, nor could I file another case with the unsolved crimes.

The door opened and in walked Dermitzakis with some computer printouts. 'Petroulias' bank statements,' he said.

Petroulias had had two accounts, one with Interbank and the other with Chiosbank. The fact that he had chosen two new and relatively small banks was enough to encourage me. Those who have shady dealings most often go to small banks, because these tend to turn a blind eye to gain custom. I tried to hold my impatience in check and examine them carefully. The Chiosbank account contained only small deposits to the amount of a hundred or a hundred and fifty thousand drachmas and correspondingly small and regular withdrawals. The usual transactions for your average man. It was as though I were looking at my own statement. On the other hand, the Interbank account showed very few deposits, once or twice a month, but large ones: from two and a half to five million. And there were very few withdrawals too. I looked at the balance: 35,522,867 drachmas. If he was engaged in moneylending, the withdrawals would have been larger and more regular. If he was on the take, the deposits would have been occasional and not so regular. So something else was going on and Sotiropoulos and I were one apiece. It seemed we were both right.

'The money in the Interbank account is no doubt money under the table,' said Dermitzakis in order to show me that he, too, had noticed it.

I paid no attention to him. I checked the dates of the three games that Nassioulis had singled out and put them next to the statement, to see whether, after all, there might be significant amounts that matched the dates of those games. I could find no deposit that corresponded with the games between Argostolikos and Anamorphosis Tripolis or between Halkidaïkos and Atromitos Sfakion. There was a deposit of two and a half million, however, prior to the game between Falirikos and Triton. It may have been a coincidence, but often coincidences which turn out not to be coincidences help to provide a clue. If the penalty that Petroulias had wrongly awarded to Falirikos were not simply bad refereeing, as Hatzidimitriou had claimed, then the boss of Falirikos had bought him off with two and a half million.

'Find out for me who the owner of Falirikos is,' I said to Dermitzakis. 'And where we can talk to him. Today.'

He came back in five minutes. 'I've tracked him down,' he said, exultant. He was about to shut the door, but Vlassopoulos stopped it and came in behind him.

'His name is Frixos Kaloyirou and he's the owner of Homelectronics, a chain of household goods stores.'

I had seen adverts for it countless times. It was one of those stores that enable you to furnish your home from top to bottom without paying anything and then they force you to sell the house to pay the instalments.

'Falirikos are playing this afternoon in Nikaia,' Dermitzakis continued. 'We can see him after the match.'

'Normally I'm the one who should go with the Inspector,' Vlassopoulos broke in. It was then that I understood why he had sneaked into my office.

'Why you?' asked Dermitzakis.

'Firstly, because I have seniority in the department and, secondly, because I'm the one who discovered Sarafoglou who plays for Falirikos and I know him personally.'

'You may have discovered Sarafoglou, but I'm the one who tracked down Kaloyirou.'

From the very first morning that Dermitzakis had joined the department, they had been at it like cat and dog. Vlassopoulos because he does in fact have seniority and considers that that gives him certain privileges, and Dermitzakis, because he's newer and wants to push Vlassopoulos aside so as to get up the ladder. And the two of them side together to get on my nerves because I am forever having to maintain a balance.

'No one is coming with me. I'm going alone,' I said angrily. 'I've a couple of questions for him, that's all. I don't need a whole squad with me for that.'

Dermitzakis turned and shot a venomous look at Vlassopoulos, who smiled smugly. He was not coming with me, but he had managed it so that Dermitzakis would not go either. He took that for a victory, one more unjustifiable penalty.

I took out a digoxin tablet, but it across the middle and swallowed one half with a gulp of my Greek and not-Greek coffee, which had lost its froth and was like dishwater.

CHAPTER 23

The only football ground I had ever seen in my life was Panathinaikos' in Alexandras Avenue. And that only from the outside. Tavros' stadium was very different. It was much smaller and much more repulsive. Perhaps because Alexandras Avenue to some extent absorbs the great size of the Panathinaikos stadium, whereas the Tavros stadium stuck out like a boil on your forehead. Whatever the case, as I looked at the second example of these multiple-function venues, for sports events, concerts, political rallies, even transit camps during the junta, it only confirmed my first impression that they resemble bathtubs for collective bathing supported on concrete pillars.

The stadium was emptying as I got there. There were not many spectators and they were dispersing quietly. At first sight, Nassioulis and Sotiropoulos appeared to have been right. There was no fanaticism or passion, but that may have been due to the fact that the local side had won, because I saw the majority of the supporters coming out full of good cheer.

I looked for the entrance to the changing rooms and found a puddle the size of a lake that you could only cross by boat. It was rectangular and lit by two twenty-five-watt bulbs behind wire meshing, barely enough to pierce the darkness. To the right was a door; to the left, two doors. From under the second door on the left came the water that was filling up the lake. The other door on the left was shut. The door on the right was open and angry voices could be heard from inside. I tried to cross the lake using my legs as stilts: with my soles in the water and my toes on end.

'You're useless!' I heard a thunderous voice from inside the room. 'We've lost every game since the start of the season. One more defeat and you go back to your village to pick olives.'

I could not see the owner of the voice, but I understood who was on the receiving end: a tall, thin fellow in a tracksuit, his head down and his arms open like wings.

'The team will come together, Mr Kaloyirou,' he said apologetically. 'We've got a lot of new players and the team hasn't gelled yet. A couple more matches and it'll all come together.'

'You asked me for new players and I got them for you. Now you're telling me that I have to wait for the team to gel, as if it were a jelly, for Christ's sake.'

The changing rooms had only two benches, joined together, and hooks on the walls for the players to hang their clothes. It looked like those temporary infernos in which they lock up refugees before sending them back to their permanent hells. The players were sitting on the benches and looking at the concrete floor.

'You're all useless, the lot of you,' Kaloyirou thundered. 'A load of sissies prancing round the field, can't kick a ball to save your lives.'

I saw Sarafoglou, who was sitting on one end of the bench, suddenly turn round. His face had darkened. 'Why are you grumbling because we're not playing well, Mr Kaloyirou?' he said to the invisible owner. 'We started training in August, we've played three matches and you still haven't paid us a penny. We have families, bills. Do you ever wonder how we get on to the field to play?'

'The fact that I keep you in the team is more than you deserve. If you don't like it, you can leave now. The back streets are full of players of your kind.'

At last I understood why Sotiropoulos had called them the dregs of the football league. They humiliate them, have them playing for peanuts and then don't even pay them that. I caught sight of two youths emerging from the stream that was filling the lake. They walked past paying me no attention.

'No water again, sodding luck!' said one.

'They're turned it off because of the leak.'

'We leave here smelling like skunks every time,' said the other.

I went through the doorway just as Kaloyirou was saying sarcastically: 'It's not as if you worked up a sweat to need a shower. Why don't you go and –'

He saw me and stopped. He was a hefty sort, like a wrestler who has given it up and turned into a tub of lard. He must have been around my age and was wearing a dark suit and open-necked shirt.

'What do you want?' he said, brusquely.

'Inspector Haritos. I'm looking for Mr Kaloyirou.' I played the innocent to make it seem that I had only just arrived.

'That's me.'

'I want to ask you a few questions concerning Christos Petroulias.' Sarafoglou turned and looked at me anxiously, but I gave no sign of noticing.

His expression softened and he did not appear to be surprised. 'If you wouldn't mind waiting outside a moment, Inspector. I won't be long.'

I went outside by the shores of the lake and someone slammed the door behind me. I could no longer hear what was being said inside, either because they had closed the door or because they were talking in low voices as a precaution. But he did not keep me waiting long. In less than a minute, he was beside me.

'Come with me. There's a café further down. We can talk there.'

He took me to an old, neighbourhood café with marble tables and wicker chairs. He insisted on getting me something and I ordered a Greek coffee. It was not from a machine or a stove, but was brewed on one of the cookers sold by Kaloyirou at Homelectronics.

He waited for me to take a first sip before saying, 'So what can I do for you?'

'We made a routine check of Petroulias' bank accounts and we found some deposits that can't be accounted for in the context of his regular income,' I said, beginning cautiously so as not to scare him and cause him to dry up. 'We are trying to trace the source of these deposits. By coincidence, one of the deposits was made a day before the game between Falirikos and Triton last May. As you knew Petroulias, perhaps you might know where that money could have come from?'

He shot me a glance and then came out with a resounding laugh that matched his booming voice. 'That's not what you're asking me, Inspector. You're asking me something else.'

'What am I asking you?'

'You're asking me whether I bribed Petroulias in the game between Falirikos and Triton that we won thanks to a last-minute penalty.'

'Which, in the opinion of the official observer, wasn't a penalty,' I added, given that he had broached the topic.

'I could answer you with a straight no, because there's no way you can prove that I bribed him, but I'm not going to. I'm going to take up a little of your time in order to explain to you the reasons why I couldn't possibly have bribed him.'

'Are there a lot of reasons?'

'Just two, but they're more than enough. The first is that almost all the owners of Third Division teams aren't interested in winning the championship or winning promotion to the next division. All they are concerned about is that their teams wallow somewhere in the middle of the table, lose money and continually need financial support.'

'Why?'

He looked at me as if he were looking at some half-witted employee. 'Listen. You no doubt know that I am the owner of Homelectronics. If you want, I can give you my company's books so you can see that it makes very substantial profits. I bought Falirikos in order to have another business alongside it that loses money in order to avoid taxation. What I pay out for the team, I save two and three times over from the reduction in taxes.'

'If that's the case, then why were you shouting at your players for losing the match?'

Again he burst into rollicking laughter. He probably liked hearing it. 'A show, Inspector. I know perfectly well that they can't win. That's why I chose them. The secret is to have a coach who is mediocre to incompetent, who doesn't have the guts to win the championship. As for the players, they don't need to be paid regularly because they nurture the hope that one day some big team will notice them and they'll be playing in the First Division. A few manage it.'

'And the rest?'

'The rest stop playing at thirty-five and go out into the world penniless and unemployed. I shout at them to show them that I mind, but also to undermine their demand for regular wages, for higher bonuses and the like. Do you understand now why it's not in my interest to bribe referees?'

'And what's the second reason?' I asked.

'What second reason?'

'You said that there were two reasons why you wouldn't bribe a referee.'

'Oh yes. The second reason is that, even if I did bribe referees, I'd never do it in a match with Koustas' team.

The name fell like a bolt out of the blue. I gazed at him speechless for a few seconds, then I thought that, no, it could not possibly be, it must be someone else with the same name and I wanted to be sure. 'Koustas?' I said.

'Konstantinos Koustas, I'm sure you know of him. He's the one who was murdered outside his nightclub.'

'Koustas was the owner of Triton?'

'Only Triton officially. Rumour has it that he also owned another two or three teams that were run by his people. The fact is that he was top dog in the Third Division. He could give the championship to one team, have another one relegated, decide whether you'd win or lose a match . . .'

So Koustas was there before me again, I thought. I did not know whether I should be pleased or go into mourning. 'And the rest of you, did you accept all that?' I asked Kaloyirou.

He shrugged. 'I told you. The players kick the ball. We play a different game and kick a different ball. Koustas didn't interfere with us in our games and we left him in peace to play his.'

Nassioulis has foreseen correctly. They all stuck together and I was up against a zone defence.

He shook his head regretfully as though he had read my thoughts. 'What do you expect from a world where all the clocks show the same time, Inspector? In the past, some stopped, others were fast, others slow. You woke up in the morning and waited for the beep from the radio in order to wind your watch. Now you wake up and all the clocks show the same time. We live in a world that's made for the Japanese.'

'What kind of games did Koustas play?'

'I don't know. There are some things it's better not to know.'

'Do you think it possible that Koustas paid Petroulias to award the penalty so that his team would lose the match and the championship?'

'It's not out of the question,' he said. 'Though, now that you ask me, I do recall something.'

'What's that?'

'Obikoue told me that after the match he'd heard Koustas and Petroulias arguing at the entrance.'

'Who's Obikoue?'

144

'A Nigerian. He's our centre forward. He's not playing at the moment because he tore a ligament and had to have an operation.'

'Do you know where he lives?'

'No, but I can find out.'

He took out his mobile phone and spoke to someone, perhaps to his useless coach. After a moment or two, he gave me the address: 22 Rodopis Street in Tabouria.

'Do you know which other teams Koustas had under his thumb?'

'No, I told you. My interest in football is personal and limited.'

He stood up. I did not try to stop him as there was nothing more I needed to ask him. Besides, I was eager to be alone, to ponder on where this new piece of information would lead me. He shook my hand, came out with a booming 'Pleased to have met you', and left.

CHAPTER 24

My first reaction was to go and see Obikoue immediately, but I decided against it. I sat at the wheel but did not have the courage to drive alone as far as Tabouria and then back to Athens. So I set off and returned to headquarters.

The traffic in Piraeos Street was slack, just as it always was on Monday and Wednesday afternoons when the shops closed early. I let the Mirafiori cruise along and racked my brains trying to remember if I had read anywhere that Koustas had been the owner of Triton. Usually, when I read a report, I can remember every word of it because I have a photographic memory, but it seemed that the camera flash had been damaged by my health problems. Anyway, it was not so important. I had something else on my mind: the question of whether the murder of a referee and the murder of the owner of a Third Division club was a coincidence or whether there was some connection between them. It may well have been Koustas who had given Petroulias the two and a half million in his Interbank account so that he would award the penalty that stopped Triton getting promoted to Division Two. Petroulias would hardly have awarded an unjustified penalty off his own bat. Not even Kaloyirou would stand up to Koustas, so Petroulias certainly wouldn't. Were the two murders unrelated or had someone else, whose interests – nothing to do with football – had been threatened, had them both killed?

Vlassopoulos saw me going into my office and came to tell me: 'Your wife has phoned twice.'

'If she calls again, tell her I'm still not back.' I wasn't in the mood for listening to her ranting, unwell as I was and up to my ears in work. 'And bring me Koustas' file.'

He wasn't expecting that. 'Are we opening up the case again?'

'I don't know yet.' And I told him what I had learned from Kaloyirou.

'Are you saying that the two murders are connected?'

'I told you, I don't know. Let's take a look at Koustas' file first.'

In less than a minute, I had the file before me, while Vlassopoulos sat opposite me watching me anxiously. I went through it carefully, read the report twice, but there was no mention of Triton.

'Nothing,' I said to Vlassopoulos.

I phoned Anti-Terrorist and asked to speak to Inspector Stellas. The officer who answered told me that he had left.

'Who else knows something about the Koustas case, the fellow who was murdered in Athinon Avenue, outside the Bouzouki Strings?'

'I'm familiar with the case. I was there.'

'Tell me, Lieutenant, do you recall whether it was ever mentioned that Koustas was the owner of Triton Football Club?'

'No, but we didn't proceed very far with the investigations, Inspector. Once we had assured ourselves that it wasn't a terrorist-related act, we left it to you.'

They ate the marrow and we were left with the bone. 'You can go,' I said to Vlassopoulos, who was still sitting and watching me. 'We can't do any more today.'

As things had turned out, I had no choice but to reopen the Koustas file and I did not know how Ghikas would take it. He had his mind at rest because he thought I had buried the case. One solution was for me to take a risk and go ahead regardless. If I didn't get anywhere with it, I could bury it again and no harm done. If I did get somewhere, then I would present him with a fait accompli. But what would happen if someone blew the whistle on me? There would be hell to pay because I hadn't kept him informed. The best course of action, I decided, would be to make things clear from the start.

I called his extension and, to my surprise, he answered himself. 'I have to see you because there have been some developments,' I said.

'Come on up.'

Koula's office was empty, with everything arranged neatly on her desk. The door of Ghikas' office was open. I went straight in. He had called me up to listen to what I had to say, but he was the Chief and his own problems came first.

'From the day she got engaged,' he said, stabbing his finger at Koula's desk, 'she's started tidying up at four o'clock and leaving. One day she disappears to go and see her fiancé, the next she disappears to take care of the wedding arrangements, before long she'll be in the family way and on pregnancy leave. That's what happens when you have women working for you.'

We are not off to a good start, I thought to myself. He's annoyed with Koula, but I was the one who was going to bear the brunt of it, and he was not going to like what I had to tell him.

I gave him the gist of my talk with Kaloyirou. 'I followed to the letter the line we had agreed upon,' I said to soften him up. 'Namely, that Petroulias had been killed because he was being bribed. Then, out of the blue, the name of Koustas cropped up.'

'Do you think that the murders are connected?'

'What can I tell you? I don't know.'

'At any rate, the killings themselves have nothing in common.'

'No, but they don't need to have anything in common to be connected.'

'I'm perfectly aware of that.' His tone was severe. For the moment he was biting the bullet, but if necessary he would bite my head off.

'We can't very well send another case to be filed unsolved just because of Koustas.'

My shot hit him where it hurt and he shut up. He fixed his eyes on his desk and sank into thought. That was a good sign. He had forbidden me to 'handle the goods', as we used to say, but now he recognised himself that we could not avoid it. He was trying to find the most painless way.

Slowly he raised his head. 'Listen,' he said. 'Officially, we are not reopening the Koustas case. We are simply investigating the Petroulias murder and may, in the course of our investigations, come across evidence relating to it. Do you understand?'

'I understand.'

'If that happens, and I pray that it doesn't, we are not investigating the Koustas case, but rather Koustas himself to the extent that he is linked with Petroulias.'

'I understand.'

'Consequently, the Koustas case will remain unsolved. And you won't make a move on it without first informing me. Do you understand?'

'I understand.'

He was priming me, just as a lawyer would his witness, or a mother her son when she wants to make him an accomplice to the lie she is going to tell her husband.

'The directive to halt the investigation concerning Koustas comes from very high up,' he said, more relaxed now.

'How high up?'

'Don't ask. You don't need to know everything. I'm just telling you so you don't go around doing whatever you feel like, as usual, and find yourself in a sticky situation.'

He opened a drawer, took out a document and began studying it to show me that the discussion was over. I had got the picture about Koustas, but I had never been able to work out what those documents were that he read all day. I had an idea that he read pulp fiction – the sort that Adriani read – but that he brought it in typed up like a document so as not to give himself away.

Before leaving for home, I made one last call – to the Koustas home in Glyfada.

'Hello,' came the sound of a stifled voice.

'I'd like to speak to Mrs Koustas.'

'She no longer lives here.'

The 'hello' had fooled me and I mistook it for the security man. After the second response, I realised I was talking to Makis.

'Is that you Makis?' I said in a friendly voice. 'Inspector Haritos here.'

'Oh, the detective. I sent my stepmother packing. She's moved out.'

She couldn't bear to see you getting stoned all day, I thought. 'Where does she live now?'

'Somewhere in Kifissia.'

'Do you have an address or a telephone number?'

'Let me look. She left me a number somewhere because she thinks I'm going to call her to see how she is, but she's got that wrong.'

He hunted for a while and then read me the number.

'Tell me, Makis, did you know that your father owned a football club? Triton?'

'Why do you ask? Are you after a transfer?'

He laughed at his own joke and hung up on me before I had time to get a straight answer.

CHAPTER 25

When I drove out of the garage of Security Headquarters, it was already dark. I thought of the abuse I was going to get from Adriani and I started to plan my strategy. Should I adopt the line of the defendant who shows remorse and asks the court's mercy, or should I play the tough cop who is always right and, when pushed, is not averse to lashing out himself? The first line of action would mean that I would have to grin and bear it till Adriani had cooled off or shut up. The second would mean that we would go at it hammer and tongs because Adriani was a long-time policeman's wife and knew that when you start yelling at your policeman husband and you have right on your side, eventually he backs down.

I was about to turn left into Dimitsanas Street when I saw someone on the pavement waving to me. I did not recognise him in the gloom at first, but when he approached the car, I saw that it was Panos, Katerina's boyfriend.

'When did you get into town?' Katerina had not mentioned anything to me.

'A few days ago.'

'Does Katerina know that you're in Athens?'

'No.'

I was quite surprised. 'You didn't call her?'

He looked me in the eye. Something was eating him and he wanted to tell me, but he did not quite have the courage. 'Can we go somewhere to talk?' he said, uneasily.

My first thought was that he was in trouble with the police. That was why he had not called Katerina but had preferred to come straight to me so that I could help him out. I opened the passenger door. He got in, but at the same time turned his head to look out of the window, as if wanting to avoid any conversation till we were somewhere quiet where we could talk in peace. I turned left into Dimitsanas Street and then left again into Alpheiou Street. I came out into Panormou Street and pulled up outside the Morocco.

The café was all but deserted at that time. There was just one couple sitting in a corner. They were rubbing noses and generally getting to know each other. Panos no longer avoided my gaze, but still said nothing. His silence made me even more worried. Was what he had to tell me so difficult? I wondered. So grave that he didn't know where to begin?

'Why didn't you call Katerina?' I said, to help him along.

His reply came after about half a minute and it was the last thing I expected to hear. 'Katerina and I are breaking up.'

If I had heard it from Katerina, I might have been pleased, but now the news was a terrific shock and I did not know whether to be pleased or sorry.

'When did this happen?' I asked him.

'A week ago.'

'Hang on a bit, Panos. Katerina was in Athens and you were in Thessaloniki. How did you break up?'

'She called and told me she was leaving me.'

'She came out with it like that, on the phone?'

He searched my face as though trying to read it. 'You mean you don't know anything?' he asked.

'What should I know?'

'Katerina has got together with your doctor.'

'She has *what*? With Ouzounidis?'

'I don't know his name, but she's with him now.'

He's lost his mind, I thought. There I was, all wired up in the hospital, with tablets and serums, being taken around in a wheelchair from laboratory to laboratory for tests and outside my room my daughter was making sweet talk with the doctor. A charming boy, I don't deny it, but I know Katerina too well. She would never do anything like that.

'Are you sure?' I asked, hoping he would give me some room for doubt.

'Unless she's lying,' he replied with a bitter smile. 'She told me that she was madly in love with her father's doctor and that she could no longer go on being with me.'

That was the final blow.

'And why didn't you ask to see her before now? Have you called her?'

'I phone her every day, but her mother answers and says she's not there.'

'Every morning she's working in the library, it's true. She's collecting the bibliography for her thesis.' I was fuming inside, but I tried to find some way to excuse her.

'I phone her at different times – morning, noon, afternoon, evening . . . It's always her mother who answers and the answer is always the same: "she's not in, Panos."'

So, with the brilliance of a retard, I realised that Adriani was in on it too. They had been plotting while I was on my bed of pain and they had kept me in the dark. Until now, I had always been convinced that Katerina was closer to me. She loved her mother, yes, I won't deny it, but she always opened up to me more, whatever problem she had she always talked to me about it. Now, I had been woken up to the fact that she had appointed her mother as special adviser and I had been forced to take early retirement. So *that* was why she had stayed on in Athens, I thought, and I felt a lump in my throat. Not to collect the bibliography, not even for me, given that I was no longer ill after all, but to be with her own private heart surgeon.

I saw Panos leaning towards me and gluing his face to mine. I thought that if we weren't careful, we too would soon be rubbing noses and people would get the wrong idea.

'I love your daughter, Mr Haritos,' he whispered. 'We've been together for four years. I love her and I don't want to lose her.'

And he burst into tears. A full-blown tower of a boy with cropped hair like a commando and a T-shirt that said 'Hellraiser', crying like a baby. I had never been fond of the academic-cum-greengrocer, but my daughter's behaviour was an insult to my manhood too and I felt a sense of solidarity with him, albeit against my will.

'What can I say, Panos?' I said, quite at a loss myself. 'What do you want me to say to you?'

'Nothing,' he replied. 'At least you sat down and listened to me.'

He got up and left without saying goodbye to me, but I did not take it the wrong way, given the state he was in. I remained there, alone, looking at the parfait ice-cream, which I hate, in front of me. The image popped into my mind of the hulk on the balcony who had started blubbering a few days ago when his girl had slapped him. I had made a mistake then. It was not only the men who grow their hair long who cry. Those who cut it short cry too; and cry like women into the bargain. The clothes are unisex, the clocks all show the same time, and the slaps are now handed out both ways. How are you to distinguish the ewes from the rams any more?

CHAPTER 26

'Good evening.'

She was sitting rigid in the armchair facing the TV, leaning forward, her elbows resting on her knees and her legs and ankles tight together. Her stance reminded me of Miss Chryssanthi, our religious instruction teacher at high school, who made us learn the Creed by heart and whenever we made a mistake would rap us over the knuckles with the edge of her ruler. Except that Miss Chryssanthi always had the missal in her hands, whereas Adriani had the remote control. And Miss Chryssanthi would come out every so often with 'blasphemer', or 'luminary', whereas Adriani appeared to be determined to stick with the 'voice echoing in the wilderness'.

'Sotiris told me you'd phoned, but I was up to my ears and I didn't have the time to call you back.'

I said it deliberately, provocatively, so she would get annoyed and react, but there was no reaction, nor did her stance shift one iota. I have to admit that her tactics were effective because they baffled me. I had expected her to start yelling and to counter her I had prepared a full-scale zone defence, which began with excuses, continued with cajolery and ended, as a last resort, with an out-and-out slanging match. But her silence blew my whole Maginot Line to bits. I sat in the armchair facing her.

'When are you going to make some stuffed tomatoes? You haven't made me any for ages and I'd really like some,' I said.

Her usual reply was, 'The only thing you'll get is gall and vinegar,' which, by the way, would have been entirely in keeping with Miss Chryssanthi. But there was no reply. She was determined to go on playing the deaf mute.

I was in a dilemma. If I were to leave, it would have been tantamount to accepting defeat. Whereas, if I remained where I was, it would force her to keep her eyes glued on the screen until she got a crick in the neck. I settled on the second solution and sat back to watch the sports report, which suddenly acquired interest because Nassioulis appeared and began to talk about Petroulias. He regurgitated our conversation of that morning, concluding that the police were investigating the possibility that Petroulias had been murdered because he had been fixing matches, but that he did not himself think that this was likely. Albeit unknowingly, he was putting me in a tight spot because just two hours earlier I had told Ghikas that I was following to the letter the line that we had agreed, and if he were watching the programme, it would make me look like a liar.

'Since when have you been interested in the sports report?'

It was Katerina's voice. I turned and looked at her. She was all dolled up, wearing make-up and ready to go out.

'Are you going out?' I asked her.

'Yes, to the cinema.'

'Regards to my doctor.'

I said it just like that, without taking my eyes off the screen, as though it were the most natural thing in the world. Out of the corner of my eye, I saw Katerina freeze. I could not wait for the moment when I would give her a mouthful, but I allowed myself a slight postponement so as to savour the sight of Adriani. Having been blatantly ignoring me all this time, she suddenly turned round and fixed her eyes on me. Anxiety, surprise, fear were all reflected in her gaze.

'I saw Panos today,' I said to Katerina, still perfectly calm.

Adriani wanted to say something, but could not find the words and looked in desperation at her daughter, who was the first to recover.

'Where did you see him?' she asked coldly.

'He was waiting for me outside headquarters. That's why I was late getting back.'

As I said this, I turned to Adriani. It was the icing on the cake. There are three things that remain with people right up to the grave: the need to pee, the need to shit and the desire for revenge.

'Didn't I tell you?' said the daughter to the mother. 'He's a fatso and a sissy. He went crying to my father.'

'What did you expect the poor boy to do? You hide behind your mother and won't talk to him.'

'We've broken up. It's over. What else is there to say?' she said curtly.

'You didn't break up. You dumped him. And by phone. Such things are not said over the phone, Katerina.'

'I told him over the phone so we wouldn't have tears and a scene.'

'He cried like a baby.'

'Never mind. He'll find some other girl and he'll get over it. Women are attracted to hulks.' As if she herself had been involved all those years with Mahatma Gandhi.

'It's not right,' I insisted. 'You don't dump a person just because you suddenly fall in love with someone else and that someone puts pressure on you to end it.'

I said this last bit because I was a moron, like every parent, and I was trying to convince myself that my daughter was an innocent who had been dragged down the sinful path by another. Her reply was brusque and final. 'Leave Fanis out of this, he's not to blame. Panos and I would have broken up anyway. We've been together for four years. The first two years were great, but then I became his mother. I had to support him in his studies, hold his hand when he did his assignments and I got tired of it! Fanis simply accelerated the inevitable. And when all's said and done,' she added in a tone which brooked no objection, 'my personal life is my own affair. No one makes decisions for me, whether it's Fanis, Panos or anyone else.'

The 'anyone else' was aimed at me.

'Anyhow, you've never liked Panos. What's suddenly got into you to make you stick up for him?' Adriani had recovered and wanted to have her say in the matter.

'Don't you see? That's just what he wanted,' Katerina said to her. 'To upset him and get him on his side.'

She came up to me from behind, put her arms round me and kissed me on the top of the head, where you usually kiss babies. 'Shall I tell you something?' she said, bending further over and looking me in the eye, 'I'm glad things have turned out this way. I've been racking my brains for so many days wondering how to tell you.'

She gave me another kiss, on my cheek this time. I turned and watched her disappearing through the door. Adriani didn't return to her Miss Chryssanthi stance, but gave me a timid smile. Now that Katerina had gone, she was trembling from top to toe in case I took it out on her. I would have done, with pleasure, but I tried to control my temper. It was our daughter we were talking about and we had to discuss the matter seriously, without any outbursts.

'Aren't you ashamed?' I said. 'All this going on behind my back and you said nothing to me.'

'She wouldn't let me. She wanted to tell you herself.'

'And while she was finding a way to tell me, you gave her your support so she could dump poor old Panos and open her arms to Ouzounidis.'

'I don't know why you're grumbling. Panos is a nice lad, I'm not denying it, but what future does an agriculturist have? At best, he's going to open a nursery or get appointed to the Ministry of Agriculture to supervise the growing of vines or broccoli. Whereas Fanis is a doctor –'

'Are you out of your mind?' I said. 'They've known each other for ten days and you're thinking of *marriage*?'

'I'm not thinking of it, but if, if it goes that far, what I'm saying is that Fanis is a senior doctor, he must be on 350,000 a month. And that's without the backhanders!'

'What backhanders?' My hairs were bristling. 'Does he take backhanders?'

'I don't know, but I imagine so. Today, all doctors take backhanders. Do you expect that he's going to say no and become a red flag to his colleagues?'

Quite right. Not a moron like me, who doesn't even take sick leave and compromises himself. Suddenly a suspicion flashed through my mind and I leapt to my feet.

'Don't tell me you gave him a backhander too,' I said furiously.

'I would have, but it wasn't necessary,' she replied calmly. 'He kept running to your room in order to see Katerina.'

'Anyway, I'm not going back to Ouzounidis,' I said flatly. 'I'll find another doctor.'

'Are you crazy? Other people beg to have their own doctor and you're going to leave him as soon as you have him?'

So that's what it had come to. I had acquired pull in the hospital thanks to Katerina. It seems that Adriani read my thoughts because she got up and came over to me. She put her hand on my shoulder.

'Costas,' she said endearingly, 'our daughter is a big girl now and she can sort out her life for herself. We can help her in her choices, but we can't make up her mind for her.'

She was thinking exactly what I was thinking. The only difference was that she had already digested it, whereas I was still trying to swallow it. On the other hand, I couldn't deny that she was right. Yes, Ouzounidis must have been on around 350,000 a month. And with the backhanders, as Adriani had said, it would have been closer to half a million. When Katerina started work, they would be earning at least 800,000 between them and they would be able to help me out with my pension. Nevertheless, I was not overjoyed about it all. Perhaps because my old-fashioned principles had been offended, perhaps because Panos used to get on my nerves and so provided me with an excuse to grumble, whereas that opportunity was lost with Ouzounidis because deep down I liked him.

'Tomorrow, I'll make you stuffed tomatoes,' Adriani said.

That was a sign that things between us were all right again. The stuffed tomatoes had become a sort of code between us. After twenty-five years of marriage, our rows sometimes lasted days, during which we would not exchange as much as a hello. And every time Adriani wants to take the first step and make up, she doesn't say she's sorry or even end her silence, but she makes a dish of stuffed tomatoes and leaves them on the kitchen table. That's the signal that the ice has melted.

Now that the affair between Katerina and Ouzounidis had been made official and the relationship between Adriani and Haritos was back to normal, I was able to get back to an idea that had been burrowing away at me since the first day I had started to investigate Koustas' murder. I was certain that Koustas had had something in his car on the night of the murder and that we had not found it. And I was almost certain that that something was money and that he must have withdrawn it from one of his accounts. I went over to the phone and called Manos Kartalis, a second cousin of mine, who was a director at the Ministry of Finance.

'Manos, I need your help,' I said to him after the usual small talk. 'Can you recommend me a smart tax inspector?'

'What do you want him for? Have they got you for tax evasion and you're looking to pull some strings?' he asked, laughing.

I almost told him that if he wanted to pull any medical strings, he should come to me, but I held my tongue. 'No. I need him to help me with a case. I have to check the books of a football club and I'm thoroughly in the dark when it comes to things like that.'

A short silence followed. 'If it's a police investigation, you'll have to go by the book,' he said uneasily. 'Through the chartered accountants body.'

'That's what I want to avoid. I want to do it on the quiet and I need someone trustworthy to help me. I'll take him with me, but I won't let on that he's a tax official. I'll make out that he's my assistant.'

'Let me think about it so I can find the right man. I'll call you tomorrow at work.'

I hung up and went into the kitchen to have some chicken broth, in expectation of the stuffed tomatoes.

CHAPTER 27

Mrs Koustas' new house was on the second floor of an apartment block in Skopelou Street, between Kifissias Avenue and Harilaou Trikoupi Street, in the suburb of Kifissia. When I rang the bell, I expected to see a Filipino maid, but it was Mrs Koustas herself who opened the door. She was wearing jeans, a sweater and slippers, and she wore no make-up. The spacious hall was still stacked with boxes from the removal. A telephone stand and a low-backed armchair had already found their places. The rest of the furniture was scattered around, waiting its turn. Mrs Koustas ushered me into a light living room, and I found myself confronted with Niki, Koustas' daughter from his first marriage, who was pushing an armchair into one of the corners. She took a couple of steps back and checked to see whether it was positioned correctly. The rest of the living room was even untidier than the hall. The boxes were everywhere: in the middle of the room, on the sofa, on the table and chairs, while the furniture was blocking the passage in between and you had to squeeze past. My hip caught on the edge of the table and I stumbled. The noise made Niki Koustas turn round.

'Be careful,' Elena said. 'I'm sorry about the mess, but I only moved in the day before yesterday.'

'I'm fortunate to find you here,' I said to Niki. 'You save me the trouble of making another trip.'

'I asked for leave from work to help Elena move in.'

The white, aristocratic cat roamed around the living room sniffing the corners, the boxes, the furniture, leaving nothing unexamined. When it saw me, it abandoned its serious work, took up position in front of me and began miaowing furiously.

'Calm down, Mitsi. Leave the Inspector in peace, he's not going to eat you,' said Elena, at the same time lifting a box from a chair to allow me to sit down. 'That's how she is with all strangers. She's selfish and spoilt,' she said apologetically, as though she were talking about a daughter.

'Why did you decide to move so suddenly, Mrs Koustas?' My question sounded somewhat ill-mannered, but it had to be asked.

'I decided to leave the house in Glyfada to Makis,' she said simply. 'It's his by right, given that he was born and raised there. After Konstantinos' death, I felt like a stranger there.'

Makis had been telling the truth on the phone. He had made her life unbearable until she had collected her things and left.

'And besides, Glyfada is a long way from the Canard Doré,' she added, as if she had read my thoughts and wanted to justify herself. 'From the moment I decided to take an interest in the restaurant, well, it was a long journey for me every evening. Whereas here, I'm on the doorstep.'

Niki Koustas had left off her work and was following the conversation. She had that same innocent smile, but in her eyes

I could see an admiration for her stepmother and I was not mistaken because I saw her coming over, hugging her spontaneously and kissing her. The truth is that I would happily have kissed her myself, not so much because she appealed to me as a woman, but above all because I really admired the way she dealt with her problems – discreetly, swallowing her sorrow. I thought that even if Makis had knocked her around, she would still have left with her head high, without saying anything that might have exposed him.

'Did you know that Konstantinos Koustas was the owner of Triton Football Club?'

'Of course,' they both answered spontaneously.

'And why didn't you tell me?'

'Because we assumed that you knew, Inspector,' Elena Koustas replied. 'If you recall, your colleagues had investigated the case before you took over. We imagined that they must have found that out. In any case, it wasn't a secret.'

Correct, it wasn't a secret and they had no reason to hide it from me. Quite simply, the Anti-Terrorist Squad had lost all interest once they were satisfied that it was not a terrorist act and they had investigated no further.

'Do you know whether your husband owned any other football club, apart from Triton?'

'No. The list of his assets given to us by his solicitor refers only to Triton. He didn't own any other football club just as he didn't own any other establishments apart from the Night Flower, the Bouzouki Strings and the Canard Doré.'

'Would you perhaps know why he wanted Triton? Why he bought it?'

Mrs Koustas shrugged. 'I told you, Inspector, Konstantinos never talked about his work. If it hadn't been for Makis, we would never have known that he'd bought it.'

'Makis?'

'Yes. He came home one day and asked his father to get him in the team. That's how we found out.'

'And how did Makis know about the team?'

'I've no idea.' She paused, then added, 'Anyway, it wasn't an irrational request on Makis' part. Makis always adored football as a little boy. He played in his school team. When his father ruled it out, Makis began pestering him to let him take charge of the Night Flower and the Bouzouki Strings.'

'That was the problem between Makis and my father, Inspector,' Niki said, cutting in. 'Makis always had small dreams, small ambitions. My father, on the contrary, had big dreams and big ambitions. All the problems between them stemmed from that distance between their dreams.'

Until, in the end, he made a junkie out of him and was left in peace, I thought. I gradually began to piece a theory together in my mind. If Petroulias had been one of Koustas' men and if Makis had known this, it wasn't out of the question that Makis had killed him in order to get revenge on his father. I would have to ascertain Makis' whereabouts between 15 and 22 June. But I did not want to ask Mrs Koustas or his sister, because they might warn him. Not to mention that he would not have had to go to the island himself. A junkie, even one from a rich family, is obliged to circulate among the lowlifes in order to get his fix. He would know everyone and everything. Albanians, Romanians and Bulgarians, as Ghikas would say. They would have bumped off Petroulias for a weekend on an island, all expenses paid.

I did not know where my theory would lead me, but it was the only one that opened up any way forward on the Petroulias murder. As for Koustas' murder, I was more or less certain that it had been carried out by professionals and that we were not going to get anywhere with it.

I got up to leave. 'Thank you, Mrs Koustas. I'm sorry if I called at an inconvenient time.' I had erased from my memory the plunging neckline and the curtain revealing Elena Fragakis' legs and I was a paragon of courtesy, because I had to take my hat off to Elena Koustas.

'Give my regards to your wife,' she said with a smile. 'You're lucky to have such a wife, Inspector.'

I knew, though I would never admit it. Niki Koustas had gone back to arranging the living room. She waved without turning to look at me.

CHAPTER 28

From Security Headquarters to Tabouria was a school day trip. There was no breeze at all and it was unbearably heavy. In the car beside me, Dermitzakis stank of sweat; outside, Athens stank of exhaust fumes. As we were passing the Social Security building in Piraeos Street, I began to feel a quickening of my heartbeat. I don't know why it took hold of me like that, even though that morning I had woken up calm and refreshed. Perhaps the heaviness or the exhaust fumes were to blame, perhaps both. I was coming up with my own diagnosis, like Adriani, I thought; I was engaging in the very thing I had sneered at. I was annoyed at myself for not having taken the Inderal with me. Ouzounidis had told me to take half a tablet whenever I felt my heartbeat racing. I sat quietly, trying to count it, to see whether it was over a hundred. I was embarrassed to be feeling my pulse and looking at my watch. The first drops of rain found us at the corner of Ermou Street, and as we got to Elaïdos Street, the heavens opened and a downpour began. I remembered getting soaked in Vouliagmenis Avenue and I felt alarmed. I wondered what I would do if we broke down now with my heart racing at top speed. I saw myself in the ambulance being rushed to hospital again. A little further on, I could see the sign of a chemist's through the rain.

'Do me a favour, Yorgos. Nip into the chemist's and get me a packet of Inderal.' I wondered how he would see me, as a frail old man or a demanding superior, but I was in no condition to stand on ceremony.

He saw me as an ailing traveller and he looked worried. 'Your heart, Inspector?'

'No, but I'm due to take one and I've forgotten to bring them with me,' I said to reassure him. 'There's a kiosk over there. Get me a bottle of water, too.'

He took the money and got out. I watched him bounding into the chemist's and then over to the kiosk and I felt an inexplicable envy, as I was never one to run anywhere.

'I'm sorry for putting you to the trouble, Yorgos,' I said, when he came back.

'Don't mention it, Inspector.'

Instead of half a tablet, I swallowed a whole one, to be on the safe side. Ouzounidis had told me that the medicine took forty-five minutes to an hour to take effect. I gritted my teeth and waited. Dermitzakis was soaking from the rain; I was soaking from sweat. Fortunately, the downpour did not last long; it had stopped inside ten minutes and in less than half an hour we had arrived in Piraeus. From the Kondyli coast road, we went up Aghiou Dimitriou Street and came out roughly in the middle of Rodopis Street. From there, we turned left towards Keratsini.

The apartment block where Obikoue lived was a flimsy, four-storey construction, which would no doubt go down with all hands at the first tremor, without leaving so much as a doorway for Adriani to shelter beneath. There were twelve doorbells, nine of which had Greek names on them, the other three being blank. We were about to play heads and tails to decide which of the blank ones to ring when a young man appeared in the entrance. We asked him where the Nigerian lived and he pointed to the basement.

'There's only one door. You'll see it when you go down,' he said.

The black woman who opened the door to us was so big that she seemed to take up the whole doorway. She was wearing a fancy, plaited dress and had a coloured scarf round her head.

'Yes?' she said in English.

'Police. Is Obikoue here?'

It seemed the word 'police' was the only Greek word she knew, because her eyes grew larger and the white in them brighter, like the white of a Cycladic island. To my amazement, she fell at my feet, wrapped her arms around my legs and began crying out. In English at first, 'No, no!' and then in some African tongue.

I tried to break free of her grip, but she was holding on to me so tightly that it was impossible for me to free my legs. 'Let me go, I've not come to arrest you,' I shouted, but she didn't understand Greek.

Four little black kids, two girls and two boys, appeared from inside the flat. The girls were clothed in what had been left over from their mother's dress, the boys were in denim shorts and red shirts. Fearfully, they watched their mother banging her head against my knees. They rushed over to her and began wailing in chorus, while from within came the sound of a man's voice shouting in the same African tongue in which the woman was keening.

There are two things I hate in life. Racism and blacks. 'Get them off me, get them off!' I shouted to Dermitzakis. I was trembling, lest the excitement sent my heart rate up again despite the whole Inderal that I had taken.

Dermitzakis managed first to pull the four whelps off me and then, after some effort, the fat mother. The whelps huddled together in a corner and, terrified, looked at their mother.

I went up to the woman, who was being held by Dermitzakis, and I touched her gently on the shoulder. Then I said 'Obikoue' and pointed to my lips with my left forefinger to make her understand that I wanted to talk to him. Her wailing had softened into a steady lamentation, and the tears rolled down her cheeks. With a nod of her head, she indicated inside the flat.

We went inside and found ourselves in a small living room, four by four metres, which recalled a stall at a church fête. The floor was strewn with cheap, plastic toys, while the two canvas balcony chairs were covered with clothes and the table with an ironing cloth and electric iron. A pungent smell pierced our nostrils, garlic mixed with onion, as though they were making cod with garlic sauce and rabbit casserole at the same time.

The woman opened a second, adjoining door and we entered the bedroom. A black man of average height with a firm, strapping body was lying on the bed. His right leg was in plaster up to the knee. The kids had drawn little men, houses, trees and clouds on it with a felt-tip pen. Two mattresses were on the floor to the right and left of the bed for the children to sleep on.

'Are you Obikoue?' I asked him in Greek.

He nodded. He looked terrified like his wife, but he did not react by yelling and wailing. The woman said something to him quickly, in their tongue.

'Why did your wife go off like that?' Dermitzakis asked him.

'I knocked, no play,' he said. 'Afraid Mr Kalogeerou send police to throw us out. I get money, send Nigeria, live two families. No send money, families no food. No play, Mr Kalogeerou throw me out, no food.'

Why would he throw him out? Either way, he wasn't paying him.

'Don't worry, we're not from the Aliens' Bureau,' I said in Greek. What with my heart and the woman's outburst, I had forgotten the little English I knew. 'Do you remember the match last year against Triton?' He nodded again. 'When you were leaving the ground, you saw the referee quarrelling with Triton's boss. Why were they quarrelling?'

'Quarrelling?' He didn't understand the word.

'Fight,' said Dermitzakis. 'Boss Triton fight with referee.'

He shrank back and the fear returned to his eyes.

'Don't be afraid,' I said. 'Mr Kaloyirou sent us. He was the one who told us that you had seen them.'

This appeared to reassure him. He thought it over for a moment and decided to talk. 'I going, pass by, and I hear,' he said.

'What did you hear?'

'Boss Triton say referee "You pay for that".'

'I'll make you pay for that?'

'Yes.'

'And what did the referee say to him?'

'Laughed. Said "You do nothing to me. I show you red card, take you out of the game."'

'He said that he'd show him a red card and send him off?' Dermitzakis said.

'Yes.'

'And then?'

'Boss Triton grab referee, like this,' and he tugged at his pyjamas with both hands to show us how Koustas had grabbed hold of

Petroulias. 'Said "Ung . . . ung . . . "' He was trying to find the word but it wouldn't come to him.

'Ungrateful?'

'No. Say he pay for ungratefulness.'

'He'd pay for his ungratefulness?'

'Yes,' he cried, enthusiastically. 'And he go.'

The combination of garlic and onion had reached the bedroom and it made me want to sneeze. The atmosphere was stifling. 'All right, we're done,' I said to Obikoue and I nodded to Dermitzakis to leave.

The woman escorted us to the front door. From her relief, she was full of smiles. As we walked away, I heard her shouting behind us 'Bye-bye, bye-bye'.

The conclusion was simple. Koustas had greased Petroulias' palm to the tune of two and a half million to make sure of victory over Falirikos and the championship. Petroulias had pocketed the money and then sold out Triton and Koustas. That 'he'd pay for his ungratefulness' made it crystal clear. But why did Petroulias take the money first and then sell Koustas out? What else was behind their dealings that made Petroulias take on Koustas, who ruled the roost in the Third Division? And what did 'he'd pay for his ungratefulness' mean. That it was Koustas who arranged to kill Petroulias? That version justified Ghikas' view that the case smelled of bribery and that we should not overlook the obvious. But if Koustas had had Petroulias killed, then who had killed Koustas? And were the murders connected?

We were on our way back to Athens. All these unanswered questions made me dizzy and I felt sick.

CHAPTER 29

The tax inspector recommended by my cousin was one Stavros Kelesidis and he worked at the tax office in Ilissia. We arranged to meet in Vassilissis Sophias Avenue, in front of the Naval Hospital, to split the distance. He asked me how we would recognise each other and I told him I would be in an old Mirafiori. I was a little afraid that he would be so young that he might never have seen a Mirafiori in his life, because it was doubtful whether there were more than four or five of them in the whole of Athens. But as soon as I had passed the Ilissia bus stop, I saw him waving to me.

He was in his thirties, with a full face and hair that went in whatever direction it wanted. He was dressed as the wholesale merchants used to dress in the fruit and vegetable market: a sports coat and a shirt with the top button fastened but with no tie.

'I'm Kelesidis, Inspector. Sent by Mr Kartalis.'

'Yes, I know. Listen. We have to move discreetly. First of all, you won't say anything about being with the tax office.'

'Mr Kartalis explained to me.'

'I'll introduce you as my assistant. Second, what are we looking for? I want you to take a look at the club's books and tell me if there were any major deposits or withdrawals between 25 and 30 August. Naturally, I could have the club's bank account opened, but it would take time. That's why I need your help.'

He laughed with a good-natured, almost childlike laugh. 'A doddle, Inspector. Inside half an hour we'll be all done and dusted.'

The offices of Triton were down Mitropoleos Street, on the second floor of a three-storey block, just after the Athens Registry Office. Its entrance stank of urine. Dogs used to pee there, now Albanians peed there. The dogs had moved up socially and now peed on the balconies where the Athenians with their mania for pets have them fenced in. There was no lift so we took the stairs. On the first floor was a clothes manufacturer's, on the second a leather manufacturer's. At one end of the second floor, squashed into two rooms, were Triton's offices.

The manager was Stratos Selemoglou, a short, fat fellow who was sweating profusely. Every so often, he took a paper tissue out of his pocket and wiped the sweat from his brow. At a rough estimate, he must have got through five packets of tissues a day. Because I had told him that I wanted to see the club's books, he had brought along the accountant, a tall chap with a crooked nose and old-fashioned, thick-rimmed spectacles.

Kelesidis got down to work straight away. He opened the books, and knew just where to look. He quickly scanned the entries and if there was nothing of note, he moved on. I let him get on with his work and walked around the two rooms. One was for administration, with a desk and two cupboards. The cupboards contained the players' contracts, the salary statements, the contract for the ground where the team trained and the correspondence with the Football Federation. The other room was a kind of storeroom, with footballs, tracksuits and boots. I did not expect to find anything of interest; I was looking simply to stress the fact that I was a policeman. The accountant remained with Kelesidis, while Selemoglou followed at my heels. Perhaps he was afraid I would steal a ball.

'How did these amounts get into the accounts?' I heard Kelesidis ask.

'From the bank, through withdrawals,' the accountant said.

'Bring me the receipts.'

I twigged that something was wrong and went back to the admin room. The accountant found the receipts in a box file. Kelesidis took a quick look at them, then handed one of them to me without saying anything. I took it and read it. It was a withdrawal receipt for twenty million drachmas.

'The books show two entries: one for five million and one for fifteen million. Why didn't you make just one entry for the whole amount, given that there was only one withdrawal?' Kelesidis said.

The accountant turned and looked at Selemoglou. 'The five million was for the wage bill for the players, the coach and the staff. It was the first of the month and we had to pay the salaries.'

'And the other fifteen million?' I asked.

'Koustas kept it,' the accountant said. 'That's why I made two separate entries.'

The date on which Koustas had been murdered was 1 September. That morning, he had passed by the bank, withdrawn twenty million from Triton's account, handed over five for the wage bill and kept the other fifteen. And I had been looking for it in the accounts of his nightclubs.

'Did he often do that?' I asked Selemoglou. 'Withdraw money from the club's account for his own personal use?'

'Yes, but not such large amounts. A couple of million, three at most.'

'Why did he suddenly need so much money?'

'I didn't ask, Inspector. It was none of my business. He owned the club, he did what he liked.'

'Could he have taken it for the needs of the club?'

He burst out laughing. 'We're in the Third Division, Inspector. Small fry. We don't deal in sums like that.'

So he had taken it to give to someone. And he had had it in his car on the night of the murder. That was why he had left the Bouzouki Strings alone. He did not want his bodyguards to witness the transaction. You only give an amount like that, at night on the sly, to someone who is blackmailing you. And that someone was not, of course, Petroulias, who was already dead. Koustas had owned two nightclubs, a restaurant and a football club. All legal businesses. His family life had been all neat and tidy. His son, at least officially, had been discharged from a detox clinic. So what was hidden behind this façade that made him a target for blackmail? Suddenly, the idea that had passed through my mind that morning at Mrs Koustas' house began to gnaw away at me again. What if they had been blackmailing him because they had found out that his son had killed the referee? And he had agreed to pay up in order to save him? But in that case, would it not have been a surer thing if they had blackmailed Makis directly? After all, he was a junkie. He would have given in straight away. No, they knew that it was his father who had the big money. That's why they went to Koustas. But what happened that made them change their minds and kill him? His killer did not even think to take the money. He left it and ran. Couldn't he have first taken the money and then killed him? And in both cases, I faced the same problem. I started with a thought, followed it through, came up against an obstacle and abandoned it.

The school trip as far as Tabouria and the return trip to Security

Headquarters, followed by the drive to Mitropoleos Street had exhausted me and I was at the end of my tether. 'Let's go,' I said to Kelesidis. 'We're done here.'

He was still poring over the books. He lifted his head and looked at me. 'Can we stay five minutes more?'

'Have you found something else?'

'No, but I want to check something just out of curiosity. Look here,' he said, pointing to a series of entries in the books, all identical: 'Sponsor: twenty million. Every month, a sponsor put twenty million into the club's accounts.'

'What idiot puts 240 million a year into a Third Division club?' I said.

'They're not idiots. That's money stolen from the tax office. They spend 240 million and they earn double and treble because it puts them in a lower tax bracket and they pay less tax. Shall I tell you the best of all? It's completely legal because they put it down as advertising expenditure. Tell me,' he asked the accountant. 'Who's your sponsor?'

'I don't recall the name, but it's a foreign company.'

'Foreign, eh? Greece has become a haven for foreigners. Bring me one of those receipts.'

The accountant went and searched again in a file. He found a receipt and handed it to him. Kelesidis read it and burst out laughing. 'There,' he said to me. 'R.I. Hellas, a research and opinion-poll firm.'

'R.I. Hellas?' I murmured, just like Ghikas, when he learns my reports parrot-fashion so as to make a statement to the press.

'What business does a research and opinion-poll firm have sponsoring a team in the Third Division?'

I didn't answer because I had something else on my mind: how was it that Koustas' team was sponsored by a firm for which his daughter worked?

'How did you come to find that sponsor?' I asked Selemoglou.

'What can I tell you? Mr Koustas came in one day and told us that he had found a sponsor for the team and that they would give us twenty million a month. From that day, at the beginning of every month, they put twenty million in the bank and we entered it in the books.'

'How long has this been going on?'

'Three years now,' the accountant replied.

Kelesidis had put aside the books and was following the conversation with some interest. 'Kelesidis, you're a genius,' I told him and I felt like kissing him.

He looked at me questioningly. 'Why?'

'Because you've turned up something that I might never have turned up. Come on, let's go.'

As I left Triton's offices in Mitropoleos Street, I had in mind an answer and a question. The answer was that I now knew where the fifteen million that Koustas had had in his car on the night of the murder had gone. My question was what dealings Koustas had had with the firm where his daughter worked. It was beyond believe that R.I. Hellas would have handed over 240 million a year of its own free will to a football team in the Third Division.

CHAPTER 30

Lambros Madas was not wearing his coat with the gold buttons or his cap with braid. Perhaps because it was still ten in the morning and it was early for wearing the uniform of a club doorman. He had squeezed his enormous carcass into a T-shirt with an extraterrestrial design on the front and was wearing a leather jacket on top of this. He was sitting at one end of the table with me at the other end, from where I could get up his nose, and with Vlassopoulos on his left. And so ends the description of the furniture in the interrogation room: a table with three chairs, surrounded by bare walls.

Nervous, Madas was fidgeting on his chair. His gaze shot from me to Vlassopoulos, but was unable to come to rest anywhere, because we remained silent and he did not know which of us was going to begin. He tried to resolve his dilemma by lighting a cigarette. The cigarette remained stuck between his lips, while his hands became free again to fumble on the table. He saw that we were delaying and that helped him to regain his composure, to feel more confident.

'So, Lambros,' I said. 'You were an eyewitness to Koustas' murder. Tell us what happened.'

'I told everything to the Anti-Terrorist Squad and I told everything to you. Do I have to go through it all again?'

'Yes, because we still don't have an official statement from you and we need one.'

Vlassopoulos took out a notepad and pen.

Madas adopted a bored expression, as if to say that we were inconveniencing him for no good reason, but because we were OK, he would go along with us. 'All right, I'll tell you again. Koustas came out of the club at around two thirty. Alone. I said, "goodnight boss", but he told me that he wasn't leaving yet. He went over to his car, opened it and leaned inside. Then I saw someone coming up to him from behind. He said something and Koustas turned round. Then this other man fired four shots. Koustas collapsed and the gunman ran towards an accomplice waiting on a motorbike a little way off. He got on the back of the bike. The accomplice accelerated away and they disappeared. I ran to Koustas, saw that he was covered in blood and went into the club to dial Emergency.'

'When Koustas opened his car door, did you see him take anything from inside?'

'No.'

'Did he give anything to his killer before he was shot?'

'No. I told you, he shot him and ran off.'

'Did you see him take something from Koustas before he took to his heels?'

'No. He ran straight to the bike.'

'When you went over to Koustas, did he have anything in his hands? A bag or an envelope?'

'No, I didn't see him holding anything.'

'We seem to have a problem, Lambros,' I said to him calmly.

'What problem?'

'Koustas had fifteen million with him on the night of the murder.

You said he wasn't holding anything. And we didn't find anything in the car. So where did the money go?'

'I don't know, but if you didn't find it, then he didn't have it with him.'

'Oh, but he did have it with him, that's for sure. He'd withdrawn it from the bank that same morning. So where did the fifteen million go, Lambros?'

His tone became hostile. 'How should I know? I wasn't his accountant.'

'No, not his accountant, his collector. You found the packet with the fifteen million and pocketed it.'

Until now his cigarette had been hanging from his lips, the bouncer's trademark when chatting comfortably and friendlily. But now he opened his mouth to protest, and the cigarette fell to the floor. He didn't bend down to pick it up because he was in a hurry to protest.

'What are you trying to say?' he shouted. 'I saw the boss fall to the ground and I ran into the club to dial Emergency. When the Anti-Terrorist Squad arrived, I told them everything exactly as it had happened. I was called into the Haïdari police station and I recognised the stolen bike. They you came round and I told you everything too. And now you tell me I'm a thief?'

'People kill for a lot less,' said Vlassopoulos. 'And wouldn't you take fifteen million if it were handed to you on a plate?'

'And where would I hide that amount of money?'

'Inside that huge frock coat of yours that you wear every night.'

As he leapt to his feet, his T-shirt came out of his trousers. The extraterrestrial receded, giving way to his hairy belly. He sat down again, lit another cigarette and squeezed it between his fingers to stop himself from shaking.

'Listen,' he said, trying to appear at ease. 'Koustas didn't have any money in his hands. He didn't have anything. If there was some money in the car, I don't know anything about it. Maybe there was and your boys from the Anti-Terrorist Squad took it.'

'What's that, scumbag?' shouted Vlassopoulos. 'Are you saying that our colleagues took the money and that we're pinning it on you to get them off the hook, is that it?'

'Calm down, Sotiris.' I leaned over and took hold of Vlassopoulos by the arm. 'Don't force him. He's going to tell us in his own good time.'

The old police trick. Good cop, bad cop. Not to mention that I didn't share Vlassopoulos' indignation. Policemen are people just like everyone else. If one of them had found fifteen million just lying around, he might have been tempted to pocket it. But I knew that Madas had taken it and that we did not need to look any further.

'Listen, Lambros,' I said. 'Let's get this over with. The longer you deny it, the worse it'll be for you.'

'It's not going to get worse for me because I didn't take it and I can prove it,' he said, but without the same conviction.

'Let me explain why things are going to turn out bad for you. Koustas was carrying all that money with him on the night of the murder because he was intending to give it to someone who was blackmailing him. We are sure about that. We are also sure that it wasn't the blackmailer who murdered him. After he'd taken the money, what reason would he have to kill him? So, he must have been going to give it to someone else. And that someone else was you. He came out of the club alone precisely in order to give you the fifteen million. Now, either he gave it to you and was murdered afterwards, or he was murdered and, knowing as you did about the fifteen million, you pocketed it and then called the police.'

'Pure fabrication, Inspector. You're fishing in the dark.'

I made no reply, but got up and went over to the door. I stopped with my hand on the knob. 'Lock him up,' I said to Vlassopoulos. 'Some people don't want to be helped. Get a warrant and turn his place over. And get a court order so we can see his bank accounts. We're sure to come up with the fifteen million and then we'll throw everything at him – the robbery and the murder, and be done with it.'

'Hold on a bit.' He jumped up again. 'You can't do that to me. After all, I'm one of you.'

'One of us, scumbag?' Vlassopoulos sneered, grabbing him by the lapels. 'They kicked you out for selling protection to nightclubs. That's how you got the dirt on Koustas and started blackmailing him. You pocketed the fifteen million and got your friends to bump him off. And now you dare to make out that you're one of us. You're scum. You and your kind make me sick!'

Well done, Vlassopoulos, I thought to myself. If we present that version to the prosecutor, Madas will go down for life, we'll wallow in self-satisfaction and Koustas' murderer will rub his hands in glee. Evidently Madas had the same thought, because he cried out: 'I didn't kill him, Inspector. I swear it. OK, I found the fifteen million lying on the ground. I got greedy and I took it. But I wasn't blackmailing Koustas and I didn't kill him.'

'Where was the money? In the car, or did he have it in his hands?'

'He had it in two large plastic bags. At first, I didn't realise that it was money. I thought it was drugs and I got scared. When the murderer spoke to him, he turned to give him the bags, but the man shot him and ran off. He never even looked at the bags. Koustas fell and the money was on the ground beside him. When I saw that he was dead, I grabbed the bags and stuffed them inside my coat – just as you said – and went into the club to telephone. Then I hid the money behind the band curtain and took it when I left.'

'What did you do with the money?'

He lowered his head and began mumbling. 'I bought a car, Mazda 323. I'd had my eye on it for some time. I spent about a million on various other things . . . TV . . . hi-fi . . . air conditioning in the house . . . The remaining ten million is under my mattress . . .'

I felt like telling him to rip the air conditioning out and to take it with him to his cell to keep him cool, so the money wouldn't have gone to waste, but it turned my stomach and I didn't want even to make fun of him. He had grabbed the money and then squandered it. If the money had been taken by an Albanian, at least it would have been put to good use – he would have opened up a business back home.

'What are we going to do with him?' Vlassopoulos said.

'He's not the one who killed Koustas so he's of no concern of ours. Hand him over to Robberies,' I said.

As I went out, something that Madas had said bothered me. The gunman had spoken to Koustas and he had turned to give him the bags with the money. The fifteen million had been intended for the murderer, but instead of taking it, he had killed Koustas. Why? One thing was sure: the killer was not black-mailing Koustas. The money was from some shady business and the murder was a cold-blooded execution.

CHAPTER 31

I got to the fifth floor and took a breather. After so many days of getting nowhere in both cases, the fifteen million that Koustas had had with him on the night of the murder was a step forward and I was in a hurry to inform Ghikas and to serve him up with the thief. During the previous few days, he had been continually on the phone asking me for some lead, some new information, which he could, at least, announce to the press. What he was about to learn was more than enough for an announcement and would keep the channels busy for two or three days. The only one to lose out was Madas, who would lose not only the millions under his mattress, but would be forced to tell everything to the press for free, just as I had foreseen. Naturally, his arrest brought us no nearer to finding the perpetrators of either murder. On the contrary, it blew apart my theory about Makis, but I had up my sleeve the discovery that the firm where Niki Koustas worked was the sponsor of her father's team. With a little embellishment, it would provide us with another announcement.

I marched into Ghikas' outer office, but there I had the wind taken out of my sails. Koula's desk was covered with scattered papers, files, and the contents of the drawers: carbon paper, staplers, correcting fluid, tweezers, a bottle of nail varnish. Koula was sitting with her elbows on the desk and had her head in her hands. She heard me come in and got up. Her eyes were red and swollen from crying.

'What is it? What's wrong?' I asked, going over to her.

'He doesn't want me any more.' At first, I thought it was her fiancé who had jilted her, but she added 'I'm being transferred,' and I realised she was talking about Ghikas.

'Why?'

'That fathead, my fiancé, is to blame.' And she started sobbing.

I presumed that Ghikas was having her transferred because now that she was engaged she left early and was no longer at his beck and call, but I asked to be sure.

'No, it's not that,' she said in stops and starts – sob, word, sob. 'He was building a two-storey house in Dionysos and the local police stopped him because his building permit wasn't in order.'

'Was it an illegal construction?'

She nodded. 'And that numbskull fiancé of mine took it into his head to tell the local police chief that his fiancée was secretary to the Chief of Security. The chief called Ghikas to confirm it and he was furious.'

'Don't carry on like that, Koula,' I said, trying to comfort her. 'There must be some solution.'

'There is. He has ordered me to be transferred.'

And she went back to her original position: elbows on the desk, head in her hands. I couldn't think of anything else to say and I went into Ghikas' office. Ghikas may have more than a few faults, but he was one hundred per cent straight. If he found out that one of his people was handing out favours or was involved in any sort of racket, then he came down on him like a ton of bricks. I found him gazing out of the window. A sure sign that he was in a bad mood, because only then did he ever get up from his chair.

'What on earth gave you the idea to come and see me?' he said. 'Lately, all you seem to do is hide from me.'

'I came to see you because there have been some developments,' I said. And I told him about the money and about Madas.

'At last, we'll be able to stop the tongues wagging for a while,' he said with a grim little smile and sat down at his desk, as he no longer had any reason to be on his feet. 'Draft a summary for me.'

He always wanted it in one page, so that he could learn it by heart and announce it from memory. If it were two pages, he would have to read it out.

'Should I mention that Koustas was going to give the fifteen million to his murderer?'

'That's what Madas says to help his own situation. Personally, I believe your version. It was Madas who was blackmailing him. He was the one the money was intended for. But he's not admitting it so as not to be sent down for attempted blackmail too.'

Now there's a thing, I thought to myself, the trick I had come up with to frighten Madas was evolving into a theory. I went on with the briefing and told him about the sponsor of Koustas' team.

'I can't see that that's of any importance,' he said, frowning. 'Every team is on the lookout for a sponsor. He found the firm where his daughter worked.'

'Two hundred and forty million a year? So much money for a Third Division team? Don't you find it strange?'

'The tax officer told you what it was all about. Legal tax avoidance.'

Again he had recourse to the simplest solution, which was not at all to my liking. I had no intention of giving up so easily, but I kept that to myself. If I told him anything more, he might forbid me to follow up my hunch and I would be left with the ace dangling from my sleeve.

I headed towards the door, but before leaving, I turned and said: 'Koula has been with you for three years. She knows how you do things and you'll miss her,' I said.

'Do you know what she did?' he said.

'Not her. Her fiancé. Koula swears that she had no idea.'

I do not know what had got into me to make me stand up for her. After all, what was it to me if Koula was transferred to some out-of-the-way police station to file summonses? Perhaps my daughter's relationship with Ouzounidis was to lame. If they caught him taking backhanders, I would do all I could to get Katerina off the hook and that led me into a strange sense of solidarity with the downtrodden and persecuted. You've chosen a tough path for a policeman, I said to myself. If Sotiropoulos were to find out, he would say it was my illness that was to blame.

'Anyhow, Koula's a good girl and she knows her job,' I continued as I was going out.

The girl in question had got a plastic bag and was collecting her personal belongings together. As soon as she saw me, she ran up to me. 'I'd better say my goodbyes, I might not see you again,' she said.

'Come on now, you're not going to find yourself overnight in the back of beyond. As soon as you hear where they're transferring you, call me and let me know.'

She stretched out her arms and hugged me. 'You were always kind to me, Inspector Haritos,' she said, on the verge of tears again, and she planted a kiss on my cheek.

In general, I am not one for emotional outpourings because they make things more difficult. Nevertheless, I saw that she was in a state and I tried to comfort her. 'Cheer up, Koula. We've all been through it. It's part of the game.' I stroked her hair and left her. She gave me a bitter smile and went back to her clearing-out.

In my office, I took a sip of my cold Greek and not-Greek coffee. Vlassopoulos sat across from me.

'How did it go with Madas?' I asked him.

'He's being held and charges will be brought.'

I reflected that Koustas' heirs should be grateful to me, because I had found them another ten million. Especially Makis, who was assured of his fix for another three months.

'Is it out of the question that Madas killed Koustas?' Vlassopoulos said.

It would suit everyone, especially Ghikas, if that were the case, but it wasn't. 'Why would he kill him?'

'No matter whether he saw or simply twigged that Koustas had all that money on him that night, he got greedy and did him in, to get his hands on it.'

'Didn't you hear what Madas said? The gunman spoke to Koustas and Koustas turned to give him the two bags with the fifteen million.'

'So Madas said. Then why didn't the gunman take the money?'

'I don't know. All I *do* know is that the money was dirty. I suspect that Koustas wanted to give it to his associates to get himself out of some grubby business. But they didn't want the money; they wanted to kill him to make an example of him. Koustas' murder was the work of professionals, Sotiris.'

I may not like simple solutions, but it had taken me almost a month to reach the conclusion that Anti-Terrorist had reached in two days, simply because, like a mug, I go straight for whatever is difficult or complex. Vlassopoulos left without raising any objections, but his expression told me that he was not convinced.

I took a sheet of paper to write the summary that Ghikas had asked me for. Through the open window of the flat opposite, I saw the hulk holding a young girl in his arms and kissing her. He must have got back together again with his girl, unlike Panos, but when they stepped apart, I saw that it was a different girl, tall with long hair. Katerina's words came to mind, that 'women are attracted to hulks'. It was not only hulks, it seemed, but also hairy types. On the other hand, perhaps it was neither the hulks nor the hairy types who were attractive to women, but rather the hulks who cried like babies. Fortunately, I have passed that age.

CHAPTER 32

The girl in the reception at R.I. Hellas greeted me with a smile, but she did not let me go straight up to see Niki Koustas. She kept me on hold while she first communicated with her. Fortunately, I was granted an entry permit and I again walked down the corridor with the cubicles. The door of Koustas' office was open, as at my previous visit. She was dressed simply, no make-up. Her short, black hair was shining and pulled back.

'We seem to be seeing each other almost every day,' she said with a smile. 'Have there been any developments?'

'No, but I have a question and I've come to see if you can answer it for me.'

'If I can.'

'How is it that Triton, your father's team, happens to have your firm as its sponsor?'

'You mean R.I. Hellas?'

'Yes.'

The childlike smile gave way to surprise. 'I've no idea. It's the first I've heard of it.' She thought for a moment and came up with an answer. 'It's not so strange, though, that I wouldn't know about it. I have no dealings at all with the firm's administration. I only deal with opinion polls and market research.'

'Perhaps you heard about it from your father?'

'I told you, I think. He never talked about his business.'

'And he never came here, to the firm?'

'Never. If he had, he would have come to see me. We may have seen each other only rarely, but we hadn't stopped talking to each other.'

'Who would know about the money given to Triton?'

'Only Mrs Arvanitakis, our director. Her office is on the top floor.'

I thought of being squashed inside the lift, which was about as big as a ship's toilet, and I decided to use the wide, wooden staircase. Besides, my heart was back on form and it was an opportunity to take an endurance test.

I passed with flying colours because when I got up to the top floor, I found I still had enough breath for another climb. The third floor had retained all the elegance of a pre-war mansion. The large salon was just as it had been and was furnished with sofas, armchairs and coffee tables. Here, no doubt, was where they welcomed the businessmen who wanted to test the response of the consumers buying their various yogurts and the politicians who wanted to test the response of the voters, before getting a taste of the yogurts, metaphorically speaking.

Along the corridor, exactly above Koustas' office, all the doors to the rooms were closed and labelled with signs: 'Accounts', 'Administration', 'Personnel'. Because none of these were of any interest to me, I walked on and at the end found the door marked 'Director'. I opened it without knocking and went in.

A thin woman of around sixty, with white hair and wearing a tight two-piece, lifted her head and looked at me over her glasses. The furnishing was in sharp contrast to the secretary – modern, metal and glass.

'What do you want?' she asked coldly, ready to send me away before I could even reply.

'Inspector Haritos. I'd like to speak to Mrs Arvanitakis.'

'Do you have an appointment?' Her tone told me that it was inconceivable that Mrs Arvanitakis could have made an appointment with a police officer.

I confirmed it. 'No.'

'I'm sorry, but she's busy.'

'I just want to ask her one small question. It won't take more than a couple of minutes.'

'I told you, she's busy.'

She obviously thought that no further discussion was required as she removed her gaze from me and began to file documents in a folder. I went up to her desk and stood over her.

'Listen,' I said to her, no longer in a polite tone. 'Tomorrow I'll have a summons served on Arvanitakis to have her appear at Security Headquarters within twenty-four hours. If she complains about being summoned in that way, I'll tell her that I came to her office to talk to her and that her secretary sent me away.'

She put down the document she was holding, looked up and tried to file me away. But she did not know in which folder to put me – with the bravos or with the braggarts. She decided to put me with the former to at least have her peace of mind.

'One moment,' she said, disappearing through the door at the end of the room. Ten seconds later she half opened it again and told me to go in, with a look dripping with gall and vinegar.

Arvanitakis could have been a younger relative of the sullen lady at the gate. At first sight, she did not appear to be more than forty. She was also wearing a tight two-piece and a white blouse. Her hair was flecked with grey that she hadn't gone to the trouble of dyeing.

'How can I help you, Inspector?' she asked, gesturing to me to sit down. She may have been put out by my being there, but she gave no sign of it.

'We're investigating the murder of Konstantinos Koustas.' I paused to see how she would react, but she simply looked at me calmly, waiting for me to go on. 'In the course of our investigations, we discovered that Koustas had dealings with your firm.'

'I don't recognise the name, but that doesn't mean that he didn't do business with R.I. Hellas. What was his line of work?'

'He was the owner of various nightclubs and a football team.'

She laughed. 'Then I very much doubt he had any professional dealings with us, Inspector. Nightclubs and football teams don't usually require market research. They can count their customers for themselves.'

'Then how do you explain that your firm is the sponsor of Triton, Koustas' football team?'

She did not reply immediately. She sat back in her chair and let out a sigh. 'That puzzles me too. I could never understand why every year we pay out so much money to an insignificant football team.'

It occurred to me that perhaps she was having me on, but her expression was totally sincere. 'Wasn't it you who decided about the sponsorship?'

'No, Inspector. R.I. Hellas is a subsidiary of an investment company by the name of Greekinvest. The directive for the sponsorship came from our parent company.'

Her answer left me floundering. I had thought I would get to the bottom of it at R.I. Hellas, but now I saw that I would have to search some more. 'How was the directive given? By phone or in writing?'

'In writing, of course. I can show you the document if you'd like.'

'Yes, I would.'

Arvanitakis pressed the intercom and told her secretary to bring the Greekinvest/Triton file. When she came in, I turned to smile at her. Her response was almost audibly sour. Not only had I obliged her to let me see Arvanitakis, but now she was running errands too. She put the file on the desk, then turned and walked out with her eyes fixed on the ceiling, at the point where the chandelier was missing.

Arvanitakis searched and found the document. It was a letter to R.I. Hellas, dated 10 September 1992.

This is to inform you that we have reached agreement with the management of Triton FC concerning the sponsorship of the aforementioned club by your firm. The total annual cost of the sponsorship amounts to 240 (two hundred and forty) million drachma, which will be paid in twelve monthly instalments beginning from the current month of September. The relevant amount will be made available by Greekinvest and will be deposited in your firm's account. The agreement is in force for a period of one year, but it may be renewed following notification by us. Please be kind enough to contact the offices of Triton FC . . .

I saw the signature and my eyes fixed on it: Christos Petroulias. So Christos Petroulias was the owner of Greekinvest and sponsoring, through his subsidiary, Koustas' team. It took me all of a minute to tear my eyes from the document and look at Arvanitakis, who was watching me curiously.

'Christos Petroulias was the owner of Greekinvest?'

She shrugged. 'I imagine so, though I don't know it for certain. He was certainly its manager, however.'

'Did he often come here, to your offices?'

'No. Only when there was something urgent.'

'So how did you communicate with him?'

'By fax or telephone.'

'Mrs Arvanitakis, did you know that Christos Petroulias had been murdered?'

She began to fidget in her seat, just like Madas. 'I heard about it,' she said, barely opening her mouth.

'So why didn't you come forward and tell us that Petroulias was the manager of Greekinvest, your owner?'

She looked at me without saying anything. She was trying to find some way to justify her inaction, but it wasn't easy. In the end, she realised that there was no escape.

'Listen, Inspector,' she said. 'We are a firm that deals in opinion polls and market research. We have dealings with political parties, politicians and businessmen. You understand, I'm sure, what it would mean for us if it came out that Christos Petroulias was the manager of our parent company. Given that his death was not in any way linked with R.I. Hellas, I decided to keep quiet, in the hope that the matter would be forgotten and that Petroulias' link with our firm would not come out into the open.'

'You mean to say that your boss dies a violent death and all you think about are the opinion polls?'

'You have to understand that no one knew Petroulias, whereas the politicians and products we deal with are known to everyone. I am sorry, of course, that he died but my duty was to protect the name of the firm I work for.'

What was it that Kaloyirou had said? 'What can you expect from a world in which all the clocks show the same time?'

'Did no one else in your firm know who Petroulias was?'

'No one.'

'All right, but Petroulias was murdered in June. It's been three months since then. Who has been giving you your directives during all this time?'

'There was a co-manager, or rather co-manageress.'

'Who was she? What's her name?'

'A Mrs Loukia Karamitris. I rarely saw Petroulias. Mrs Karamitris I have never seen at all. I only know her from her phone calls and from the signature on her faxes.'

The name of Loukia Karamitris meant nothing to me, but then I do not keep notes like my assistants. I make a mental note of everything. 'You'll have to come to Security to make a statement,' I said to Arvanitakis.

'May I ask you a favour?'

'What kind of favour?'

'Please don't do anything to encourage Petroulias' link with the firm to come out.'

'If there's no specific connection with his death it won't.'

She breathed a sigh of relief. 'I'm sure there's no connection. May I have the document?' she said, pointing to the letter with Petroulias' signature that I was still holding.

'Yes, but I'd like a photocopy.'

She got up from her desk and walked with me into the outer office. Curious and displeased, her secretary stared at her for having gone to the trouble of accompanying me. Arvanitakis made the photocopy herself. She handed it to me, keeping hold of the original.

As I went down the wide, wooden staircase, I cast one more glance over the photocopy and the letterhead caught my eye. Greekinvest's address was 8 Fokianos Street. The offices of R.I. Hellas were in Apollonos Street. The offices of Triton in Mitropoleos Street. They were virtually only a block apart. I did not think that it was a coincidence.

I was in a hurry to get back to my office and I ran down the stairs. When I got to the second floor, however, I changed my mind. I turned and went back into Niki Koustas' office.

'Did you speak with Mrs Arvanitakis?' she said, with her usual smile.

'Yes, and I want to ask you one more thing. Does the name Christos Petroulias mean anything to you?'

'No, should it?'

It shouldn't, given that Arvanitakis had kept it a secret. 'I was asking in case your father had ever mentioned him to you.'

'Never.'

'Have you ever heard of a Loukia Karamitris?'

Her smile vanished and she became serious. She fell silent and bit her lower lip. Yet when she spoke again, her voice was calm. 'I've certainly heard of her,' she said. 'She's my mother.'

I stood staring at her. Which mother? 'You don't mean Mrs Koustas?'

'No, I don't mean Elena. I mean my actual mother. The one who brought me into the world.'

I went down the two remaining flights of stairs without being aware of them. I forgot to say goodbye to the girl in reception and, finding myself outside, I came to a halt outside the door because my thoughts had cut the legs from under me.

How was it that Petroulias and Koustas' ex-wife were managers in the same company? And how was it that they had both agreed to give 240 million a year in sponsorship money to Koustas' team for three years running? Even if I were to accept that Petroulias had some other form of dealings with Koustas, what about his ex-wife? She had left him for a singer. She had cut all ties with her kids and yet was funding her ex-husband's team? And why had Petroulias awarded an unjustifiable penalty *against* the team he was sponsoring, causing them to lose the championship?

I arrived at my Mirafiori without realising how. I sat with both hands clutching the wheel, gazing through the windscreen, seeing nothing. As to Petroulias' dealings with Koustas I could think of various explanations. But Karamitris' relationship with her ex-husband left me at a loss.

CHAPTER 33

From early that morning, a minor skirmish had broken out between me and the Adriani–Katerina bloc, which of late had adopted a common front against me, rather like the EEC with the Bosnian Serbs. It was the day I had to go to the hospital for tests. Katerina insisted on coming with me, but I was adamant. It was enough that I'd have to see Ouzounidis and I didn't know how to behave towards him. If Katerina came too, I would constantly have the feeling that they were exchanging glances, smiles and nods, and it would get on my nerves. Well, perhaps they wouldn't and it was just my imagination, but I couldn't get it out of my head. I made the suggestion that I go alone, but it came up against the wall that was Adriani and bounced off. And so we arrived at a compromise solution: I would go with Adriani and Katerina would get on with her research in the library.

'When do you think you'll be through so you can return to Thessaloniki?' I asked her.

She stared at me, but without her usual ironic smile. 'Do you want to get rid of me?' Her look was hostile, but the question was an aggrieved one.

I could see that my relationship with my daughter had been going downhill of late and I had done nothing to stop it. I felt that I was to blame, but I was bothered by the thought that she wasn't staying in Athens because of the bibliography, but because of Ouzounidis, and that was enough to make me want to pack her off to Thessaloniki. In the past, I would be down in the dumps whenever the time came for her to leave. I would be now too, I knew it, but I wanted to get rid of her all the same.

'You'll get behind with your research because of me and then I'll feel bad.' It was a half-lie and like all half-lies it was effective because she put her arms round me and kissed me.

'Oh Dad, will you ever be free of your preconceptions,' she said, laughing.

Never, I thought to myself. A policeman without preconceptions is a bad policeman. The situation cooled down somewhat, but I left home with my nerves on edge. We agreed that Adriani should come at eleven thirty to pick me up and take me to the hospital, and now I was standing in the canteen waiting for Aliki to give me my Greek and not-Greek coffee. I saw her smiling to one of her colleagues and I felt like shouting at her, but I held my anger in check.

Holding my coffee, I went to the office of my two lieutenants in order to find Dermitzakis, but he wasn't there. 'Where's Dermitzakis?' I asked Vlassopoulos.

'He must have gone somewhere.'

'Of course he's gone somewhere. The question is whether he told you *where* he was going or whether anyone can leave any time they feel like it without saying anything.'

'No, he didn't tell me.'

'Send him into my office the instant he gets back. I want him.'

No sooner had I taken the first sip of my coffee than the door opened and in walked Dermitzakis.

'Have Makis Koustas and his sister brought here. I want to cross-examine them.'

'Has there been some development?' Dermitzakis asked timidly.

'I'll tell you after I've had a few words with those two. Go on, off with you. And another time when you leave the office, make sure you tell someone where you're going.'

'I didn't go far. I only went to get some cigarettes.'

'Even if you go for a pee, we want to know where you are.'

He seemed to be trying to find an explanation for my vile early-morning temper, but he couldn't. But I looked at the medicines lined up on my desk and I knew. I was riddled with anxiety about what the tests would show. In recent days, when I had felt fine, I had begun smoking the very occasional cigarette – on the sly in my office, never at home – and I trembled at the thought that Ouzounidis might find out from the X-ray. It was the first time after a good few days that my heart was racing again and I took a whole Inderal instead of the usual half so as to be calm when I went to the hospital and outwit the cardiograph.

It was ten o'clock and I still had an hour and a half before Adriani came for me. I had time to inform Ghikas about all that had happened the previous day. Now that the link between Koustas and Petroulias had been verified beyond doubt, we could no longer leave the Koustas case with the unsolved crimes. The developments would not please Ghikas one bit but they pleased me and raised my spirits somewhat. I was about to pick up the phone when Sotiropoulos walked in.

'What's all this that Ghikas has been telling us? That Koustas had fifteen million on him on the night of the murder and his doorman robbed him of it as he was lying dead?' he said in a disbelieving tone.

'It's as he's told you. Why are you asking?'

'Because that's not all. There's more to it and you're keeping it from the public.' He looked at me with the expression of an underfed dog.

'That is all. There is no more. Do you want me to repeat it so you can digest it?'

'Digest what? That after a whole month of investigating, instead of the killer, you've caught a two-bit thief? I'm going to have to work very hard to make a story for the news bulletin out of that little scrap.'

And draw it out for three days showing the photograph of Koustas' dead body every night, I thought.

'Do we have any news about Petroulias?'

'Not yet.'

'I told you, it's your illness that's to blame.'

I pictured his expression if I told him about the link between Koustas and Petroulias, and Koustas and his ex-wife, and that raised my spirits even higher. I again picked up the phone to call Ghikas, but I saw that I only had three-quarters of an hour. If he kept me talking, I might miss my appointment with the doctor. As it was, Adriani came half an hour early out of fear of our being late.

It took us a quarter of an hour to get from Alexandras Avenue to the State General Hospital. During that time, all remnants of my good spirits vanished and anxiety and despondency took their place. The appointment was for noon, but Adriani hurried into the surgery to announce our arrival. She came back with a nurse.

'The doctor has arranged for you to have your tests so that you'll be ready when your turn comes,' she said, smiling with satisfaction at the special treatment.

The nurse was a short, bandy-legged woman with sideburns and a moustache. 'This way,' she said curtly.

Fortunately, this time I was given a reprieve from the wheelchair, not to mention the personal cistern. I was given priority in all the examination rooms and had to suffer the disgruntled, sometimes murderous, looks of those who were waiting in line. They undoubtedly thought that I had given someone a backhander. They could not know that my privileges derived from elsewhere.

Within a quarter of an hour I was finished and sitting in a plastic chair outside the surgery, holding the three folders with the test results tightly in my sweating palms. The surgery door opened and the bandy-legged woman told us to go in.

I suddenly saw before me a different Ouzounidis. This was not the cordial, smiling young fellow that I had known earlier. He was formal, cold and said only what was necessary. He looked grimly at the results and told me to take off my shirt and lie down. The experience of the policeman took over for a moment from the anxiety of the patient and I immediately understood what was behind his manner. Katerina had told him that I had found out about their relationship and he wanted to take the wind out of my sails before I could raise the subject myself. I had not intended saying anything to him, but his attitude got up my nose and I decided to act cold and formal myself.

And so a contest began.

'Take a deep breath.'

No reply.

'Does that hurt?'

'No.'

'Remain seated.'

No reply.

'Has your heart been racing?'

'Very little.'

'OK. You can get dressed.'

No reply. While he had his stethoscope to my chest, it suited us both, because we did not have to look at each other. Once I had got up, the problem of avoiding each other's eyes returned.

'You're fine,' he said to me coldly at the end, while filling in his report card. 'The tests are clean and the cardiograph much improved.'

I suddenly felt as light as a feather. My first thought was to apologise to Vlassopoulos and Dermitzakis for bullying them that morning.

'Yes, but he tires himself out, Doctor,' Adriani said, who had made an art of spoiling my delight. 'He goes out at eight in the morning and comes back at seven in the evening.'

'Never mind, the walking is good for him. Given that he's all right, he should carry on normally.' He was investing in Adriani all the cordiality he had denied me. I was glad to escape the chuckles and nods that passed between him and my daughter, but now he was doing it with my wife.

He turned back to me and his cold expression returned. 'Stop all the medication apart from the digoxin. And make an appointment to come back to see me in three months.'

You can say what you like, I'm going to keep taking half an Inderal for my peace of mind, I thought.

'You see, and you wanted to change your doctor,' Adriani said with satisfaction as we were walking back to the car.

I thought about raising the matter of his expression, but I did not want to spoil my well-being. Besides, it would be three months before I saw him again – *if* I saw him again.

CHAPTER 34

'Have you caught the men who killed my father?'

'No, why would you think so?'

'I thought that that was perhaps why you'd called us here.'

They had pulled up their chairs and were sitting beside each other. He in his leather jacket, jeans and cowboy boots. She in a skirt with a hemline just above the knee, blouse and cardigan. They gave the impression of wanting to hold each other's hands and yet they were so different. Anyone not knowing them would have sworn that they were not brother and sister. Makis was unshaven, sullen and looked older than he was. Niki was dressed simply, but with taste, and her smile made her look younger than she was. I had sent for them to get certain information before seeing their mother, Loukia Karamitris. I also wanted to get a clear picture of Niki Koustas' relationship with R.I. Hellas.

'If I were going to announce your father's killer to you, I would have sent for Mrs Koustas too.'

'Maybe she was the one who killed him and you've already got her locked up,' said Makis, breaking into a laugh.

'Makis, don't talk like that about Elena. It's not right,' his sister said sternly.

The first difference between them was already evident. That's what I was counting on – on the differences between them.

'Do you know whether your father still had contact with your mother after they separated?'

'They didn't separate, she left him,' Makis answered. 'We woke up one morning and our mother was gone. Dad told us she had left and wasn't coming back. From that day on he never spoke about her again and he forbade us even to mention her name.'

'Was your mother a woman of independent means?'

Niki smiled that innocent smile of hers. 'When she left, Makis was fourteen and I was twelve, Inspector. We had no notion of property or means.'

'So you don't know whether she had her own business, for example?'

'She didn't while she was living with us because she spent all day in the house. If she had any businesses after she left, that I can't say.'

'How did you come to work for R.I. Hellas?'

'When I came back from England, I began looking for work. My father told me about a firm that was recruiting research analysts. I went to see Mrs Arvanitakis, told her about my studies and she hired me.'

She had studied in England and research analysts weren't ten a penny like lawyers or engineers. Though perhaps Koustas had had Karamitris or Petroulias have a word with Arvanitakis so that she would hire her.

'Are you sure that your mother had no hand in your being hired?'

'Why would she have?'

Makis leapt to his feet. 'You keep going on about my mother. What possible connection would she have with my father's murder? She left him fifteen years ago. Do you think she waited until now to kill him?'

'Do you know someone by the name of Christos Petroulias?' I asked him.

'Is he the one you asked me about this morning?' said Niki, cutting in.

'Yes.'

'And how would we know him?' Makis asked.

'You might because you're crazy about football and you wanted to play in your father's team. You might know him as a referee.'

'I only ever played football in the street. I didn't become a footballer because my father didn't want it. Where would I ever meet a referee, for God's sake?'

'Because he was an associate of your father's.'

'You mean that my father was bribing him. So what? He wasn't the only one.'

'I didn't say that he was bribing him. I said that they were associates. And an associate of your mother's too,' I added, and watched him to see how he would react.

'Leave my mother out of it!' he shouted. 'My mother had no dealings with my father or with any crappy referees!'

'Your mother was in partnership with Petroulias,' I said mildly. 'They jointly owned or ran a company called Greekinvest. It's the parent company of R.I. Hellas, where your sister works. R.I. Hellas was, at the request of your mother and Petroulias, sponsoring a team owned by your father. That's why I asked you whether your mother still had any contact with your father after they separated.'

They both looked at me dumbfounded. Makis began to mumble something, but gave up. Niki's eyes were fixed on me and her mouth half open. 'Are you sure about that?' she asked eventually.

'That's what Arvanitakis told me.'

'Does Arvanitakis know that Loukia Karamitris is my mother?'

'No, but she confirmed that by order of Greekinvest, R.I. Hellas was sponsoring Triton to the tune of 240 million a year.'

The innocent smile had vanished and her gaze filled with hate. 'Why don't you go and arrest that useless mother of mine and ask her what she has to say about all that? As if it weren't enough that she abandoned us to our fate, she comes back to haunt us now.'

'I won't have you talk about our mother like that, Niki.'

Makis slumped into his chair and covered his face with his hands. Niki went and put her arms around his shoulders. 'OK, OK, I take it back,' she said. 'You're right, I shouldn't talk about her like that.'

Makis raised his head and looked at her. 'I went to see her,' he whispered.

'When?'

'Just after she left. I found out that she was living in Varybobi. Don't ask me how I managed to get out there to the back of beyond when I was only fourteen, but I did. "Mum, it's me, your son, Makis," I said when she came to the door, "I've come to see you." She looked at me for a moment without saying anything. Then she said, "Go away. Go away and don't come back." And she shut the door in my face.' He said all this neither to Niki nor to me, but to himself. 'She did not want to set eyes on her son, but she went on doing business with my father after she'd left him.'

Niki had taken his head between her hands and was caressing it, comforting him.

'Someone was blackmailing your father,' I told them. 'On the night he was killed he had fifteen million on him and had gone to his car to get it. The most probable thing is that he was going to give it to someone. And that someone is the one we're looking for.' And I told them about Madas.

'He must have been giving it to someone who had the dirt on my stepmother,' cried Makis jubilantly. 'To keep his mouth shut.'

'What dirt?' I asked.

'Makis!' Niki's tone was somewhere between fear and warning.

He paid no attention to her. His eyes lit up again, just as they did every time he got angry. 'Ask her where she's been going every Tuesday afternoon for the last three years. Every Tuesday afternoon, Dad went to the team's training session and she would sneak out of the house. She never missed even one Tuesday! Ask her where she went! I'll tell you – she was cheating on him! At least my mother had the guts to leave him, whereas this one was two-timing him.'

'Makis, Elena wasn't cheating on our father. It's only your hate that makes you say things like that.'

'You weren't at home, so you don't know,' he whispered, suddenly deflating. It was as though all his strength were in one breath that he had released.

A fine pair, I thought. The son squeals on the stepmother and worships his mother and the daughter squeals on the mother and worships her stepmother.

Niki helped him slowly up as though lifting a crystal vase that she was afraid of breaking. She put her arm round his shoulder to support him. Then she turned to me. 'If you don't want us for anything else, we'll be going, Inspector,' she said, almost imploringly.

'No, there's nothing else.'

When they had gone, I reflected that although I had been trying to get information about Karamitris, I had found out something more about Elena Koustas. I called Dermitzakis in.

'Have someone watch Elena Koustas' movements,' I said, telling him everything that Makis had told me.

He looked at me in surprise. 'Do you believe the word of a junkie?'

'No, but check it out. It may be a lead.' I refrained from telling him that I could easily have a soft spot for Elena Koustas and I knew I had to put a brake on my liking for her.

'I'll get Antonopoulos on to it. He's a smart lad,' Dermitzakis said.

He was a newcomer who had been transferred to us from the Vice Squad. Bland and prosaic, he was by nature inconspicuous. Dermitzakis had made a good choice. I sent him off and collected my papers together to go home.

CHAPTER 35

'Dad, will you drop me off at Iroon Polythechniou Street? I have to go to the campus,' Katerina said to me that morning as I was getting ready to leave.

'Of course I will.'

We got into the Mirafiori and set off in silence. I had my gaze fixed on the road ahead; Katerina had hers on the pavement to the right of her. She was watching the pedestrians scampering past, and the people jostling at the bus stops and pushing and kicking to get on the bus. When we got to Hymettou Avenue, she broke her silence.

'I asked you to give me a lift because I wanted to talk,' she said. 'But not in front of Mum. Just the two of us.'

She came straight out with it, no beating about the bush, and she took me by surprise. I turned to her, but she was still looking at the pavement. 'OK, let's talk,' I said. 'What do you want to tell me?'

'Not in the car. I want us to talk somewhere quiet.'

I felt my heart pounding. She has decided to abandon her studies, get a steady job somewhere and marry Ouzounidis, I thought. I bet that's what she wants to tell me. That's why she wants to take her time, to give it to me gently. So many years of studying, so much money forked out, not enough for holidays even in rooms-to-let, and suddenly along comes some doctor, gives you a purge, and you fling everything to the wind. That's how it is, sparrows reach the skies in one of two ways: either they fly or the cat carries them up on the roof tiles in its mouth. Katerina was moving from the former to the latter. Common sense told me to be patient, but I couldn't restrain myself.

'Is it about your studies?'

'No, it's not about my studies. It's something else I want to talk about.'

I swallowed my breath to hide my sigh of relief. If it wasn't about her studies, I was confident that a solution could be found for everything else.

'Let's not do it today, as I don't know what time I'll get free,' I said, and I was suddenly gripped by another fear, that she might take it the wrong way. 'I'm not trying to put it off,' I said, justifying myself. 'It's just that I've been shouldered with two murders and I'm up to my ears.'

'I know.' It took her from Aristokleous Street to Ethnikis Antistaseos Street to give me a smile. 'There's no need to go inside the university. Leave me at the lights.'

She got out as soon as the light was at red. I watched her crossing the street and wondered whether I was beginning to resemble Koustas, who never changed course when it came to his son, so that he kept running aground on the reefs, until in the end not even a tugboat could free him.

The same thought was still in my mind as I drove north up the National Road to get to Karamitris' house in Varybobi. I had phoned her to say I would be coming some time that same day.

When she started to protest that I was keeping her indoors all day waiting for me, I suggested that she could, as an alternative, come to Security Headquarters. She backed down straight away, because no one wants to be questioned there.

And so I was cruising in the right-hand lane of the National Road. It was virtually empty and the few cars overtook my Mirafiori as a conger eel does a jellyfish. Good luck to them, it did not bother me at all, firstly because in the Mirafiori I was used to being overtaken even by tricycles and, secondly, because like that I could give some thought to Katerina. Once I was over my alarm concerning her studies, I was able to take some pleasure in the fact that she wanted us to have a chat and it lifted my spirits somewhat. It meant that she had not forgotten the time when the two of us would conspire behind her mother's back. I didn't have to rack my brains to guess what it was she wanted to tell me. As it was not about her studies, it would be about Ouzounidis. She no doubt wanted to explain his behaviour at the hospital when he had been as cold as an Eskimo. Even so, the fact that she did not want her mother as a support and preferred to talk to me was a good sign.

Waiting for me just after the turn for Nea Erythraia was my second pleasant surprise of the day. All the conger eels who had overtaken me on the National Road had been brought up short and were shouting, swearing and honking their horns. After waiting a good ten minutes, I got out of the car to see what was happening. A hundred and fifty metres further on, the road was blocked by cars, lorries and trucks that had been parked across the National Road. Behind the vehicles I could see a crowd of people. Some were holding banners, which were impossible to read, and one man with a loudhailer was shouting slogans, all of them impossible to decipher. On both sides of the road, in front of the roadblock, riot police, vans and patrol cars were lined up.

The truck driver who was in the same line as me had a cigarette hanging from his mouth and was sticking two fingers up to everything framed by his windscreen: the landscape, the vehicles, the police and the demonstration.

'What's happening, why have we stopped?' I asked him.

'The locals from Menidi have blocked the National Road in protest against the new rubbish dump being sited there.'

'Is there a dump planned for Menidi?' It was the first I had heard of it.

'No.'

'Then why are they protesting?'

'Because the Ministry is looking into setting up a biological cleansing plant in one of ten municipalities in the Athens area.'

'And that's what they're protesting about?'

'Menidi is one of the ten and they want to be excluded now, so that the other nine will be left fighting between themselves.'

In front of the truck was a white BMW. Its driver was leaning against the bonnet. In his right hand he was holding a cigar and in his left a mobile phone and he was talking in English. 'Yes, yes,' he was shouting in order to be heard. 'Not more than an hour.'

If he means that he won't be held up for more than an hour, he must be from another planet, I thought.

'What fault is it of mine, can you answer me that?' muttered the truck driver next to me. 'I'm carrying a perishable cargo, frozen fish, and if the block continues till tonight I'll be looking for a pan to boil the grey mullet or a grill for the red mullet, otherwise they're going to start smelling and I'll have to ditch them. Every lousy yob and village with a gripe has taken to blocking the roads in Greece and honest people can't do a day's work.'

'You're carrying fish?' I heard someone beside me say. I turned and saw the driver of the BMW, cigar in his mouth, coming over to the truck driver's open window. 'What about me? I have foreign clients waiting for me in Thessaloniki to close a deal worth billions and I risk losing it.'

'I don't give a shit about your millions,' the truck driver replied. 'My job is to bring food to people.'

The driver with the cigar looked at him ironically. 'Not to me, it isn't. I wouldn't put your frozen fish in my mouth. I only eat fish that smells of the sea.'

'You know what you need?' the truck driver yelled at him. 'For me to empty my fish all over your flashy car and make you walk to

Thessaloniki, you turd. Ten years ago your kind were still shitting out in the fields and now you're playing the billionaires.'

I left them to their class struggle and cursed myself for having taken the National Road to avoid the traffic in Kifissia. I glanced behind in case I could get away in reverse but the queue was almost as far back as Treis Yefyres. About a hundred metres up ahead, two police officers were leaning against their car and watching the situation resignedly. I walked up to them.

'When are they going to open the road?' I asked, after explaining who I was.

'What can I tell you, Inspector?' one of them replied. 'They said four hours, but now their coordination committee is having a meeting. They might prolong the block for another four hours, or twenty-four, or even indefinitely. It's their deck and they're the ones with all the aces.'

I told them where I was going and for what reason. 'We understand, but all we can do is take you there ourselves,' the other replied.

'And what about my car?'

He laughed. 'It'll most probably still be in the same place when you come back. But if they open the road, we'll take it to the station at Nea Erythraia and you can collect it from there.'

I walked back with him to show him the Mirafiori. Fifteen or so drivers had gathered in front of the truck. The truck driver and the driver of the BMW had come to blows and the others were keeping them apart, though the fists were still flying.

The police officer glanced at them indifferently. 'Madhouse,' he said and walked past them. It was none of his business, he wasn't a psychiatrist.

CHAPTER 36

The patrol car brought me, by a roundabout route, to a street named after the first victim of local community associations – Aristotle. I stood and looked at the house before approaching it. At first sight, it revealed a faded splendour. It was one of those old summer houses that had been built when Varybobi's illegal plots of land had begun to be sought after by the inhabitants of Athens. Someone had had it built with great care and had then abandoned it to its fate, apparently having lost all interest in it. Its white colour had become a dark grey, the plaster had begun to come away and the few flowers in the garden were stifled among the nettles and weeds. The front gate was unlocked and creaked as I opened it. The concrete path leading to the front door was cracked and in places invaded by grass.

I climbed the steps and rang the doorbell. It seemed that she had been eagerly awaiting me as the door opened immediately. The woman standing in the doorway must have been in her fifties, but looked ten years older. Her hair was dyed a startling red and curled around a face that was either fat or swollen – you couldn't tell. She may have been beautiful once, but now her flesh was loose, like an overused corset.

She showed me through a door on the left into the living room. The same picture of faded splendour. Chairs whose gloss had faded, sofas and armchairs covered in a shiny green cloth – make-up to hide their abysmal state, just like Karamitris' hair. One of the armchairs was occupied by a man of indeterminable age given that his face was covered with a black beard, black hair and black glasses. He reminded me of those Islamic theologians from Egypt or Palestine that I had seen on TV.

'This is Kosmas Karamitris, my husband,' said Mrs Karamitris. 'I told him to stay because our discussion concerns him too.'

Mr Karamitris looked at me coldly, making not the slightest gesture to greet me. I remembered that he was once a popular singer. If his wife's son was the bouzouki-club cowboy, her husband was the cabaret-club ayatollah.

'Do have a seat,' she said, pointing to one of the armchairs covered in the shiny green make-up.

I came straight to the point. 'I want you to tell me about the company you represent, Greekinvest.'

'What can I tell you? I don't know anything,' was her reply. It seems she read the disbelief in my expression because she rushed to add, 'I know, it sounds strange, but you'll understand when I tell you the whole story.'

'Go ahead.' I did not know whether I was going to get the whole story or a trumped-up rigmarole. But I decided to let her speak before pressing her.

'You know, of course, that I was married to Konstantinos Koustas.'

'Yes.'

'Then you'll also know that I left him.'

'That too, yes.'

She paused, evidently to give thought to what she was about to tell me. 'Konstantinos Koustas wasn't an easy man to live with, Inspector. He was abrupt, authoritarian, always wanted his own way. I was still a young girl, I needed to be cosseted and he treated me like a rag doll. I wanted to live my life and he gave me two kids to look after and kept me shut up in the house.'

She stopped and glanced at her present husband. Perhaps she was waiting for him to say something to help her out, but he sat there expressionless, like the blind beggar without his accordion. She realised that no alms were in the offing and elected to carry on as best she could.

'I put up with it for fourteen very long years. My only fun was at the Bouzouki Strings. Konstantinos had just opened it and I'd sometimes go at night to pass the time. That's where I met Kosmas. He began phoning me at home. It seems I needed an excuse to get away from Konstantinos and so we were drawn together. I went through a year of terror, terrified that Konstantinos would find out because he would have made mincemeat of us. Kosmas saw that the situation couldn't go on like that. He told me to leave Konstantinos and to go and live with him. One night, when Konstantinos was at the Bouzouki Strings, I threw a few clothes into a bag, left everything else behind, and walked out. With the money he'd made from singing, Kosmas opened a small record company, Phonogram. At first, we lived in hotels. Then we rented this house. It was a wilderness here when we came here, but we wanted to get away from Konstantinos.'

There was another pause. I heard her talking and my mind went to Elena Koustas, who, according to Makis, disappeared from the house every Tuesday afternoon. Karamitris must have done the same.

'Can I get you something to drink? A coffee perhaps?' She was trying to buy time, either because she could not bear to come out with everything, or because from that point on she was going to have recourse to lies and she wanted to organise them in her mind.

'No, I don't want anything. Thank you.'

She had half got up, but now sat back down again. She took a deep breath. 'I expected that Konstantinos would come after me, search for me, but he did nothing. Neither sight nor sound. The one thing he did was to make sure every door was closed to Kosmas. No one would give him work. And his record company wasn't going well. Every time he was about to sign a contract with some star or other, the deal mysteriously fell through. In the end he ran out of money and was forced to borrow from loan sharks.'

She fell silent and again looked at her husband. Her look implored him to pick up the story, but he remained expressionless.

'One evening, it must have been around nine o'clock, the doorbell rang. A van was pulled up in front of the door and the garden was littered with all the clothes I'd left behind when I walked out. Konstantinos was standing there and laughing. "I've brought you your wardrobe," he said. We had been together for all those years and I'd never seen him smile other than at Christmas and Easter. Now he was splitting his sides with laughter. I was frightened. Do you know what I mean: when you're used to dealing with an unsmiling man and suddenly you see him laughing his head off, it's not happiness you feel – it's terror. "Let's go inside, I want to talk to you," he said and walked in as though it were his own house. "How's it going, Kosmas?" he said to my husband. "I hear business is bad." And all that in a cordial manner, as though he were talking to a friend. "I've something that belongs to you," he said to him. He opened his wallet and took out a cheque.

'It was a cheque for fifteen million that Kosmas had given to a loan shark as security for a loan.' Karamitris suddenly cut into the conversation, without warning, like an actor waiting for his cue to speak. 'How he'd found it and redeemed it was a mystery. He asked me whether I could pay it. He asked deliberately in order to have his fun. He knew that we barely had enough to eat, that I couldn't even pay the interest. Then, he made us a proposal.'

'What proposal was that?'

'He said that he wouldn't present the cheque and that he would add the interest I owed to the loan, but on two conditions.'

'What conditions?'

'First, that I would never ask to see my children,' said Mrs Karamitris, taking up the thread again. 'I didn't understand why he made that one of the conditions. I'd never tried to see either Makis or Niki.'

I understood, however. Makis was suffering then, he needed his mother, and Koustas wanted to make sure that Loukia would not give way if Makis came to her, which is exactly what had happened.

'And the second condition?'

'That I become manager of one of his companies and do whatever he told me. "As long as you do what I tell you, you have nothing to fear because I won't cash the cheque," he told us.'

'And you accepted?'

'What else could I do? When you're drowning, you'll clutch at anything.'

'Why didn't you sell your company in order to get out of trouble?' I asked Kosmas.

'Are you serious, Inspector? It was going under with so many debts, I wouldn't have got as much as a million for it. And then –' He started to say something, but abruptly stopped.

'Then, what?'

'Koustas offered to put money into the company. He invested another twenty million, I signed another cheque, and Phonogram was saved. Since then, we have been able to get by, but I never made enough to pay off Koustas. He had us in the palm of his hand.'

And then, as though only just realising that Koustas had

manipulated him for so many years, the distant expressionless Karamitris leapt to his feet. He was shaking with rage and his glasses teetered on his nose.

'We were his slaves,' he barked. 'Just imagine, I can't even divorce her.' And he pointed to his wife. 'If I divorced her, he threatened me, he would immediately present the cheques and I would end up in prison. Do you understand what I'm saying? I'm stuck with her for the rest of my life.'

He was done and let his body slip back into the armchair. He wore glasses but his short-sightedness was elsewhere. If he divorced Loukia, she would have no obligation to him and she could have thrown Greekinvest in his face.

She looked at him, but now her gaze was full of contempt. 'Don't complain, you didn't do so badly,' she said. 'After all, what were you before? A third-rate singer who went first onstage to warm up the audience. I'm the one who lost out. Konstantinos may have been what he was, but he kept me in feather down. And I left the feather down for foam rubber.'

'Then why didn't you leave me if you were better off in the past?' Kosmas said. 'We'd both have been better off.'

'Because I loved you.' She said it and observed a minute's silence for her lost love, though no one stood up in its memory. Neither her husband nor me.

'And what did you do at Greekinvest?' I asked her.

'Nothing. All these years, Konstantinos never bothered me at all, so much so that I had forgotten about it. It was only after June that he started sending me papers to sign.'

Because till then, he had arranged everything through Petroulias. He had had two strings to his bow. Once Petroulias had been killed, he had turned to Karamitris. In the end, no matter how much Elena might have complained that her husband kept her shut up in the house with her Filipino maids, she had been the luckier wife. Perhaps smarter too, if what Makis had said about Tuesday afternoons proved true.

'What kind of papers did he give you to sign?'

'I have no idea.'

'You don't *know*? Don't disappoint me now. Didn't you read what you were signing?'

'There was nothing to read. They were blank sheets of paper with the name of the company and a pencilled cross where I had to sign.'

Koustas had had her sign and then he had added whatever he wanted, carte blanche. That's how he had given the order for his team to receive the sponsorship money. 'Did you ever meet Christos Petroulias?'

'Who's he?' she said.

'Your joint manager at Greekinvest.'

'First time I've heard of him.'

She wasn't lying. Koustas would never have brought his two joint managers into contact.

'Is it the same Petroulias who was murdered, the referee? Or is it just someone of the same name?' asked Kosmas.

I turned and looked at him in surprise. 'Did you know him?'

'No, but I'd heard of him. From the time Koustas saddled me with a football team, I've been forced to follow the matches.'

'What team did he saddle you with?'

'Jason. In the Third Division.'

I remembered what Kaloyirou had said, that Koustas owned only one team, officially Triton, but that he ruled the roost in the Third Division. Now a second team had come to light with Koustas as its hidden owner. As I was reflecting on this, another idea occurred to me. Perhaps Greekinvest sponsored Koustas' other teams too.

'I want the keys to Greekinvest,' I said to Loukia. 'We have to search the company's offices.'

'Go ahead, search them, but I don't have the keys.'

'Look,' I said to her, 'don't make things any worse. Right now I'm asking you to help me. If I don't get it I can get a warrant and break down the door.'

'Go ahead, break it down,' she said. 'By all means set fire to it, why don't you? Konstantinos never gave me any keys. Whatever papers he wanted me to sign he sent to the house.'

It occurred to me that we had not found any keys at Petroulias' place either. If he had had any, they would have been taken by those who searched the place before we got there.

'Inspector.' Kosmas Karamitris stopped me as I made to leave. 'What will happen if during your investigations you come up with the cheques with my name on them?' Despite his expressionless look, his tone betrayed his anxiety.

'When we're through, they'll find their way to the rightful heirs.'

'To his children, you mean. Who knows, perhaps things will change now,' he said. 'I'll divorce their mother and in exchange they'll give me back the cheques.'

'Don't be in too much of a hurry,' she replied. 'My kids don't even want to see me dead after the way I treated them.'

Niki yes, Makis no, but she did not know that. 'Where were you on the night that Koustas was murdered?' I asked Kosmas.

'When was he murdered?'

'On Tuesday 1 September, at two thirty in the morning.'

'At home with Loukia. We ate, watched a bit of TV and then went to bed.'

'Do you have a witness to verify that?'

'No,' he answered and I detected a faint smile behind his beard. 'But if I had known he was going to be murdered, I'd have asked a few friends round to celebrate.'

'Do you suspect Kosmas?' his wife cut in. 'Why would he murder Konstantinos? What did he have to gain by it? Even now that he's dead, he still has the debt hanging round his neck.'

Yes, but the debt apart, he had found himself the owner of a football team and his wife the owner of Greekinvest. I bit my tongue and decided to say nothing. I first wanted to search the company's offices, to find out what other teams Koustas owned in what other people's names before reaching any conclusions.

Loukia Karamitris came with me to the door to show me out. 'Your son came to see you and you sent him away,' I said as she opened the door for me.

She sighed. 'It happened three or four times after our meeting with Konstantinos and I was afraid,' she replied. 'I thought it might be one of Konstantinos' tricks to test me.'

'If you hadn't been afraid of your former husband, would you have let the boy in? Would you have spoken to him?'

She thought for a moment and then shrugged. 'I don't know. Perhaps.' She paused again. 'They were never my kids,' she said as if wanting to justify herself to me. 'Makis and Niki were both Konstantinos' kids. Even their names. Makis was given the name of Konstantinos' father and Niki of his mother. It never occurred to him to name one of them after my parents. He never even discussed it, because he considered them his alone. I just gave birth to them.'

Two blocks away, in a street named after Venizelos, another victim of local community associations, I found a taxi to take me to the police station in Nea Erythraia to collect the Mirafiori. During the journey I tried to decide whether what I had learned from Karamitris and her husband belonged with the billion-drachma business of the BMW owner or with the truck driver's rotting fish.

CHAPTER 37

The first thing I did when I got back to Alexandras Avenue was to summon Vlassopoulos and Dermitzakis.

'Get a warrant to search the premises of Greekinvest,' I told Vlassopoulos. 'Call the public prosecutor and get his approval on the phone. They can send the papers later.' Not that we would find anyone at the offices of Greekinvest to show it to.

'When are we going there to search the place?'

'As soon as you've got the word from the prosecutor. And arrange for a locksmith to come with us.'

'Shall I come along to help?' Dermitzakis asked. 'I've nothing pressing.' He was afraid we might come up with something and that he wouldn't get his name in print.

'I've another job for you. Call the Football Federation and have them fax us a list of all the owners of teams in the Third Division. I want it now. If they start being difficult, put pressure on them.'

He didn't care for the division of labour, but he said nothing. Normally, I should have been banging my head against the wall for having waited for Karamitris to open my eyes and for not having asked to see the list of owners earlier. Of course, it wasn't going to be easy for us to locate the fronts used by Koustas, but we would go through the names one by one in the hope of coming up with something.

It occurred to me that I ought to inform Ghikas, but I decided to leave it until later. It was better to finish first with the search at Greekinvest's offices and then present him with the whole bed of roses. My mistake up to now had been my hastiness. Perhaps the fact that I had not been assigned to both cases from the very start was to blame. Petroulias' murder had not been discovered for three months and not at the place where it had happened. And I had been bequeathed Koustas' murder by Anti-Terrorist only after they had decided that it did not suit them. Though again, perhaps the fact that I had been searching in the dark was to blame. I had had nothing to go on and in my efforts to find a lead I had proceeded in stops and starts. But if I had some excuse for that mistake, I could not forgive myself at all for the next one. I should have investigated which other teams in the Third Division were owned by Koustas. The more teams he had, the more involved he was with Petroulias. Thank God I had thought of questioning Niki and Makis about their mother and I had found out about Elena Koustas. Of course, it might have been just hot air on Makis' part, but if it were true, then I had committed another blunder: I had allowed my liking for Elena Koustas to get the better of me.

Having made three mistakes, I decided to take it step by step from now on. Because on the one hand the two cases were becoming clearer, on the other they were becoming more intertwined. It was clear now that Koustas and Petroulias had been hand in glove. But that was also the problem. Why did Koustas need Petroulias? To fix Triton's matches? He could have simply greased his palm each time. Why have him as a front at Greekinvest to fund his team, given that both businesses belonged to him? Why take the money from one pocket to put it into the other? As if he had got the idea from the public sector, where the State pays taxes and contributions to itself. The only explanation was the one Kelesidis had come up with – tax evasion. But why would he involve his ex-wife and her husband? To take revenge on them? If he had not enlisted Loukia Karamitris after Petroulias' death, I might possibly have believed that. He had kept her on ice for years to be able to use her in time of need, as he had done. It was not revenge that was eating at him. Koustas, at least as I pictured him through the descriptions of his daughter, his son and his two wives, was a cool customer, not prone to passions. His game was elsewhere – but where? Perhaps searching the offices of Greekinvest would provide me with the answer. That's why I decided to wait.

Vlassopoulos poked his head round the half-open door. 'We're all set to go.'

'The locksmith?'

'He'll meet us there.'

We took a patrol car rather than the Mirafiori. We made the journey in silence. I didn't know what Vlassopoulos was thinking. Perhaps he wasn't thinking of anything, but on seeing me pensive didn't want to disturb my thoughts. My mind was still on Koustas' relationship with Petroulias, his ex-wife and her husband. If Koustas' murder hadn't been the work of professionals, then Karamitris and her husband were the only ones to have any reason for bumping him off. The story they'd told me was no doubt true. They knew that I could have easily verified it and they wouldn't have lied to me. They did not kill Petroulias because they did not know him. Just as Petroulias most certainly did not know Loukia Karamitris. Koustas had kept them apart and had used them according to his needs. But after Petroulias' murder was in the news, they might have learned who he was and grabbed at the chance of a lifetime. They bumped off Koustas so that Greekinvest together with R.I. Hellas would pass into Loukia Karamitris' hands, and her husband would remain the owner of Jason. Even if the cheques turned up, they could settle with their holders from a position of strength.

'What are we looking for?' Vlassopoulos said as we turned into Mitropoleos Street.

'What are we usually looking for when we investigate, Vlassopoulos?' I said testily, because he had interrupted a line of thought that I liked a great deal and it was as though he had woken me from a pleasant dream.

'I mean, are we looking for something in particular?'

'No. We'll take whatever we find, just like in the sales.'

Greekinvest's offices were in Fokianos Street, number 18. The locksmith was already waiting for us outside. We entered the premises through the open front door and began searching the names on the doorbells. We did not have to search for long. The doorbell on the left-hand door on the ground floor bore the name of 'Greekinvest'. The locksmith glanced at the lock. It took him no more than a minute to open the door and we entered a flat that was pitch dark because all the shutters were down. Vlassopoulos opened one of them and the dull light from the window lit up a small two-roomed flat. There was no hallway and the door opened directly into one of the rooms. Next to it was the kitchen. At the end was another room and a tiny bathroom. In the first room were a desk, a chair and a cupboard fixed to the wall. A basic workspace. On the desk was an electric typewriter and a telephone and fax machine. The other room was empty and smelled musty from being shut up. In the kitchen there were no cups, no glasses, not even a gas ring for making coffee. It was the same in the bathroom: just a roll of toilet paper, no soap or towel.

'We'll be through in a quarter of an hour,' said Vlassopoulos, and I was filled with disappointment.

It was clear from the first glance that Greekinvest had no staff, just like all bogus companies. Whoever came here stayed just as long as it took them to write a letter or to send a fax and then left. The desk drawers were not locked and why would they be? They had nothing to hide. The first contained Greekinvest headed paper; the second contained some pens and an ink cartridge for the typewriter and the third was empty.

The locksmith went over to the cupboard, which was locked, and set about opening it. Vlassopoulos remained standing in the middle of the room watching us, having nothing to do. The cupboard had three drawers. In the first I found files. The one on top was marked R.I. Hellas. I took it over to the desk, sat down and opened it. Since I had finished with the cupboard, Vlassopoulos began looking through the other drawers to pass his time.

The first document I picked up was a letter dated 26 August 1995 and signed by Karamitris, saying that the funding of Triton would continue for the following year. Underneath, I found a copy of the original fax concerning the sponsorship that had been sent to Arvanitakis and signed by Petroulias. As I dug deeper, I found a batch of letters that were requests for popularity ratings for a number of politicians. The name of the former minister whose popularity rating was greater than that of his party leader appeared three times. The last request had been in August and was signed by Karamitris. It must have been the request that Niki Koustas had been working on when I visited her the first time at R.I. Hellas' offices. I came across the names of two more politicians. They were both well-known politicians and active in Parliament, which meant that they were both frequent speakers on radio and TV. Each of the other requests for ratings had been signed by Petroulias.

'Inspector.' I turned and saw Vlassopoulos with a pile of ledgers. 'The company's books,' he said.

There was no point in me looking through them, because I would not understand a line of them. 'Take them and we'll get them checked,' I said and went back to the R.I. Hellas file.

Why had Koustas instructed R.I. Hellas to carry out polls on politicians? I mean, that was what the firm did, but opinion-poll firms usually get requests from parties, newspapers and TV channels. What was Koustas' interest in these particular politicians? Arvanitakis hadn't said anything to me about getting requests for opinion polls from Petroulias or Karamitris. Another mystery, I thought to myself, but not one I could solve there and then and so I put the file to one side.

I took the other two files from the cupboard. One was marked 'Athletico'. It didn't take me long to discover that it was a sports shop in a shopping mall in Maroussi. A sports shop hidden away in a shopping mall wouldn't even make enough to pay the rent. Even I knew that, though I hate sports and shopping. I began leafing through the file and came across a fax identical to the one that R.I. Hellas had received concerning the funding of Triton. Except that Athletico had been instructed by Petroulias to sponsor Jason, the team that Koustas had entrusted to Kosmas Karamitris.

The third file was marked 'Wall of China', a Chinese restaurant in Livadia. Who on earth would open a Chinese restaurant in the provinces? People in Livadia fast during Lent by eating souvlaki – they weren't suddenly going to get a craving for Chinese noodles. I suspected that here too I would find instructions to fund some football team and I was right. This time it was Proteus, the Livadia team. I didn't know who the owner was, but it wouldn't be difficult to find out. And in the case of both Jason and Proteus the instructions were identical to those concerning Triton. The sponsorships were provided by Greekinvest. Proteus, Jason, Triton and the imitation caryatids in his garden in Glyfada. It seemed that Koustas had a thing about antiquity.

I put these files aside too and once more sank into deep thought. How much did I have to go on? First, that by means of Petroulias and Karamitris, Koustas secretly controlled Greekinvest. Second, that Greekinvest openly controlled R.I. Hellas, the Athletico sports shop and the Wall of China restaurant. Third, that all three sponsored teams were, directly or indirectly, controlled by Koustas. I suddenly felt that I was in a vicious circle. I had started out with Koustas at Greekinvest and had ended up with Koustas by way of the Third Division. I could not believe that tax evasion was the only reason for all this recycling.

'Bring the ledgers and the files and let's be on our way,' I said to Vlassopoulos.

If there were something behind all this, we would only find out from the books. And that's why I would need an expert, but before going to an expert, I would have to get Ghikas' approval. I was afraid that before long I'd find myself back in Ouzounidis' hands.

CHAPTER 38

I got into the lift with Vlassopoulos, but we parted at the third floor, he to go to his office, I to continue to the fifth.

'What shall I do with these?' he asked, indicating the books and the correspondence from Greekinvest that he was carrying.

'Lock them up in your office and I'll let you know.'

After, that is, I had seen Ghikas to find out just how far I could go in untangling the web of Koustas' businesses. Until now, he had found ways of putting the brakes on me, but now I had evidence that he could not overlook without compromising himself. I had been wondering why he had kept putting obstacles in my way, but the letters to do with the politicians' popularity ratings explained everything. I still did not know what the purpose of these had been, but Ghikas' constipation most certainly was caused by this and the purgative I was about to present him with was not going to be to his liking.

In the outer office, I was greeted by Koula with a friendly 'Good afternoon', garnished with a big smile.

'What, still here? Not gone yet?' I said, unable to master my surprise. It was clumsy on my part, as though I were in a hurry to be rid of her, but I still had in my head the image of her crying and collecting her things together.

'I'm not going,' she said. 'Someone else has gone.' And as confirmation, she stretched out the fingers on her hand to show me that she was no longer wearing an engagement ring.

'What on earth happened?'

'I sent him packing. I can't say I was keen on getting hooked to a con man who used my name in his dirty dealings. Mr Ghikas was right.'

'You mean the Chief told you to break up with him?' I couldn't believe my ears. Since when had Ghikas ever concerned himself with our personal lives? He had not even come by the hospital to see how I was and now suddenly he was worried about Koula's future?

'He didn't tell me to break up,' she said. 'He simply said that if I wanted to get on in the Force, it wasn't enough that I was clean, the people around me had to be clean too. I thought about it and decided it was better for me to break up with Sakis rather than get transferred to some suburban station and end up making coffee for the sergeant.'

'How long were you together?'

'Five years.'

'And didn't it hurt you, Koula, to break up? Weren't you in love with him?'

'Does it matter that I'm more in love with my work?' she said coquettishly. 'If I were to leave here, when would I find a post like this again? Whereas I can find as many men as I want. Fortunately, there's no shortage.'

Just look how Ghikas had turned my advice to his own advantage, I thought. He not only got her to break up, but he also made sure she would be in her office till nine at night given that now she wouldn't be running off early to see her fiancé. Love, engagement, confetti: all were gone – without even a commemorative photograph.

I caught Ghikas doing one of the two things he does to fill his day: sitting in his chair or talking on the phone. He was doing the latter and I waited for him to finish. I knew he wouldn't be long, not because he was polite and didn't want to keep his subordinates waiting, but because he had a strange sense of secrecy and he didn't want others listening to his conversation. And I wasn't wrong; in less than fifteen seconds he had put down the phone.

'What news is there?' he said.

I began my report with Karamitris and her husband, then told him of the search at Greekinvest's offices, the businesses that Koustas had owned and the funding he had been providing to teams he controlled. I left until last the opinion polls for politicians carried out by R.I. Hellas on Koustas' instructions. Ghikas was not particularly tall and he seemed to shrink as my report went on. When I got to the bit about the popularity polls, only his head was visible behind his desk, confirming my suspicions that pressure was being put on him by politicians.

'I don't intend investigating the politicians,' I said and I watched him sit up again in his chair. 'After all, R.I. Hellas is an opinion-poll firm and it's quite natural that they should carry out polls for politicians.'

'Quite right.' His relief poured out in those two words. 'Though I don't like all that mess with Koustas' businesses. Usually, when you don't want to have everything in your name, you put it in your wife's name or your kids' names. He used a football referee, his ex-wife and the ex-wife's husband, although they loathed each other.'

I clenched my fists so as not to rub my hands with delight. I had got him exactly where I wanted. 'He may have done it for tax reasons,' I said in order to play things down. 'We might find out if we investigate his books. But I need a specialist for that.'

'What kind of specialist?'

'Someone from the Association of Chartered Accountants.'

He heaved a sigh. 'If we get involved with the Association of Chartered Accountants, tomorrow it'll be the talk of the town and his heirs will be screaming their heads off on TV. I'm not saying that Koustas was a major businessman, but he did have eight or nine companies. The time's long gone when you had to be a mogul to come out and speak. Now every kiosk owner has a statement to make about chewing gum.'

He wasn't wrong, but I had his sedative ready. 'I could do it discreetly. I can hand it over to a tax officer I know. He's smart and trustworthy.'

'All right,' he said, satisfied again. 'Let's see what the books throw up and then we'll decide how to take it from there. And don't let Karamitris' husband out of your sight. He may be the solution to our problem,' he called after me.

'I don't intend to.'

On my desk I found the list of the owners of the Third Division teams. I looked for Jason first. Owner: Kosmas Karamitris. Somewhere in the middle, my eyes fell on the name Proteus. A surprise was waiting for me in the adjacent column. Owner: Renos Hortiatis. Well, well, the manager of the Bouzouki Strings nightclub was the owner of a football team in Livadia that was funded by Greekinvest through the Wall of China, a local Chinese restaurant. And yet, if you thought about it, it wasn't all that strange. Koustas had given his second team to Karamitris, someone he had in the palm of his hand, and his third team to Hortiatis, someone he could trust. I suddenly recalled a scene from my visit to the Bouzouki Strings. Makis yelling at Hortiatis that he would get rid of him and Hortiatis laughing hysterically. At the time, I had wondered why Hortiatis had laughed. Now I knew. He laughed because he was sitting pretty. Even if Makis got rid of him, he would still collect the funding from the Wall of China now that Koustas was dead.

I picked up the phone and called Kelesidis at home. 'How long do you need to check a company's books?'

'It depends on the company and their books.'

'An investment company, an opinion-poll firm, a sports shop, two nightclubs, two restaurants and two football clubs.'

'Has it got to do with that football team whose books I saw? Triton, wasn't it?'

'Yes.'

'A month working an eight-hour day, without overtime.'

There was no way I could drag the two cases out for a month until the checking was complete. 'All right, let's do it another way. Let's start with the investment company's books and see where that leads us.'

There was a silence and then I heard him say in a somewhat strained voice: 'I can't check the books of companies that belong to other tax offices, Inspector. It's not the same as my coming once, unofficially, to help you. What you're asking is a breach of regulations.'

'What if you're instructed by the Ministry of Finance?'

'That would change things.'

'OK, I'll arrange it. You be at my office at Security Headquarters at nine o'clock in the morning. And say nothing to anyone.'

Manos Kartalis, my second cousin, was amused when I told him that I needed Kelesidis again. 'You'll end up taking him from the tax office to the police force,' he said. 'But, I'll take care of it.'

I looked at my watch. It was already seven o'clock. I wanted to question Hortiatis that night. There was no point in my going home.

It was better that I went early to the Bouzouki Strings so that I could speak to Hortiatis before it got too noisy.

I called Adriani and told her not to expect me for supper.

'So you're working all night again?' she said sourly.

'I'm not going to be all night. I'll be home by midnight at the latest. After all, Ouzounidis told me to work normally.'

'And so you decided to change jobs and become a nightwatchman,' she said sarcastically and hung up.

CHAPTER 39

Three days of thunder and lightning had given way to a light drizzle, which didn't justify the wear and tear on the windscreen wipers. It was nine o'clock and I was trundling slowly from the lights of Panepistimiou Street towards the darkness of Omonia Square. The motorbikes and cars were jostling around the worksite for the new underground station.

Aghiou Konstantinou Street had shed the mountains of rubbish it had had the first time I was at the Bouzouki Strings. On the corner of Menandrou Street, in front of St Constantine's, two shady types were huddled together, presumably dealing in dope. Either the patrol car in front of me did not see them or simply did not attach any importance to them, like me, because no police officer stops to pick up pushers and junkies without having been specifically instructed to indulge in what would be a pointless exercise.

In Athinon Avenue the traffic was heavy, the lane going towards Skaramangas full of lorries, the lane towards Athens full of coaches. The drizzle had worsened and it took me half an hour to get to the Bouzouki Strings. I found the space where Koustas parked his car empty and I parked in it.

Madas' place at the door had been taken by a tall, sallow-faced fellow.

'Is Mr Hortiatis here?' I said.

'Why do you want him?'

'Never you mind why I want him. Is he here? I ask, you answer.' The 'I ask, you answer', was the code to let him know that I was police.

'Go on in,' he said, opening the door for me.

The place had not changed from the previous time. The same liver-coloured upholstery and the lame baklava slices, the same arrangement of the tables and chairs. The only thing missing was the singer licking the microphone. The girl at the bar was busy, as ever, shining the glasses.

'Where can I find Mr Hortiatis?' I asked her.

'He's in his office,' she said, looking at her face in the glass that shone like a mirror.

'And where is his office?'

'Third door on the left down the corridor.' And she pointed to the doorway, which I knew from my previous visit.

I glanced into the dressing room used by Kalia or Kalliopi, but it was empty. I knocked on the third door on the left and before hearing 'Come in', I was already inside. Renos Hortiatis jumped up and held out his hand. The action was mechanical. Whenever he saw anyone, he held out his hand, as though he had been working for years on the Athens–Lamia toll road.

'Inspector! What brings you here?'

'I need some clarification concerning Konstantinos Koustas' business activities.'

'Do have a seat.'

We both sat down and I left him looking at me for a moment so that he could get used to me. 'Mr Hortiatis, are you the owner of a football team called Proteus?'

He was disconcerted, but soon recovered his bonhomie. 'Are you a football fan, Inspector?'

'I wasn't, but your late boss has made me one and the way I'm going, I'll probably end up a hooligan. Are you the owner of Proteus?'

'I am.'

'And Proteus is a team in Livadia?'

'I'm from Thessaloniki originally, but I grew up in Livadia. I came to Athens when I got out of the army.'

'Is that why you started a team in Livadia? Because you grew up there?'

'I didn't start it. It already existed, but it had reached rock bottom. I decided to buy it and help it to get back on its feet, so that Livadia would have a team to be proud of, albeit in the Third Division.'

'So that is why you became involved, or was it perhaps because the Wall of China restaurant, which funded your team, was also in Livadia?'

He smiled and answered without batting an eyelid. 'It's only natural, Inspector, that a team from Livadia would find a sponsor in Livadia. It's not going to find one in Athens.'

'Did you know that the Wall of China belonged to Koustas?'

This time his surprise looked genuine. 'No, I did not.'

'And it wasn't Koustas who proposed the restaurant to you as a sponsor?'

'No,' he replied again. 'As far as I know, they came of their own accord. They said that since we were a Livadia team, they would like to be our backers.'

'What was the amount of the sponsorship?'

'One hundred and twenty million a year.'

And another 240 to Triton gave us a grand total of 360,000. Now, all I needed was for Kelesidis to tell me the amount paid to Jason, Karamitris' team.

He wasn't lying, but he was giving me only half the truth. Koustas had no reason to reveal to him that he was involved in the Chinese restaurant. He had told whoever was in charge to approach Hortiatis and that's what he had done.

'What hold did Koustas have over you?' I asked him abruptly.

'What do you mean?'

'Proteus didn't belong to you, did it, Mr Hortiatis? It belonged to Koustas. You were no more than a front.'

'Wrong,' he barked in his shrill voice and sprang up. 'The team is mine, in my name.'

'It may be in your name, but behind you was Koustas.'

'Definitely not. My relationship with Koustas was completely above board.'

'And just what was the nature of that relationship?'

So far, he had managed very well, but now would begin the humming and hawing. 'When I was considering buying Proteus, I didn't have the money and Koustas offered to lend it to me.'

'And you paid him back?'

He avoided my gaze. 'No. In point of fact when he saw that I was in trouble, he suggested that he should become a silent partner in the team and so even up our accounts like that.' He looked at me again. 'It's not against the law for me to have a silent partner. There are businessmen who silently control a dozen businesses.'

'Keep calm, Mr Hortiatis, no one's accusing you of anything. What was his percentage of the partnership?'

The evasiveness threatened to return, but then he said: 'At first it was 25 per cent. By the time he died it had reached 60.'

'Why? Had he lent you more money?'

'No, but he funded my buying of new players.'

He had been saved by pure chance, I thought. If Koustas had not been killed, he would have got total possession of the team and Hortiatis would have remained as owner in name only. Now that I had three different cases before me, I could see more clearly the different tactics that Koustas used in order to acquire partners. He had one relationship with Petroulias, who was obviously dependable, one with Hortiatis, who was his employee, and a different one again with his ex-wife and her husband, who were his enemies. The only common denominator was the recycling of money. What had seemed to me to be a vicious circle at first was but the revolving movement of a laundry machine. Koustas was laundering money; it was the only solution that made sense. If my suspicion was confirmed, then we would be closer to the conclusion that both Petroulias and Koustas had been murdered by professionals. The Anti-Terrorist Squad had been right in one thing, except that it was not racketeers who had killed Koustas, but organised crime. My heart sank because I knew that the bird had flown. I could uncover the whole case, but I would end up only with a blank.

'That's all I wanted to ask you. We're finished,' I said to Hortiatis and I got to my feet. In his mechanical way, he held out his hand to me. I shook it and left.

As I was passing her dressing room, I saw Kalia putting on her make-up.

'How are things, Kalia?' I asked her.

She stopped what she was doing and looked at my reflection in the mirror. It took her a few seconds to remember who I was. 'The inspector, right?' she said.

'The inspector,' I confirmed and went in. 'What was it Koustas wanted from you on the night he was murdered?' I hadn't swallowed what she'd told me about his having threatened her because she did not look sexy enough on stage.

She shrugged. 'What would he want from a girl like me? At most, he might ask me to open my legs for him, but he didn't have to. He could find much prettier girls than me if he wanted.'

'You told me he'd threatened to have you mopping up because you didn't swing your hips enough.'

'If that's what I said, that's the way it was.'

'That's not the way it was. It was something else, wasn't it? What was it, Kalia?'

'Look, I don't remember what I said to you or what Koustas said to me. Now leave me alone because I have to get ready.'

And she turned back to the mirror. I could have marched her down to headquarters and leaned on her, but what good would that do? What I had found out about Koustas was enough for me to understand what kind of operation he had going. In any case, he wouldn't have said anything remotely useful about his dealings with the underworld to Kalia.

Leaving her dressing room, I bumped into Makis, in his cowboy outfit. I wondered whether he ever sent it to the cleaner's. His fiery gaze fixed itself on me.

'Well, did you look into what I told you about my mother-in-law?' he said.

'Since when did you start telling me what to do?'

I got home at a quarter to twelve, a quarter of an hour earlier than the time I had set for myself. Adriani was sitting in front of the TV. Usually she went to bed at around eleven.

'Why aren't you in bed?'

'I thought I'd wait for you, in case you wanted something to eat.'

I asked her to fix me a snack just to keep her from feeling annoyed that she'd waited up pointlessly.

CHAPTER 40

Before leaving that morning, I arranged with Katerina to meet in the afternoon so we could talk. She suggested we went to the Morocco, because it was close to Security Headquarters, but my mind went immediately to the academic-*cum*-greengrocer crying his eyes out and I was afraid it might have an effect on me. In the end, we settled on the Magic Flute, at six.

Kelesidis arrived at headquarters at nine thirty. I met him at the entrance and immediately locked him in the interrogation room. I served him up with Greekinvest's books, together with the bank accounts and for dessert I gave him Petroulias' tax declaration.

I left him looking greedily at the books and went up to my office. I took pencil and paper and began to draw up a table, in the hope that it would help me to find the missing link between the businesses controlled by Koustas.

BUSINESSES OWNED BY KOUSTAS
Bouzouki Strings
Night Flower
Canard Doré
Triton FC – sponsor R.I. Hellas

BUSINESSES OWNED BY GREEKINVEST
R.I. Hellas
Athletico (sports goods)
Wall of China (restaurant)

BUSINESSES OWNED BY KARAMITRIS
Phonogram – no connection with Koustas except for loan
Jason FC – sponsor Athletico

BUSINESSES OWNED BY RENOS HORTIATIS
Proteus FC (Koustas 60 per cent ownership) – sponsor Wall
of China

At first sight, nothing seemed to link Koustas' businesses with Greekinvest, Karamitris' businesses or Hortiatis' football team. The only link was the sponsoring, but that, too, was a weak one. R.I. Hellas' sponsoring of Triton linked R.I. Hellas, and consequently Greekinvest, with Koustas, but there was nothing to link him with Greekinvest's other businesses, just as there was nothing to link him with the businesses owned by Karamitris or Hortiatis. I would ask Kelesidis, but I was certain that if some tax inspector were to carry out a check on any of the above businesses, it would be impossible for him to find the link that led to the others and with Koustas as the final recipient. And moreover, all the businesses operated legally, so he wouldn't be able to find the least irregularity. All right, perhaps the amount of funding they gave to Third Division teams was large, but it was their money and they could do what they liked with it. However, the tax inspector's weakness was my own weakness. If he was laundering money, how was he doing it? Through sponsoring his team and Karamitris' and Hortiatis'? If I were to add it all up, it came to around 500 million a year. Had he set up this whole network of businesses to launder 500 million, which was peanuts in money-laundering terms? I looked at my table, but I could get nowhere and all my hopes were now resting on Kelesidis, even though I wasn't going to tell him: he would get above himself.

The door opened and in walked Sotiropoulos. He no longer knocked, he walked straight in like it was his home. I made a note to have a key made for him so he could get in when I was out.

'What do you want?' I asked sharply to take the wind out of his sails, at the same time taking out a blank sheet of paper to cover the table before he got to my desk.

'I want you to give me something new. From the day you gave us Koustas' doorman, everybody in here has clammed up.'

'There's nothing new. When something comes up, you'll hear about it.'

He stared at me with a look full of suspicion. 'You're not being straight with me,' he said. 'You're up to something and you're keeping it from me. I'll be forced to go on the air and say that the police are deliberately keeping the public in the dark.'

'You can say we've come up against a Byzantine wall that not even dynamite can bring down.'

A smile spread over his face and his satisfaction made him forget his suspicion. 'I told you you'd land yourself in a mess with Koustas. Everybody knows that he was mixed up in various rings, but he was a crafty devil and no one could get anything on him. And Petroulias?' He stopped suddenly and his suspicions returned. 'Well? Do you think the two cases are connected after all? Perhaps you were right and not Nassioulis?'

I was in a difficult position because I couldn't reveal to him that the two cases were not only connected, but in fact related by blood. Fortunately, I was saved by the internal line. I lifted the receiver and heard Kelesidis' voice.

'Inspector, can you come down here for a moment. I think I've found something.'

'Ghikas wants me,' I said to Sotiropoulos, putting down the phone and getting up in a rush.

'You didn't answer me. Are the two cases connected after all?'

'I told you, we haven't come up with anything.'

He screwed up his face, but I didn't give a monkey's. The lift was playing its tricks again. It went up to the fourth floor, changed its mind and continued going up. I wasn't in the right mental state to take a patience test, so I got out and began going down the stairs two at a time. I tried to imagine what Kelesidis could have found that had escaped me, but then again he was a tax officer; he saw companies and money with a different eye.

Kelesidis was in the interrogation room with all the books spread out around him. 'What have you found?' I asked.

He was so absorbed that he raised his head almost in alarm. He saw that it was me and smiled. 'A mill,' he said. 'At a rough estimate, I'd say that Koustas was laundering about three billion a year. Of course, in order to confirm it, I'll need to see the books of his nightclubs and compare them with the bank accounts. But I don't think I'm far out.'

'What do you expect to find from making a comparison?'

'Let's start at the beginning – from the sponsoring.'

'I realised that myself,' I cut in. 'He was laundering around 500 million a year. So that leaves another two and a half billion roughly. How was he laundering that?'

'The 500 million was half the profits from Greekinvest's businesses. The other half went into its coffers, but Greekinvest never showed any profit.'

'How come?'

'Because every year Greekinvest took a loan for around 500 to 750 million from an account at the Ionian Bank. I'm certain that the amount of the loan came from dirty money and it channelled this into its subsidiary companies in the form of funding for sponsorship. At the end of the year the loan had been paid off from the legal profits of Greekinvest's subsidiary companies and it was renewed for the following year. It took out loans in dirty money and paid them off with legal money, apart from the sponsorship funding it received, also legally, through the football teams. I don't know who the account at the Ionian Bank belongs to, but I'm sure that if you open it, you'll find Koustas behind it. Add to that another 150 million that he laundered through the State.'

I gazed at him like a moron. 'What are you saying? That the State laundered money for him?'

'Every team in the Third Division gets around fifty million a year from the State. All official and above board. Times three, that comes to 150.'

'And the rest? How did he launder that?'

Kelesidis smiled at me with the look of a teacher opening his pupil's eyes. 'That's why I need the books of the nightclubs and his bank accounts. And I can tell you what I expect to find. His establishments, like all establishments, should show a regular turnover. But some days that turnover would be trebled and quadrupled. That means that on those days Koustas made out false receipts, artificially increasing the takings in order to present the dirty money as part of the establishments' income and launder it.'

'But he paid taxes on it.'

'Who told you that there's no cost attached to dirty money?' he replied laughing. 'Those he was laundering the money for would have paid the taxes as well as giving a cut to Koustas. If he was on 25 per cent, which is reasonable, then he was making 750 million a year untaxed apart from the legal profits from his clubs.'

I listened to him and I could have kicked myself. If I hadn't been in so much of a hurry to take a quick look at Koustas' accounts and I'd had them opened properly, I would have picked up the thread much sooner. Suddenly, Koustas' accounts made me think of another detail from Petroulias' tax declaration.

'How did Petroulias get away with not declaring even a penny from Greekinvest?' I asked.

'Because he wasn't receiving any salary as manager of the company. As soon as a company doesn't show any profit, why would anyone check the manager's tax declaration? But there's still something I don't understand –' Kelesidis broke off, picked up Petroulias' bank statement and began thumbing through it. 'It's easy for me to locate the dirty money that he was getting from Koustas. I can see deposits sometimes of one million, sometimes three million, sometimes five million . . . Those are from Koustas. But suddenly there's a deposit of 150 million. It's the only one and I can't understand how it suddenly went up to that amount.'

'When was the deposit made?' I asked.

'On 25 May.' He seemed surprised at my concern.

My legs went from under me and I collapsed into the chair. 'Look at when Greekinvest made the payments on the loan to the Ionian Bank.'

He looked, then raised his head in amazement. 'Usually at the end of every month,' he said. I don't know what amazed him: the discovery he had made or my brilliance, but if it was the latter, he was mistaken.

Now I knew who had had Petroulias killed: it was Koustas himself. The argument between Petroulias and Koustas that the Nigerian had overheard after the match hadn't been about the penalty, but about something much more important. The penalty had simply ignited the fuse. Petroulias had wanted something from Koustas, or there had been something between them, and he had warned him that he would make it worse for him. That's what he had meant by the red card. And on 25 March, he had shown it to him. Instead of paying Greekinvest's payment on the loan, he had deposited the money in his own account. Koustas had found out and had had him done in. But who had killed Koustas? I didn't have time to think about it, because another thought came into my head, ousting the other.

'Koustas was laundering money for others and had to account to them,' I said to Kelesidis. 'So somewhere he would have to record what he received and what he paid out.'

'No doubt, but you'll have to find the second set of books for that.'

'What second set?'

Now it wasn't my brilliance that amazed him but my stupidity. 'Most companies keep two sets of books,' he replied. 'An official set that they use for the balance and for tax purposes, and a second set, an unofficial one, that gives the true picture, which the tax office doesn't learn about. If you find that second set, you'll find out how Koustas got hold of the money and how he returned it.'

'And where am I going to find this second set?'

He laughed. 'If it were so easy for the tax office to find, Inspector, half the businessmen around would be behind bars now.'

'All right. Keep going and I'll bring you the books from Koustas' clubs and his bank accounts,' I said, getting to my feet.

The Anti-Terrorist boys were idiots and I even more so for relying on what Elena Koustas had said and for not searching his house.

CHAPTER 41

This time we didn't take the coast road to Koustas' house in Glyfada, but went down Vouliagmenis Avenue. The drizzle was continuing for the second day in succession. It didn't look like turning into a downpour or clearing up. Just the odd drop every so often that got on your nerves. Like having a temperature of ninety-eight – neither one thing nor the other. Lousy weather.

'What do you want the wipers for?' I said to Dermitzakis. 'They're no help, they just obstruct your view.'

He turned them off and I got some peace, because I found them distracting and I couldn't think. In the end, what Nassioulis had said had proved to be prophetic. Koustas had set up a zone defence which was impossible to break through even after his death. You broke through the first line, which were his clubs, and you came up against Greekinvest. You broke through the line of Greekinvest and you found yourself facing Karamitris. You got past Karamitris and you ran into Hortiatis. And when you eventually managed to get past all of them, looming before you was the goalkeeper – his secret books and his mysterious underworld associates. And the ball had come to me and I could neither score nor pass it to anyone else. Who knows, maybe the Anti-Terrorist Squad and Ghikas had given it to me for that very reason, because they were sure that I wasn't going to break through Koustas' zone defence. I was on my way to search his house, but my initial enthusiasm had gone and I was doing it half-heartedly. A crafty old devil like him wouldn't have hidden his secret records at home. Once it was only the Foreign Office that had secret records and whenever anyone managed to get hold of a bit of paper, all hell broke loose. Now every Tom, Dick and Harry had secret records.

Koustas' house had the same look of Alcatraz that it had had on my first visit, but the similarities stopped there. I rang the bell, there was the sound of a click and the gate opened of its own accord. No security man and no Filipino maid cooking soya. In the garden, the few flowers were mournfully bowing their heads from lack of water and the caryatid copies had turned grey from the dirt, as if they had aged centuries.

The front door was closed so we rang again. The door suddenly opened with a 'Come on in, where've you been, dammit,' that belonged to Makis, but when he saw us, the wind was knocked out of him. He had a worried, distracted look and he was on edge. Evidently he was expecting his pusher to bring him his fix, but we had turned up and he was gripped by panic.

'What the fuck do you want again?' he shouted in a voice fluctuating between fear and despair.

'Calm down, Makis,' I said gently. 'We want to search the house, because we believe that your father hid some documents here and we need them.'

'You can't, I'm expecting company. You should have called.'

His company was his dealer. 'It won't take long. We'll search his office, that's all.'

He laughed. 'What office? My old man didn't have an office. Either here or anywhere else. He didn't want a permanent base, so that he'd be difficult to pin down.'

'Then we'll take a look round the house.'

He wasn't thrilled by the idea, but he didn't want any trouble with the police. 'Search all you want,' he said, going into the living room.

Everything in the living room was in a state of dissolution. There was an exhibition consisting of shirts, trousers and jackets draped over the sofa and armchairs. The two wooden chairs were now covered with wine bottles, whisky bottles and Coca-Cola cans, while lined up on the mantelpiece was a collection of various glasses. Makis collapsed into an armchair, on top of his clothes.

'Where's the staff?' I asked.

'Walked out,' he replied, his face suddenly beaming with satisfaction. 'My father and stepmother had them to spy on me.

Watchdogs in my own home to follow me all day, where I went, what I did, what I ate, what I drank. As soon as I'd got rid of Elena, I sent them packing too and found a bit of peace.' He said it with the delight of a child who has come of age and freed himself of one form of dependence in order to surrender himself body and soul to another.

'What other rooms are there on the ground floor?' I asked him.

'Dining room, kitchen and bathroom. Upstairs there are three bedrooms and two bathrooms. In the garden, next to the kitchen door, you'll find some steps leading down to the basement.'

'Let's start with the basement,' I said to Dermitzakis. If Koustas had had anything hidden in his house, he would most likely have put it there.

As we were going out again into the hallway, I saw a closed door facing me. I opened it and found myself in a dining room with heavy drapes. It seemed that Makis didn't use it because everything was in perfect order, like a museum with exhibits from the period of Elena Koustas. The table was large and rectangular, easily accommodating the ten chairs around it. The sideboard with its four cupboards covered the whole of the right-hand wall. Arranged on top of it was a collection of crystal: vases, plates and fruit bowls, while on the facing wall all the silverware was exhibited inside a glass case. There were three paintings – two portraits with a landscape between them – hung over the sideboard. The only blemish was the vase of flowers that had wilted, shedding the leaves all over the table.

The kitchen was next to the living room; it was large, spacious and nauseating. If Adriani had been with me, she would have fainted. The dirty plates were piled up in the sink, and on the marble surface to the right and left of the sink were various boxes with the remains of pizzas, greaseproof paper with bits of souvlaki, uneaten chips and the carcass of a roast chicken. Something like orange squash or Coca-Cola must have fallen on to the floor, because as soon as we took a step inside, our shoes stuck.

Once we were outside, we both began taking deep breaths to clean our lungs from the stench. There were only four steps leading down to the basement. The wooden door was unlocked, so we pushed it open and went in. The basement was darker than the house. Dermitzakis fumbled around and found the light switch. At least Makis hadn't forgotten to pay the electricity bill.

The basement spread out under the whole expanse of the house and was part wine cellar, part utility room. Against the wall on the left was a washing machine and a spin dryer. Beside these were two huge baskets, probably for the dirty clothes. Dermitzakis went over and took a look. He also opened the drum of the washing machine. He was simply doing his job and, as might have been expected, he found nothing. Leaning against the far wall were two bikes. The one must have been Niki's and the other Makis' from their childhood. On the right-hand side was the wine rack: four shelves with holes in order to keep the bottles flat with their necks pointing slightly upwards. I looked at the labels: they were all foreign, but not in English because I would have been able to pronounce them. Most likely, they were French. From the orders he placed for the Canard Doré, Koustas evidently took a few bottles home to drink in comfort. I went over to the wine rack. It was a frame with a plywood back that was up against the wall without being fixed to it.

'Help me to move it aside,' I said to Dermitzakis. If Koustas had a hideaway for his secret documents, this was the only spot where he could have built it.

'The bottles will fall out,' said Dermitzakis.

'Let them. The one who put them there doesn't need them any more and his son would do well to stop drinking.'

We got hold of the rack from both ends and tried to pull it away from the wall. It was so heavy we couldn't budge it. With a great deal of effort we managed to tip it forward slightly. The wall was green from the damp, and there were patches of mould here and there, but no safe or hideaway.

I took another look around, mostly to assure myself that there was nowhere else that Koustas could have hidden the books. 'Let's go,' I said to Dermitzakis. 'There's nothing here. The basement was our only hope. We'll search the bedrooms too, but I don't expect we'll find anything.'

The scene upstairs was the same as that on the ground floor.

Makis' bedroom was like a pigsty, and the other two were neat and tidy. We were in Koustas' bedroom looking in the drawers and under the mattress like two Hollywood detectives – who discredit the police force worldwide with their inanities – when Dermitzakis' beeper went off.

'It's from headquarters,' he said, and went into Makis' room where there was a telephone.

I went on searching, without reason and without success, until I heard Dermitzakis' voice from the next room.

'It's Vlassopoulos, Inspector, he wants a word with you.'

I felt almost relieved that I had an excuse to stop. 'Inspector, I've just had a call from Antonopoulos. Elena Koustas is at this moment in a flat in Kypseli. Antonopoulos is outside and he wants to know what he should do.'

'Stay outside and wait. Give me the address.'

'It's 4 Prinopoulou Street, second floor.'

'Let's go,' I said to Dermitzakis after hanging up. 'Besides, we won't find anything here.'

'Where are we going?'

'To Mrs Koustas' love nest: 4 Prinopoulou Street, Kypseli.'

As we went past the living room, I saw Makis sitting in the same chair and staring with glazed eyes at the wall facing him. If he saw us leaving, he certainly didn't show it.

CHAPTER 42

On the way back, Dermitzakis made use of the siren. It pierced my eardrums, but I put up with it because I wanted to catch Elena Koustas. Thanks to the siren, we were at Prinopoulou Street within three-quarters of an hour, but we got stuck at the top of the street because outside number 6, the block next to the one where Koustas was, two patrol cars and two ambulances had pulled up and a throng of idlers had gathered to watch. Antonopoulos was not outside the entrance to number 4 as agreed. I looked around for him and saw him next to the patrol cars, standing in front of the spectators. From the crowd rose the screams and screeches of a plump woman of around forty. Her fat arms were extended to the skies with clenched fists, then they plummeted down on to her head. Two paramedics carried a stretcher covered with a sheet from inside the entrance. The woman let out another scream and rushed towards the stretcher, but two police officers caught hold of her and held her back.

Antonopoulos saw me standing outside the entrance to number 4, turned his back on the spectacle and came running over.

'What happened?' I asked him.

'A family of Russo-Pontians in the basement. They went inside in broad daylight and killed them. Father, grandmother and two kids, all of them. Most likely the work of Russian mafia; the father was involved with drugs. The wife had gone to the supermarket and thereby saved her life. She's the one tearing her hair out.'

'And why did you leave your post?' I asked him once he had finished his unofficial report. 'Were they short of officers so you had to run and help?'

'I only went over for a moment to see what was happening.'

'And if Mrs Koustas had left in the meantime?' He had no answer to that one. 'Well, did she leave or not?' I kept on.

'I don't know.'

'It's your job to know.' Every day there were massacres with Albanians, Arabs, Russo-Pontians and anyone else who got in the way. It had reached the point where they no longer sent the cases to Security Headquarters; they were dealt with by the local police, who turned up then simply filed them with the others. Now we were standing and looking on literally as well as metaphorically. I went over to the entrance to read the names on the doorbells.

'She's on the second floor,' Antonopoulos said from behind me. 'The bell says Triandafyllidou. I've already checked it,' he added, pleased with himself.

'Good job you managed it before the Russo-Pontians let in their visitors.'

The front door was ajar. I pushed it and went inside. Dermitzakis followed, but I stopped him. 'You stay with Antonopoulos.' He looked at me with a grieved expression. 'There's no need for any drama, we're not the Vice Squad,' I explained to him. He stayed behind and I took the lift to the second floor.

I did not make him stay downstairs because I was afraid of any fuss, just that I did not want to embarrass Elena Koustas. I did not want anyone else to set eyes on her if I caught her in flagrante. The thought of it annoyed me, because I did not know what was making me give her the kid-glove treatment. Perhaps it was remorse for having taken her for a floozy when she had turned out to be a lady. But if I now found her with her lover, then my first impression would be confirmed and Elena Koustas/Fragakis would be a suspect for the murder of her husband. Nevertheless, I did not want to embarrass her. I put it down to my heart condition, just like Sotiropoulos, who was a sucker for easy solutions.

The flat with the name 'Triandafyllidou' was the last one on the right. I rang the bell and the door was opened by a white-haired woman in her sixties, dressed in grey and black – grey blouse, black skirt, grey stockings, black slippers, old-fashioned clothes from the time when we still called Maroussi Amaroussion. Our surprise was mutual, because she had not expected to be confronted by a stranger, nor I by a sixty-year-old woman in a love nest. Unless she rented out her flat. Rooms-to-let for love-nesting.

'What do you want?' she said.

'Inspector Haritos. I'd like to speak to Mrs Koustas.'

I watched the alarm in her eyes, but she quickly recovered. 'You've made a mistake. There's no Mrs Koustas here.'

'Listen, are you going to let me come in or do I have to use force?'

'Show the inspector in, Kaiti.' I heard Elena Koustas' voice from inside and my threat had gone to waste.

The woman stood aside and let me into the bare entrance hall. In a doorway on the left stood Koustas smiling at me. 'This way, Inspector,' she said.

I found myself in a sparsely furnished living room. A table and four chairs and an armchair in each of two corners was all the furniture there was. Sitting in a wheelchair next to the table was a young man. His head was leaning to one side, as though he were looking at the world askance. His mouth was half open and his tongue was resting on his lower lip. His gaze was fixed on a cuckoo clock on the wall he was facing. I stood there, taking him in, but he seemed not to have registered my presence. His hands were resting on his knees. He raised them, clapped twice and let them fall back again. Before long he raised them again, without taking his eyes off the clock, clapped twice and let them fall again. Behind me I heard the voice of Elena Koustas.

'My son,' she said. I was utterly astonished.

She smiled at me with a faint, bitter smile. The cuckoo sprang through its little door and let out a 'cuckoo, cuckoo' to mark the half-hour. Elena's son raised his hands again and clapped them four times on this occasion, letting out a cry of pleasure.

'You're surprised, aren't you?' Koustas said. 'No doubt you were expecting something else.'

'Yes.' How could I tell her that I'd been sent up the garden path by Makis and that I had come here certain that I would find her with her lover.

'There is nothing else, Inspector. This is Stefanos, my son. I had him when I was twenty-five. Now I'm exactly double his age.' She said all this calmly, almost blandly, as though she were making a statement.

'How did you find me here?' she said.

'We had some information that you were in the habit of leaving your house each Tuesday afternoon and returning late.' Putting it like that made it plain that we had been watching her, but I did not dare say so straight out.

'Who told you that?'

'I'm sorry, but I can't say.'

She smiled. 'I can easily guess,' she said. 'Niki had left home, my husband is dead, Serafina, my Filipino maid, never spoke to you. That leaves the guards and Makis.' She waited for my response, but I said nothing. 'It can only have been Makis,' she said. 'So, what did he tell you?'

There was no longer any point in my hiding it from her. 'That you went out every Tuesday afternoon to meet your lover.'

The bitter smile gave way to a bitter laugh. 'Poor Makis. Not that he was wrong. How could he ever imagine, not knowing anything? That was always his problem. He always set off on the right foot and ended up on the wrong one.'

'Did your husband know?'

'About Stefanos? Yes, from the very beginning. When he proposed to me, I told him that I wanted him to come home with me so that I could show him something. So he met Stefanos and I told him that he was illegitimate and disabled.'

Elena Koustas went over to her son and hugged him from behind. The young man did not feel the hug and paid no attention. His whole attention was fixed on the clock, but he was no longer clapping. Perhaps he realised that it would be some time before the cuckoo came out again or perhaps he had just got bored with it.

'And how did he react?'

'He told me it didn't matter to him.' She smiled again and repeated wryly: '"It doesn't matter to me," those were his words, as though it were some trivial detail. He told me to find a flat and a trustworthy woman to take care of Stefanos. He would deal with all the costs, but on one condition: that I agreed never to see him again.'

'And did you agree?'

'My first reaction was to say no. But then I thought that Stefanos would at least be secure for the rest of his life. Whereas with me and the kind of work I did, that wasn't guaranteed. I found Kaiti, a distant cousin of my mother, and I brought her here from Katerini to look after him.' Her voice had acquired a certain passion, as if she were belatedly justifying herself to her husband. 'But I couldn't bear not to see Stefanos,' she said. 'I managed it for six months, but my life was hell. One Tuesday afternoon, when I knew that Konstantinos would be going to his team's training session, I left the house and came to see him. I was terrified in case he found out. But he didn't and so, almost every Tuesday afternoon, I'd sneak out of the house, like a thief, and come here to see Stefanos.' She stopped to take a breath and smiled at me. 'Now you know everything, Inspector. There are no other secrets in my life.'

Now I knew everything, but it was of no use to me, apart from a bit of information that was of little importance. Either Koustas had already set up his money-laundering business from that time or he had been about to set it up. That's why he had wanted Elena to break off with her son. He had not wanted to be vulnerable with the work he was engaged in. And Elena's disabled child was a vulnerable spot that had to be erased from the face of the earth. He had not wanted to lose Elena, but nor had he wanted her incurable son to provide a target for threats and blackmail.

I held out my hand to Mrs Koustas. 'I'm sorry to have troubled you,' I said like a twerp, but I did not know what else to say.

'Goodbye, Inspector,' she replied. 'And now that you've learned everything, I hope you'll stop having me followed.'

It was said without reproach or spite, and that made me feel even more of a heel. I was overcome by a desire to explain to her, to tell her how ashamed I was for thinking so poorly of her and, at the same time, how I had hoped to be proven wrong and that what Makis had told me would not be true. But her bitterness that she knew how to turn into dignity, coupled with all the policeman's hang-ups that I had, left me speechless.

CHAPTER 43

I arrived at the Magic Flute half an hour late. I had passed it thousands of times, but it was the first time I had ever gone inside. The clientele were the highbrow type: architects, engineers, lawyers and the like. They seemed to realise, either from my look or my off-the-peg suit, that I was a policeman. They all turned and stared at me. I could not have cared less and I looked around for Katerina. I saw her sitting in the last of the booths lining the left-hand side of the place. She had a coffee in front of her. I sat down opposite her.

'I'm sorry I'm late,' I said.

'Never mind. I have a policeman for a father and I know that policemen usually arrive late on the scene.'

We both laughed and that made me feel somewhat more at ease, though, on the one hand, I didn't like the surroundings and, on the other, my mind was stuck on Koustas' secret books and, generally speaking, I wasn't in the best of moods. If I had known that morning that the rest of the day would go the way it had, I wouldn't have agreed to meet her. The waiter was standing over me and to get rid of him I ordered an orange juice.

'So, what do you want to talk about?' I asked her.

She didn't answer straight away. She played with her cup and looked at me. 'Before you arrived, I'd made up my mind exactly what I was going to say to you, I'd got everything worked out, but now I don't know where to begin,' she said with a faint smile.

'Begin where you want,' I said. 'Is it so difficult for you to talk to your dad?'

'Sometimes it is. And much more often, lately,' she murmured.

'Tell me. Whatever it is I'll listen to you and we'll talk about it. We could always talk about things.'

She again looked at me without saying anything, as though doubting my intentions. Then she sat up straight. 'OK. I want to ask you what you have against Fanis. Why do you behave to him like that?'

I was caught off guard. 'Me?' I said. 'How do I behave to him?'

'The other day when you went for the tests, the poor guy took one look at your expression and froze.'

'*My* expression? What about his own?'

'Don't shout.'

'Do you know how he treated me? Like someone on social benefit –'

'Don't shout.'

'– that the doctors want to get shot of as quickly as possible. He barely said good morning to me and spent more time looking at my tests than at me. In the end –'

'I said, don't shout.'

239

'– what he had to say he said to your mother, as though I were a child and he was talking to my guardian. And then he wonders about my expression. What did he want me to do, bow and scrape?'

'Please. Don't shout.'

Only then did I realise that I had raised my voice. The highbrow customers turned once again to look at me, but I was choking with indignation and I didn't give a damn.

'Dad, the night before, Fanis was looking forward to seeing you. But when you walked into the surgery, he saw the look on your face and froze.'

'Did he freeze with my look or I with his?'

'I don't know. I wasn't there to say. But I asked Mum and she said the same, that you had a look as though you wanted to –'

'What? To kill him?'

'No. To cuff him and take him down to headquarters. Fanis saw it and was afraid you might cause a scene and embarrass him in his own surgery.'

We looked at each other. I tried to bring Ouzounidis' expression to mind. Cold, professional, that of a doctor who does not let his patients even ask questions. Was it my expression that had caused his reaction, as Katerina had said, or was it his expression that had caused mine? Another case that would remain unsolved, like Koustas' murder. Firstly, because there was no mirror for me to see my expression and, secondly, because Adriani was biased in favour of Ouzounidis, so that he was bound to be right and I wrong.

'Do you know why I want to be with Fanis? Have you understood?' Katerina said.

'Because you've fallen in love with him. Just like you'd fallen in love with Panos.'

'Panos had to do with my moving to Thessaloniki. I'd just finished high school, it was my first time away from home, I was lonely and I needed someone to hold on to. I don't know, maybe that's why I chose someone big and muscular, so I could feel safe with him – though he turned out to be a milksop. I knew you couldn't bear him, and, deep down, I couldn't bear him either.'

'And what about Ouzounidis?' I could not bring myself to call him Fanis. 'What's the difference?'

She stared into her cup and tried to put her thoughts into some order, to explain it to me. 'The other day I told him that I was finishing with the bibliography and I'd be returning to Thessaloniki –'

'You didn't tell me that.'

'Because whenever I go away, you go into mourning and it's easier to tell you at the last minute. Do you know what Fanis said when he heard it?'

'What?'

'He told me that he understood, but that he had his patients and his night duties and that it wouldn't be easy for him to fly up to Thessaloniki that often to see me. "I might be able to get away for a weekend," he said, "but don't be upset if we don't see each other again till Christmas."' She paused to see how I would react. I said nothing so she went on. 'That's what I like about Fanis: he loves me, but he also loves his work and he has no intention of sacrificing it for me. And that means that he understands that I've no intention of giving up my studies for him. Whereas Panos had become like a leech towards the end.'

Up until now, I had always felt proud that my daughter had taken after me rather than her mother. Now I was slowly discovering that she hadn't taken after me either. I'm good at analysing murderers and criminals, at discovering their motives, but when it comes to myself, I haven't a clue. Most of the time I don't know what gets into me, why I react as I do or what I want from those around me. Katerina, on the contrary, could read herself as if she were an open book; she went over her motives with a fine-tooth comb. Suddenly, I thought of Elena Koustas and her son. I imagined her getting home at midnight from the theatre and running to the bedside of a disabled child to see whether he was asleep. And later, sneaking out of Koustas' house to go and see her son for a few hours. I was annoyed that Elena Koustas was coming between my daughter and me, but the image was wedged in my mind and wouldn't go away.

'What are you thinking about?' Katerina asked, bringing me back to reality. 'Are you tired of listening to my problems?'

'No, of course I'm not tired, dear. It's this case that's going round in my mind all the time.'

'Which case? The Koustas one?'

'Yes.' I didn't want to tell her about Elena Koustas and her child, so I said: 'I'm looking for some accounts belonging to Koustas and I've no idea where they might be. I searched his house this afternoon, but I didn't find anything.'

'Why don't you ask his accountant?'

And why didn't I, dammit? Why hadn't I thought of Yannis, Koustas' accountant who worked at R.I. Hellas? Perhaps because I had identified him as closer to Niki than to her father.

'Once, in a seminar on commercial law, the lecturer brought a tax official to talk to us. He told us jokingly that a businessman might keep secrets from his wife but never from his accountant. His accountant knew about everything, from his mistress to his business's unofficial books.'

'Katerina,' I said, 'you may have just given me the solution.'

She laughed. 'Well, that's something,' she said, 'even if it's not exactly what I wanted.'

'Do you intend to marry him?' I asked.

'Who? Fanis?'

'Yes. Do you intend to marry him?'

'Now you're talking like Mum and it doesn't suit you,' she said, suddenly becoming serious. 'All I'm bothered about, Dad, is finishing my doctorate and then I'll decide what I'm going to do afterwards. Marriage is not part of my plans for the time being.'

'Tell my doctor to come round one Sunday for lunch before you go back to Thessaloniki.'

She looked at me for a moment to make sure I wasn't joking and then her face lit up. She was about to lean over and kiss me but she held back so as not to make a scene. She took hold of my hands and squeezed them. 'You don't know how happy you've made me,' she said.

'Because I've invited Fanis over?'

'No, because I talked you round.'

Once we were outside in the street, she took my arm and put it round her shoulders. We reached the Mirafiori like two lovebirds who had just bought their first old banger and were off for a spin in it to celebrate.

CHAPTER 44

Yannis Stylianidis, Koustas' accountant, was sitting in the same chair that Kelesidis had sat in the previous day. His face was visible only from his chin upwards as it was hidden up to that point by three ledgers, two belonging to the Bouzouki Strings and the Night Flower and one from the Canard Doré. I picked up one and began flicking through it. The entries meant nothing to me, but I perused them with the eye of an expert about to set a fine of fifty million for tax evasion. Vlassopoulos was standing over Yannis to make his presence felt and make him feel uncomfortable.

'Are these all?' I asked, after silently flicking through them for some time.

'Yes.'

His voice revealed his willingness to cooperate. I sat down in the chair facing him and folded my arms. 'Why are you lying to me?' I asked mildly.

'I'm not lying to you, Inspector. I brought them all. Income and expenditure books, entrance books, till receipts, purchase invoices, everything.'

'Everything except Koustas' second set of books.'

He was taken aback, but kept his composure. 'What second set? I don't understand.'

'Don't play the hero, Yannis, because it would not be in your best interests. I'm talking about Koustas' secret books, where he recorded his illegal dealings.'

'There are no such books, or, if there are, he never showed them to me.'

Vlassopoulos suddenly grabbed him by the shoulders and began

243

shaking him. 'Listen here, you little sod, there are other ways of getting you to talk! Tell us where Koustas kept his other books so we can all go home!'

'I told you, I don't know!' he shouted in fear. 'If there are any other books, I don't know where they are.' He didn't dare look at Vlassopoulos and his gaze fell imploringly on me.

'Yannis, we're not tax officials,' I told him.

'I know.'

'So we're not interested in any tax evasion. Our interest is in something else.'

'What?'

'How your boss laundered three billion a year and who gave him the money to be laundered.' From his expression I knew that I had him and I continued in the same vein. 'You were his accountant, you saw nothing but receipts and invoices. Maybe you cottoned on to what was concealed behind his businesses, maybe not. So if you tell us where Koustas kept his second set of books, no one is going to come after you for money-laundering. But if you continue to play dumb and we find them, you're the one who'll come out of it badly. Koustas is dead and we can't do anything to him. But we can throw the book at you for being his accomplice.'

While I talked, he was twining and untwining his fingers, till in the end he did not know what to do with his hands. 'I don't know whether Koustas had any secret books,' he murmured eventually. 'If I knew, I'd tell you.'

'Who kept Koustas' official books?'

'I did.'

'Where?'

'At home.'

'And who brought you the papers for the entries?'

'One of Koustas' bodyguards.'

'Where did he bring them? To your home or to the office?'

'To my home. Every Monday afternoon, he brought me the receipts from all three establishments for the previous week.'

'And you say that he never showed you his second set of books?'

He hesitated again. 'No, never.'

244

Vlassopoulos grabbed him by the shoulders again, but this time he lifted him up like a sack and held him pressed against the wall. 'Who are you trying to fool, you little squirt!' he shouted, giving him a couple of slaps. 'What do you take us for? A couple of your mates to be taken for a ride?' Another slap. 'You kept the books at your place, they brought you all the papers, by hand, and you're telling me that you've never set eyes on the unofficial books? You think you can make fun of me, do you, you scumbag?' He held him there with one hand and turned to me. 'Inspector, we're wasting time. Let me have him and I'll beat it out of him.'

Stylianidis heard Vlassopoulos asking for my permission to let him beat the information out of him and instinctively closed his eyes so as not to see the blows when they started raining down on him. I wondered why he persisted in keeping his mouth shut. Then I suddenly recalled the scene from my first visit to Niki Koustas' office and it all became clear to me.

'Let him go,' I said to Vlassopoulos. 'He's not going to talk because he wants to play the gallant protector.' I got up and went over to him. 'Who is it you're protecting, Yannis?'

'No one,' he murmured.

'It's not Koustas, because he's dead. You're afraid that if you talk, you'll incriminate Niki Koustas, that's it, isn't it?'

He opened his eyes and looked at me. Vlassopoulos let go of him, but he didn't move away. I remembered how Yannis had looked at Niki that day and I knew I was right. 'Listen to me,' I said. 'Niki Koustas had no connection whatsoever with her father's affairs. We're certain about that. She lived on her own, had her own job and rarely saw him. So she's not in any danger.'

He was not convinced. 'Are you being honest with me? Or are you trying to trick me to make me confess?'

'No. We need the books to find out who murdered Koustas. And neither you nor his daughter are suspects.'

'Koustas had a warehouse in Karanaou Street, next to the Armenian Church,' he said hesitantly. 'I'd go there every fortnight, in the afternoon, and he had me doing the entries for two books.'

'Did he bring them with him?'

245

'No. He had them locked up in a safe in the warehouse. There were no receipts or invoices. He told me what amounts to write in each book. He always had them with him, written out on a bit of paper.'

'And he never told you what those amounts were for?'

'Just once he told me that he was cheating the tax office, like all businessmen, and that I shouldn't say a word to anyone either about the warehouse or about the books.'

'And you kept your mouth shut?'

'No accountant would ever inform on his boss that he was cheating the tax office, Inspector. After all, the job of every accountant worth his salt is to do just that.'

Except that Koustas wasn't cheating the tax office. He was laundering money. Perhaps Yannis had realised this from the entries, perhaps not. Whatever the case, Koustas must have been paying him plenty to keep his mouth shut.

'OK, Yannis,' I said. 'That's all, you're free to go.'

Stylianidis stared at me disbelievingly. He could not believe that he was getting off so easily. He glanced at Vlassopoulos, saw that he was now smiling at him too, got to his feet and made for the door. Before going out, he stopped.

'Please don't do anything to hurt Niki Koustas,' he said to me. 'If any harm were to come to her because of me, I'd kill myself.'

It was quite possibly the first time that he had admitted his love for Niki Koustas and he was admitting it to me. Wrong person, wrong time.

'Don't worry, no harm will come to her.'

He went out, closing the door behind him. 'Get a car ready,' I said to Vlassopoulos. 'And get a locksmith from Forensics. Have Dermitzakis find out from the land registry whose name the warehouse in Karanaou Street is in.' Something told me it wouldn't be in Koustas' name.

The previous day's drizzle had stopped and we were experiencing scattered cloud with periods of sunshine. In Sarri Street, we ran into a wall of traffic and left the patrol car on the pavement. The storeroom was in a basement. The door was made of steel with a security lock. We stood outside waiting for the locksmith, who arrived a quarter of an hour later, annoyed and flustered.

'You don't know what I went through to get here,' he said. It was the same locksmith who had opened Greekinvest's offices. He studied the lock. 'It's not difficult, but it'll take me a little time.' Ten minutes later, he pushed open the door and in we went.

In the large basement, three piles of boxes were lined up against the wall on the right. Against the left-hand wall was a desk with a swivel chair, a telephone and fax machine. The safe that Stylianidis had told us about was next to the desk and reached halfway up the wall. The locksmith peered at it, then took out his tools and began fiddling with it. Vlassopoulos started searching the drawers in the desk.

I was left with the boxes on the opposite wall. Two of the piles had a label on them with the name 'Sofrec'. I opened the first two boxes and came across two different kinds of packaged cheese. The third pile consisted of bigger boxes and the label on them said 'Tripex'. In the first box I found six bottles of red wine. Evidently, it was French produce that Koustas had purchased for the Canard Doré. I left the boxes and went back to Vlassopoulos.

'Nothing. They're empty,' he said, indicating the drawers.

I had not expected them to contain anything interesting to us. Only the safe would reveal Koustas' secrets to us and the locksmith was still working on it. I went and stood over him. What if he can't get it open? I thought to myself. It seemed he sensed my concern because he looked up and smiled.

'Don't worry,' he said. 'I've brought some dynamite along. I'll blow the lock if I have to.'

Another quarter of an hour went by with Vlassopoulos and me on tenterhooks. Eventually, I watched the locksmith turning the key four times in the lock, lifting the handle and swinging back the door of the safe.

'All done,' he said, stepping aside.

The safe had three shelves. The top shelf was a cupboard, another safe inside the safe. 'You're not finished yet,' I said to the locksmith. And I pointed to the cupboard. Vlassopoulos leaned over me so that he could take a look too.

'That's child's play,' he replied, picking up his tools again.

On the second shelf I found the two books that Stylianidis brought up to date every fortnight. I flicked thorough them. They were full of figures that meant nothing to me. 'Take them,' I said to Vlassopoulos. 'They're for the experts.'

On the bottom shelf was a thick folder. I took it out and put it on the desk. I sat down in the swivel chair and opened it. It was full of receipts for bank transfers, all in German marks, ranging from 50,000 to 300,000 marks. The transfers were made by way of a foreign-currency account at the Ionian Bank and always to the same branch, Unibank, Vaduz. I was damned if I knew where Vaduz was. The beneficiaries were Sofrec and Tripex.

So far, I didn't need an expert to explain things to me. These were bogus companies that were sending dirty money and getting it back all washed and ironed. Koustas had opened an account in foreign currency and used this to move his associates' money. They brought it into Greece, either in cash or by various money transfers, Koustas laundered it through his businesses and sent it back to them all cleaned. The wine and cheese was simply wool over the eyes. Most likely he made the loan to Greekinvest from the same account at the Ionian Bank.

That's why he hadn't wanted his son to take over any of his establishments. He preferred to send him for treatment every so often and pay for the detox clinic rather than have him under his feet. I thought of Makis with his leather jacket, his cowboy boots and his eyes, sometimes glazed, sometimes blurred, and I felt a twinge of pity.

'Got it,' said the locksmith, and I went back to the safe.

Koustas had three brown envelopes locked away in the cupboard. The first contained photocopies of documents concerning a transfer of property that made everything clear. The owner of the property, a four-roomed flat, was Konstantinos Koustas and he was transferring it to one of the politicians with the high popularity ratings.

I opened the next envelope and two photos fell out – of the island where Adriani and I had gone for our holidays when the earthquake happened. One was a postcard, one of the pretty postcards that you find at every street kiosk or tourist shop. An idyllic image, taken from a ship or fishing boat. The other had been taken by an amateur photographer. It showed a rise, a spot that I didn't remember having seen and that at first meant nothing to me. But then I made out the bay with the *pension* where Anita and her English friend had stayed with the lion-taming philosopher and I suddenly understood. It was the spot where they had buried Petroulias before the landslide had happened and where eventually I had been lumbered with his body.

I went on looking at the photograph and gradually my thoughts began to fall into place. That was why Koustas had wanted the fifteen million on the night he was murdered. Someone knew where Petroulias was buried and was blackmailing him. That was what was behind the two pictures of the island. Koustas had known his murderer; he was the one blackmailing him. That was why he had turned round when the murderer had spoken to him. Yet the photos confirmed something else: that it was Koustas who had planned Petroulias' murder. Otherwise, why would he have succumbed to blackmail?

I left that conundrum for later and opened the third envelope. Inside was a strip of film and a colour photo. It was of a man lying naked on a bed. He was turned towards the lens, with eyes closed and mouth half open. Probably he was groaning with pleasure as there was a naked girl sitting on top of him. Her head was tilted back, her eyes open and her face stony and expressionless. It was Kalia. And the man lying on his back was the former minister with the popularity ratings higher than those of his party leader.

In the end, the politician came out of it better than the former minister, I thought. He got a four-room flat while the former minister had to be satisfied with Kalia. The fate of whoremongers. That's why Koustas had wanted R.I. Hellas. He kept them both for security. If the money-laundering came out into the open, he would get the politicians to use their influence to put a stop to the investigation. And because simply being politicians wasn't enough – they had to be high-ranking ones too – he increased their status through rigged opinion polls. Something told me, however, that he didn't intend to stop there; he was aiming much higher. If the government remained in office, the politician with the flat would no doubt be rewarded with a Ministry, given his popularity ratings. If the government fell, then the former minister was in line to become the next prime minister. I reflected on what it would have meant for Koustas to have had in his pocket a prime minister with Kalia on top of him. And his daughter had processed the false figures. Now I knew who had wanted to stop the investigations into the Koustas case: it was the politician and the former minister.

I also knew now what Koustas had been discussing with Kalia on the night of the murder. Evidently he used to send the girl to various friends of his to have fun with and she had reacted. That explained the heated tone. Besides, Kalia had told me indirectly when we had talked the second time. She had said that the only thing Koustas could ask of her was for her to open her legs for him. Except that she didn't open them for him, but for others, whom Koustas had in his pocket.

But why hadn't the blackmailer taken the fifteen million from Koustas? Why had he killed him instead? I had no answer to that. As one mystery was solve, another arose. Unless the one who killed him was not the one blackmailing him. Koustas had been expecting the blackmailer, to give him his money, but the murderer had arrived first and done him in. It was the only explanation, but it did not bring me any closer to finding his murderer.

CHAPTER 45

When I got home, I had to take an Inderal and then lie down because my heart had started racing again after many days of inertia, chugging like a motorboat leaving harbour. And why wouldn't it race, what with the secret accounts, the documents and, above all, the photographs Koustas had in his warehouse? The whole business was becoming more complicated as things got clearer and I was between a rock and a hard place. If I were to take a step forward and show Ghikas the two photographs of the island together with the documents transferring the flat to the politician and the photo of the former minister with Kalia, he would no doubt have a heart attack before I did. At best he would uncover Koustas' money-laundering business so as to establish his motive for instigating the murder of Petroulias. But he would hush up the involvement of the politician and the former minister, so the Koustas case would go up the spout because it was highly probable that these two, or one of them at any rate, had been involved in Koustas' murder.

Then again, if I were to take a step backwards and continue the investigations without informing Ghikas, I ran the risk of being brought to task on some trumped-up accusation of harassing or blackmailing political figures, and the case would once again be hushed up and I would – at best – be put out to grass.

I thought about it this way and that way and was unable to come up with any solution. In the end, I decided to put my dilemma on hold and concern myself with Kalia, the club plaything, who you could push around, hit, even screw in the toilet without anyone taking it amiss.

I jumped up from the bed and took the three envelopes out of my jacket pocket. I kept the envelope with the photo of the former minister and locked the other two in the drawer of my bedside table.

Adriani was watching the reality show with Methenitis, who was this time wearing a blue jacket, white shirt and grenadine trousers.

'I'm going out,' I called to her.

She turned and looked at me anxiously. 'Will you be long?'

'Perhaps, but don't start your nagging because I've got enough on my plate,' I said, and that took the wind out of her sails. She took one look at my expression and didn't dare persist.

Once again, I found myself in the thick stream of traffic going towards Omonia Square, with the usual build-up first in Panepistimiou Street and then in Aghiou Konstantinou Street. I would find no one but the waiters at the Bouzouki Strings, I thought. We were bumper to tail as far as Sarakaki Street, and that suited me. I preferred to be on the road than to arrive early and have to sit at a table like a salesman come to sell taramasalata and waiting for the manager.

The beanpole doorman recognised me and stepped aside. The tables were all laid and were ready for the customers. The musicians in the band were all bent over their instruments and were whispering to each other. Sitting at the last table next to the door was the club's photographer, who was assembling his equipment. I watched his fingers handling the films with the ease of the expert and an idea began to form in my head. I went over and sat down in the chair beside him.

'Good evening,' I said.

'Good evening, Inspector,' he replied, attaching the flash to his camera. 'You're early. Mr Hortiatis never gets here before ten.'

'It's not Hortiatis I wanted, it's you.'

'Me?' He looked up in surprise.

'Yes. I'm going to show you a photograph and I want you to tell me who might have taken it.'

I took the photograph showing the former minister with Kalia out of the envelope and laid it in front of him. He picked it up and looked at it. His hands started to tremble, but he did his best to present himself as the objective professional. He studied it for some time, then turned it over and looked at it from behind, supposedly to see the name of the photographer. He was doing a little number to stall for time and regain his composure.

'I can't tell you,' he said. 'It's been developed in a private laboratory.'

'When did you take it?' I said.

It seems he was expecting the question, because his eyes fixed on me innocently. 'It's not one of my photos.'

I leaned over and brought my face up close to his. 'Tell me the truth. I know that you took it on Koustas' orders.'

'I didn't take it,' he insisted.

'You know what will happen if the photo gets into the hands of the politician? He'll realise at once that it's yours and he'll make sure every door is closed to you. You'll end up in Syntagma Square taking snapshots of kids and tourists feeding the pigeons. Whereas if you tell me how and why you took it, you'll come out of it clean and I won't say a word to anyone.'

He took hold of the print and looked at it again like an artist admiring the work. 'OK. You're right. Koustas asked me to take it. I told him I didn't want to get involved, but he insisted. If I'd said no, he would have fired me. The club was full every night then and I was making good money.'

'When was that?'

'Over a year ago.'

'What did he say to you exactly?'

'He gave me the keys to Kalia's place. He told me that Kalia would be bringing someone home that evening and that he wanted me to photograph them together naked on the bed. I took my other camera with me, the one with the built-in flash. I went outside on to the bedroom balcony and left the shutters half open. I positioned the camera in the gap between them and waited. When I saw the man giving it all he'd got on the bed, I began. I used up half a film, but he was so far gone that he had no idea. A few days later, I happened to see his face on TV and it was only then that I realised who I had been photographing. I was scared shitless, but Koustas told me it would all be OK.'

'What did you do with the film?'

'I developed it in my own darkroom and gave it to Koustas, together with five prints I made. I didn't keep even one, I swear.'

He didn't have to swear. I knew he wouldn't play tricks with Koustas. It occurred to me that perhaps he was the one who had taken the photograph of the island, but I rejected the idea. That one had been taken by someone like me, who points the lens and then presses the button. But why had Kalia played Koustas' game? Was he paying her or did he have her in his pocket too and was blackmailing her?

'Is Kalia here?'

He stared at me in astonishment. 'You haven't heard?' he said. 'Kalia's dead.'

The news hit me right between the eyes. 'When?' I asked him, after it had taken me a good half-minute to find my voice again.

'Her body was discovered in her home four days ago. Died from an overdose. She hadn't been to the club for two days and wasn't answering the phone. Hortiatis thought she'd left, but Marina, the girl she went onstage with, was worried because she knew that Kalia was into hard drugs. She got a locksmith to go round to the flat with her. When they went in, they found her dead in bed.'

'Where can I find this Marina?'

'She may be here already, getting dressed for the show. Otherwise, Hortiatis knows where she lives.'

The light was on in Kalia's dressing room and sitting in her chair was the auburn-haired girl I had seen onstage with Kalia and the gypsy with the sideburns.

'Are you Marina?' I asked.

She didn't look at me in the mirror as Kalia had, but swivelled round in her chair.

'Yes, I am,' she replied with a politeness becoming a girl with auburn hair.

'Tell me about Kalia.'

She bit her lower lip. 'What do you want me to tell you?'

'Where you found her. How you found her. Everything.'

She told me the same story that I had heard from the photographer. Her voice trembled at first, ready to break, but as she went on, it levelled out.

'Where was she when you found her?'

'In bed. Her body wrapped in a towel. It seems she had taken a bath in order to relax and then . . . she had taken her fix.'

'What did you do when you saw her?'

'I don't know, I don't remember. At some stage I saw two police- men standing there. The locksmith told me that I'd become hysterical and he had called emergency. I don't remember anything.'

'Where did Kalia live?'

'Oinois Street, number 7, in Nikaia.'

'Thank you,' I said.

As Kalia had died in her home, the local police station in Nikaia would have taken care of the formalities, that is, calling the coroner to identify the cause of death and then handing the body over for

254

burial. With two or three junkies kicking the bucket every day from overdoses, the police stations had turned into funeral parlours. But I felt her photo resting against my heart and I was beset by questions. She had died naked, wrapped in a bath towel. Who was to say that she hadn't been with the former minister or some other 'client' before taking her fix? And if she had been, had her lover left any clues behind?

CHAPTER 46

At half past ten the traffic in Athinon Avenue had thinned out. I got stuck behind a darkened coach. On the back seat, a passenger was nodding. His head kept falling forward and swinging back and forth. Every so often, he tried to keep it upright, but it only fell again like a coconut falling from its stand. In the opposite direction, a convoy of lorries was occupying the whole of the left-hand lane and was headed towards Skaramangas. I could not make out what got into them all of a sudden and made them honk their horns together. Terrified, the few cars kept to the right-hand lane out of fear of being crushed by them, but no one in the darkened windows woke from their slumber.

I turned right into Thivon Street and passed by the Third Cemetery in order to come out into Petrou Ralli Street. I tried to keep my eyes on the road ahead as I had no wish to see graveyards in my sleep. I did, however, take a glance, wondering whether Kalia was buried there.

I found the police station at the corner of Panayi Tsaldari and Alatsaton Streets. It was a flimsy three-storey construction of concrete blocks and cement, like all those built to order nowadays.

The duty officer was young and his expression had not been soured by the Force. His eyes were fixed on a couple standing in front of his desk. The man had not shaved for a week and it was hard to distinguish his features. He was holding an accordion against his chest. The woman was wearing a red blouse and black skirt. Round her neck was a laminated photograph showing her holding two little girls. On the photo's white surround, written in felt-tip pen, were the words 'Serbo-Bosnian refugees'.

'Give me a minute to finish here and I'll be with you,' the officer said after I had introduced myself. He turned back to the Serbo-Bosnians. 'The complaint says that you went to the café in order to steal,' he said sternly, addressing the man.

'No steal!' cried the man. 'We do music, make money to get food for kids.' And he pointed to the two girls in the photo. The woman, it seemed, did not speak Greek. She kept looking first at her husband and then at the officer.

'I know. You went to make money by pinching from the customers while they were watching the match on TV.'

'I no thief, I muzisan,' the man insisted. And to prove the truth of his words, he unfastened his accordion and began to pump it and press the keys. The sound of the melody spread throughout the station with the assaulted, the junkies, the pickpockets and the officers gathering in the doorway and staring. The woman thought they had been brought there to play and she began to sing a sad, plaintive song that sounded to me like a lament for the dead. We were all overcome by grief and only the two girls in the photograph smiled.

'OK, OK, off with you!' said the officer, cutting them short. 'And next time they throw you out of a place, make sure you leave before they make a complaint and you end up in hot water.'

The man immediately stopped playing, took his wife by the arm, kept repeating, 'Thank you', and hurried out with her. The officer watched them leave arm in arm and turned to me.

'In the Academy they kept telling us all day long that our job was to enforce law and order, track down criminals and rid society of its parasites,' he said. 'No one told me that one day I'd end up feeling sorry for the parasites.'

He did not know that I, too, was there to ask him about another 'parasite'. 'A few days ago, you found a girl who died from an overdose at 7 Oinois Street.'

'Yes, Kalliopi –' The full name escaped him. He got up to get the file. 'Kalliopi Kourtoglou.'

'Do you have the coroner's report?'

'No, but I can tell you what the coroner told us. She died from an injection of pure heroin.'

'Did you find anything in her flat to suggest any criminal activity?' He looked at me sharply. 'Her death may be connected with another murder we're investigating,' I explained.

'No, we found nothing suspicious.'

'Fingerprints?'

He again flicked through the file. 'The only fingerprints we found were hers. Apart from –' He stopped and read the report more carefully.

'Apart from what?'

'On the bedside table we found two glasses and a bottle of whisky. One of the glasses had her fingerprints on it, the other was completely clean.'

'What about the bottle?'

'Clean too.'

Normally, I should have congratulated myself for not being satisfied with what the photographer and Marina had told me, but I felt like shouting. 'What, didn't you find it suspicious that there were no fingerprints on the other glass or on the bottle?' I asked the sergeant. 'Somebody was with her when she died. And he wiped his fingerprints off so as to leave no trace. How do you know that he wasn't the one who injected her with pure heroin?'

He gave me a look as if to say that he was dealing with a retard and so had to be especially patient. 'We found her wrapped in a bath towel, Inspector.'

'I know that. So?'

'The man who was with her must have been a junkie, a friend of hers, who'd gone round to get stoned with her. Junkies often do that; they don't like getting stoned on their own. He must have seen her die, got scared and taken off so as not to get involved.'

'And why would he wipe his fingerprints clean?'

'If he was a known addict, he was probably afraid that we'd find him easily.' It was a reasonable explanation on his part and he looked at me, satisfied with himself for having silenced the head of the Security Homicide Division.

'Did you find her handbag?'

'Yes. It contained a purse with her identity card, five thousand drachma and an address book.'

'Bring me the address book.'

He went out and, before long, came back with the book. I opened it and found the name of the former minister together with his phone number. It seems he wasn't just a screw-and-scram kind, as Dermitzakis might have said, but a regular client. Evidently, Koustas still had not said anything to him about the photos and the former minister was happily making the most of Kalia's charms.

'I want to take a look at the flat.'

'You're in the nick of time,' he said. 'We're handing it over tomorrow.'

'Can you spare me an officer to drive me there?'

'I can spare you an officer, but I don't have a patrol car. We only have two and they're both out.'

'Never mind. I have my own car.'

'Kondokostas!' shouted the sergeant, and a young uniformed officer immediately appeared at the door. 'I want you to take Inspector Haritos to Kourtoglou's flat at 7 Oinois Street.' He opened his drawer and took out the keys.

'Who found the girl's body?' I asked Kondokostas as we were driving up Beloyanni Street.

'I did, together with Balodimas, a colleague. We got a call from a locksmith that her friend had taken along to open the door.'

Oinois Street was a back lane leading off Solomou Street. Kalia or Kalliopi lived in a ground-floor flat. The door was still sealed with yellow tape. Kondokostas removed it and opened the door with the key given to him by the duty officer. It was a two-roomed flat, cheaply furnished, but clean and tidy.

'Show me where you found her.'

I followed him into the bedroom. The bed was in one corner and was unmade, with the cover and outer sheets rolled back. The pillow still had the depression in it from Kalia's head.

I found nothing suspicious. Everything was in its place. I opened the bedside drawer. It was full of cosmetics. On top, I found a strip of elastic and a handful of disposable needles. Kalia was in the habit of taking her fix in bed. That's what she had done on the night of her death.

'Where were the glasses?'

'On the bedside table. The bottle was on the floor next to the bed.'

Thrown over the back of a chair next to the door were a T-shirt, a pair of jeans and a jacket. A pair of trainers looked lost by the chair's legs. I opened the wardrobe on the wall. Another pair of jeans, two pairs of tights and two dresses, on hangers. The top drawer was full of underwear, the next of T-shirts and in the third were three pullovers. No one could have searched the drawers because all the clothes were in tidy order.

I went out of the bedroom and into the kitchen opposite. Kondokostas followed at my heels, either because he was afraid that I might steal something or because it was the first time he had set eyes on an officer from the Homicide Division carrying out a search and he wanted to learn something. But there was nothing in the kitchen either, that struck me as being out of place. In the cupboards, the plates and glasses were all arranged neatly and the sink was clean. I had served for years in narcotics and it was the first time I had ever come across a tidy junkie. I thought of Kalia with her constant cynicism and it occurred to me that she had had to die for me to discover what was behind it.

The same tidiness also characterised the small living room. I was about to leave when my eye caught the TV table. Next to the TV was a picture frame face down. I picked it up and the glass came away from the frame. It was empty with the photo missing.

'What's this here?' I asked Kondokostas, indicating the frame.

'A frame.'

'And didn't it seem odd to you that it was empty? Didn't it tell you anything? Do you have empty frames in your home, Kondokostas?'

'No.'

'Then where's the photo?'

He shrugged. 'I don't know.'

I was going to tell him that whoever wiped his prints off the glass and bottle also removed the photo from the frame, but I thought better of it. There was no point in my explaining to him that on the night that Kalia had taken an overdose, she had been with someone very close to her, whose photo she had kept beside the TV, to be able to see it while she was watching Methenitis' reality show. If he had not been the one to kill her, then he may have seen her dead body, got scared, removed all traces of his having been there and disappeared. I could, of course, go through the names in her address book, but it would have been damn near impossible to check every alibi. Besides the photo revealed something more. If it had been her boyfriend, or a relative, he may not have taken it. When all's said and done, just because she had his picture in the living room didn't mean he was with her when she died. No, the man in the photograph was either someone of consequence or someone connected with the case. And the only person of consequence connected with the case was the former minister.

'We're done,' I said to Kondokostas.

I dropped him at the station and headed back to Athens. It was one o'clock by the time I arrived home. I opened the door and found all the lights on. Adriani was standing in the hallway, waiting for me.

'What time do you call this?' she said angrily.

'I told you, I had work to do.'

'And was your work so important that you don't think about your home or your health or your daughter who's leaving in a few days? It's not your heart that's your ailment, it's your work, and that's one sickness Fanis can't cure.'

I pounced on the opportunity of hearing Ouzounidis' name. 'And what do you plan to cook for my doctor on Sunday?' I asked her, thinking that this might calm her.

She glared at me. When I got to the bedroom, I heard her shouting behind me: 'Is that all you've got to say to me, then? Is that all you've got to say?'

I was already in bed when she came into the room. We'd been married for so many years and she was still embarrassed about getting undressed in front of me. She took her nightdress and went into the bathroom to put it on. Then she lay down beside me and turned her back to me.

'I'm thinking of making stuffed tomatoes for him,' she said as I was turning off the light. 'You don't mind me making them for him, too, do you? It's just that I can always rely on them.'

Well, I never! Now I have a rival for stuffed tomatoes, I thought to myself. 'Go ahead, but ask Katerina if she's serious about him, because once he's eaten your stuffed tomatoes, he's sure to ask her to marry him.'

She turned and put her hand on my chest. 'Goodnight,' she said sweetly and closed her eyes.

CHAPTER 47

The next morning, I woke up resolved to give myself another twenty-four hours, which meant keeping away from the office. If I was away, I could not keep Ghikas in the picture and consequently I could keep the transfer documents and the photographs for one more day. It was my last possible deadline. If by the end of the day I had not managed to discover whether the former minister had been involved in Kalia's death, I would hand all the evidence over to Ghikas for him to sweep under the carpet and close the case. Because there was no way the Koustas case could be brought out into the open in all its intricacies without revealing the involvement of the former minister.

I phoned Vlassopoulos and told him I wanted to clear up some loose ends in connection with the Petroulias case and that I would be late getting to the office. I made no mention of Koustas. There was the danger, of course, that Ghikas would ask for an update from Vlassopoulos, but I didn't dare tell him not to say anything about what we had found the previous day in Koustas' warehouse. I relied on my experience of Ghikas, who nearly always only accepts reports from the heads of departments.

My second call was to Markidis. 'Does the name Kalliopi Kourtoglou mean anything to you?' I asked him.

'No, who is she?'

'A girl who was found dead from an overdose five days ago.'

'Korkas must have dealt with her. Hold on.' He came back a couple of minutes later. 'Just as you said,' he told me.

'Meaning?'

'She died from an overdose.'

'Good, so they weren't lying to me. Anything else?'

'There was sperm in her womb. She must have had sex half an hour or an hour prior to her death.'

'And why wasn't that in the report made to the police station in Nikaia?'

'Because no one called to ask us and the report still hasn't been typed up yet.'

'How many days does it take for you to type up a report?'

'For God's sake,' he shouted, 'the girl was a regular user and died from an injection of pure heroin. What does it matter whether she'd had sex beforehand or eaten pasta? Do you know what extra work we have with all these junkies? I've only got two secretaries and one of them is on maternity leave. How do you expect me to manage?'

'OK. When the report is ready, send me a copy.'

'Why is it of such concern to you?' curious, at last, in spite of himself.

'Because the girl worked in one of Koustas' clubs and she may have some connection with his murder.'

There was a pause, then an 'Oh boy!' and he rang off.

Then the most important call. I dialled the number of the former minister and his secretary answered. I asked what times the honourable former minister was available to the public, without mentioning who I was. I simply let it be understood that I was a voter who required a favour. The secretary informed me that the honourable former minister received people at his office every day between eleven and two.

I looked at my watch. It was ten o'clock and before going to call on the former minister I had to know how he secured his high popularity ratings, because the information might come in handy.

Niki Koustas was surprised to see me. At first, she seemed uneasy, perhaps because she recalled our last meeting in my office.

'I need to pick your brains,' I said.

'Why? Surely you don't need to check your popularity ratings.'

'Me, no. But if someone wanted to show high ratings for a politician or for a product, could they fabricate them?'

Her uneasiness passed and she laughed at me. 'Of course they could. You're a police officer, you for one should know that fraud is possible everywhere.'

'If you wanted to fabricate an opinion poll, how would you go about it?'

'I'm an analyst, Inspector. I process the data that I'm given. The fraud is in the collecting of the data, of the sample, as it's called, and that's why it's difficult for anyone to detect it.'

'So you get the data already prepared?'

'Exactly.'

'From whom?'

'From those responsible for collecting the sample.'

'And who decides how the sample is collected?'

'Mrs Arvanitakis.'

'Thank you,' I said, getting to my feet.

'How come this sudden interest in opinion polls?'

'There's a point I want to clear up.'

'Does it have to do with my father's death?'

'Maybe yes, maybe no.'

I left her wondering and went up to the third floor. The elderly secretary was wearing the same tight two-piece and had the same spectacles perched on her nose. She saw me enter, but her expression remained fixed. It could not become any more unfriendly than it naturally was.

'I want to see Mrs Arvanitakis. It's urgent and I don't care how busy she is,' I said.

She glanced at the telephone in front of her. 'She's on the phone. You'll have to wait.'

Arvanitakis may or may not have been on the phone. Perhaps she told me that simply to make me wait and get one over on me. Anyway, I had to wait five minutes before her ego was satisfied and I was allowed to go in.

Arvanitakis was studying some spreadsheets. It was eleven in the morning but she was dressed as though for an official reception: a dark blue outfit with a light blue handkerchief in the jacket pocket, a white blouse and whatever gold was left over from the votive offerings of the faithful.

'To what do we owe the pleasure, Inspector?' she said with a forced smile.

'I need you to clear up a few things that have emerged from our investigations.'

Her smile evaporated and her expression showed that my opening words were not to her liking. 'Concerning Greekinvest?'

'And R.I. Hellas. Whatever you say will remain between the two of us,' I said, taking a seat.

'Fair enough, though I can't really see what secrets the two of us might share.'

I ignored her irony because she would no doubt change her tune when I got to the crux of the matter. 'Mrs Arvanitakis, from what I've discovered, you carry out research for the popularity ratings of a member of the government and a member of the opposition.' And I gave her the name of the former minister and of the politician who received the flat from Koustas.

'Yes.'

'Who commissions the research?'

She tried to get out of it. 'You realise, I'm sure, that this information is classified.'

'Listen. I came here informally and I've assured you that whatever is said will remain between us. Or would you rather that I summon you officially to make a statement?'

She let out a sigh and said: 'We received the request from our parent company, Greekinvest.'

'How was the request made?'

'By fax.'

'Could this research have been, let's say, selective?'

'*Selective*?' she repeated, taken aback. 'What *do* you mean?'

'Carried out in such a way that the method of research might predetermine the result.'

'Opinion-poll agencies are private businesses, Inspector. They provide a service and are required to conform to their clients' wishes. If the client requires the research to give objective results, then the research is carried out objectively. If he requires a result that will please him, then the research leads to the conclusions that the client desires. Of course, firms want to protect their good name, which is why they take certain precautions.'

'What sort of precautions?'

'If the research states that it was carried out on the basis of a "representative" sample, that means that it was objective. If the word "representative" is not mentioned, that implies that it may not have been so objective.'

'And what does a "representative" sample mean?'

'Let's take the case of a political party. If the sample covers the whole of Greece, then it's representative. But if we take the sample only from those areas where the party is traditionally strong, then, as you can understand, its popularity ratings will appear to be higher, and the sample won't be representative.'

'And what happened in the case of the two politicians?'

She let out another sigh. 'The person commissioning the research determined the method.'

'Which was?'

'He requested us to take the sample from the politicians' own rallies or only from their own constituencies.'

'And because the political rallies are usually attended by the politician's supporters and because the politician is particularly popular in his own constituency, his popularity ratings always appear high.'

'Precisely.'

'And how is it that the former minister always had popularity ratings higher than those of his party leader?'

She looked me in the eye. 'You put me in a difficult position, Inspector.'

'I'm in a difficult position myself, Mrs Arvanitakis.'

'I have your word that this will remain just between us . . .?' She was no longer being ironic: she was imploring.

'Yes, you do. It's simply for my own information.'

'Theoretically, I could carry out research concerning the party and its leader on the basis of a representative sample, but compare the leader's ratings with a sample taken only from the former minister's constituency. In that case, the former minister's ratings would always be higher.'

'Isn't that fraud?'

'I prefer to call it a strategy, Inspector.'

And because today we all live by using strategies, there is no longer any fraud. It is something that Niki Koustas with her innocent smile simply could not conceive.

'And if someone were to uncover your strategy?'

For the first time she laughed spontaneously and sounded completely at ease. 'Come on, who's going to take the trouble to investigate? Usually those who get the high ratings gloat, and those who get the low ratings say that the poll was rigged. But neither of them has the data to prove one thing or the other. We keep the data in our files. And because those with the low ratings invariably denounce the poll, the public believes us and not them.'

Now I knew how Koustas had fabricated the popularity of the two politicians for his own ends. I had also found out how opinion polls are rigged and I congratulated myself on never setting store by them.

CHAPTER 48

The former minister had his office in Akadimias Street, in one of those blocks that house the offices of lawyers and public notaries. Most likely he had been a lawyer too before Parliament had got lumbered with him, to the relief, no doubt, of the Lawyers' Association. Useless economists become accountants and useless lawyers become politicians. That's the way of the world. I entered a large room. All around the walls were wooden chairs and in the middle of the room was a coffee table with old magazines. The walls belonged exclusively to the honourable minister, in a variety of poses. A portrait that smiled down on his voters; a photograph from a pre-election rally with him waving to the crowd and with the party banner in the background; another photograph of him beside the party leader, and many more: with foreign dignitaries, industrialists and military officers. I wondered where the photograph of him and Kalia would best go.

Sitting on the chairs were an elderly man, a middle-aged man with a package in a plastic bag at the side of him, and a woman wearing a scarf. At the far end of the room was a glass partition. At the desk in front of it was a rather plain-looking girl. No doubt she was the daughter of a voter and was waiting to be appointed to the public sector by the back door and in the meantime was helping out her patron.

'Inspector Haritos. I would like to see the minister,' I said. She raised her arm and pointed to the chairs, so I added 'on an official matter'. Her arm stopped halfway before she lowered it again.

'Please wait,' she said, and disappeared behind the partition. Before long, she reappeared. 'Mrs Koutsaftis will see you.' And she pointed to the partition.

Mrs Koutsaftis was the minister's private secretary and she looked just that. A woman with grey hair, a green dress with a huge brooch on her right shoulder and a scarf round her neck. To her right was the Pearly Gate, in other words, the door to the minister's office, its dark padding and studs making the plastic seem like pieces of burned *baklavas*.

'What is the nature of your business with the minister?' she enquired.

'I told the young lady outside that I wanted to see him on an official matter,' I said. 'Evidently, she didn't inform you.'

She pursed her lips and her nose took an upward incline, but she was in no position to raise any objection.

'Take a seat,' she said, pointing to one of the armchairs. She went through the Pearly Gate, closing it behind her. Presently, she reappeared and told me to go in.

It is disconcerting to see before you a man dressed impeccably in a dark grey suit, blue striped shirt and grenadine tie while you are imagining him naked on a bed with a girl perched on top of him. I bit my lip to stop myself chuckling. The former minister got to his feet and held out his hand. He had the same smile on his lips as in the photograph in the waiting room where he was greeting the crowds.

'Do come in,' he said. 'I'm so pleased to meet you. I've heard a lot about you.'

He had heard nothing, of course, but all politicians want to make out that they have a particular concern for the security forces and that they know all the officers by name. Even though they remember them only when there are rallies, demonstrations or football matches.

'Forgive me for not making an appointment, Minister,' I replied, paragon of politeness that I am. 'But we are investigating the murder of Konstantinos Koustas and a number of questions have arisen.'

He did not appear to be worried. On the contrary, he adopted the expression of a grieving relative. 'Tragic business,' he said, shaking his head. 'Great loss.'

'Did you know him?'

'But of course. He had a fine restaurant with French cuisine in Kifissia, the Canard Doré. And because I adore French cuisine, I go there often. I can assure you that it is on a par with the best.'

'He also had two clubs, the Night Flower and the Bouzouki Strings.'

'Yes, I have visited both of them a couple of times, though I'm not overly fond of popular music. But, I'm sure you'll understand, we politicians are obliged to put in an appearance now and again in such places. It's good for our profile.' He stopped and looked at me. 'But beyond that, I had no other dealings with Konstantinos Koustas and I wonder how I may be of help to you.'

'During the course of the investigations, I found something that belongs to you and I thought I should return it to you personally.'

'To me? What could Koustas have possibly had that belonged to me?' He looked at me enquiringly, but he still did not betray the least anxiety.

I took the envelope with the photograph out of my pocket and put it on his desk. I had left the film at home. He picked up the envelope and opened it. You know how clover sprouts up from dry earth after the first spring showers? That's exactly how the beads of sweat sprouted on his brow. His hands trembled and he clutched the photograph tightly between his fingers so as not to drop it.

'I've never seen this before,' he mumbled.

'And the girl?'

'I saw her once, when I went with a group of my voters to that club owned by Koustas – what did you call it?' He pretended to have forgotten the name, though he might have suffered amnesia as a result of his shock.

'The Bouzouki Strings.'

'Yes, the Bouzouki Strings. My voters were captivated by her and Koustas sent her to our table to entertain us. It was the early hours of the morning when we left. We had all drunk a lot, I was quite tipsy and I offered to give her a lift home in my car out of politeness. When we arrived, she asked me in for a drink – and . . . that's what happened.' He fell silent and again stared at the photograph, which he had put down on his desk. 'How was I to know that it was all a set-up and that Koustas had had someone hidden in the flat to photograph us?'

'Did you see her again?'

'No, never.'

'Then why did she have your telephone number in her address book?' I reached into my pocket and took out the page from Kalia's address book where his telephone number was written and handed it to him.

'I've no idea,' he replied. 'Ask her.'

'Unfortunately, I can't ask her, Minister. She's dead.'

'Dead?' He stared at me in amazement. His surprise may have been genuine, though politicians are actors. It's part of their profession.

'Yes, five days ago, from an overdose. Someone was with her at the time of her death and left having first removed all traces of himself.'

He stared at me. 'And you believe that I was this person?' he asked me slowly.

'Were you?'

'No.'

'Where were you on Monday night?'

'We had a marathon party meeting, went on till late.'

'How late?'

'Till eleven.'

'And then?'

'I went home.'

'Was anyone with you?'

'No. I'm divorced and I live alone. I had a snack, watched the late-night news and went to bed.'

'So there's no one who can support your claim that you were at home all night.'

Suddenly, the politician inside him awoke again. 'Do I require a reliable witness?' he asked in the severe tone of a minister taking some head of department to task.

'What can I tell you, Minister? Whoever was with her did not want his identity to be revealed. And the death of Kalia or Kalliopi was to your advantage. Koustas was already dead so there was no one left to expose you or blackmail you on account of your . . . your indiscretion.'

'That's absolute rot!' he hissed. 'My political record won't allow such insinuations, Inspector. I've been a Member of Parliament for twenty years, I've served as a minister and I've never given anyone any cause to blackmail me.'

'Koustas, at any rate, was blackmailing you or intended to blackmail you. Otherwise, why did he have the photograph taken? What was your relationship with Koustas, Minister?'

'I've already told you what my relationship was. It was epicurean, nothing else.'

'I'm sure he wasn't blackmailing you to make you eat at the Canard Doré.' I felt like mentioning the raw cut that they had given me to eat, but I couldn't remember its name. 'Did he have any connection with your popularity ratings?'

'What connection is there between my popularity ratings and Koustas' death? Those were carried out by R.I. Hellas, a firm that belongs to someone called Petroulias.'

'Who has also been murdered. But Petroulias was only the front. Behind him was Koustas, as you very well know. What was it Koustas asked from you in exchange for presenting your popularity ratings as being higher than those of your party leader? Was it perhaps that he wanted your protection for the three billion in dirty money that he was laundering every year?'

He turned white. But his voice remained cold and clinical. 'Are your superiors aware that you came here to subject me to these questions?' he said.

'No, they're not. If I'd told them, I would have had to have shown them the photograph and the page from Kalliopi Kourtoglou's address book with your telephone number. I preferred to keep it to myself and give it to you personally so as not to cause you embarrassment.'

'Thank you. I am most grateful.'

He still had not realised that his gratitude was not worth as much as a cheese pie. 'In exchange, I was hoping you would enlighten me concerning your relationship with Kalia and with Koustas.'

'I've told you all I know. There's nothing else.'

'Very well.'

I did not hold out my hand because I did not want to shake his again. I had reached the door when behind me I heard 'Inspector' and I turned round.

'Is this the only print?' he asked, indicating the photograph.

'Yes, that's the only one, you have my word.'

'Thank you again. And I knew nothing about the girl dying until you told me,' he added.

Normally, I should have asked him for a sperm sample to compare it with what was found in Kalia's womb, but it was out of the question – sperm was subject to parliamentary immunity.

I wondered whether I had played my cards right. The problem was that I was only holding two: the photograph and the page from Kalia's address book. I was missing the ace of spades and I was bluffing with the opinion-poll card. If he had swallowed it, he would make a move and expose himself. I was certain that on the night of Kalia's murder, he had been with her in her flat. The explanation that the duty officer had come up with, that it was a junkie who had got scared and vanished, was not convincing. No stoned junkie thinks to wipe away his fingerprints and remove a photo from its frame. He leaves everything as it is and takes to his heels, bumping into doors and furniture. Only a clear mind that is able to consider the consequences removes all the traces one by one. And the clear mind belonged to the former minister, not to some junkie.

Intercourse. Liddell & Scott gave four meanings: 1. being with another or similar, for the purpose of eating or conversation; association, relationship, society, conversation. 2. without speaking . . . but intercourse by continual dealings, relations. 3. listening to the teaching of a master. 4. carnal union, intercourse between male and female, Plato, *Sympos.* 206E.

So 'intercourse between male and female'. Certainly the former minister had not gone with Kalia 'for the purpose of eating or conversation', nor, I surmised, for 'listening to the teachings of a master', even if Kalia had probably taught him a thing or two. He would have opted for the 'carnal union'.

I lay on the bed with my dictionaries around me in order to relax, but I could not get the former minister out of my head. I tried to calculate what his next move would be. Most probably he would contact Arvanitakis and ask her to destroy the data from the opinion polls. He would have gone through Petroulias, had he been alive, but that door was shut for good. He would know nothing about Karamitris, as Koustas had kept her in reserve, so he would try to get out of it on his own and would expose himself. Because from the moment that he began trying to get rid of the data, he would reveal that he knew the opinion polls were fixed and that he had been protecting Koustas in return for his high popularity ratings.

It occurred to me to have his office and home lines tapped. If he were to contact Arvanitakis, he would hardly dare present himself in person, he would do it by phone. I rejected the idea, however, because I would have to go up the hierarchy to get permission to tap a suspect's line and I would never get it. The best thing to do was to wait a couple of days and then take out a search warrant to search the offices of R.I. Hellas. Arvanitakis had told me that morning that she had the data in her desk. If we didn't find it, it would mean that she had disposed of it as a favour to the former minister, and so he had his hands dirty. My only hope was that he would make his move quickly, because the next morning I would have to hand over the evidence I had found in Koustas' warehouse to Ghikas and from then on it would be a matter of hours before he called a halt to the investigation.

I got up from the bed to stop my thoughts racing. Adriani was in the kitchen. All around her, she had spread out tomatoes and peppers, all with their tops cut off, in a pretty, symmetrical arrangement, green, red, one pepper, one tomato. In front of her was a bowl with the filling. She took a pepper, filled it and put its top back on. Then she took a tomato and did the same thing. She worked with amazing speed, as though she had learned the skill in a plastic-toy factory.

'It's a bit early to be preparing them, isn't it?' I said.

She looked up and smiled at me. 'No. They're better if they're left overnight to absorb the oil. Tomorrow, I'll cook the grouper *à la Spetsiote*.'

'What? You're doing fish too?'

'We can't offer the poor man only one dish when we've invited him for lunch. He'll take us for penny-pinchers.'

Quite right. And besides, given that we had not given him a backhander, he might get the wrong idea about us. Adriani went back to her assembly line. I sat and watched her filling three peppers and two tomatoes. Then the phone rang. I went into the living room to answer it and it was Koula.

'Mr Haritos, the Chief Superintendent says that you should be in the office of the Secretary General at seven o'clock.'

I was surprised. I only saw the Secretary General of the Ministry twice a year, if that. 'Did he tell you what he wanted me for?'

'No, only what I've told you.'

'Thank you, Koula.'

I put the phone down and stood there a moment collecting my thoughts. For him to ask to see me at seven in the evening was not a good sign. I went into the bedroom and took out of the bedside drawer the three envelopes – the one containing the film of the former minister, and the other two. To be on the safe side, I took them with me. You never knew.

'I'm going out,' I called to Adriani on my way to the front door.

'What time will you be back so I can have your meal ready?'

'I don't know. The Secretary General wants to see me.'

It was almost six thirty and the traffic was as bad as it could get. Crawling along like that was not the best possible thing because it gave me time to think and I could not get my mind off the Secretary General. If he had simply wanted to be briefed, Ghikas would have found a way to exclude me, because he wanted to have the monopoly on the contacts with the political hierarchy in the Ministry. Was it that he wanted confirmation that there had not been any notable progress in the Koustas case so that he would have an excuse to bury it? If so, Ghikas no doubt wanted me with him to make me the scapegoat. Given that Haritos has not managed to get anywhere, what else can we do but close the case? I would come out of it incompetent, they would come out of it unscathed and the case would get filed. I did not like that scenario one iota, but what could I do? After all, I was still looking for the killer and I was still in the dark. If I had listened to Stellas from Anti-Terrorist from the very beginning and had put the case on file, I would not now be getting burdened with the failure.

When I arrived in the Secretary General's outer office, I found Ghikas sitting in an armchair, waiting. I sat down next to him.

'You've put your foot in it,' he said in a whisper that sounded more like the hissing of a snake. It was accompanied by a venomous look.

'Me? What have I done?'

'You'll find out. But know this: I can't cover for you. You'll have to get out of this one yourself.'

I had no time to reply because the secretary came out of the Secretary General's office and told us to go in.

The office was small and shoddily furnished. The Secretary General was ensconced behind an enormous desk. He neither got up nor held out his hand to greet us; he simply nodded to two chairs in front of his desk. Ghikas sat down and half turned his back so as to face the Secretary General and avoid looking at me.

The attack began with a volley, without warning. 'Mr Haritos, I always thought of you as an extremely able officer, but today you have proved me wrong.'

'Why, Mr Secretary?'

'Who gave you the right to blackmail a Member of Parliament and a former minister at that? Who gave you approval?'

'First of all, I didn't blackmail him.'

'You threatened him in order to obtain information from him. If you wanted to find out what connection he had with Konstantinos Koustas, you should have come to me, or Superintendent Ghikas. The man sounded as though he was shaking from indignation over the phone. He assured me that his only connection with Koustas was that he ate at his restaurant. He is preparing a question for the House and is going to ask the minister to account for your conduct.'

The swine, I thought. As soon as he was sure that there was no other print of the photograph to expose him, he had phoned the Secretary General to get me out of the way.

'Did he say nothing to you about a photograph?' I asked innocently.

'What photograph?'

I took the three envelopes out of my pocket. I chose the one with the film of the former minister and Kalia and handed it to the Secretary General. I kept hold of the other two so as not to use all my ammunition in one go. He raised the film to the lamp on his desk to see it in the light. It seemed that he saw something, because he let it fall immediately, as though it had burned his fingers.

'What is that?' he asked.

'A film with photographs showing the former minister in bed with one of the girls who worked at Koustas' club, the Bouzouki Strings. We found them in a warehouse where Koustas kept his secret files. The girl died of an overdose and I have reason to believe that the former minister was with her at the time of her death.'

'Do you think that he killed her?'

'I have no evidence yet to prove it. But Koustas was blackmailing the former minister and that was the second reason for my having visited him.'

'Why would he blackmail him? What grounds did he have?'

'Using his clubs as a front, Koustas had organised an entire money-laundering operation.' And I gave him the whole zone defence that Koustas had set up. Ghikas had made a ninety-degree turn and was watching me squint-eyed. He would hold it against me, I knew, until one of us retired, but there was nothing I could do about it right then. The Secretary General had his chin resting on his hands and his eyes closed.

'And that's not all, there's more,' and I served him up with the other two envelopes for dessert.

He opened his eyes reluctantly and took the large envelope, the one with the transfer documents for the flat. He read the name of the politician, who belonged to his own party, and, not knowing what to do with the documents, handed them to Ghikas. Then he took the other envelope with the two photographs of the island. He looked at them and handed these too to Ghikas. They looked like two family friends gazing at holiday snapshots: the one looked at them and then handed them to the other.

'What's the significance of these last two photographs?' the Secretary General wanted to know.

'The first is a photograph of the island where the body of Petroulias was found. The second is a photograph of the spot where his body was buried. As for the significance, it is certain that Petroulias was murdered on Koustas' orders. Somebody knew it and was blackmailing Koustas. That is why he was carrying fifteen million on him on the night of the murder.'

'Who was blackmailing him?'

'I don't know that yet. Perhaps the killers themselves were blackmailing him in order to get money out of him. Perhaps he was being blackmailed by the blonde who was with Petroulias and who we have still not been able to track down.'

'When did you come up with this evidence?'

'The day before yesterday.'

'And why didn't you immediately inform your superior officer? You found evidence incriminating political figures and you kept it to yourself?'

'And after I'd stressed that you weren't to make any move without first informing me,' Ghikas added, digging my grave deeper.

'I had every intention of turning it over.'

'You turned it over today because I summoned you and you're trying to get out of the difficult position you find yourself in. Otherwise you might have kept it in your pocket for another couple of weeks.'

I knew that this was my weak spot – in the ordinary way I should have informed Ghikas immediately, but I took a risk and now I was struggling. So far I had been the star of the show, rather like Karteris, Koustas' singer at the Bouzouki Strings. But now I was in danger of becoming the Kalia of the Police Force.

'I wanted to verify the evidence, to be able to give a complete report to the Superintendent.'

'And just when would you have verified it? After having blackmailed the politician that Koustas had given the flat to?'

'I have my hands full with two murders and a money-laundering operation. I considered it my duty to get to the bottom of it.'

'Your duty is to inform your superiors when political figures are involved in your investigations and to wait for instructions. You have been a long time in the Force and you know very well that that is a basic rule. Instead, you took an initiative without informing anyone. Your conduct was not professional, Inspector.'

'It was professionals who built the *Titanic*, Mr Secretary,' I said. 'But the world was saved by Noah, who was an amateur.'

I watched him turn as green as a crab apple. 'You will hand over the case files to Mr Ghikas,' he said angrily. 'And as of today, consider yourself suspended. I'm going to have you sent before the disciplinary board for breach of duty.'

'I did no such thing. When I have my hands full with two murders that are connected, I am obliged to investigate every avenue.'

'You are also obliged to act within the limits of your responsibilities. You are not Noah and we are not going to sink the ark on your account. We're done.'

Of course we were done. Given that they now had the film, the transfer documents and the two photographs of the island, what else did they have to say to me? I got up and went to the door without another word. The members of the disciplinary board would take me for an idiot for having put the noose round my own neck, whereas I could have given the evidence to Ghikas and put the responsibility on him. After all, that's what everyone does and that's how they preserve their peace of mind. All I had to do was to take a walk round the archives to see the mountain of unsolved crimes and confirm what a twerp I was.

'I want the two files on my desk on Monday morning,' I heard Ghikas say behind me.

I did not even acknowledge it. I opened the door and went out.

CHAPTER 50

I had been struggling with my dilemma from the previous evening: should I or shouldn't I tell Adriani and Katerina that I had been suspended? Usually when you share your pain with someone, it's like taking out a loan. You get some breathing space, but you spend months paying back your temporary relief with onerous terms. If I were to say that I had been suspended, I would at least get it off my chest. The price would be that Adriani would get upset and she would start nagging at me out of fear of my suffering a heart attack. Besides, there were two other arguments in favour of my keeping silent. Katerina was leaving the next evening for Thessaloniki and I didn't want her to have to be worried about me. And Ouzounidis was coming for lunch. It would not have been right on our part to receive him with long faces, as though we had invited him to a wake.

This dilemma only added fuel to my anger. With the evidence that I had toiled to gather, the Secretary General had two politicians by the throat. He could now stop the former minister bringing his question to the House, but at the same time he had sugared the pill by having me taken off the case. The two politicians had simply changed master; from being Koustas' pawns, they were now pawns of the Secretary General. I wondered what was more painful for them: being at the beck and call of Koustas or at the beck and call of their peers. They may very well continue to boost their popularity, to upgrade them from water pistols to armoured cars so they might possess weapons with a greater range. Ghikas would sweep the case under the carpet and continue to aim for Chief of Police. As for me, I was the Kalia of the Police Force, as I had predicted. And I had to bear my cross alone, just as Kalia had borne hers to the very end.

'Aren't you going to get dressed? It's already eleven.' I turned and saw Adriani in the bedroom doorway. She had been wearing her Sunday best since first light, as though she had been to the Easter matins.

'What time is he coming?'

'We didn't mention a time, but are you going to welcome him in your pyjamas?'

Reluctantly, I got out of bed. Adriani noticed. 'What's wrong?' she asked anxiously.

'Nothing. The usual Saturday doldrums.'

'Come on, get yourself dressed and into the kitchen and tell me if the fish is all right.'

'Why? If I tell you it's not, are you going to cook it again?'

'Oh, very witty,' she said and went out laughing.

I put on a clean shirt, the trousers from my best suit and a pullover. I was not going to wear a tie for Ouzounidis. Besides, the disciplinary board would most probably suggest I take voluntary early retirement so that I would have no black marks on my records.

Then I would be going round permanently without a tie, which would be just fine.

I quickly shaved and made my way to the kitchen, where waiting for me was my coffee and Adriani, fork in hand.

'Taste it.'

She had been a touch enthusiastic with the pepper, but I didn't say anything so as not to send her into a flurry of despair. 'Very tasty,' I said.

'I don't believe you, just look at you!'

I turned and saw Katerina. She was without make-up and was wearing jeans, a pullover and slippers.

'What's wrong with me?'

'Couldn't you have worn a dress at least?'

'Daddy, where's my ball gown?' I laughed despite my black mood.

'Bumpkins the both of you!' said Adriani scornfully. 'I wonder at how anyone falls in love with her.'

She remained wondering until a quarter past twelve when the doorbell rang. Adriani grabbed me by the hand and rushed me into the living room, where the table was laid: white tablecloth, the best dinner service given as a wedding present by my godmother, the lawyer's daughter, the best glasses that we got at half-price through collecting coupons from the newspapers, all perfectly arranged, as if the distances between them had been measured with a ruler. Of course, the cutlery let us down. She had been going on at me for years to get a set of good cutlery but I had always turned a deaf ear.

Katerina brought him to the living-room doorway and pushed him inside, saying, 'Go on in, you don't need introducing,' while she went into the kitchen with the cake brought by Ouzounidis.

The welcome would have been appreciably shortened had it not been for Adriani's gibbering, all that 'at last' and 'we're so pleased', as if we had all been living on tenterhooks, wondering when he would come round. When my turn came to greet him, we were both so uptight that it was a wonder our hands didn't shake of their own accord. We both smiled uncomfortably.

The small talk came out with difficulty and dried up every so often. We remarked on how fickle the weather had been. We all agreed, and the conversation stopped there. Then, Ouzounidis told us that there had been a lot of traffic on the roads because Athenians went out every Saturday to shop for new shoes. We all laughed and the conversation came to a halt again. In the end, my effort to appear a good host was too much for me and I felt my spirits sagging. Fortunately, we were soon sitting at the table, the *à la Spetsiote* came, and the compliments began. Ouzounidis told us that his parents lived in Veria and he lived alone in Athens and how much he missed home cooking. Adriani sat enraptured, with a smile on her face, and they all forgot about me.

If the two politicians had not been involved in the case, perhaps I would not have been so worried. The worst thing was that I could not be sure how far the Secretary General wanted to take it. If he had taken me off the case so as to sweep it under the carpet, then I was not going to be in too much trouble: I'd get away with a verbal warning. But if he had decided to keep the two politicians in his pocket, then he might have me pensioned off to make them grateful to him and thereby even deeper in his pocket. And how would we get by on a reduced pension? House, rent, Katerina's studies? She still needed at least another two years to complete her thesis. What would I say to her? Stop your studies because your father's an outstanding moron who thought he could take on the politicians.

'Daddy!'

At any rate, I couldn't expect any support from Ghikas. I had succeeded in alienating him altogether. If I had taken care to keep him on my side, he might have put in a good word. After all, he was Chief of Security and his word carried weight.

'Daddy, where are you? I'm talking to you!'

I raised my head from the grouper as if waking from a slumber and saw three pairs of eyes staring at me. Adriani had the poisonous regard of the mother who silently reproaches her child for his bad table manners, while Katerina was waiting for her astonishment to pass first before becoming angry. But worst of all was Ouzounidis' look. He was gazing at me in the same icy way he had gazed at me that day in his surgery, as though he were about to hand me my prescription and kick me out. Now, I've done it, I thought. Now he's going to think that I don't like him for sure and I'm even showing it in my own home. There was no way now I could convince Katerina that he was the one who had behaved coldly and not me.

'I'm sorry. Something happened yesterday at work and I'm still a little upset –'

'Your mind's never off your work,' Adriani interrupted. 'Even when we have guests. What is it this time, some detail you missed? It's always something of the sort that's eating away at you.'

Suddenly it was all too much for me: the Secretary General, Ghikas, the lecherous former minister and his photographs, the money being laundered by mafiosi that no one seemed to care about, the injustice that I should end up carrying the can – for all of it. A hand was tightening round my throat and I felt that if I didn't cry out, I would suffocate. When I did eventually speak, however, my voice didn't come out loud, only hoarse and broken.

'I've been suspended.'

There was a sound like that of a bell ringing. It was Adriani's fork as it fell to her plate. Ouzounidis' expression did a volte-face and the iciness turned to alarm. He turned to Katerina, full of concern. Perhaps he was afraid that she was going to faint, but my daughter was more composed than any of us.

'What happened?' she said calmly. 'Why have you been suspended?'

Someone once said that the elephant is the slowest animal in the world until it gets going. The same was true of me. Till then, I had been holding it all back. As soon as I opened my mouth, however, it all came out. I started from Petroulias' body on the island and finished with my meeting the previous evening with the Secretary General. My confession confirmed what policemen always say: confess and you'll feel a weight lifted off you. As soon as I was through, I felt at peace, and relieved.

'And you were suspended for interrogating a politician?' said Katerina, unable to believe it.

'A former minister.'

'Even so.'

'We were better off during the junta, if you ask me,' Adriani cut in. 'At least, then, the State respected its police officers.'

'That's enough, Mother!' Katerina said. 'They didn't respect them. They had them to torture the poor man in the street.'

'Did your father ever torture anyone?' As if I'd ever tell her if I had.

'What's that got to do with anything?'

'It has. That's why he's been suspended now.'

'None of this has any connection with the junta, Mrs Haritou,' said Ouzounidis gently. Then he turned to me. 'You know, when I was appointed to the hospital, all my colleagues couldn't do enough to help me, to explain things to me, and I was overjoyed. After about six months, they began distancing themselves. They avoided me, talked in low voices to each other and gave me sideways looks. I did all I could to find the cause, until one day the director called me to his office and asked me whether I took bribes from the patients. "Whoever said I take bribes is a liar," I told him angrily. "You're right not to," was his reply, "but don't let it be known. Make out that you do."'

'You mean he wanted you *not* to take bribes, but to lie and say that you *did*?' I asked, astounded.

'I was equally astonished. Do you know what he said to me? "I'm telling you for your own good. Otherwise they'll make your life hell and your patients will end up by paying for it."'

'And what did you do?' Katerina said.

'A variation on a theme,' he replied, laughing. 'I still don't take bribes, and I don't say that I do. I simply let people assume it.'

I reflected that I had been unable to realise what the doctor had realised: that the difference is not between ethicalness and unethicalness, but between what seemingly was or wasn't. The former minister was on the take from Koustas, but seemingly made out that he wasn't. The doctor wasn't on the take from his patients, but seemingly made out that he was. The one was seemingly ethical, the other seemingly unethical. So I should have realised that the former minister was involved in Koustas' money-laundering operation, but have made out that I didn't realise it, so that I could seemingly be a police officer and have my peace of mind.

I saw Adriani, who all this time had been biting her lip, get up and leave the room. I knew she was going into the kitchen to cry and let it out. It wasn't that she was afraid of my being suspended, but the fact that I had been dealt with unjustly offended her egoism. I got up to go after her and comfort her, but Katerina held me back.

'Leave her, she needs it,' she said.

And before long, she came back with a smile on her face. If she had been crying, she must have rinsed her face so it wouldn't show. The one good thing about my confession was that it warmed the atmosphere and we all felt much more at ease. When, at around six, the doctor and Katerina decided to go out, we had already promised not to lose touch now that Katerina was leaving. As it turned out, I had been wrong both about the former minister and about the doctor. I had underestimated them both. Adriani went into the kitchen and Katerina went to get ready.

'How old is the Secretary General who suspended you?' Ouzounidis asked me once we were alone.

'Around forty-five.'

'We had a professor of psychiatry at the university. Do you know what he used to say to us?'

'What?'

'Heaven help us when the polytechnic-school generation starts performing operations. But he was wrong.'

'Why?'

'Because the polytechnic-school generation doesn't perform operations. They all found a nice little niche for themselves in politics. That's the tragedy of it.'

I couldn't see the tragedy myself. We used to knock them around, now they knock us around. That's all there was to it.

CHAPTER 51

What Saturday didn't bring, Sunday did. To be more precise, the night between Saturday and Sunday, I felt a terrible discomfort. I woke up every half-hour, then tossed and turned for another half-hour until I fell asleep again. Beside me, Adriani sensed I was restless and opened her eyes a couple of times, but then I pretended to be asleep.

I woke properly at nine in the morning feeling exhausted and with my heart racing. I measured my pulse rate and it was 105. I took an Inderal and lay on my back, with my eyes fixed on the ceiling. I thought of taking down a dictionary to relax a bit, but I didn't have the energy to go as far as the bookcase. Eventually, Adriani came into the bedroom and in a worried voice asked me what was wrong.

'There's nothing wrong. Don't start on at me,' I said curtly to stop her getting worked up.

By eleven, my heart rate hadn't eased up, my pulse was still up to a hundred and I took a second Inderal. I had started to think that I would end up in the hospital again, when Katerina came in.

'My bags are ready,' she said as she walked in, but she saw me motionless, with my gaze fixed on the ceiling and stopped. 'What's wrong?' she asked.

'Don't say anything to your mother, but my heart is going nineteen to the dozen. I've taken two Inderal, but it's not had any effect.'

She went out without saying anything and before long came back with a glass of water and half a tablet.

'What's that?'

'Lexotanil. It's from Fanis.'

'Is he here?'

'No, he got them last night from a chemist's. "If your father has any problems with his heart," he told me, "give him half a Lexotanil and it'll help." Come on, take it.'

I was in no position to argue and I swallowed it without a word.

'If Mum were to see us at this moment, she'd say "See how useful it is to have a doctor in the family,'" and she laughed. Then she leaned over and hugged me. 'Don't worry, they won't do anything to you,' she said. 'It's not in their best interests to go all the way with it. They'll shove the case under the carpet and forget about the disciplinary board.'

'Ghikas won't forget it.'

'Ghikas will do whatever his superiors tell him. That's why he got to be Chief while you remained an inspector.'

'Does it bother you that I am only an inspector?'

'Of course not. Fanis, too, will end up staying where he is with that mind of his, but that doesn't bother me either.'

After three-quarters of an hour I had to admit, albeit belatedly, that Ouzounidis knew his stuff and I got up. I went into the kitchen where Adriani and Katerina were chatting.

'So you're up?' Adriani said, relieved. 'Shall I get you a coffee?'

'Naturally.'

While I was drinking my coffee, the phone rang and Katerina answered it. 'Daddy, it's Fanis and he wants to talk to you,' she called from the living room.

'How did you know my heart was going to play up?' I asked him when I picked up the receiver.

'It wasn't difficult to diagnose,' he said cheerfully. 'It has nothing to do with your heart, it's the stress. How are you feeling?'

'Better.'

'Good. If it plays up again tomorrow when you hand over the files, don't be alarmed. Take half a Lexotanil again. If it doesn't ease up, phone me. Katerina has my home number and the number of the hospital.'

'Thanks.'

'Don't thank me. After all, I'm your doctor.' He paused for a moment, then added: 'Don't stay in today. Take your wife and Katerina and go and eat out somewhere before you take her to the station.'

I was still in a state of shock and I followed his advice without protest. I told Adriani and Katerina to get ready to go out. It was drizzling and because it was Sunday there was only light traffic on the roads. We were only the third group of people in the taverna. The rest of the tables were empty. I ate with my gaze fixed on Katerina. She was upset at leaving us, upset at leaving Fanis, but managed to hide it and was all smiles.

After the meal, I took them to Kifissia for coffee and by the time we arrived at Larissa station, it was already six thirty. Katerina's train was at seven and she told us not to wait, but we insisted on seeing her into the carriage. We had done that the first time she had left for Thessaloniki and since then it had become an unwritten law. Before we parted, she put her arms round me and held me tight.

'Don't worry,' she whispered in my ear. 'And if you have any problems, call Fanis.'

'I'll be fine,' I said, also in a whisper, to reassure her.

'I know you. You won't say anything to Mum, so at least tell Fanis. And I'll call you tomorrow to find out what happened.'

After having had Katerina staying with us for so many weeks, the house seemed empty, lifeless. Adriani pricked up her ears, as if waiting to hear some sound, something to tell her that Katerina was still in the house. But she heard nothing; there was absolute silence and her eyes filled with tears.

'She's gone,' she said in a broken voice.

I made the mistake of holding her to me and she burst into tears. She put her head on my chest and began sobbing silently.

'Don't carry on like that. It'll be Christmas in a couple of months. She'll be home again.'

I had no idea how those couple of months would pass, but the first couple of hours passed in front of the TV watching *Blind Date*. At first, I was bored stiff, but I sat with Adriani to keep her company. Slowly, however, I began to discover the beneficial effects of those programmes. You watch them blind – as the title says. Your eye is on them, but you see nothing of the gold lamé that passes before you, hear nothing of the inanities that the people come out with and you let your mind drift off elsewhere. Mine drifted to the conversation I'd had with Ghikas and the Secretary General. Perhaps I should not have handed over all of the film, should have kept some negatives to have them developed and to show to the disciplinary board. The same with the transfer documents. I should have made photocopies before handing them over. I thought that I would impress them with the evidence I had and I got caught out like a tyro. Now how was I going to convince the members of the disciplinary board that I had had incriminatory evidence when I had gone to interrogate the former minister and how could I convince Ghikas to get it out from his drawer? On the one hand I was afraid they would hush the matter up and, on the other, I had handed them everything they needed on a plate in order for them to do just that. My only hope was what Ouzounidis and my daughter had predicted: that they would let it all blow over and forget about the disciplinary board.

These thoughts kept revolving in my head until I heard the sound of the news bulletin and I got up. I had no wish to listen to the news on a Sunday evening. I had reached the door of the living room when I heard, among the main stories, 'Upheavals in the Police Force in connection with the Koustas case' and I made an about-turn. Adriani shot me a questioning look, but I shrugged. I had no idea what they were going to say, whether the Secretary General had spoken, or if Ghikas had made a statement to the press, but I felt my heart pounding again.

I waited patiently during the news of flooding in Achaea, of a junkie who had been found dead in Kolokynthou, of the twenty-two violations of Greek airspace by Turkish fighter planes, of two Albanians who had killed a farmer just outside Yannena, until at last the newscaster said:

'Turmoil prevails in the ranks of the Greek police in connection with the still-unsolved murder of Konstantinos Koustas. More from our special correspondent, Menis Sotiropoulos.'

Sotiropoulos appeared on cue, in his Armani shirt and Timberland shoes, standing in front of the entrance to Security Headquarters in Alexandras Avenue.

'Good evening, Nikos, good evening, ladies and gentlemen. From his grave, Konstantinos Koustas has managed to turn the Police Force on its head. Unconfirmed reports say that the Security's Head of Homicide, Inspector Costas Haritos, has been suspended from all duties.'

'And do you believe, Menis, if it's true, that this is connected with the investigations into the murder of Konstantinos Koustas?'

'Nikos, the police have never before kept their cards so close to their chests. And there's a reason for that. It's an open secret that Koustas was involved in a number of suspicious activities, even though no charge was ever brought against him. The rumours say that Inspector Haritos set out to interrogate certain political figures who, it appears, were involved in a money-laundering operation that had been set up by Koustas.'

'And do you think that this is the reason for the Inspector being suspended?'

'We can say nothing for certain at the present time. However, Inspector Haritos is one of the most honest and most able officers in the Force and if it proves to be true that he has been suspended, then it is not improbable that an attempt is being made to cover up the case in order to protect certain political figures.'

'So, in other words, Haritos is being made the scapegoat?'

'I hope that's not the case. But if it is, I can assure you that the public will learn the truth and the attempted cover-up will fail.'

'Thank you, Menis.'

The topic changed and the leader of the Opposition appeared in Gavdos, wearing a pullover and no jacket, denouncing the government.

Why had Sotiropoulos done that? He was not particularly fond of me and, for my part, I could not stand the man. And yet he had gone on the air to defend me. Why? To get a story? He could have done that without singing my praises.

I turned and looked at Adriani. She was smiling from ear to ear and her eyes were sparkling. 'Did you hear what Sotiropoulos said, and you can't bear him?' she said.

'And just think, he's not even a junta supporter,' I replied.

CHAPTER 52

'Guess whose name Koustas' warehouse was in,' said Vlassopoulos the next morning when he saw me walking down the corridor. 'Loukia Karamitris.'

'It's of no concern to me. Bring me the files on Koustas and Petroulias,' I told him and turned rapidly into my office in order to avoid the expressions of support and the variety of looks – some of sympathy, some of understanding, some of spite, all of which would annoy me equally.

I didn't get a coffee or a croissant, partly because the coffee would accelerate my heart rate, partly because I wanted to convince myself that I was only passing through, that I would simply hand over the files to Ghikas and then go. How I would spend my days idly at home, bickering all day with Adriani, was another matter, and I preferred not to think about it for the time being.

Vlassopoulos brought the two files and left them on my desk. 'I heard it last night on the news,' he said, 'but I thought it was just TV talk.'

'I don't want to discuss it, Sotiris.'

'OK, I understand.'

He went out and closed the door quietly behind him. First, I opened Petroulias' file. Everything was there: the statement by Anita and her English boyfriend, the statement by the philosopher-*cum*-lion-tamer together with the additional statement he had made in Germany, Markidis' report, as well as the statements by the president of the Association of Referees and Petroulias' neighbour. And all my own notes. I put it aside and picked up Koustas' file. I went through his file more thoroughly. I did not want to leave out any document and have them accusing me of deliberately concealing evidence. Under normal circumstances, I would have written a detailed summary of each case for Ghikas, the better to put him in the picture, but he had only asked me for the files and I was not prepared to add so much as a full stop.

Sotiropoulos found me arranging the documents in chronological order. Usually, he came around eleven, but he had come earlier to see how I had taken last night's report. I was at a loss because I didn't know whether I should thank him or pretend I hadn't seen it. Fortunately, he got me out of my difficult position.

'You're smarter than I thought,' he said. 'You made me think you knew nothing, whereas you'd succeeded in unearthing everything concerning Koustas' little operation. But that was your mistake.'

'What? To have unearthed it?'

'No, that you said nothing. If you had come out with even one little piece of information, they wouldn't have dared to lay a finger on you. But, on the one hand, you play the faithful little hound and, on the other, you do as you please. The one undermines the other and that's why you always come out the loser.'

'Why did you do what you did?' I asked him.

'What did I do?'

'That story last night. Go on the air and sing my praises. Why did you do it? We've known each other a long time, I know, but it's not as though we see eye to eye exactly.'

He shrugged. 'I didn't do it for your sake; I did it for my sake.'

'For your sake?'

'Yes. The job goes from bad to worse and I'm swimming in a cesspool all day. Now and again I have to lift my head to get a breath of air. So that I don't suffocate. You were a good opportunity, that's all.'

I looked at him, standing there in front of my desk, in all his brand names. Somewhere deep down, the commie inside him was still smouldering. He turned to go, but at the door, he said: 'Anyhow, it's still not too late.'

'For what?'

'For you to talk. If they do suspend you, let what you know leak out. They won't dare to lay a finger on you, I guarantee it. You have my phone number.'

I watched him disappearing through the door. He, too, had taken the same course: from commie to seemingly ethical. He was seemingly swimming in a cesspool, but he got his rake-off from his good deed. I put the two files under my arm and went out into the corridor. As I passed Dermitzakis' office, I saw him chatting with Sotiropoulos. Whatever they were saying, I did not want to know.

The lift was waiting for me, with open arms, as though overjoyed that it would soon be rid of me. I pressed the button for the fifth floor.

'Heavens, what's happening today?' Koula said on seeing me walk in. 'The phones have been ringing all morning. The Secretary General has called three times alone, not to mention the reporters.'

He had called three times because he was desperate to know whether I had handed over the files. 'Don't worry, they'll stop calling soon,' I replied and walked straight into Ghikas' office without knocking. Given that they were in such a hurry to get the files, formalities were of little importance.

Ghikas was at the window, admiring the view, namely the church of Aghios Savvas and the old Panathinaikos Stadium. He heard the door closing and turned. He saw that it was me and sat down at his desk to take custody of the documents in an official pose. I put the files on his desk.

'The files of Petroulias and Koustas. Nothing missing.'

He looked at me without touching them. I knew he was going to pretend to be devastated, but he would also say that it was my fault. He would want *me* to be plagued by remorse for putting *him* in a difficult position and being unable to help me.

'The files are to remain with you,' he said. He registered my surprise, but he gave no inkling of pleasure. 'The minister saw Sotiropoulos' television report last night and is furious with the Secretary General. He has ordered that the investigations continue, without any attempt to cover up the involvement of the two politicians. He said that they are protected by parliamentary immunity and it's for the Parliament to decide whether it will be lifted or not. The Police Force is to do its job.' He paused and we looked at each other in silence for a good half-minute before he took up again. 'Keeping the evidence you found in Koustas' warehouse from me wasn't right,' he said. 'You did it because you thought I would hush the matter up and that upset me.'

Of course he would have hushed it up, but now he had the weight of the minister behind him and he could talk without fear. I leaned over and picked up the files from his desk. Ghikas still had his gaze fixed on me. As if he wanted to say something, but couldn't get it out. What I had heard was so incredible that I knew at once it could not possibly be the whole truth. No minister goes to such lengths for an officer in the Homicide Division as to take his Secretary General to task and incur the displeasure of the Chief of Security. He would be more likely to replace him than come into conflict with two of his close associates.

'It's not only Sotiropoulos' report. There's something else that you haven't told me.'

'Yes, there is something else,' he said, in a tight spot now.

'What?'

'This morning, Loukia Karamitris was found dead in her car. Someone had put a bullet in her head.'

So that was it. Any cover-up was now going to be even more complicated. They now had a fourth murder on their hands and suspending me would have been that much more difficult to justify.

'Where was she killed?'

'She was found in the forest at Varybobi, by a young couple passing on a motorbike.'

His words reached me as I was going through the door. 'When you come back, write me a brief report so I can make a statement. We can't keep it under wraps any longer.'

He had got himself out of it and now he wanted his little spiel written for him. He was not remotely concerned about Karamitris. She was my headache.

CHAPTER 53

Loukia Karamitris was lolling back in her seat and staring through the windscreen at the tall pines on both sides of the road. Her right arm was resting on the passenger seat. Her mouth was half open.

Beneath her red jacket, she was dressed any old how, in a yellow blouse and blue skirt. As if someone had phoned her and she had put on whatever she first laid hands on and rushed out to meet whoever it was. Markidis was bent over, examining her.

'Found anything?' I asked.

'Don't be in such a hurry. I've only just got here.'

'I let him get on with his work. The patrol car was parked twenty metres off, and on the other side of the road, a young lad of around twenty-two was leaning against a 1000cc motorbike. He was wearing a black leather jacket, black leather trousers and black boots. If it had not been for the dark glasses, I would have taken him for an office armchair. When he saw me walking to the patrol car, he followed me.

Sitting on the back seat of the car was a girl, also wearing leather gear. Most likely they shopped at the same store and so got a reduction. She was nervously squeezing a cigarette between her fingers. Every so often, she put it to her lips, drew on it deeply and then looked at the ash to see if it had grown any longer.

'Was it you who found her?' I asked.

She nodded her head, ready to burst into hysterical sobbing.

'Keep cool, girl!' her friend called to her. 'Keep cool and tell him what he wants so we can be off.'

'Get him out of here,' I said to the officer who was sitting in the passenger seat.

He needed no persuasion. He got out of the car, grabbed hold of the lad by the arm and started pushing him away forcibly.

'What's your name?' I asked the girl.

'Maria . . . Maria Stathakis.'

'Tell me exactly what happened, Maria. Take your time, no urgency. All you have to do is tell me and then you can go.'

She drew again on the cigarette. 'Stratos and I were on our way to Oropos, to catch the ferry,' she whispered. 'I wanted to go via Varybobi because it's nice riding through the forest in the morning. But we got lost and didn't know how to get back on to the National Road. We saw the car parked there and Stratos sent me over to ask for directions. The woman was sitting – sitting, like you saw her. I tapped on the window, but she didn't turn to look at me. I thought it strange.'

She started to tremble and burst into tears. I was afraid that the nervous outburst would make her tongue-tied, but she went on in a whisper.

'I thought there must be something wrong with her and . . . and I opened the car door . . . I touched her, but she still didn't move . . . Then . . . then I saw the bullet hole in her head.' She started sobbing again.

'And you realised that she was dead?'

She nodded. 'I called Stratos. He said that she was dead and phoned Emergency.'

'Where did he call from?'

'From his mobile.'

'Calm down, Maria, we're done. As soon as I've spoken to your friend, you can leave.'

She lit another cigarette. The young man was astride his bike with the engine running, ready to pounce. He was irked because we had pushed him around a bit.

'What time was it when you called Emergency?' I asked him.

'Nine thirty.'

'How long was that after you'd seen that the woman was dead?'

'I don't have my eyes on my watch all the time,' he said, deliberately provocative.

'Five minutes? Ten? An hour? How long roughly?'

'Ten minutes.'

'While you were here, did you see anyone else?'

'Like who, for example?'

I felt like thumping him. 'How should I know? I'm asking you. A pedestrian, a car, a motorbike, anything at all.'

'No, we didn't see anyone. Who'd be fool enough to ride through a forest at that time apart from us?' And Karamitris who was killed, I thought. 'But we did see a car as we were coming here.'

'Going which way?'

'Towards Athens. A Toyota Corolla. About five hundred metres from here.'

295

'Did you notice anything about its number plate?'

'No.'

'The driver?'

'Yes.'

'Out with it then. Don't piss me around,' I said angrily.

'I saw him out of the corner of my eye as he had the window wound down. He had white hair.'

'White hair?' Lambros Madas, the doorman at the Bouzouki Strings had told me that Koustas' murderer had had white hair. 'And his face? Did you notice anything?'

'I didn't have time. He was going at some lick.'

I called one of the officers from the patrol car. 'Take their particulars. We need them to make a statement,' I told him. 'Then let them go.'

Could it be that the same person had murdered both Koustas and Karamitris? The fact that he had sped off when he saw the young couple seemed to lead to that conclusion.

Markidis had finished and was collecting his things together. 'So what do we have?' I asked.

'She has been shot at point-blank range in the right temple. Do you see?' he said, leaning inside the car to show me Karamitris' temple. 'You can see the imprint of the mouth of the barrel. The hole is perfectly round and the surrounding hair singed. The black grease from the bullet is quite visible around the edge. The bullet came out of the left temple, hit the side window and ricocheted. You'll no doubt find it in the car.'

'When did the murder take place?'

'Two hours ago at most.'

I looked at my watch. It was eleven. 'Were there any signs of struggle?'

'No.'

'What type of weapon was it?'

'At first sight, it looks like a .38, but I'll be able to tell you exactly following the autopsy.'

In the distance I could see the ambulance coming to collect Karamitris. It drew up beside the patrol car and two paramedics got out carrying the stretcher. I shouted to Dimitris from Forensics. 'See if you can find the bullet, it should be somewhere in the car.'

If the gun was a .38, then the murderer in both cases was the same white-haired man. But instead of making things clearer, this only complicated matters. All right, he had killed Koustas because he was the brains behind the operation. But why had he killed Karamitris? Something wasn't right. Unless this same white-haired man had also killed Petroulias and it was a clean-up operation. Someone was eliminating all traces. But that was something we could only find out from the murderer or from the blonde, and we didn't know who she was or where she was.

As the ambulance pulled away, a silver Nissan drew up next to me. The door opened and Kosmas Karamitris got out.

'They notified me just half an hour ago. Is it true?' he asked in a fluster.

'Yes. Someone shot your wife at point-blank range. Where were you when they notified you?'

'In my office.'

'What time did you leave home?'

'Eight thirty, just like every morning.'

'Was your wife at home when you left?'

'Yes. She still hadn't got up.'

So, the murderer either knew when Karamitris left home or was following him and saw him leave. Then he had telephoned the wife and had arranged to meet here. But why would Loukia Karamitris rush out of the house because some stranger phoned her? Had she known her murderer, too, like Koustas? If she had, then she was more involved in the business than she had admitted to me.

Dimitris came over to me holding a small plastic bag with a bullet inside. 'We've found it, Inspector. It's from a .38. I'd bet money that it's from the same gun used to kill Koustas.'

'Koustas?' Karamitris asked in astonishment. 'What are you saying? That whoever killed Koustas also killed my wife?'

I didn't reply because, at that moment, another possibility suddenly flashed through my mind. What if I was wrong? What if Koustas and his ex-wife had not been killed by his underworld associates, but by someone else, who would benefit from having them out of the way?

'Let's go to my office for a chat,' I said to Karamitris. 'In any case, I need you to make a statement.'

'They said I'd have to go to the mortuary to identify the body.'

'There's no rush, it's only a formality. Besides, I was able to identify her given that I knew her.'

He looked at me curiously, but was in no position to object. 'Let's go,' he said.

'Would you object to our searching your house first?'

That put a flea in his ear and he stared at me. 'Am I under suspicion?'

I shrugged. 'In a murder case, people in the immediate environment are always under suspicion until it's verified that they had no connection,' I replied, as vaguely as I could. 'If you allow us to look round voluntarily, it means you have nothing to hide.'

He hesitated a little, but then agreed. 'All right, but I want to be present.'

I grabbed hold of Vlassopoulos and Dermitzakis, who had been sent off to look for eyewitnesses, but had returned empty-handed. Karamitris led the way in his car and we followed behind.

Vlassopoulos and Dermitzakis began searching, while Karamitris and I sat in the living room in the two armchairs covered in the shiny green material. I looked around. It seemed nothing had changed since my previous visit. There was the same image of faded splendour attempting to conceal itself behind a veneer of make-up, but without success.

'My employees will confirm that I arrived at the office around nine fifteen, like every morning,' Karamitris said.

'I have no doubt that they will.' I already knew that the murderer was the white-haired man, but I kept that to myself.

'Then why are you searching my home?'

'Because we may find some piece of evidence that will help us.'

The evidence came ten minutes later and Vlassopoulos was holding it in his hand. 'Look, Inspector.'

He handed me an open cheque for fifteen million. The signature on it was legible enough for me to see that it belonged to Kosmas Karamitris.

'What's this?' I asked him.

'A cheque.'

'I can see that. It's one of the open cheques that Koustas was holding in order to blackmail you. How did you get your hands on it?' I added, before he was able to reply, 'And take care not to lie to me, because I'll have your accounts checked and I'll know if you redeemed it.'

'It came by post,' he mumbled.

'By post? What do you take me for, Karamitris?'

'No, really. It came by post the day before yesterday.'

'And where's the envelope?'

'I threw it away.'

'Where's the second cheque for twenty million that you'd given to Koustas?'

'I don't know. That's all that was in the envelope.'

The case was starting to make sense. I had been searching for racketeers and mobsters and the solution had been right in front of my nose. I had suspected him from our very first conversation, but Koustas' money-laundering had led me in the wrong direction.

'Mr Karamitris, you're coming down to Security HQ with me because you have a lot of explaining to do,' I told him.

'The cheque came by post. I'm telling you the truth.'

'You're making it up. Who makes a gift of a cheque for fifteen million and through the post at that, not even by special delivery. Look around for the other one,' I said to Vlassopoulos.

They looked, but found nothing. The other cheque had to do with his record company and he had most likely taken it to his office. Karamitris' car remained parked outside his house and we all left together in the patrol car.

CHAPTER 54

Vlassopoulos and Dermitzakis locked Karamitris in the interrogation room. I left him to steep in his anxiety and headed for my
office. If I had wanted everything to be above board concerning
regulations, this would have been the moment to inform Ghikas, but
I wanted to interrogate Karamitris first.

I was going into my office when the phone rang. It was Adriani.

'You said you'd be back soon. What happened?' she asked, her
voice full of worry.

'I'm staying here. The situation has changed and we're back to the
old routine.' I explained everything to her in detail.

'Serves them right,' was her gleeful comment. 'Will you be late?'

'Don't ask. I've no idea.'

'All right. Come whenever you're done.'

Everything was going my way, I thought. The minister had
revoked the order to suspend me, and Adriani had given me leave of
absence for an unspecified time.

There followed a second call, straight after the first. This time it
was Katerina. 'What happened, Dad?'

'Did you arrive safely?'

'Never mind whether I arrived safely, what happened with you?' I
told her the story of my day from the beginning.

'I said they wouldn't dare do anything to you and I was right,' she
said in a satisfied tone.

'What am I supposed to do now with the Lexotanil?' I said to tease
her.

'Hold on to them. The way you take everything to heart, you'll be
needing them again soon.

I hung up and summoned Dermitzakis. 'Send the young couple
that found Karamitris' body to the artist at Forensics. I want a
picture of the driver.'

'OK, but from what they said, they only caught a glimpse of him.'

'When they put their minds to it, they'll come up with other
details. If necessary, get Madas too. He saw him at night but he

might remember some details. And I need a search warrant for Karamitris' office.'

I got up to go to the interrogation room, but I was stopped yet again by the telephone. I was surprised to hear Elena Koustas' voice.

'I've just heard on the news that Konstantinos' ex-wife has been murdered. Do you think I may be in any danger, Inspector?'

'No, Mrs Koustas. You're in no danger. Loukia Karamitris was involved in your husband's dealings. You were not.'

There was a short pause. 'Is it true that Konstantinos was laundering money?' she said.

I did not want to upset her, but there was no point in lying. In any case, the bombshell would drop in the next few days. 'Yes, it's true.'

'And you say that I'm in no danger?'

She hung up before I had had time to tell her that the dirty money her husband had been laundering had no direct connection with the two murders. Someone else had killed Koustas and Karamitris and for some other reason.

When I walked into the interrogation room, I found Karamitris sitting at the end of the table. Vlassopoulos was standing over him just as he had done with Yannis, Koustas' accountant.

'On the night that Koustas was killed, I was at home with Loukia. You asked me and I told you,' he said.

'You told me, I remember.' I sat down beside him.

'Unfortunately, Loukia is no longer alive to be able to confirm it.'

'It's not necessary, I believe you.'

He was surprised, but seemed relieved. 'And this morning, I left home at eight thirty. Loukia had only just woken up. I arrived at my office at nine fifteen. You can check to confirm that.'

'I will, but I have no doubt that is the case.'

He felt more confident on seeing that I believed his alibi and raised his voice. 'Then why have you dragged me down here?'

I leaned over and looked him in the eye. 'I've dragged you down here so you can tell me about the white-haired man,' I said calmly.

'What white-haired man?'

'The one you had kill Koustas and then your wife.'

301

His gaze froze. 'I had someone kill Koustas and my wife? Are you out of your mind?'

'Karamitris, you were smart, I'll give you that. Of course, you were helped by Koustas' criminal associates. When I learned that he'd been killed by a white-haired man, I thought at first that it must have been a professional hit man. And I would have gone on believing it if you hadn't made the mistake of sending him to kill your wife.'

He had begun trembling. 'You're wrong,' he murmured. 'I didn't send anyone to kill either Koustas or Loukia.'

'I can understand about Koustas,' I told him calmly. 'He had you dancing to his tune and he was prepared to cut your legs from under you at any moment. You thought that if you got him out of the way, you'd have some breathing space and then you'd have all the time you needed to find the cheques. If you'd stopped there, Koustas' murder might have remained unsolved because we were targeting his associates and you would have got away with it. But your greed got the better of you. When you saw how easy it was to get rid of Petroulias, you thought of getting rid of your wife in the same way so that you'd be left with the businesses that, on paper at least, were in her name – the opinion-poll agency, the sports store and the Chinese restaurant.'

'Why would I kill Loukia? She was my wife and in any case would share the businesses left to her after Koustas' death.'

'Because you were at daggers drawn. I saw it with my own eyes. Do you want me to remind you what you said to me when I came to your house the first time? You said that you couldn't divorce her because Koustas wouldn't let you. And she called you a third-rate singer. You were afraid that now Koustas was dead, she would divorce you. Who knows, maybe she even told you she would and that's why you were in a hurry to get rid of her. You are an accessory to two murders.'

His fear put fire in his belly. He began to shout. 'I didn't kill anyone, dammit! You're trying to pin the killings on me because you are too incompetent to find who really is responsible.'

'We'll find the white-haired man, don't you worry!' Vlassopoulos said. 'But that won't change anything as far as you're concerned. You'll go down for life as an accessory to the fact.'

My mind suddenly tripped over a detail that I had discovered at the start of the investigations. I hadn't attached any significance to it at the time and had forgotten it. I racked my brains trying to remember what it was.

'I'm not an accessory to anything,' Karamitris was shouting. 'And your white-haired man has nothing to do with me at all.'

'Then how did the cheque for fifteen million come to be in your house?' I said.

'I told you. It came by post.'

'When?'

'The day before yesterday.'

'How did it come? Regular post, recorded delivery, how?'

'I don't know. We found it pushed through the letter box. Loukia's name was on the envelope.'

'Who sent it?'

'There was no name. Not even a stamp. Someone just pushed a cheque for fifteen million through the letter box and didn't wait for a receipt.'

'What do you take us for, you moron?' With one hand, Vlassopoulos grabbed him by his jacket collar and lifted him up. He began shaking him. It was like Adriani making her egg and lemon sauce. 'First you said it came by post and now you tell us someone pushed it through the letter box. Do you take us for dimwits, you scumbag?'

'I don't know. It may sound strange, but that's exactly what happened.'

'Where is the other cheque you gave Koustas? The one for twenty million?'

'I don't know. There was only the one cheque in the envelope. I've no idea where the other one is. You searched my house an hour ago and you didn't find it. You can search my office too. You won't find it there either.'

'We won't find it because you tore it up,' Vlassopoulos said, pinning him to the wall.

303

'So why didn't I tear up the other one, too?'

'Maybe you kept it to make it out to the white-haired man,' I said. 'His fee for killing Koustas, getting rid of your wife and finding the cheques for you.'

'Is that it, you sod? Is that why you kept it? Speak!' Vlassopoulos bellowed, now pinning him against the wall.

'You can't treat me like this! I've done nothing! I want to see my lawyer!'

'You'll see your lawyer as soon as you've confessed,' I said.

The interrogation went on in much the same vein. We leaned on him, but Karamitris continued to protest his innocence. And all the while I searched my memory to resurrect the elusive detail that I had forgotten, but it wouldn't come. After two hours, I took Vlassopoulos outside the interrogation room.

'Lock him up with some bum,' I told him. 'He'll have a rough night and he might break. In the meantime, we'll search his office, even though we won't find the second cheque. He tore it up. That's why he doesn't mind our going there to search.'

I got into the lift and took a breather in Ghikas' office. I found him with Stellas from Anti-Terrorist. Time for him to learn his lesson, too: that we don't put cases on file before solving them.

'Any developments?' Ghikas asked.

'We're still looking for the killer, but we've found an accessory to both murders.'

'Who is it?' he asked me, leaping to his feet. He was still terrified it might be one of the two politicians.

'Kosmas Karamitris, the husband of Loukia Karamitris. First he had Koustas killed because he was holding cheques of his for a total of thirty-five million, and then he had the same man kill his wife so that he could get his hands on what Koustas had owned and was in her name.'

'Why would he do that, given that they were married?' Stellas said.

I thought of suggesting him as Karamitris' lawyer. 'Because they both wanted a divorce. It seems that Loukia intended to make the first move, Karamitris got scared and had her killed before she had time to start proceedings.'

'Do we have enough evidence to make your case?' Ghikas said.

I had the cheque ready and handed it to him. 'It's one of the two cheques that Karamitris had given to Koustas.'

'And how did he get his hands on it?'

'He says it came in an envelope pushed through his letter box.'

They both laughed. 'Prepare a report for me so I can make a statement. We don't have the murderer yet, but the accessory is enough for us to be able to say that we've effectively cracked both cases. The case of Petroulias has already been wrapped up.'

'You'll have it tomorrow morning.'

'Congratulations, you managed it,' he said to me as I was leaving. He had never congratulated me, but he found it a good bit easier than apologising to me for having colluded in my suspension.

'You lot in Homicide are downright ferrets,' Stellas said. 'You don't give up, do you?'

That is why every now and again we catch a killer, while you never catch any terrorists, I wanted to say, but I kept my mouth shut.

I walked out of Ghikas' office like a turkey that's been fattened up a week before Christmas. I called Dermitzakis and asked him what had happened with the sketch of the man with white hair.

'The young couple are working on it now with the artist, but I don't think they'll be finished this side of midnight,' he said.

'Did you have Madas brought from Korydallos Prison?'

'No. I thought I'd wait and see what the two kids came up with.'

'Have him brought in, don't waste time. Where's the search warrant?'

'We'll have it tomorrow morning.'

There was nothing else to be done and I was getting ready to leave when the phone rang again.

'Stratopoulou here.' It was a woman's voice. 'Do you remember me, Inspector?' The name meant something to me but I couldn't quite recall. 'From San Marin. We chartered the sailboat to Petroulias, the man who was murdered,' she added, when she realised my hesitation.

'Of course I remember.' Was that the detail I had forgotten? No, it was something else, but I still couldn't recall what.

'I phoned you to tell you that we had sent the boat to the repair yard. When we got it back they gave us some things belonging to Petroulias. It seems he had put them in a little cupboard behind the helm and no one had thought of searching there. Do you want me to bring them in to you?'

'If it's not too much trouble.'

'I'll stop by tomorrow morning on the way to the office.'

'Thank you, Mrs Stratopoulou.'

Not that they would be of any interest now, but it wouldn't be right to discourage members of the public who wish to help the forces of law and order.

CHAPTER 55

Gloat: to look at something or think about it with satisfaction, often in an unpleasant way. I felt the dictionary slip from my hands. It seems I fell asleep gloating over the misfortune of the Secretary General that had happened at just the right time to coincide with the murder of Loukia Karamitris. It was the first time in three days that I had slept like a baby, no interruptions, no nightmares.

I woke up in the morning feeling cheery and also impatient. I was in a hurry to get to the office to close the file on Kosmas Karamitris. Walking down the corridor on the third floor reminded me of the good old days. Cameras, microphones and a pack of reporters were blocking the door to my office.

'Patience, everyone. Superintendent Ghikas will be making a statement presently,' I said, pushing past them.

'Is it true that it was Kosmas Karamitris who murdered Koustas and Loukia Karamitris?' shouted someone from the back.

'I told you, there'll be a statement. Have a little patience.'

'You managed it again,' Sotiropoulos whispered as I passed in front of him. 'Don't forget what you owe.'

I had not asked him for anything and I did not owe him anything.

Whatever he did, he did for himself, but he was one of those who volunteer for things because they dream of a medal. In my rush I had forgotten to get a coffee and croissant, but I could not be bothered to go out again because the vultures would swoop again. I was about to begin my report for Ghikas when I was interrupted by Dermitzakis.

'I've brought Madas from Korydallos. He's with the other two and they're trying to come up with a picture of the white-haired man.'

'Fine,' I said. 'As soon as it's ready.'

'I've also got the search warrant.'

'Take Vlassopoulos and go and search Karamitris' office. I have to write the report for the Chief.'

I was certain that they would not find anything and so there was no point in three people wasting their time. I got down to the report, trying to fit three cases – Petroulias, Koustas, Karamitris – on to one page, so that he could learn it by heart for the reporters.

Then I was interrupted again, this time by Mrs Stratopoulou. I had clean forgotten about her and our telephone conversation of the previous day. She had a bag over her shoulder. In her right hand she was carrying a briefcase and in her left a plastic bag.

'I've brought you the things, Inspector,' she said, planting the plastic bag on my desk.

'Thank you, Mrs Stratopoulou. I'm sorry we put you to so much inconvenience.'

'Never mind, it suits us to be on good terms with the police. We often have run-ins with the port authorities because of our work and a good word from you wouldn't go amiss.' She gave me a big smile and left.

I opened the plastic bag. Inside was a blue sailing T-shirt, wrapped up like a meat loaf. I unwrapped it and found Petroulias' passport. My first thought was that he had been getting ready to run off. His going to sea had been to throw people off the scent. As soon as he had taken care of his affairs, he was going to disappear.

As I flicked through the passport to see whether it had been stamped with a visa for some Third World country, a 7x10cm photograph dropped out of it. I picked it up and froze. I shut my eyes and opened them again to make sure I wasn't dreaming. The photograph showed Petroulias naked from the waist up. He was wearing a sailing cap and sticking out his hairy chest.

Beside him, with her head resting on his shoulder and with a familiar smile, was Niki Koustas. Her hair was blonde and fell loose over her shoulders.

So here was the mysterious blonde under my nose. I had spoken to her so many times, except that in the meantime she had cut her hair and dyed it. She had changed so much since then that I wouldn't have recognised her if it had not been for the childlike smile, which was in the photograph as it was in real life, and the playful eyes.

When, after a good few minutes, I had recovered from my shock, my reaction was to run into the other office to catch Vlassopoulos and Dermitzakis, but they had already left.

'Contact the patrol car,' I said to Athanassopoulos. 'Tell them to leave Karamitris' office and bring Niki Koustas from R.I. Hellas here, now, to headquarters.'

I left him getting on the radio and went to take a breather on the fifth floor. The reporters were clustering outside Ghikas' office, talking all together, and Koula's look told me that she was ready to kill someone. The reporters swarmed up to me.

'Will you make a statement?'

They were eager to get their share of slops from the kitchen. There was no point in saying the same thing over and over again. I pushed through them and into Ghikas' office.

'Is it ready?' he said. 'They've been driving us crazy since this morning.'

'No, it's not. They'll just have to go on waiting.'

'Why?'

I took the photograph of the couple out of my pocket and handed it to him. 'One is Petroulias. Who's the other?' he asked me. He realised it was the blonde we had been looking for, but he had never seen Niki Koustas.

'Niki Koustas. Koustas' daughter.'

It was his turn to be struck dumb. 'And now what do we do?' he said at last.

'We postpone the statement until I've had a chance to interrogate her. I've told Vlassopoulos and Dermitzakis to bring her in. She may have been involved in the murder.'

'Right, but make it as quick as you can.'

'If we get delayed, you can make an initial statement and we'll come out with a later announcement concerning Koustas.'

'It would be better if I had something I could say about Koustas. It'll sound more impressive.' He said it as though Niki Koustas were going to come and take a sample for his popularity rating.

As I pushed my way through the pack, I caught sight of Sotiropoulos' suspicious and searching gaze. I went back to my office and within a minute he was standing before me.

'Something's going on,' he said. 'Something new. I can see it in your face.'

'Don't tell me that I owe you,' I said to take the wind out of his sails. 'All I owe you is a big thank you for helping me out in a difficult moment. But if you want to get a story, stand outside my office and wait.'

'What story?' he asked with a glint in his eye.

'I'm not saying. But if you want it, you'll wait.'

He opened the door and rushed out, afraid of being two seconds too late and missing the story. But he didn't miss it, because a quarter of an hour later, the story arrived escorted by Vlassopoulos and Dermitzakis. Niki Koustas was furious.

'What kind of behaviour is this?' she shouted at me. 'When have you ever called me for questioning and I refused? Did you have to send two of your underlings to frogmarch me here and embarrass me in front of the whole firm?'

'When did you cut and dye your hair?'

That caught her off guard, but she soon regained her composure. 'When I came back from my holidays. When did you start becoming interested in my hairstyle?'

'I'm not at all interested in your hairstyle. I'm interested in a blonde who was with Petroulias when he was killed.'

I took the photograph from my drawer and handed it to her. She looked at it for a long time, as if she wanted to be sure that she was the one with Petroulias.

'Where did you find it?' she asked. Her voice was trembling now, like the hand that was holding the photograph.

'In a cupboard behind the helm of the sailing boat that you chartered with Petroulias. Together with these.'

I took the T-shirt and Petroulias' passport out of the plastic bag and handed them to her. She started to tremble even more and looked ready to cry.

'Can we talk in private?' she asked in a broken voice.

Perhaps if we were alone, she would confess more easily. I nodded to Vlassopoulos and Dermitzakis to leave.

'I'm listening,' I said. 'What do you have to tell me?'

'I was having an affair with Christos.'

'I know. Just as I know that Petroulias was murdered on your father's orders. What I don't know is to what extent you were involved in the murder. That's what I want you to tell me.'

She took out a handkerchief and wiped away her tears. Then she gave me that innocent smile of hers, but this time it was mixed with bitterness. 'I'm the victim who survived,' she mumbled. 'Because I was Koustas' daughter.'

'What's that supposed to mean? Let's have an end to the lies, Niki. You've caused us enough sweat. Tell me how you got involved in Petroulias' murder. Were you doing a favour for your father?'

She sat down in the chair opposite me and looked at me in silence for a while. 'I met Christos at the beginning of January,' she said eventually. 'He had come to the office on business, I don't recall what business, and we had chatted a bit. When I left the office in the evening, I bumped into him outside. He said it was a coincidence, but it may not have been. Anyway, he invited me to go for a drink and I accepted. After three dates, we started having an affair.'

She closed her eyes, and heaved a deep sigh. 'He was a very charming man. He could be funny and tender at the same time. He won you over from the first meeting.'

She fell silent. Her description of Petroulias was a ploy to delay what was more difficult. 'Four months went by like that. We were together every night and every weekend, sometimes at my place, sometimes at his. Around the middle of May, my father phoned me one day and asked to see me. I was surprised because he rarely called me. Usually I was the one who called home and got the news from Elena or Makis. When I saw him that evening, he asked me to break it off with Christos. I don't know how he had found out, but he knew how long we'd been together, where we saw each other, everything. I told him that I didn't intend dumping Christos and that he had no right to interfere in my life. Then he began cursing him, saying that he was a corrupt referee and a lowlife, that behind his clean appearance he was up to the ears in filth and that, one day, I'd find his body lying on the rubbish heap. We had a real set-to and from that day we severed what little contact we'd had. When I told Christos, he laughed. He confessed to me that he had once had dealings with my father, that things hadn't gone at all well, and from that time my father had hated him. The explanation wasn't necessary. From the way that my father had spoken about Christos, I'd already realised how much he disliked him. To cut a long story short, at the end of May, we decided to go on holiday, sailing round the islands. I told no one, not even Elena or Makis, I just said I was going on holiday. Naturally, my father would have understood who I'd gone with, but I didn't care. We had a marvellous time, we were so happy, till one day . . .'

She stopped. We had arrived at the murder and I said nothing. I waited. Niki was trembling from head to foot. She bit her lip to stop herself crying.

'We had come from Santorini to the island where . . . to the island where you found him buried. We'd been moored there for two days when, on the second day, at around six in the evening, two men appeared on the quayside and jumped on to the boat. One of them told Christos to go with him into the cabin so they could talk. When they came out, Christos was deathly pale. "Get hold of your father," he said to me as he stepped on to the quayside between the two of them. "He's sent them to kill me." I went crazy. I tried to run after them, but one of them gave me a murderous look. But it wasn't that that stopped me, it was Christos. "Don't come with me," he shouted. "Call your father." I watched them bundle him into a car. I began trying to find my father, using my mobile phone, but I couldn't find him anywhere and his own phone was switched off. After about an hour, I gave up and started searching madly for Christos. I didn't find either him or the other three.'

'Three? You told me there were two of them. And according to the coroner's report, he'd been killed by two men.'

'There were three. The third was the driver, a man with white hair.'

'White hair?'

'Yes. I asked in the cafés, in the shops. No one had seen them.' And then, not being able to hold it back any longer, she burst into tears. But she went on talking to me through her sobbing. 'I went back to the boat and all night long I tried to find my father. Late at night, Elena phoned and told me that he'd called to say that he was on business in Larissa. Day broke and Christos still hadn't returned. I ran to the harbour and took the first boat leaving the island. I had a mad hope that maybe they had taken him to Piraeus. I saw the car with the three of them driving on to the boat without Christos and I realised he wouldn't return. I gathered our things together, phoned the charter firm and told them that Mr Petroulias had fallen sick and had to be taken back to Athens. Then I took the next ferry.'

'Why didn't you report it to the police?'

She stopped again and took a deep breath. She managed to hold back her sobbing and smiled bitterly. 'When I got back to Athens, I went straight to my father and told him everything. "I told you to break up with him, because he was bad news and would get himself killed, but you wouldn't listen," he said coldly. I threatened to go to the police. "Go," was his reply. "How are you going to prove that I had any connection with him? Because he said so? On the day he was killed, I was in Athens and later in Larissa. I have twenty witnesses to confirm it. One day you'll thank me for freeing you of that scumbag." That was his last word on the matter. Even if I had gone to the police, what could I have said? I had no proof, Inspector. Only what Christos had told me and Christos was dead. And even if I had had proof, how could I tell them that Christos had been killed without revealing that the murderer was my father? Could I send my father to prison? And if I did send him, would it bring Christos back?

312

From that day, my father and I never spoke again. The next day, I cut and dyed my hair. I couldn't bear seeing myself in the mirror with long, blonde hair. I felt as if I'd always see Christos beside me.' She took another deep breath and added, almost with relief: 'That's the whole truth, Inspector.'

'Why did he have his passport with him?'

'I had mine too. We were planning to go across to Turkey from Samos.'

You may have been planning to go to Turkey, but Petroulias was planning to make a run for it, I thought. I wondered whether I should keep her in custody. But her story was in keeping with what our investigations had come up with. And the way she had spoken, with tears and sobbing, seemed to suggest that she wasn't lying. Besides, the photograph was, in fact, in her favour. If you plan to kill someone, directly or indirectly, you don't have yourself photographed with the victim.

'Why didn't you tell me all this when I questioned you after your father's murder? He was no longer in danger of you getting him sent to prison.'

'For me, his murder was a punishment. If I'd told you, it wouldn't have changed anything, but it would have upset Elena and Makis, who knew nothing of all that. Especially Makis. He has enough problems.'

'Did you send the photographs to your father?'

'What photographs?'

'One of the island and another of the spot where Petroulias was found. They were in your father's safe. Did you send them?'

'Do you think I was in any state to be taking photos of the local sights?' she said bitterly.

'I don't know, perhaps. Perhaps you took them in order to blackmail him.'

'Why would I do that? I could have whatever money I wanted without blackmailing him.'

She was right. Koustas would have been only too pleased to give her money to keep her quiet. 'I want you to look at a sketch of the white-haired man that we're putting together and then you can go,'

I told her. 'But I might need you to come in again to make a formal statement.'

She shrugged. 'Whenever you like. Phone me and I'll come in on my own. I'd rather you didn't send an escort and embarrass me like that again.'

I called Dermitzakis and asked him what was happening with the sketch.

'It's almost ready. You'll have it in five minutes.'

The five became fifteen and we sat through them in silence. The girl was deep in thought, and I tried to put into some sort of order what I would give to Ghikas. At last Dermitzakis came in and handed me the sketch. The artist had made the sketch using a black background in order to highlight the hair. I gazed at a face of a man, possibly in his fifties, a man completely unknown to me.

'Is this the white-haired man?' I asked Koustas, passing her the sketch.

She took it and stared at it for some time. 'Broadly speaking, yes, it resembles him,' she said, somewhat hesitant.

'Do you have any observations? Any alterations you would make?'

She shrugged. 'I saw him only fleetingly as the car passed me. No, I've nothing to add.'

'All right, you can go.'

At least now we knew roughly what the white-haired man looked like. I called Ghikas and told him everything that Niki Koustas had told me.

'Do you believe that she's not involved?'

'I'll look into it, but I don't think that I'm going to find anything to contradict what she has now told us. Besides, it confirms what we already know. The only new element concerns the man with white hair.'

'Send the sketch to all stations. And let me have a copy to give to the media. Maybe something will come of it.'

'Maybe. If he's not already in Moscow drinking vodka.'

I hung up and tried to fit the information that Niki Koustas had given me into what we had already. It was obvious that Petroulias had not got together with her by chance. He had planned it. First, he had got hold of Koustas' daughter for security, then he had undermined his team to force him to back off, and when Koustas had not given way, he had grabbed the payment on the loan and run off with the daughter. But he had not reckoned on the fact that Koustas wouldn't give way for his daughter's sake. Perhaps he was in too deep a hole himself. The money wasn't his. It belonged to his associate and he was in danger from them. I shudder when I think of Koustas. He had his daughter's boyfriend killed, turned his son into a junkie, and forced his second wife to stay away from her disabled son. And all that for a few hundred million tax-free every year.

Again I racked my brains trying to recall the detail I had forgotten. Nothing came. All I could think of was that I had to show the sketch to someone, but to whom?

CHAPTER 56

In the end, it came to me when I was hardly expecting it – in my sleep. I opened my eyes and reached for the alarm clock on the bedside table. It was ten past three. Beside me, Adriani's calm, regular breathing. I hopped out of bed and went into the living room. I rang the police to get the telephone number of the officer at the Haïdari station. That excessive zeal of mine always landed me in trouble, but I was like a cat on hot bricks. I phoned the station and asked to speak to Sergeant Kardassis.

'He's not here, Inspector,' the duty officer told me. 'He comes on at eight in the morning.'

I went back to bed, but I could not get to sleep. I stared into the darkness. I reached for the alarm clock again and saw that it was almost four thirty. I went into the kitchen to make coffee. I rarely make it for myself and it came out like dishwater. I sipped at it and thought of where the detail that I had at last remembered might lead me.

I made the mistake of leaving home earlier than usual because I was all wired up. I got caught in the rush hour. All the roads were jammed and I cursed myself for not taking one of Ouzounidis' Lexotanil to steady my nerves and for not leaving at the usual time.

The moment I walked into my office, I picked up the phone and once again asked for Sergeant Kardassis. This time, thank God, I found him.

'Inspector Haritos,' I said. 'Do you remember the night I came to the station?'

'Of course, Inspector.'

'Do you remember that fellow who wanted to bring charges against his best man because he made a pass at his wife?'

'Oh, him? He piped down and at last we got a bit of peace and quiet.'

'You'd told me something else then, that he had also brought a charge against someone else, on the night that Koustas was murdered. Do you remember?'

'Now that you mention it . . .'

'You found the bike used as the getaway by Koustas' killer in Leonidou Street, outside the Haïdari tax office, right?'

'Yes, that's right.'

'And where did the incident with the car take place?'

I heard him going through his papers. 'The car was double-parked in Anexartisias Street and was blocking the entrance to Pavlou Melas Street.' He realised where I was leading and added: 'Pavlou Melas Street is parallel to Leonidou Street in the direction of Prophitis Ilias.'

'Presumably you have both their addresses, given that he brought charges.'

'Yes, I have them here. The man you saw at the station is Aristos Moraïtis and he has a car-repair business in Patroklou Street in Aigáleo. The other is Prodromos Terzis and he has a children's clothes factory in Kachramanou Street in Nea Ionia.'

I took the sketch of the man with white hair and hurried out of my office. Before leaving, I stopped at the office of the two lieutenants.

'I'm going out and I don't know when I'll be back,' I said to

Vlassopoulos and Dermitzakis. 'Don't go running off because I might need you.'

'What are we to do with Karamitris?' Vlassopoulos said.

'We'll interrogate him when I get back. Let him get used to prison life.'

If I found the man with white hair, I would have found the killer in all three murders and I would have Karamitris where I wanted him. The only thing that did not fit was how Petroulias' murderer then became the murderer of Koustas and Loukia Karamitris. It might just have been a coincidence. Coincidences get you out of a fix where there are no logical explanations.

To judge by the cars lined up in front of the garage, Moraïtis must have been doing a roaring trade. Two youths in overalls were playing about with a Suzuki Swift.

'Where will I find Mr Moraïtis?' I asked one of them.

'Inside, in the office,' replied the other. The one I had asked did not even turn to look at me.

The office was a square partition at the back of the shop, made of plywood and glass and with the dimensions of a bathroom. From a distance, I could see Moraïtis' head, but when I entered the office, I had difficulty in recognising him. Not that I remembered him particularly well, but I had retained the impression of a hefty man. This one was shrivelled, unshaven, with a lifeless gaze, and looked as if he had just got up after some grave illness.

'Are you Aristos Moraïtis?' I asked, just to be sure.

'Yes.'

'Inspector Haritos. I don't know if you remember me, we met one evening at the Haïdari police station. You had come to press charges against someone who had made a pass at your wife.'

'Don't speak of her,' he shouted. 'Don't remind me of the bitch!' He saw that I was surprised and hastened to explain. 'She left me.' He jumped up and his voice rang through the work-shop. 'She ran off with a meat merchant. I treated her like a princess. All the cars you see here paid for her dresses, her shoes, her rings. Every night, she was at the bouzouki clubs, dancing on the table, with me showering her with flowers. I was a doormat for her to wipe her feet on and she dropped me for a meat merchant.'

He said it all in one breath and sat down again, panting. He mentioned nothing of the fact that he had driven her crazy with his comings and goings at the police station. Not to mention that his wife, juicy and plump if I recall her correctly, was much more suited to a meat merchant with a red Mercedes.

'Things like that happen,' I said to soothe him, and to win his sympathy.

'Has it happened to you?'

'No, thank God.'

'So don't *you* tell *me* that it happens,' he said crossly.

The conversation was going off on a tangent, so I came directly to the point. 'Listen, I came to ask you something. Do you remember that a few days prior to the night we met, you'd gone again to the station to bring charges against someone who had blocked you in with his car and the two of you had come to blows.'

'Oh, him,' he said dully. 'I withdrew the charges. Since Fofo buggered off, I'm in no mood for messing with courts.'

'When you left the station and went to Anexartisias Street to get your car, do you by any chance recall seeing a Yamaha with two men on it, anywhere thereabouts?'

'Are you serious? I wanted to kill the guy and you're asking me if I saw a motorbike . . .'

'Sometimes you remember things later that you thought you hadn't noticed. Look at this please. Does it remind you of anything?' And I showed him the sketch of the man with white hair.

He looked at it reluctantly. 'I don't remember getting into the car, so how do you expect me to remember this dickhead?' he said.

He was not going to like the next question, but I had to ask it. Perhaps his wife had seen the Yamaha. 'Where is your wife living now?'

His gaze darkened and fixed on me. 'How should I know? With the meat merchant. Ask in the meat market if you want to find her.'

He said it out of spite, but it wasn't such a bad idea in fact. The meat merchant would be shouting his mouth off and swaggering for having got his hands on a woman like that, so it wouldn't be difficult for me to find out in the market where they lived.

Moraïtis had once again lapsed into despair. I left him with his bitter memories of his plump wife.

To get from Aigaleo to Nea Ionia, you need two Inderal and three Lexotanil. It was two o'clock in the afternoon and the heat in the Mirafiori was unbearable. I was sweating, but I kept the windows closed so as not to have to inhale the exhaust fumes. I gritted my teeth until I turned into Konstantinoupoleos Avenue, but there I gave up. I opened the window and surrendered unconditionally to the exhaust fumes. I turned right into Aghiou Meletiou Street and came out into Ionias Avenue. After about fifty metres, I got stuck in the traffic and looked for a way out. I found one by turning into Sarandaporou Street, and from Laskaratou Street, I took Herakliou Avenue. Not that there was any great difference, but at least the traffic kept moving, albeit at a snail's pace. When I turned into Alsaton Street to get to Kachramanou Street, I glanced at my watch and it was twenty-five to four. It had taken me an hour and thirty-five minutes to get from Patroklou Street to Kachramanou Street.

Prodromos Terzis' children's clothes factory was housed in a large ground-floor space, with small-paned windows recalling an old machine shop. Inside, there were three counters and an ironing press. At two of these some women were making clothes. The ironing press was having a day off.

'Which one is Mr Terzis?' I asked one of the girls.

She pointed to a man of around forty-five, who was bent over the third counter at the far end of the room. Standing opposite him was a couple watching him as he was showing them children's shirts and shorts. Terzis was beefy if your gaze first fell on his physique and portly if it fell on his belly. Roughly as Aristos was before he had shrivelled through pining for his wife.

'Mr Terzis?' I asked, going up to him.

'Yes.'

'Inspector Haritos. I'm here about an incident that doesn't concern you directly, but to which you may have been an eyewitness.'

'I'm up to my ears. Can't it wait for some other time?'

'I'm afraid it can't. It's urgent.'

'Excuse me,' he said to the couple. 'I'll be right back.' Then he turned to me. 'This way.'

He opened a door at the far end and walked ahead of me down to a basement that was used as a storeroom. In one corner, he had put his desk and a chair for visitors, which was presently occupied by a bag. I put it on the floor so I could sit down. He immediately rushed over to pick it up and put it on his desk.

'Sorry, but it gets dirty easily,' he said. Then he took out a duster and began dusting his desk.

I'm dealing with a flea-catcher and I'm not going to learn anything, I said to myself, disappointed. My only hope was Aristos' wife.

'Mr Terzis, do you recall an evening about a month ago when you went to lodge a complaint at the Haïdari police station, together with a certain Mr Moraïtis?'

'Oh, that bum.' His fury had not abated. 'I had gone to show some samples to a client and was forced to double-park, because it was impossible to find a parking space. I thought that if someone honked their horn, I'd hear them and go outside to move it. But that scumbag lunged at me as soon as I went outside. I'd been showing samples all day, I was dead tired and he dragged me along to the station at one in the morning.'

'When you went back to get your car, do you recall having seen a Yamaha with two riders?'

He screwed up his face in an effort to remember. 'I didn't see any motorbike,' he said after a while. 'But I did see two men getting into a car.'

'Where did you see them?'

'I saw them as I was turning into Thralis Street. The car was parked in front of a school complex. It looked like an Opel Corsa from what I recall.' While we had been talking, he had dusted his desk again and emptied the ashtray three times.

'You didn't notice anything about the number plate?'

'No, but it was pale green.'

'And the people who got into the car?'

'One was white-haired.'

There he was, the white-haired man again. They had abandoned the motorbike and made their getaway in an Opel Corsa. We would find it no doubt among the list of stolen vehicles, but I was equally sure we would not find any fingerprints or any other clues. I took out the sketch and showed it to him.

'Was this the man?'

He looked at it, though his expression told me that he did not recognise him. 'Perhaps, I can't be sure. It was dark and the only thing I could make out was his white hair.'

'And the other man?' I asked, praying that he would describe Karamitris to me.

'Not man, woman.'

'It was a woman?'

'Yes. At first I took her for a man because she had short hair, like a boy's. But as I overtook them, my headlights fell on her and I saw that it was a woman.'

I said nothing. I simply stared at Terzis, duster in hand, who was looking at me curiously.

Suddenly, the solution to all three cases was there, before my eyes, as if it had been presented to me on a plate.

CHAPTER 57

It was half past seven when we knocked on the door of Niki Koustas' flat at 12 Fokylidou Street. At first she was surprised to see us, but then she broke into a laugh.

'Well, either you have me brought to you with an escort or you come with an escort yourself, Inspector. Come in.'

She showed us into the living room, which was sparsely furnished with two armchairs, a glass table and a few cushions scattered around the floor for you to get a stiff back. In one corner was a TV with a huge black screen.

Elena Koustas was sitting in one of the armchairs. Her face was pale and her eyes swollen from crying. 'Here again, Inspector?' she said wearily. 'No one ever cared about my husband as much as you. I wonder if he deserves it, even now.'

'That's the fate of police officers, Mrs Koustas. To care about people who normally don't deserve it. Would you be kind enough to leave us alone?'

'No, let her stay,' Niki cut in. 'Besides, she knows everything you know. There was no point in hiding it any more.'

Vlassopoulos and Dermitzakis took stock of the cushions and preferred to remain standing. As did I. Niki saw me hesitate and went and sat on one of the cushions, leaving the armchair to me.

'Where were you on the night your father was killed?' I asked.

'Here, at home, with Makis. I told you that the first time you asked me.'

'All night?'

'Yes.'

'You're not telling me the whole truth. Makis was with you, but the two of you did not stay here all night.'

She glanced at me and immediately gave in. 'Yes, we went out for a while. Makis wasn't feeling well and we went out for a drive so he could get a bit of air.'

'Why didn't you tell me *that* the first time I asked you?'

'Because Makis had only just got out of rehab. I didn't want you to think that he was still taking drugs. The police don't take kindly to junkies.'

I looked at her. She was composed, with that innocent smile on her face.

'You didn't go out for a walk, Niki. You got on to a stolen Yamaha and went to the Bouzouki Strings, where Makis killed your father. The plan was yours. Makis is permanently stoned, he couldn't have come up with a plan like that. From the moment he had had Christos killed, you planned to take revenge on your father. That's why you took the photographs. You came back to Athens, cut and dyed your hair, allowed some time to pass so that people would get used to your new look and then you put your plan into operation.

Except that you couldn't carry it out on your own; you needed a partner. And where would you find a better partner than Makis? He hated your father, too. He didn't give him any money, he hadn't let him play football and he wouldn't give him one of his clubs to manage . . . He had closed every door to him. Your plan suited him to a T. He could take revenge on your father and at the same time get everything he had been deprived of for so many years . . . Money . . . the clubs . . . everything he wanted . . .'

Elena had jumped to her feet and was looking at me with horror stamped all over her face. 'What you say cannot be true,' she said, terrified. 'None of it is true.'

'Let him finish, Elena.' Niki was still composed.

'First you sent him the two photographs. You wanted him to believe that it was blackmail. That's why he had the fifteen million with him on the night he was murdered, but it wasn't the money that you were after. You'd inherit everything anyway. You did it to get him out of the club without his bodyguards, which is precisely what happened. On the night of the murder, you left here on the motorbike. You dropped Makis off to hide next to the Bouzouki Strings and you stopped a little way off with the engine running. Koustas came out alone at the time arranged. He bent down to get the money out of his car and Makis stepped out of the darkness. He told him to turn round and shot him four times. Then he ran to you, jumped on the bike and you sped off. It was a clever plan, I have to admit. Your father owned several nightclubs, we would believe he had been threatened by racketeers and had been killed for not meeting their demands. But I knew something didn't ring true from the beginning. Professional hit men use only one bullet, two at the most. Makis, however, was not a professional. He shot him twice in the heart, once in the chest, once in the belly. Out of hate? To make sure of killing him? Who knows?'

Elena had turned to stone. She looked first at me and then at Niki. Perhaps Niki was still smiling because she thought that all this was just my own hypothesis. She still could not know that I had an eyewitness, Terzis.

'You abandoned the bike in Leonidou Street, outside the Haïdari tax office,' I went on. 'You had a car parked in Thrakis Street. You got in and you drove off. I don't know whether the white wig that Makis wore was your idea or his. Anyhow, the trick worked. The lane in front of the Bouzouki Strings is dark. Madas, the doorman, saw the white hair and was taken in. As for you, you were wearing a helmet.'

Vlassopoulos and Dermitzakis were just standing there, staring at me. I had given them a rough briefing on the way, but they had not imagined that Koustas' murder had been so simply and so cleverly planned.

'Take her down to headquarters for formal interrogation,' I said to Vlassopoulos.

Suddenly, Elena leapt between us, blocking my view of Niki. 'It's not true, Niki! It's all lies, isn't it?'

'No, it's not all lies. A part of it is true.' She leaned to one side, so that she could see me. 'Your hypothesis is correct up to a point, Inspector,' she said.

'It's not a hypothesis. I have an eyewitness who saw you getting into the car in Thrakis Street and he recognised you.'

'Of course he recognised me – because I was there.' She said it straight out, as if she had been there to buy a car or bathroom tiles.

'So you're admitting, then, that you were an accomplice to the murder.'

'I was an unwilling witness to the murder of my boyfriend and an unwilling witness to the murder of my father.'

'What's that supposed to mean?'

'Listen,' she said, heaving a sigh. 'On the night of the murder, Makis had been fixing again and was very uptight. He was calling our father every name you can imagine. I'd been through everything, you know, and I couldn't bear to listen to him. To calm him, I suggested that we went out. At first I thought of taking my car, but he'd come on the bike and so we took that.'

'Was the bike stolen?' I cut in.

She shrugged. 'He told me he'd borrowed it from a friend.'

'Did Makis steal the bike?'

'Who else? My father never gave him any money, I told you that.

And when you're an addict, you'll do almost anything to get your fix. Anyhow. Because I'd had a bike when I was studying in England, I made it a condition that I drove. I didn't want him driving in the state he was in. Once we were in Vassilissis Sophias Avenue, he began guiding me step by step. At first, he told me to go down Panepistimiou Street. When we arrived in Omonia Square, he said he wanted to go to the Bouzouki Strings because he'd proposed something to our father and he was waiting for a reply. If I've learned something from Makis, it's to never refuse anything to junkies. They go crazy. When we reached the Bouzouki Strings, Makis got off and walked over to the club. I didn't want to go anywhere near my father. I lost sight of Makis and assumed that he'd gone inside. Presently, I saw my father coming out alone. He went to his car to get something and Makis suddenly appeared behind him. I don't know where he had sprung from. Probably he'd been hiding as you said. He said something and Dad turned round. Then I saw Makis take out a gun and shoot him. My father collapsed and Makis ran in my direction. He jumped onto the bike and told me to drive off. What was I supposed to do? He was under the influence of drugs, had a gun in his hand and might have shot me, too. Makis guided me to the spot where we abandoned the bike. And on the other road, he had parked the car. We got in and drove away.'

'Didn't you ask yourself where he'd found the car?'

'He told me it was rented. If you search, you'll find the name of the company he rented it from.'

'And the white wig?'

'He had it with him and put it on while he was hiding. He took it off in the car and put it in his pocket.'

'And why didn't you report the murder to the police when Makis left you?'

'For two reasons, Inspector. The first you already know. I couldn't turn my brother in to the police because he'd killed my father, just as I couldn't turn my father over when he killed my boyfriend. The second reason is that Makis didn't deserve to go to prison. My father destroyed all of us. He had turned Makis into the wreck he is, killed the man I loved, separated Elena from her son . . . And all that for money, as if he didn't have enough already.'

For the first time, I detected loathing and passion in her voice. I saw Vlassopoulos and Dermitzakis standing there, open-mouthed. And who could blame them? The plan was even better than I had thought. She had persuaded Makis to kill her father, but she had planned it so that if the worst came to the worst, she could hang it all on her brother, the junkie, just as she was doing now.

'And what about the white-haired man who you said was with those who took Petroulias?'

'You showed me a sketch and I told you that it resembled the man I'd seen on the island. The sketch doesn't look remotely like Makis. Besides, Makis was in Athens when Christos was killed and he can prove it.'

'There *was* no white-haired man. You said it deliberately as a red herring.'

She shrugged. 'All you have to do is find the white-haired man.'

She knew we wouldn't find him because he didn't exist. 'You can put all that in your defence plea,' I told her. 'But no court is ever going to believe you.'

'You're wrong,' she said. 'I'm a victim. My father's men killed my lover and I saw my brother kill my father. What court would fail to understand the double tragedy I've suffered? At most, I'll get a suspended sentence.'

As if wanting to strengthen her self-confidence, Elena Koustas ran to embrace her. 'You won't go to prison,' she said. 'I'll find the best lawyers.'

That's how she would persuade the court, in the same way that she had just persuaded Elena. The jury would listen to her and the tears would flow in buckets. Perhaps I would have felt sorry for her too, if she hadn't hung everything on her brother.

Niki clutched Elena to her. 'Thank you, Elena,' she whispered. 'It's lucky I have you. I know you'll help me prove that I'm innocent.'

'And you'll let your brother die in prison,' I said.

'No one has done as much as I have for Makis, Inspector,' she said angrily. 'But it's not me who's killing him. Makis died the day he got into drugs.'

He's already dead, why should I die too. That's what she was thinking. As I looked at her, she reminded me of some second-rate film from a video club, *The Demon With the Angelic Face*. She was extremely clever and yet she had murdered her father out of love's passion. Love had clouded her reasoning and she couldn't understand that she was a pawn between her father and her lover.

'Do you want to take anything with you?' Vlassopoulos asked her.

'There's no need. Tomorrow I'll be out on bail.'

She walked to the door without looking behind her. Vlassopoulos followed her and I heard the front door close.

'You'll have to leave too, Mrs Koustas. We'll have to seal the flat.'

'Will you be going for Makis now?'

'Yes, so we can get it over with.'

She looked at me. 'May I come with you?' she said, finding it difficult to get the words out.

'Why?'

She breathed a sigh. 'Makis will need clothes. And given the state he's in, he can't do it himself.' She saw me hesitate. 'Please,' she implored.

Where was the Elena Fragakis of old, with the irrepressible breasts and the curtain for her thigh? Elena Koustas was a hen looking after her brood – a disabled son and two stepchildren who had killed their father.

'OK, you can come along.'

'Thank you,' she said.

CHAPTER 58

When a case closes, there are some who benefit and some who pay. I benefitted by having cleared up three of the murders, having caught two of the three culprits, and like that I get up the nose of those who would like to trip me. Ghikas benefitted because both cases had closed in the least painful way and there was no need for any cover-up. The two politicians benefitted because they had had no direct involvement in Koustas' murder and so wouldn't appear in court and could continue to make statements on TV. Niki benefitted, albeit on balance, because she had hung everything on her brother. The heaviest price would be paid by Makis, who would take the rap not only for the murders, but also for premeditated murder. But Elena would pay too because everything had collapsed around her and she would be running from the prison to the courts and then to her son.

All this was going through my mind as we were driving down Vouliagmenis Avenue. Dermitzakis was driving while Mrs Koustas and I were in the back seat.

'The other day, you told me that I wasn't in any danger.' I heard her voice and woke from my thoughts. 'Did you believe it, or did you just say it to reassure me?'

'I believe that you're not in any immediate danger.'

'But what will I do if my husband's associates turn up and want their money? I've no idea how much he owed. If they threaten me, can you protect me?'

'What do you reckon, Dermitzakis?'

'Are you joking, Inspector?'

I would have said the same, but I wanted him to say it. If I had said it, it would have got around that I consider the Police Force incapable of protecting citizens.

'They have more money and are better equipped than the police, Mrs Koustas,' I explained to her. 'In addition, we have laws and codes of conduct that bind us. They are free to do as they like.'

'And what do you advise me to do?'

I reflected a while. 'Are you concerned about hanging on to your husband's fortune?' I asked her.

'Only the Canard Doré. I'm fond of it and I'd like to go on running it.'

'OK, sell the rest, collect the money and deposit it in the bank. If your husband's associates ever show up, you'll give it to them and then they'll leave you alone.'

'You're right. That's what I'll do.'

I turned and looked at her. She tried to smile at me, but her eyes were tearful. I had been holding back a question for some time, but it kept popping up.

'It was Niki who planned her father's death,' I said. 'Makis was only her instrument. Surely you can see that she's hanging it all on her brother to save herself? And yet you offered to help her. Why? Doesn't Makis deserve more than a bag of clothes? Is everything else going to go to Niki?'

She sighed and remained silent for a while. 'You have met my three children, Inspector,' she said eventually. 'My own child and my two stepchildren. If you found them out at sea struggling against the waves and you only had one lifebelt, which one would you throw it to?'

From the day I met her, that woman had had a way of reducing me to silence.

When we arrived outside Koustas' house in Glyfada, it was already ten o'clock. I looked at the dark building and I recalled the first time I had gone there, again with Dermitzakis. High walls, barbed-wire fencing, security guards, closed-circuit TV, but nothing had been able to protect Koustas. He had taken every possible measure to guard himself from the underworld and he had been killed by his own children. Now that Makis would be going away, Elena Koustas would put it up for auction, to be bought by the next high-security freak.

We rang the bell and before long the gate opened on its own. One of the few mechanisms still working. Fortunately, it was dark and Elena Koustas couldn't see what a mess the garden was in. Makis was surprised to see me.

'Here again? Not fed up yet?'

He was wearing the clothes he always wore. His jacket was fastened up to the neck. Elena Koustas came in last. He was even more surprised to see her.

'What do you want?' he asked her.

'I came to get something I'd forgotten and the Inspector was kind enough to bring me,' she said.

He said nothing but his gaze remained fixed on her, as if he were trying to think of something. He gave up and headed towards the living room. We followed him while Mrs Koustas went upstairs.

The living room was a rubbish heap, as it had been on our last visit. The light was dim like the light in a cell. He sat on the sofa and unzipped his jacket, but he kept it wrapped tightly around him as though he were cold. I sat in the armchair facing him, while Dermitzakis stood by the door just in case.

'Out with it then, why are you here?' he said.

I wanted to get it over with. 'I've come to arrest you,' I said. No beating about the bush. 'For the murder of your father.'

'So you've cottoned on at last,' he said, unconcerned.

'Yes. It took me a little time, but I've cottoned on, yes. You and Niki killed him. She devised the plan and you carried it out.'

'Don't spoil it for me,' he shouted. 'I'm the one who killed him. If it wasn't for me, he'd still be alive. All my life he called me idle, worthless and incompetent. I had to kill the bastard for him to realise that I'm more than able to start something and finish it.'

Is that what Koustas had thought of when he saw him pointing the gun at him? 'Yes, but you were helped by Niki. You planned it together.' He remained silent and looked at me. 'Makis, you've got a lot to answer for,' I said. 'Don't add to it by taking on what you didn't do as well. Talk to me if you want to alleviate your position, because you're going to prison for a very long time.'

He burst out laughing. 'I'm not going to prison, I'm going to paradise,' he replied. 'If you have money, prison's a paradise for junkies.'

Why was he doing it? To protect his sister? Because he wanted all the kudos for himself, without any partners? Perhaps for both those reasons. If he kept it up, Niki would get off scot-free.

'Why did you kill your mother?'

'When I went to see her, to talk to her, she slammed the door in my face,' he screamed, furious. 'And she was conniving with my father behind our backs. She abandoned us because supposedly she couldn't bear him and yet the next minute she was doing business with him.'

The hate and pain had taken root inside him and there was no point in my trying to explain to him that things had not happened exactly like that.

'Was it you who put the cheque through Karamitris' letter box?'

'Yes. I found the cheques by chance in an old wallet in Dad's bedside table. There were other cheques in it too. I read the signature and realised who it was.' He gave a high-pitched laugh. 'The same trick I played on him too,' he said proudly. 'And they both fell for it. I sent the two photographs to my father and phoned him. I told him the time had come for him to give me the money he'd deprived me of for so long. He wanted to give it to me at home, but I said no. I told him that I didn't trust him and to meet me alone outside his club. The scumbag walked right into it. Just like my mother. I waited till her husband had left and telephoned her. I told her who I was and that if she wanted the other cheque, she would have to meet me. She agreed.' He stopped and his expression darkened again. 'Do you understand?' he shouted. 'A fourteen-year-old kid and I made a long journey to see her and she shut the door in my face. And it was only when I told her about the cheque that she wanted to see me.'

'Where did you find the photographs?'

'They were Niki's. She'd taken them to remember where her boyfriend was buried.'

She had not taken them for that reason. She had taken them because she intended using them in exactly the way that she had. It was her one weak spot, but not a significant one. She could quite easily claim that she had not given them to Makis, but that he had found them on his own and taken them.

'What did you do with the wig that you wore?'

'It's around here somewhere. You'll find it.'

'And the gun?'

'I'll tell you that too. Everything in its turn.'

I was going to insist, to be sure of getting the gun from him, but another thought flashed through my mind. I had been wrong about the former minister and Kalia. He wasn't the one who was with her on the night she died.

'And Kalia? What had she done to make you kill her?' I said.

331

He shrank into his seat and avoided my gaze. 'I felt sorry about Kalia. But she had to go,' he said, heaving a sigh. 'Kalia and I were once together. She was the one who taught me how to get stoned and like that I was able to get some relief, to forget, to be somewhere else. But my father found out and threatened her. He told her he'd fire her and make sure she never got a job anywhere else. She was frightened and broke off with me. When I sent him the two photographs and phoned him, my father went to her and told her to talk me round, but she said no. She called me and told me about it.'

So that's what Koustas and Kalia were talking about on the night of the murder. He wasn't threatening to fire her, he'd done that before. He was asking her to talk to Makis on his behalf.

'When I saw you in her dressing room asking her questions, I got scared,' Makis said. 'You know, we junkies don't have much endurance and I was afraid that if you put pressure on her she'd confess. I let a couple of days go by and then approached her. I told her that now my father could no longer stop us, we could get together again. She was pleased. The second time we saw each other, she took me home.'

He stopped, raised his eyes and looked at me. 'You know, she loved me,' he said, as though he found it strange that someone could love him. 'She had my photo next to her TV.' He thought about it again. 'You'll tell me she put it there for my benefit. You never know with junkies. We made love and then I prepared our fix. I gave it to her first.'

He fell silent again and his gaze turned inwards. 'She felt nothing. She died in my arms like a little bird,' he whispered.

At that moment, Elena Koustas came into the room. In her right hand she was holding a bulging travel bag. She put it down, next to me. She stood there and looked at Makis. Her eyes were full of tears.

'Makis, I want you to know that I always loved you,' she said softly. 'And now, whatever happens, I'll stick by you.'

Makis had his eyes fixed on her, but said nothing. Suddenly, he made a rapid movement. He stuck his hand into his jacket and pulled it out holding the .38. He jumped up and turned to me.

'You wanted the gun, didn't you? Here it is,' he said, pointing it at

Elena. 'You're the last one,' he said to her. 'As soon as I've taken care of you, I'll be done.' He saw Dermitzakis moving in from the doorway. 'Careful, copper,' he shouted. 'Careful, or you'll get it too.'

I took advantage of the fact that his eyes were on Dermitzakis and got to my feet. 'Put it down, Makis,' I said as gently as I could. 'There's no reason for any more killings.'

He turned to me, keeping the gun pointing at Elena. 'Stay where you are,' he said. 'I'm going to finish what I have to do, then I'll give you the gun and I'll come quietly. You can write whatever you want and I'll sign it. I won't cause you any trouble whatsoever.'

I glanced at Elena. She was looking at him with a calm, sad smile on her face. Oh God, not Elena too, I thought to myself. He's killed his father, his mother, his girlfriend, but not Elena too. I was surprised to discover that, even though I see so many corpses, there are still some deaths that cause me pain.

Makis' hand had begun shaking. I took a step to the left, to get between him and Elena. I heard the shot and, at the same time, I felt my chest burning and exploding. The bullet's momentum knocked me backwards and I lost my balance. I caught sight of Dermitzakis lunging at Makis. Then –

STUFFED VEGETABLES
(CONSTANTINOPLE STYLE)

Ingredients

1 kilo tomatoes
500 grams green peppers
1 kilo onions
250 grams white short-grain rice (not parboiled or basmati)
500 ml olive oil (not sunflower oil)
Some pine nuts and currants
Salt, pepper and spices

Instructions

- Chop the onions, put them in a pan and leave to fry over moderate heat.
- Slice the tops from tomatoes, remove pulp with a spoon and keep aside.
- Do the same with the green peppers, removing the seeds.
- When the onions are ready, add 250 ml of oil to the pan, together with salt, pepper and spice. Stir for a few minutes before adding the rice.
- Stir the rice and onions before adding the pine nuts and currants.
- Meanwhile, crush the tomato pulp with a potato masher. Add half of the pulp to the rice. Stir the mixture for a while, remove from heat and allow to cool for a short time.
- Arrange the tomatoes and peppers in an ovenproof dish and, using a spoon, carefully fill them with the mixture. When

finished, replace the tops and pour 250 ml of oil over them, together with the remaining tomato mixture diluted with a little water.

- Cook in oven for 20 minutes at 250°C and then for another 40 to 50 minutes at 180°C.

BY PETROS MARKARIS
ALSO AVAILABLE FROM VINTAGE

☐ The Late-Night News	9780099464624	£6.99

FREE POST AND PACKING
Overseas customers allow £2.00 per paperback

BY PHONE: 01624 677237

BY POST: Random House Books
C/o Bookpost, PO Box 29, Douglas
Isle of Man, IM99

BY FAX: 01624 670923

BY EMAIL: bookshop@enterprise.net

Cheques (payable to Bookpost) and credit cards accepted

Prices and availability subject to change without notice.
Allow 28 Days for delivery.
When placing your order, please mention if you do not wish to receive
any additional information.

www.vintage-books.co.uk